Beyond The Veil

The Legend of Mortem | Book Three

J.L. Weir

Trigger Warnings

Beyond the Veil contains content which may trigger some readers. If you are bothered by torture, kidnapping, or mentions of rape, please consider carefully before reading this book.

CHAPTER 1

Evanora was still at large and they were hoping the archaic orb Aiden secured from Abigor's personal chamber would serve a purpose at some point; whatever it was, they did not know. Until the enchantress was located, Santiago and Jabari mutually decided Santiago's clan would remain in Seba. Seba was no small oasis by any means. It was a myriad of the most opulent, fertile landscape the girls had ever seen, stretching on for miles. It was the clandestine, pulsing heart of the surrounding desert, teeming with wildlife from the sky above to the waters below.

Colorful butterflies fluttered about the lush vegetation; snakes writhed their way through the trees; the larger predators skulked within the shadows. Reptiles and crocodiles glided through the river, and the melody of birds split the silence, while flocks of colorful feathers looked like clouds of stained glass drifting beneath the serene, celestial blue skies.

Santiago met with the Circle of Lords, who decided to bestow Dante and Aiden the honor of becoming titled after all they had done to save Silas, Dante, and Jadis; Dante had not only saved Jadis's and Silas's lives, he'd also put an end to Abigor's sadistic rein.

The ceremony was the talk of Seba and was just two days away. All who lived there wanted to be a part of the ceremony or at least witness it. Word spread to the far reaches of the oasis on the wings of busy bees.

Rumors about the Dhamphyr spread just as quickly as no one had actually come across an original descendant of Hecate, much less a legendary hybrid, and the whispers were no longer adequate. They needed to see the mythical being with their own eyes, which caused as much of a stir as Dante and Aiden being titled.

The excitement surrounding the ceremony also drew a lot of unwanted attention to Silas, Dante, Eden, and Aiden. To their mates' dismay, it put them in the forefront of everyone's mind, especially the unmated brujas, who were desperate to claw their way into the bed of an Aristocratic Nosferatu. Mated or not, they did all they could to get in 'good graces' with the girls for no other reason than to gain an invitation or an offer of employment during the ceremony. Jadis and her girls preferred to remain in the shadows and the influx of false pretenses made them feel as if they were walking barefoot through saw grass; it also made Jadis feel like an aberration. Silas and Dante had enough and asked Jabari to close the temple grounds to everyone other than clan members, or those involved in their business-related matters.

Once again, the girls could go about their daily lives in peace, while their mates went about their business with their clans. Their mates left before the girls had woken up and didn't return until the evening. Santiago was all business and made sure everyone toed the line.

Jadis reached out, and neither Silas nor Dante was in bed. She sat up and scanned the room, and her apprehension had a vice-like grip around her heart; she still suffered from bouts of anxiety and night terrors.

Dante was standing at the window with Silas when he noticed her stir. "Hi, baby, you're finally awake."

"There's my girl." Silas uncrossed his arms, walked over, and plopped on his back on the bed, then pulled her on top of him.

"What's wrong, darling?"

"Nothing. I'm fine now." She lay on top of his body with her head on his chest as he wrapped his arms around her.

"Your fear still plagues you?" Silas asked.

She stretched her arm and held her hand out for Dante without answering Silas. The moment Dante ran his hand over her head, the incessant anxiety disappeared.

"How long have you been up?" she asked.

Dante lay down next to them, bent over, and gave her a gentle kiss. "Not long. Are you hungry?"

She slipped halfway off Silas and playfully nipped at Dante's neck. "Yes."

"Maybe it's feeding time?" Dante suggested.

"*Maybe* we should have breakfast in bed," she replied.

"A mate after my own heart." Dante winked.

"Before we head out, I believe we should all have breakfast in bed," Silas offered.

He playfully wiggled his body under hers, and his hardened shaft pushed against her stomach. She rolled over and straddled him. He squeezed her butt cheeks and slowly moved her hips back and forth.

"I suggest the two of you take off your sweats, unless you know something I don't."

Silas flipped her onto her back, causing her to yelp as he and Dante removed their sweats and repositioned her body between theirs.

She rolled off of Silas, straddled Dante, and bent down. The soft warmth of his tongue brought about a heated desire in them both.

Silas moved behind her and began rubbing her shoulders, moved her hair to the side, then bent over and kissed the back of her neck and shoulder.

Dante pulled his mouth away ever so slightly. "I can't get enough of you," he whispered with a wink and a nod for her to move down.

Silas let go of her shoulders and drew back. He grabbed either side of her hips and pulled her body toward his.

She moved farther down, kissing and licking her way over Dante's chest. As she suckled and teased Dante's nipples with her tongue, he let out a raspy moan.

She sat up, leaned into Silas's chest, reached behind her, and grabbed the back of his head.

Silas turned her head and swept his tongue over hers while cupping her breast in one hand and placing the other on her stomach.

"Ah, mon chéri, I want it rough," Silas whispered.

Dante continued to massage her thighs before he moved his hand up and began rubbing her sex with his fingers. She let out a gentle moan, and her pulse quickened beneath his touch.

She pulled her face away from Silas and he placed his hand on her back, pushed her body forward onto Dante's, and lifted her hips to meet his groin.

She ran her tongue up the sides of Dante's shaft before sliding it into the heat of her mouth.

"Fuck—" Dante growled. The warmth of her firm grip, the softness of her skin rubbing his, and how her tongue teased his shaft, sent a surge of heated sensations through his body.

Silas teased her sex with one hand and slid his fingers in and out of her body with the other. "You are so wet for me, baby," he groaned as he placed the tip of his vein against her wet opening and gave a harsh thrust, reveling in the tightness of her core that enveloped him.

As soon as Silas shoved himself in, she had to let go of Dante's shaft. She gasped and placed her forehead on his hip.

"Shit," she moaned.

She continued rubbing Dante's vein and squeezed tighter, twisting her fist up and down, using the slick drops seeping from the tip.

Damn, she thought. The sensations roaring through her body when they took her together were like nothing she had ever experienced.

Dante had a fistful of her hair and he gently pulled her head back up, urging her to take him again. Her sexual, enticing thoughts only ramped up his desire.

She kept Dante's vein in a tight grip and slowly stroked the full length of his shaft while teasing the tip with her tongue again.

"Just like that," Dante mumbled.

She picked up on his desperation and need to consume her sexually, which only stoked her own arousal. The sensations rose to the surface as Silas relentlessly rocked himself in and out.

Dante felt her body trembled, and he chose not to hold back any longer. He let out a groan from deep within his chest as his release surged to the surface. "Ah, mon amour."

She swallowed the salty liquid while her own orgasm rocked her body.

"Pedicabo me," Silas exclaimed. He gave another hard shove and held himself steady, as deep into her core as possible. He let out a deep-throated growl and grasped her shoulder tighter with one hand, squeezing the tender flesh on the back of her hip with the other as he pulsed inside her.

After they finished, she rested her head on Silas's chest, and he gently stroked her hair while Dante lay beside her with his arm draped over her body.

"I love you, baby," Silas said warmly.

"As do I," Dante stated as he landed a hard slap on her ass.

She yelped and jumped, which caused them both to chuckle. "I love you, milords, but dammit, Dante, the two of you really need to stop doing that!"

"*Milords*?" Dante repeated.

"Seems we should do this more often if this is all it takes for her to address us appropriately," Silas teased.

"Seems I've moved up from nanny to lord. Good to know," Dante said.

"Tonight's the night, baby," she stated. Tonight, you will become a lord and I'm elated.

"It's going to be one hell of a party, brother," Silas added sincerely.

"Ah—don't swoon on me now, my dears," Dante joked.

They found themselves laughing aloud, remembering back to where the statement came from.

The temple staff was busy completing the details for the ceremony. They worked around the clock, making sure every detail was in place for a month.

Jadis walked through the grounds with Mag, Limi, Sindri, and Badru in tow, on her way to see the rooms where the ceremony, feast, and Grand Ball would commence. The staff had transformed the gardens into a fairy tale of sorts. Large white swans with their webbed feet lazily paddled in the decorated pools while colorful flower pedals gently floated with the soft, rippling waves. She took in the fragrance of tropical flowers that wafted through the air. Peacocks with long, tapered, colorful feathers and eyes of emeralds freely walked through the gardens. Hundreds of flowers of every shape, size, and color had been woven into exotic vines and draped around the trees and temple columns.

Sindri and Badru had Jadis fully amused as they jumped and lunged, trying to catch a couple of butterflies; so much so she hadn't noticed Mag and Limi stalking the swans in the pool. They suddenly jumped in, causing a large splash, which sent waves of water cascading over the edge of the pool. An abundance of flower pedals followed the water, flooding the ground at her feet. She looked up, and the swans were flapping their enormous wings, trying to fly away from Mag and Limi. The loud bugling caught two of the young girls' attention, who had been helping to make the arrangements. They began yelling at the wolves to get out of the pool and thought Jadis was another staff member.

Jadis was yelling at Mag and Limi to come to her when she heard a loud crash behind her. Sindri had jumped after a monarch and climbed one column, knocking over a couple of enormous bouquets. As Sindri climbed the floral garland wrapped around the stone columns, she pulled half of it down. The commotion caused by the swans, wolves, and cubs, as well as the mortified staff, had her howling in laughter.

"You can't be here—look what they have done! Get the dogs out of here and take those fucking cubs with you!" one of the maidens screamed.

The young gal was running around trying to catch the swans and each time they hissed at her, she would yelp and run back.

As Jadis looked at the catastrophic scene before her as well as the five maidens yelling at her, picking up flower pedals, chasing swans, and trying to fix the hanging, torn garland, she struggled to contain herself.

Another followed suit. "Get out. You have no right to be here—look at the mess!" she yelled.

A male voice spoke from behind Jadis. "What's all the commotion, milady?"

She abruptly turned around and Sigurd was standing there holding Badru. He looked both amused by the scene and angry.

"Sigurd?" was all she said in-between her hysterics. "They—it was a butterfly and the swans."

The maidens stood as frozen as opaque statues at the sight of Sigurd. Their senior grounds keeper, Anat, had made his way over and was proceeding to yell at the maidens to watch their tone.

"You will bow your heads and address milady Montiago properly! That's Silas's and Dante's Mate," he scolded.

"I'm—so—sorry. I did not realize, milady." The first who had yelled at Jadis stuttered her apology to Jadis's continued amusement; she added a curtsy, which caused Sigurd to chuckle.

"Anat, I assume you will deal with them appropriately?" Sigurd asked, sounding serious again.

"No, Sigurd, it's okay. They aren't from the oasis, they had no idea," Jadis stated, trying to quell her amusement.

Sigurd tilted his head toward Jadis, curious why she was defending them.

"Mag, Limi, veni!" They finally rushed to her side and sat obediently. Jadis walked over, leapt into the air, and grabbed Sindri from the top of the column.

"I'm sorry. I didn't mean for this to happen," Jadis stated, addressing Anat.

"Milady, all is fine. We shall have this back together in no time," he replied, along with a polite nod.

"This isn't your doing. I will fix it."

"No, milady, we will take care of it. No need to worry or bother yourself." Anat smiled.

"Sigurd, will you hold Sindri for a minute?"

He smiled warmly and reached for Sindri.

"Quod si quarum turbata," she whispered, along with a wave of her hand.

To everyone's shock, with the exception Sigurd, the chaos warped and waned. After a few minutes, the garland was in place, planters were upright, and the waves of pedals were back in the pool. Jadis fixed the entire catastrophic scene in a few minutes.

"I'm sorry, Anat, I'll take them from the gardens." Jadis smiled.

"All is well, milady. Thank you and I will speak to the girls," Anat replied.

"Please, no need. I don't want to see them getting into trouble. They've worked really hard. Everything is beautiful." She winked at the girls, subtly telling them it was going to be okay.

"This way, milady." Sigurd put Sindri and Badru down and walked with Jadis toward the temple entrance.

"I feel terrible. They were so scared." She chuckled.

"Aye, that they were," Sigurd replied.

They walked into the elaborately decorated dining hall. "I'll leave you to it. Do you think you can keep them under control—aye?"

"What? He jokes?" she teased.

"Aye, milady." He winked before disappearing.

She looked around and noticed dozens of large, hand-carved, wood chandlers hanging from the cathedral ceiling on ornate, iron chains over each of the three expansive tables; each containing at least a hundred fat, tapered candles. The Great Hall was three times as long as it was wide.

The Temple has never been so busy. The air is filled with the scents of exotic foods, flowers, and garnishments. I can settle into its fragrance like my cubs when they curl up beneath the warmth of the early morning sun, she thought.

Four large, gray stone fireplaces sat against the walls, lining both sides of the expansive room. Each fireplace had a large, intricately carved stone mantle that was impeccably decorated. *The age of the hearths is like a passage in time. I can already imagine the beauty of the bright orange flames as they flicker and spit at the curved, blackened ceilings.*

Tall black iron candelabras lined the center of the expansive wood tables. Beautiful china and crystal glasses, along with solid silver flatware, sat at each seat regardless of who would dine on food.

Luciana sure has a knack for this, Jadis thought. Luciana, of course, controlled every detail of the entire ceremony.

Jadis leisurely strolled into the Ceremonial Hall, where Dante and Aiden would receive their titles. Garlands made of fresh, beautiful flowers hung from the ceiling and columns similar to the ones in the gardens. The staff had placed enormous bouquets and tapered candles around the room. A long, woven Persian rug, infused with vibrant scarlet colors, geometric motifs, and angular patterns, ran from the top of the decorated altar, down the three steps, and along the length of the expansive room.

An enormous tapestry hung behind the ceremonial altar. It stretched from floor to ceiling and was a symbol of their status, wealth, and nobility. It took dozens of ladies a month to hand-weave the intricate designs, using silk, cotton, and gold thread.

Damn, she thought as she stared at its beauty. Four Roman soldiers who were sitting atop regal, black stallions and surrounded by the chaos of a battle stood forefront on the tapestry. Flags from various clans were being held up against a rolling, dark sky, while warriors fought with raised swords clashing against their enemy's shields in the background. They also depicted the warriors in hand-to-hand combat while arrows zipped across the smoky valley. Bodies were strewn about and lying lifeless on the blood-stained ground and under the horses' dark hooves; two of whom had risen up on their hind legs. Staring at the tapestry, the scene reminded her of a poem she'd once read. *How can man die better than facing fearful odds, for the ashes of his father and the temples of his gods.*

"Beautiful, isn't it?" Luciana said.

Her voice startled Jadis, and she jumped.

"I didn't mean to startle you, dear. I see you approve?" She wrapped her arm around Jadis's back and rubbed her hand up and down her arm.

"Yes, very much so—it's stunning." She slid her arm around Luciana's waist and stood in awe of the power radiating from her.

"I had no idea you liked poetry, Horatius nonetheless."

"Yes, I spent a lot of years alone before finding Silas again."

"I understand loneliness all too well, dear. However, you and I will never experience it again. My sons have been given a divine gift and my heart is full. I wouldn't have picked a better match for my bairns had I searched the heavens myself."

"I don't have the words to describe what that means to me."

"Darling, there are no words to describe the happiness you have brought into our lives." She paused briefly, admiring the tapestry with Jadis. "I would like you to stand with me tonight."

"It would be my honor, but shouldn't you stand with Santiago?"

"Yes, which means you will stand with Santiago and myself, while they grant Dante and Aiden the title. You are now part of the vampirian elite.

Tonight is the perfect time and place for you to be recognized for who you are."

"I would love to, but this night should be about Dante and Aiden."

"My dear—just another reason I adore you so." She smiled.

She turned Jadis around and gave her a tight embrace. She reveled in Luciana's luxurious scent and the calmness penetrating her body, so much so she felt the tears pool in her eyes.

Luciana gently stroked her hair. "Every girl needs a mother. I understand you have Hecate, but you also need a semi-living mother." She chuckled. She moved back and cupped either side of her face in her hands and looked directly into her eyes. "Your emotions speak for themselves. You are far too young to have walked this earth alone. It's unimaginable, and it ends tonight. It will be made clear you belong to us, with us."

Jadis wrapped her arms around Luciana and clung to her. Her words brought about a fury of emotions she didn't realize she carried.

"What do we have here?" Silas's voice pierced the emotional silence.

"What are you two doing?" Dante asked.

"Nothing. I was just wandering around, checking everything out." Jadis wrapped her arms around Dante, while Silas greeted his mother.

"Mother," Silas stated as he kissed her cheek. She returned the gesture before Dante greeted her in the same manner.

"Hi, baby," she stated and wrapped her arms around Silas.

"Everything okay, mon chéri?" Silas asked, sensing Jadis's emotions.

"Baby?" Dante questioned as he moved in next to Silas and pulled her into his body.

"Everything is fine. I have asked her to stand with your father and me tonight during the ceremony, is all," Luciana said.

Jadis realized how happy that made them, as they looked at her and then back at Luciana.

"It's about time, Mother," Silas joked.

"I agree," Dante added.

She poked Dante in his chest and winked. "You two stop," Jadis stated, a bit embarrassed. "Tonight is about you, wizard, not me."

He grabbed her finger, pulled her in for a tight embrace, and stole a little tongue.

"It's a family celebration, baby," Silas said. "Now come here."

Dante let her go and she leapt into Silas's arms; he too stole a heated kiss. "We can't wait to get your ass back to bed," Silas whispered into her ear.

"Silas!" she said telepathically. *"Your mother is standing right here."*

"It's no matter. I agree with Silas." Dante laughed, embarrassing her all the more.

"Since we are on the subject, is there a time we might expect a little wizard or assassin to grace us with their presence?" Luciana asked.

The flush in Jadis's cheeks immediately grew in intensity, and she shifted her glance between the three of them. "What—I mean—" She fumbled for words, to everyone's continued amusement.

"We'd be happy to accommodate your request, Mother. We should skip the ceremony altogether and get started," Dante stated jokingly as he smacked Jadis's butt.

"Dante, stop." She chuckled and slapped his hand away.

"Well, hell, I believe I am capable of multitasking. I can give Dante his title and we can give mon chéri here a title of her own." Silas swept her into his arms, acting as if he was going to carry her out.

"Silas, put me down," she urged.

"Unfortunately, we will all have to wait. As much as I would ap-preciate a beyorn gracing us with their presence, no one will skip the ceremony," Luciana stated. "Say your goodbyes. We all need to be getting ready."

Silas, Dante, and Jadis looked at each other, not wanting to be separated. They had something else on their minds.

"Perfect, everyone is together as it should be," Santiago stated as he entered. He walked over to Luciana and pulled her in for a passionate kiss.

"I hear there was a little situation in the courtyard earlier?" Santiago asked.

Jadis looked at her wolves and cubs, trying to come up with an explanation. "What do you mean?"

"I believe you and your companions caused quite the ruckus," Silas stated as he raised his eyebrows and cocked his head in a joking manner.

"Everything looked okay to me," she replied with a coy smile.

"You sure about that?" Dante asked.

"Stop teasing her," Luciana replied. "I think the courtyard looks exquisite."

Santiago winked at Jadis before turning his attention back to Luciana. "My love, I assume you have informed them of our decision?"

"Yes, my love. Jadis will stand between us during the ceremony. I have already made the arrangements."

"How does that not surprise me?" Santiago smiled. "Come." He held his hand out to Jadis and pulled her in for a hug. "You deserve nothing less than to stand at our side." He kissed the top of her head, placed his hands on her shoulders, and looked directly at her. "What joy you have brought to all of us, dear child, not to mention your loyalty to our sons. You will forever remain in our hearts and our home. Most are defined by insatiable ambition. You are solely defined by emotion and love. You are their match in every way. You have proven your loyalty to our sons and the family without regard for yourself and it has not gone unnoticed."

Jadis had her sisters, but belonging to such a large family was a little overwhelming emotionally.

"It seems the gods were listening," she replied.

Santiago smiled warmly and kissed the back of her hand. "Well then, it's time we part ways until tonight."

Silas swept her off her feet, and she wrapped her arms and legs around his body. "I love you, vampire."

"And I you, mon chéri." He handed her to Dante, who wrapped her tightly in his arms.

"I love you, wizard, and I am so proud of you."

"And I love you will all my heart."

He set her down, and Luciana took her hand and led her away. Jadis stopped momentarily and placed her hand on the corner of the stone wall. She looked back at her perfect mates.

"Is my gift for Dante here?" Jadis asked Silas privately.

"Yes, baby, they are being cared for as we speak."

She gave a slight nod of acknowledgment and left with Luciana.

"What was that look she gave you about?" Dante asked, knowing Silas had cloaked her words.

Silas placed a couple of hard pats on Dante's shoulder and jokingly shook him back and forth. "She said you're ugly."

Dante gave Silas an exaggerated eye roll and the three of them laughed aloud.

CHAPTER 2

Mercia and Aisley were sitting in their decrepit one-room apartment after another all-night bender. "I can't believe those bitches got us exiled," Mercia stated.

"Well, if you hadn't been all over Dante, this wouldn't have happened," Aisley scolded.

"Me? I think you're the one who said you wanted to do more than spread your legs for him. So don't put this all on me." Mercia stood up and threw her pillow against the worn headboard.

Aisley began to cry. "I might have said that, but you were actually stupid enough to bat your fucking eyes at him in front of Jadis."

"I wish the bitch were dead and gone. I would move on Dante before her body had finished burning." Mercia still had a seething hatred for Jadis and Aria.

Aisley wiped her eyes and plopped down in the tattered chair across the room, pulling her knees tightly to her chest. "What makes you think he would want you? He wouldn't so much as acknowledge your presence."

"And you could do so much better? What makes you think he would want you either?" Mercia walked over to the table and grabbed the half-empty bottle of vodka.

"Stop being a bitch, Mercia, I'm not in the mood to argue over who could fuck him first."

Mercia took another sip and plopped down on the bed. "Whatever, but we should pay that bitch back."

Aisley thought momentarily as she held her hand out for the bottle. "Maybe we should?"

"What? I didn't mean that literally! You think either of us is a match for her? Not to mention we wouldn't be able to get within an inch of her. I think you have cried your fucking mind out!"

Mercia also wanted to get rid of Jadis but knew the impossibility of the task. *Unless.* "What if we somehow summon the Enchantress everyone whispers about?"

"*Summon the Enchantress*? Exactly how are we to do that? Everyone knows she has disappeared." Aisley liked the idea, but the mere thought of messing with the Enchantress sent a wave of fear and caution up her spine. "If the rumors are true and she is as evil as they say, it may cost us our lives."

"I have an idea," Mercia said. "Maybe we can summon her if we call out using Jadis's name?"

"What are your plans if she decides to kill us once we let her know how she can get to Jadis?" Aisley asked.

Mercia thought momentarily before deciding it might be worth a try. "Maybe we can make a deal with her? I don't know, Aisley, why don't we figure something out instead of sitting here crying all the fucking time? I want that bitch to pay for all she took from us."

Aisley looked out the window and then back at Mercia. "I do too. There just might be a way."

The ladies-in-waiting were seeing to the blood hosts who were being impeccably dressed in an area outside the temple. They would soon line the back of the Dining Hall under guard. It was an honor every unmated bruja in the oasis begged for, and it caused more than one fight; it was all the females of Seba talked about. They had been going to a rehearsal of sorts for weeks in order to ensure their behavior, as well as who they could and could not approach. Luciana made it very clear to each one of them.

Each vying to become more than just a blood host; most of whom would do whatever it took to be bedded by one of the Aristocratic Nosferatu who would be in attendance. The highest-ranking members of every clan had been sent an invitation.

There were only thirty lords altogether and it wasn't a title given out randomly or without permission from the Circle. Most of whom were ancient Nosferatu as old or older than Santiago. There were only a handful that matched the young age of Silas, Eden, and now Dante and Aiden.

Jadis, Luciana, her sisters, as well as Aria and Maddie, were in one of the large bed chambers dressing. They had a dozen familiar handmaidens helping them to dress; most of whom were from a lineage of families who had worked in the temple for generations. Their families were loyal and trusted.

Jadis sat quietly, watching the ice clink against her glass as her fingers toyed with the condensation, trying to calm her racing thoughts when Skye's laughter broke her from her transfixed state of mind.

"Jadis, are you listening?" Skye asked.

"Yes, I'm listening."

"Well, your blank stare says otherwise."

"Somebody's nervous," Aria replied.

"You all are ridiculous," Jadis chuckled.

"We were just wondering how you are going to follow the rules now that you will be mated to two lords?" Skye joked.

Jadis rolled her eyes. "It won't be any different than it is now. We're already mated, least you forget."

"Well, we all think you're going to be on lockdown more times than not," Maddie joked.

"That's rich coming from you. Eden has you on a very tight chain," Jadis teased.

"I'll hold your freedom for you. We know they'll snag it the next time you pull some fuckery on them." Aria laughed.

"I can say the same about you when it comes to Aiden," Jadis added.

Skye crossed her legs and adjusted her robe. "Jadis, we all know you are screwed, and the sooner you admit it, the better off you'll be,"

"Really, just me? Doesn't Syth own a little anklet?" Jadis clapped back in a joking manner.

Luciana was fully amused with the girls as they bantered back and forth. "Come, gather around. I have something for my girls," she stated, interrupting the conversation.

They followed Luciana and Jadis could tell by Maddie's smile, she knew something they didn't.

Luciana held out her free hand, and one of the chambermaids walked over and handed her a long box. "It's tradition, a gift for a son's new mate. You will have to excuse me. I'm a little late with the gifts. Jadis tends to cause a few distractions."

Jadis's eyes widened, not having expected the playful jab, which sent everyone but her into another bout of laugher.

Ivory nudger her shoulder in a joking manner. "What, you're speechless? Who would have thought?"

Luciana opened the box and resting in black, padded velvet were four beautiful platinum chokers that looked like a modern version of an Iphenorian Priestess's Senebtisis. Running the length of the choker were raised, black diamond studs having been inlaid in the center. Rubies surrounded each stud while diamond-shaped, garnet pendants hung gently from the choker and seemed to move like raindrops under a gentle breeze.

Their brilliant red hue is so vivid it reminds me of the bright crimson rays of a full Blood Moon. "They are stunning," Jadis stated.

"I can't believe this. I don't know what to say," Aria added.

"We can't have you all walking around with a bare décolletage," Luciana stated.

"How do we ever thank you?" Ivory looked at Skye, who had the same shocked expression.

"It's a tradition dating back a thousand years. Only the mates that are taken by an original descendant of Prince Vladislav Aramastus Davoran the First are gifted one."

They looked at each other in awe; they never thought about how ancient their family's lineage truly was. However, looking at Luciana and Santiago, their nobility spoke for itself.

"Come, darling, let me." Luciana gently turned Jadis around and fastened the choker around her neck; she then moved to Skye, Ivory, and Aria.

Jadis looked at Maddie, and she was fastening the exact same choker around her neck. "Welcome to the family," Maddie stated as she held up her glass.

"We have no more time to waste." Luciana motioned for the chambermaids, who began feverishly moving about while the girls sat in their emerald-colored silk robes with a drink, laughing and chatting with one another as they were being attended to.

Jadis sat with one hand resting demurely in her lap and a drink in the other. After Talula, the eldest, had finished her hair, she handed her a large silver hand mirror. Jadis held it up in front of her, and as soon as she saw her reflection, she was speechless. She had a large beehive like updo with one long curled strand running down her back. *The awkward mess resembles that of a woman right out of the seventeenth century!* She reached up to mess with the curls and was immediately stopped by Talula.

"Milady, don't touch it, you'll mess it up." Talula placed her palms on the sides of Jadis's head as if she was flattening her hair and pulling it back. "There—that should do."

Jadis heard Luciana snicker, and as she turned and glanced at her, Luciana had covered her mouth with her hand. *She either saw the expression on my face or read my thoughts. I figure it's the latter.* "You're laughing at my hair. I look ridiculous!"

"I'm sorry, but yes, it's quite the mess," Luciana agreed.

"You have a Queen's bouffant," Aria yelled out.

"Your hair looks exactly like mine, so laugh it up," Jadis snarked back.

There is no way in hell I'm going to show up at the party looking like this! Silas and Dante will surely laugh their asses off, she told herself.

"Get her a tiara," Ivory announced.

"Jadis, it's not that bad." Maddie was trying to be polite but ended up in hysterics herself.

"Let me—" Luciana stood and walked over to Jadis, dismissing Talula. She pulled all the pins out, freeing her hair from the hideous mess, and combed it tightly to the sides of her head and pinned it down just above her ears. She then pulled on the long locks and brushed them out before pulling the top back and creating a slight poof that ran from her forehead to the back of her head, letting her hair cascade softly down her shoulders and back in gentle waves.

"There now, why hide all that mahogany beauty? Let them see how stunning you are." She played with it for a few minutes, making sure there was nothing left of the Queen's bouffant before handing Jadis the mirror. "Here, darling."

As soon as Jadis saw her new style, she was elated. *It's beautiful. In ten minutes she fixed the hideous mess.* "I love it. Thank you so much. I would have been mortified."

"We all would have been, dear. Now what do you say we get dressed?"

Jadis glanced at her girls and started laughing at their sour expressions. "Who's laughing now?" she joked.

I will not show up with my hair looking like this while Jadis looks like a medieval princess, Aria protested.

"All right. Everyone, take your hair down. You look ridiculous," Luciana stated as she held out her glass, waiting for it to be refilled.

In unison, they were quickly pulling out pins, brushing out the curls, and helping each other fix the mess. Luciana walked to each of them and made sure their hair looked exactly alike.

Jadis heard a thump and looked at Talula. She had plopped the hairbrush on the bureau in a huff; she was an age-old maiden who had not adapted to modern customs and didn't appreciate the changes Luciana had created.

"Talula, I would like my hair to match the girls." Luciana sat back and took a drink with a devious smile.

The girls tried their best to hide their amusement, knowing Luciana was putting Talula in her place.

"Milady, your dress is ready," Kaleen said sweetly before following Talula to fetch another dress.

"If you and Aria expect us to call the two of you *milady*, you have another thing coming," Ivory stated firmly.

"You will address me accordingly. After all, you are just a commoner," Jadis replied.

Skye furrowed her eyebrows at Jadis. "*A commoner?* We are mated to the same family."

"And if we demand the two of you bow to us during the ball, I bet you do," Aria teased.

Maddie tipped her glass toward the girls. "It seems the peasants have graced us with their presence tonight."

Luciana leaned farther back into her chair and clapped her hands together as the laughter escaped her mouth.

Ivory and Skye did all they could to curtail their obvious annoyance, not wanting to encourage the girls' humor at their expense.

"As entertaining as you all are is, it's time to dress." Luciana stood as their dresses were brought into the room.

They matched perfectly. *Apparently, it's customary for each clan to dress alike, having chosen a specific color, not to be repeated. Simply put, it's a quiet expression of unity amongst each clan, according to Silas,* Jadis thought.

Their cobalt blue satin dresses accentuated their thin waists and hugged their hips. The dresses were trimmed with braided, gold edging and had a low-cut front and back. The V-cut back plunged down past the small of their backs while the low-cut neckline in the front partially exposed the inner edge of their cleavages, leaving just enough for the imagination. The thigh-high slit on the left would give onlookers a glimpse of their toned legs while the long, satin material on the right pooled at their feet in a soft, folded pile.

Luciana was adorned in exquisite jewels while archaic, gold brooches pinned the dress at her shoulders. Her hand-sewn, cobalt blue gown draped eloquently over her body, while a curtain of pleated silk cascaded down from her waist to the floor. The silhouette of her body was barely visible through the fine linen that drifted across the dark, stone floor as she walked; the girls stood gawking at the vision before them.

"Oh, my—you are all simply divine." Luciana walked around each of the girls, making sure their dresses were a perfect fit before stepping back as if she were studying them. "It seems something is missing."

She walked to the ornate bureau and opened a drawer as the girls side-eyed each other. They followed Luciana, and she pulled out two beautiful, hand-carved wood boxes. She opened the first, exposing three stunning gold wrist cuffs. A directionless fog rolled over the edges and swirled around the cuffs, having been disturbed by the lid's movement; the Archaic energy was undeniable.

"Jadis, Aria, and Maddie, these are gifts to you from your lords. It's another tradition we hold to the highest of regard. Silas, Dante, Eden, and Aiden created the designs for each of you."

The bodies of three snakes formed the shank of Jadis's cuff and each head faced in opposite directions, while a large cabochon-cut, red garnet sat in the center.

While Luciana placed one on Jadis, Aria, and Maddie, Jadis noticed hers had three intertwined snake bodies and three heads, while Aria's and Maddie's only had one. She admired the beauty and effort it must have taken to create it when it dawned on her. *The snakes are the Pagan symbol of rebirth.*

Luciana looked at Jadis and winked. *"Silas, Dante, and Aiden knew you would figure it out. They forged it themselves,"* she stated telepathically.

"Aiden created this with Silas and Dante?"

"He did. It's our little secret." Luciana winked.

"This means more to me than they could understand."

Luciana wrapped Jadis in her arms. *"And you, my dear, mean more to them than you can understand."*

"I don't know what to say," Aria stated, interrupting Luciana and Jadis's private conversation.

Luciana and Jadis kept an arm wrapped around each other as they turned to face the girls.

Maddie stood quietly, admiring the cuff and thinking about the effort Eden had put into designing it.

"They're beautiful," Skye stated as she stepped forward.

"They are stunning," Ivory agreed.

Luciana opened the second box and the same featureless white fog rolled over the edges and swirled around the box. Two solid gold cuffs were tucked into folded black velvet. They were inlaid with rubies, and Egyptian inscriptions had been etched into the gold along with a raised, chiseled figure of a scorpion.

"These are for the two of you." Luciana turned to Skye and Ivory. "Syth and Agaeus also created them." She placed them on their wrists, along with a hug.

A sudden knock at the door interrupted them. "Milady, it's time."

"Well, this is it. Let's take our places," Luciana stated.

Jadis felt slightly lightheaded and had to place her palm on the wall. "My heart is in my throat," she whispered to the girls.

"I'm just as nervous," Aria admitted. Even though she would not be standing next to Santiago and Luciana, it was still unnerving.

They lined up along the corridor leading to the stairs. Skye and Ivory would appear together, followed by Aria, Jadis, and finally Luciana. They held hands, trying to calm themselves.

It was the moment Jadis, Skye, and Ivory dreaded; they were being introduced to as the daughters of Hecate; their true identities revealed to all clans and covens. It was also time to let it be known they belonged to the House of Montiago.

The girls listened to the boisterous voices, laughter, and excitement radiating from the jubilant crowd in the Grand Hall. After a few heart-pounding moments, the tempo changed, and the orchestra began playing a waltz known as Vienna Blood.

Luciana stepped before the girls. "It's time, girls. Shall we?" She gave Skye and Ivory a tight embrace and a kiss on either cheek before motioning them to head for the stairs.

"Miladies Skye and Ivory Montiago!" They took one step forward before being motioned down the stairs.

Jadis tilted her head to the side, listening to the whispers that immediately followed the announcement. "It's them—they are Hecate's daughters," she heard. The whispers carried on for a few silent, deafening minutes before they quickly became that of enthusiastic cheers.

Syth and Agaeus stepped forward and patiently waited. As soon as Skye and Ivory appeared at the head of the stairs, Syth and Agaeus glanced at each other.

They are strikingly beautiful. They wear their darkness like shrouds on silent queens, Syth thought.

Agaeus shifted his stance and looked up at his beautiful mate. *Time has once again drawn us back together, and this is just the beginning of our destiny.*

Syth and Agaeus held their hands out to their mates and escorted them back to where the rest of their clan was standing.

"Have I told you yet how much I love your darkness?" Syth whispered.

Skye looked into his beautiful eyes and smiled. "And I will love you with all of it."

"The whispers, they can't believe they are Hecate's daughters," Jadis said quietly to Aria.

"I'll be at the bottom waiting for you. You can do this. We all know they are going to be stunned by your appearance. Don't let it get to you," Aria stated as she gave her a tight embrace.

"It's your turn, dear." Luciana kissed Aria on either cheek and motioned her forward.

Aria and Jadis gave each other's hand a gentle squeeze along with a wink.

"Milady Cirillo!" The crowd cheered and clapped, knowing her mate was about to be titled.

Aiden stepped forward and nervously messed with his tunic. As soon as his eyes met hers, thoughts swirled. *She's captivating, and she deserves all of me. Not the unspoken, desperate desire I have for another that feels like a rope twisting around my heart. I will no longer love her from a distance. I will surrender my torment and put my desires and sleepless nights to the grave.*

Aria looked at Aiden and had to take a moment to gather her composure. *My god, he is gorgeous.* She took a couple of deep breaths and made her way down the expansive stone staircase.

Aiden smiled wholeheartedly at his beautiful mate as he reached out for her hand before taking their place with their clan.

Eden patted Aiden on the shoulder, knowing how entangled his emotions were. *"The past is the past, brother. Your regret is in vain."*

Aiden answered his silent statement with a simple nod.

"Damn, you look amazing," Aiden stated.

"And you, milord—are gorgeous."

Aiden chuckled at Aria calling him *milord*. "About time you fell into line," he joked.

"Don't think it's going to happen again."

"We shall see." He winked.

"It looks like it's just the two of us, my dear."

As happy as Luciana looks, there's something she isn't saying. "What is it?" Jadis asked as she placed her hand on her stomach, waiting to hear the bad news.

"There is no bad news tonight," Luciana replied, responding to her thoughts. "However, you must know no one has ever met, much less seen a Dhamphyr. They have been waiting to glimpse the mythical creature since word spread regarding your existence. You are also the one who was bestowed Hecate's powers. The two combined have created quite the stir."

"I'm well aware," she mumbled.

"You are what myths and legends speak of. There will be a lot of chatter, stares, and they will try to greet you personally." She paused momentarily. "There is just one thing you need to know."

"Yep, here it is, just say it." Jadis motioned her hand for Luciana to land the final blow.

"How do I say it politely? You carry—a certain enticing energy and your allure is intoxicating. Unfortunately, the males of our kind will be drawn to you. It will attract a lot of unwanted attention."

"In other words, it will draw them to me the way a courtesan is to cheap perfume," Jadis mumbled.

Luciana laughed aloud. "I was going to put it a bit more eloquently, but yes. Rest assured, we have made preparations. Sigurd is a revered guest tonight. However, he has insisted he stand at your side at all times. If you need anything, you reach out to anyone of us immediately. Come, child." She lovingly wrapped her arms around her daughter.

It suddenly became so quiet you could hear a pebble roll in the sand. Luciana stepped back and squeezed her hand, motioning for her to walk out.

Silas and Dante stepped forward and stood shoulder to shoulder. Dante looked at Silas, who gave him a larger-than-life smile. They placed one arm behind their backs and bent the other across their stomachs, and looked up.

"Milady Montiago!"

Jadis appeared at the top of the staircase and hushed gasps, whispered chatter, and transfixed stares greeted her.

Silas put his free hand on Dante's shoulder the moment he laid eyes on her; he and Dante glanced at each, awestruck.

Dante placed his hand over his heart and took a deep breath. "Prince Vladislav himself would have taken her as his mate—look at her."

"She is a vision to behold. Even her gods would be envious." Silas slightly adjusted his stance, trying to quell the beating of his heart.

The moment she laid eyes on Silas and Dante, she stopped mid-stride. The roars and cheers that erupted from the quiet crowd became indistinct as her attention was solely focused on her mates. *They are stunning. Drenched in regality. No one has ever captured my eyes the way they do.* They captivated her. She felt as if her heart had just rolled over, and her nerves demonically morphed from fluttering butterflies to untamed bats.

They were both wearing semi-form-fitting, dark blue leather trousers that laced up the crotch. Their pant legs were slightly bunched in piles above the top of their black leather boots. Their tunics matched her dress perfectly; intricate patterns with very specific symbols were sewn into the material with braided, black and gold thread. Puffy, white pleats on the shoulders of their shirts stood out from beneath the dark blue sleeveless tunics. The low-cut shirt exposed part of their chests and there was a deep richness to their chestnut-colored skin that was enhanced by the white silk of their shirts. The tunics opened in the front, not having buttons or ties, and the trim matched that of the black and gold edging on her dress. They also had matching amulets hanging between their pecs, complementing her cuff.

Their amber eyes glowed like swirling pools of tranquility, and hidden within the heated passion of their gaze was a promise of protection and possessiveness.

Silas watched the way she gracefully walked down the steps, looking as refined and sophisticated as any royal. *There is something dark, something sinister. The temptress is slowly seducing my demons. Her heart has caged two darkened, feral things.*

Dante watched the way her hips gently swayed from side to side. With each delicate step, the split in her silk gown parted, allowing a glimpse of her toned leg, leaving him longing for more. *She is the madness that forces me to crave her chaos, the lost whisper claiming the last of my sanity, and she is mine.*

She made it to the last step and took their hands in hers, and they pulled her in, pressing her body between theirs. They bent their heads down on either side of hers and she reached around and gently slid her hands around and held the back of their necks in a tight embrace. She could feel the warmth of their breaths on the nape of her neck and the desire coiling in their bodies. They each had a hand firmly placed on her lower back and the other on her hip.

"I beg to lick your lips and seduce your tongue. Show us your demons and we shall show you ours," Silas growled with a wicked tone.

Jadis let out a low rumble. "My hungry lovers, my demons want to devour yours."

"And ours want to ravage your body until the darkness turns to dawn," Dante said.

They slowly pulled away and walked arm in arm back to their clan, and took their places front and center. The sexual tension between them was as thick as the sweltering heat of a tropical summer.

They tried to focus on Luciana's appearance, but try as they might, their lust-filled desire was getting the better of them. All Jadis could think about was how badly she craved them.

"We like the way you think." Silas winked.

She looked at each of them before looking back at Luciana. *Just in case the two of you are wondering—I'm not wearing panties,* she stated telepathically.

Their eyebrows shot up, and their heads tilted in her direction, and she looked back at them with a mischievous grin.

"You don't play fair, mon chéri. I believe I have a hard-on," Silas growled as he casually hid his crotch with his free hand playing around.

"I just came in my pants," Dante teased, with squinted eyes as he subtly pulled at the front of his laces in a joking manner.

Silas and Jadis almost bellowed aloud; it took all they had to contain their heated laughter. She couldn't look at them; she had to divert her eyes and look at the floor, knowing full well if she caught even a glance, she could not curtail her laughter.

"Lady Montiago!" As Santiago took Luciana's hand, they turned and headed to the Ceremonial Temple.

They lined up on either side of the altar, and Jadis stood in-between Santiago and Luciana. Aria stood two steps below Santiago while the rest of the clan lined up on the other side. The entire room was lit by candles, and the shadows frolicked and played on the stone walls. Hundreds of gentle, amorphous flames sputtered and flickered with the soft whiffs of air. The heat of restless flame compelled the wax to cascade down the sides of the candles like a slow roll of molten lava.

Four large candelabras, forged from black iron with twisted rods, held dozens of candles. They were standing at an angle on either side of the enormous tapestry, bringing the subdued hues to life; it was truly a masterpiece of gallantry and stories untold. As Santiago stepped forward, Jadis looked at her mates with pride and adoration.

Santiago stood before Dante and Aiden on the altar. "Tonight, you stand ready. Do you accept the distinction and title of lord, bestowed upon you by the Circle and all that it entails?"

"Aye, milord," Dante and Aiden agreed.

"Your lords and brethren shall bequeath you the Amulet of Nosferatu. Your achievements in the fields of battle have honored not only our family, but all clans."

Santiago stepped back and stood next to Jadis, while Silas and Eden stepped before Dante and Aiden.

Silas stepped forward first and was holding the Amulet of Nosferatu. "Warrior."

Dante kneeled before Silas, grasped the handle of his sword in a fist-like grip with both hands, placed the tip on the rug, and bowed his head slightly above his bent arms.

Silas placed his hand on the top of his sword. "Do you swear by the decree of Nosferatu to defend all clans, protect all mates, and honor all brothers?"

"Aye, milord, with my life."

"Dante, I place the Amulet of Nosferatu around your neck. Shall shame never find you nor battle take you. Wear it honorably and proudly. May it never be cut off for dishonor, degradation, or cowardice." Silas placed the Amulet around his neck.

Silas stepped away and Eden stepped forward, holding the Amulet of Nosferatu. "Warrior."

Aiden kneeled before Eden, grasped the handle of his sword in a fist-like grip with both hands, placed the tip on the rug, and bowed his head slightly above his bent arms.

Eden placed his hand on the top of his sword. "Do you swear by the decree of Nosferatu to defend all clans, protect all mates, and honor all brothers?"

"Aye, milord, with my life."

"Aiden, I place the Amulet of Nosferatu around your neck. Shall shame never find you nor battle take you. Wear it honorably and proudly. May it never be cut off for dishonor, degradation, or cowardice." Eden placed the Amulet around his neck.

Santiago stepped forward again and stood between Silas and Eden. "Rise now," he said.

Dante and Aiden stood and placed their swords in their sheaths attached to their hips. "May you protect those who stand behind you, fight with those who stand beside you, and defeat those who stand against you. We have granted you the title. Lords, step forward and swear your fealty to the Circle."

Dante and Aiden turned toward the Circle of Lords, who were standing front and center, and swore their fealty together.

"I swear by hand, heart, and blade, never shall we stand alone. We shall rise before our brothers with sword, shield, and stone, till death doth take me home. We shall be the hunter, not the prey. We shall fear no enemy, neither living, nor by the grave. We shall wear their bones and spill their blood. We shall stand between our enemies and our home, till death doth take me home."

Santiago took another step forward and placed one hand on either of their shoulders. "Clans, you shall swear your fealty to your coveted lords, forged in iron and stone."

"Aru—Aru—Aru!" All members in attendance shouted out the wordless chant before kneeling before their new lords with their heads bowed. They placed one fist on the ground, holding their swords, and held their other fist to their hearts.

"Aye, milords, we swear our fealty in your honor. We shall stand beside you blood, body, and bone. Should we ever raise our blade to you in malice or deceit, may it be the iron that seals our fate." They then stood and faced Dante and Aiden.

Santiago, Silas, and Eden stood shoulder to shoulder with Dante and Aiden.

"The Circle has spoked and your words shall be law. May the feast commence in your honor!" Santiago announced.

The entire room erupted in cheers, chants, and bellows, and they swiftly moved in and greeted Dante and Aiden.

Jadis stood and watched as they grasped forearms, patted Dante and Eden on the shoulders, and greeted them with so many words and expressions of congratulations she couldn't make it all out; she was beyond honored to witness the event.

She stood quietly, lost in thought. *It's one thing to hear all the gossip and chatter, but to witness it is on a whole other level. I now understand the excitement and desire to be a part of it. Watching Dante and Aiden bestowed such an honor—there are no words.*

She was bewitched with emotion and pride. It took all she had to keep from crying in front of an entire legion of aristocratic Nosferatu, who stood stoic and dignified. *I could never have imagined the depth of their words, the truth in their eyes and power it yields. Even my gods would be pleased.*

Silas and Dante walked to Jadis as Jabari led the exuberant crowd to the Grand Hall, allowing the family a few moments of privacy.

Dante swept her into his arms. "Your gods are pleased?"

She wrapped her arms around his neck. "Very much so, as am I." She pulled her head back and her lips fell to his. "I'm proud of you. You deserve nothing less, milord."

"*Milord?* Well, I'll be damned." Dante smiled.

Silas walked over and stole a heated kiss before looking at Dante. "I believe it's tradition the mate bends the knee to her lord," he stated.

"Yes, I believe it is," Dante agreed.

Jadis furrowed her brows and gave them a coy smile. "Luciana said I don't have to."

"I promise you will be on your knees tonight," Silas rumbled, forcing Dante to laugh in agreement.

"Come, let us enjoy the feast!" Santiago announced.

Jadis looked over to see Aiden set Aria down. He caught her eye and winked, and she smiled and winked back with a nod, letting him know how proud of him she was.

CHAPTER 3

There were three hundred guests in attendance for the feast. Just as Jadis had envisioned the four, enormous fireplaces lit the dining hall with their forked flames, spitting toward the blackened ceilings. Their entire family sat across from one another in the center of the main table while Jabari and Santiago sat at the head of the table, with Luciana seated between them.

Jadis tipped her glass to Sigurd, who was sitting across the table, in appreciation of his offering to stand by her. He returned the gesture with a lustrous smile and a wink. "'Tis my honor, milady—no need to thank me."

Jadis smiled. "I truly appreciate it." He nodded and tipped his cup to her.

The brujas dined on food while the Nosferatu sipped on unlimited amounts of alcohol. Their meal was being served by a multitude of flawlessly dressed wait staff. They carried in the food on large, silver platters on the shoulders of the servitors. They set the layers of food that looked more like works of art down in the middle of each table, expanding its length. It was a delicacy of bread, fruits, cheeses, and vegetables of every variety, along with a multitude of meats decorated with sprigs of parsley, sage, and rosemary. Their combined fragrance was enough to make one's mouth water.

They had been drinking for a couple of hours while their guests feasted on the elaborate meal. The boisterous voices and laughter grew as the night went on and the alcohol continued to flow.

The Nosferatu had picked their blood hosts and the eloquent looking ladies sat in their laps, allowing them to drink from their vein at the table. It became apparent how quick and dangerous pack feeding could become. Once a few of the vampires began feeding, they all followed suit. Their insatiable hunger only seemed to grow as the night went on; even Jadis felt the pull. However, the eldest clan members and wizards controlled the enormous group's blood lust, keeping it from becoming a bloodbath.

Jadis felt Dante place his hand on her inner thigh and began sliding up between her legs, pushing her dress aside, and she grabbed his hand.

"Dante!" she whispered. "Stop it, someone will see."

He and Silas placed one of their elbows on the table to face her and gave each other a mischievous look.

"You two better not!"

"Oh, so serious." Dante winked.

"Maybe we should show our mate we can play games too," Silas stated as he looked at her with a devious, half-cocked grin.

"There will be no games at dinner." She tried to sound serious, although her chuckling gave her away.

They picked up their cups and took a drink. However, they each kept a tight grip on her thigh. She noticed Jabari whisper to Santiago and they motioned for their silver goblets to be filled with absinthe and knew she would be safe. She moved her hands onto their thighs, leaned back into her chair, and slid them toward their crotches. As she slid her hand up their thighs, their eyes swirled with excitement.

Silas and Dante peered at her over the rims of the cups, wondering just how far she was going to take things.

"What if the two of you—feed from me at the same time weee—you know?" she suggested.

Their bodies went rigid and she felt their desire as their canines slipped from their gums with the mere thought.

She squeezed tighter and slid her hand all the way up, only stopping once she reached the swelling heat between their legs and gave them a gentle rub.

Dante looked at her with a burning stare of desire. "It would be fucking amazing. Be careful what you wish for. I might just pick your ass up right now."

"These little sexual games you play, baby, are going to be repaid in kind." Silas slid his chair back, acting as if he was going to pick her up.

"Silas—don't you dare!"

They let out a throaty groan, and she prayed Jabari would stand. Her pulse quickened, and her heart was pounding against her breast. *They are going to take my ass right here,* she thought.

Jabari stood and held his silver goblet up. "I believe a toast is in order!" Jabari shouted, to her relief.

Everyone in attendance pounded their fists on the table, picked up their goblets, and stood with cups held high. "Aru—Aru—Aru!"

Silas and Dante looked at her like she had just pulled the rug out from under them. She pushed her chair back and stood, bringing their devious intentions to a halt.

"What's the matter, having trouble standing?" she asked.

They stood and casually cupped their hands in front of their crotches, acting as if they were adjusting their necks, but she knew full well they were hiding their arousal. They picked up their cups with one hand, keeping the other in place.

"We'll remember this," Silas growled.

"We are going to punish you in so many ways tonight," Dante rumbled.

They gained their composure as Jabari spoke. "Lord Montiago and Lord Cirillo, tonight, we drink for lovers, brothers, and lords!"

"Aru—Aru—Aru!"

"May you never look down upon your brother, unless he is on bent knee."

"Oooo—" The crowd erupted in subdued, drawn-out, wordless expressions following his statements.

"Save your lust for war on the battlefield and your lust for love in your bed."

"Ayyyy—"

"May your mates be hard on the battlefields and soft beneath your bodies."

"Ahhh—"

Silas and Dante crossed their arms over each other's behind her back and grabbed her ass. Jadis was mortified and felt the heat flush across her face. She was so taken aback, she fumbled with her cup and almost dropped it.

"Yep, no panties," Silas whispered.

Dante nodded and tilted his glass to Silas. "Bare ass, I like it."

"What's wrong, mon chéri? No words? Someone got you by the ass?" Silas joked.

"Fight the enemy who hardens your heart and love the mate who warms it," Jabari continued.

"Ahhh—"

"May you be the Lord of Darkness and shadow. May your mates be the light guiding you home."

"Ayyyy—"

"Let us drink to lovers, brothers, and lords!" Jabari nodded and tilted his cup to the crowd.

"Aru—Aru—Aru!"

They stood before the entrance into the main temple and waited before being motioned into the grand ballroom. The music from the orchestra filled the room and spilled out through the doors. *The harmony from the multitude of instruments is speaking to my soul. As Luciana would say, it's hauntingly beautiful,* Jadis thought.

As Jabari introduced each clan, they entered the temple. Nosferatu placed their fists against their hearts and raised their swords while their mates curtsied and nodded.

Jadis, Maddie, and Aria looked at each other and then back at Ivory and Skye and watched as they curtsied and nodded to them.

"We will never let them live this down," Jadis whispered.

"No, we will not." Maddie chuckled.

"Not a chance in hell," Aria whispered back.

As amused as they were, they weren't about to laugh aloud; it was the most sumptuous event that had taken place in years.

The look Ivory and Skye just shot our way says it all. They know they'll be the butt of our jokes for the rest of the night and longer. Jadis chuckled to herself.

"So, you play games with your sisters as well?" Silas whispered.

"It appears we need to up our game," Dante replied, agreeing with Silas.

"The two of you will behave yourselves. Everyone is looking at us."

"All the more entertaining, darling," Dante said.

Guests filled the room with chaotic chatter, dancing, and drinking. The orchestra was at the opposite end of the temple near the doors, so the guests meandering in the illuminated courtyards could also enjoy the drifting melodies.

The mates wore elegant, detailed dresses with a décolleté revealing their shoulders, arms, and cleavage. They also had refined hairdos and jeweled accessories adorning their bodies. The colors matching that of their clans, and their mates dressed as well as and similar to Silas and Dante.

They had been strolling through the ballroom for what felt like hours, giving everyone a chance to greet their new lords and congratulate them.

Searing looks of curiosity and whispers regarding Jadis did more than ramp up her anxiety. *I feel as if the air in the room is being constricted from my chest,* she thought.

Sigurd remained at her side and made it known to her, as well as a few others, more than once. They would have to go through him to get to her. It also allowed Silas and Dante to enjoy themselves without having to intervene, unless, of course, someone crossed the line. Then all bets were off.

The orchestra stopped, and Santiago stepped before the jubilant crowd. "Milady Montiago has a gift for her lord. Bring them!"

She took a deep breath and placed her hand over her heart to stop the erratic hammering.

The crowd parted way near the main entrance and surrounded Silas, Dante, and Jadis in a half circle and waited. The looks of excitement and curiosity apparent in the various expressions; all waiting to see what the mythical Dhamphyr had gifted her lord. She looked at Dante and smiled.

"What are you up to, darling?" he asked as he pulled her in tight.

"I have something for you. Silas helped me pick them."

Dante looked at Silas and chuckled. "*Ugly*, huh?"

"I couldn't spoil the surprise. I believe I would have suffered the wrath of the gods," Silas joked.

"I can't disagree." Dante laughed.

Silas stepped behind Dante and Jadis and placed his hands on Dante's shoulders and shook him back and forth, joking around. "I believe you will be pleased."

The crowd gasped when three black Friesian Stallions pranced into the center of the temple with one handler on either side of their enormous bodies. Their black leather harnesses had triangular, dark green emeralds lining the center of each strap in their entirety, and the parts of the tug straps had intricate designs etched into the platinum Jadis had designed.

The stallions were exquisite; their prancing nothing short of spectacular and powerful. Their black, wavy manes, which they wore like crowns on kings, and tails of black scroll ink, were stunning. They tossed their heads up and down, and huffed and grunted while their large front hooves met the floor and sounded like iron hitting stone.

Dante stood wide-eyed and Jadis could see the emotions that crossed his face. He looked at Silas, whose smile could light up the bleakest of nights.

Dante gave him an endearing nod and then looked back at Jadis. "Mon amour, you remembered the story after all that happened?"

"How could I forget anything that meant so much to you, not to mention how much your story meant to me in that moment." She backed away and playfully pulled him toward the stallions. "Let's meet them."

Dante ran his hands over the stallion's face and looked into his eyes as if speaking to him. There was deep intelligence, soft and warm, behind his brilliant hazel eyes. The stallion blinked multiple times as if he was understanding Dante. He walked around its entire body, patting and rubbing his back and hips before stopping at its mane. He ran his hands through the soft, lush locks, giving it a couple of hard pats of approval.

The stallions stand tall and strong, and I look like a child in comparison, while Dante and Silas look like gods standing there. They also remind me of Silas and Dante; intelligent, unbroken, and regal; not to mention spirited and headstrong, Jadis thought.

"We're *spirited and headstrong*?" Silas questioned, having read her thoughts.

Once again, she rolled her eyes, to their mutual amusement.

"I assume we have a stable suited to the lords and lady's stallions?" Dante questioned, knowing full well she had seen to their every need.

"Do you have to ask? It took the staff a month before our mate here would approve it," Silas explained.

"I have no doubt."

Jadis looked up at Dante. "You like them?"

"Like? Mon amour—there is no other gift in our world that could mean to me what they do." He swept her off her feet and held her in his arms. The depths of his love for her were like an antiquated flame he couldn't control.

He held Jadis in his arms but didn't speak.

His silence, the strength, and the power of his embrace say more than any words, she thought.

He set her down after a heated kiss and the three of them admired their stallions along with the rest of their family before being escorted back to the stables.

The orchestra began playing, and the crowd moved back to the dance floor and their entire clan gathered together to enjoy the rest of the night with each other.

"Milady," a voice said from behind Jadis.

She spun around. "Aiden!" Jadis gleamed as he pulled her in for a tight embrace. "I believe congratulations are in order?"

He pulled back slightly. "I believe you should address me accordingly—as in milord," he replied.

"Not a chance in hell—*milord*. The one and only time," she teased.

"I'll take what I can get," he replied as he gave her another tight embrace.

"Well, what do we have here? Two lords and a lady?" Aria announced.

"Yes, don't remind me." Jadis chuckled.

Aria moved in and gave Dante a hug. "Congratulation, milord." She smiled.

"Keep it up and we might have to make you address us formally all the time," he joked.

Aria raised her eyebrows in a questioning manner. "Good luck getting your mate to follow along."

"Where are the pheasants?" Maddie yelled out.

Ivory and Skye rolled their eyes, unamused. "If you all think we are ever curtseying again, it's not happening," Ivory stated firmly.

Jadis placed her hand on Ivory's shoulder. "We'll see about that."

"Yes—we will," Skye chided.

"What say we take our mates to the floor?" Eden suggested.

"I would love to take my mate to the floor," Silas replied.

Jadis poked Silas in the chest. "Don't even start that shit."

"Shall we?" Dante asked as he and Silas bent over, placed their hands behind their backs, and held the other out to her.

"We shall." Jadis took their hands, and they spun her around between them, moving amongst the crowd.

They easily fell into step with each other, and their smiles spread across their faces. The entire crowd flowed in unison to the humming of the waltz; their movements in tune with the vibrations of the music. Dante, Silas, and Jadis moved together, one step with every movement as they glided around the floor. They kept her between them, moving around each other; each step, twist, and turn smooth and graceful.

Silas and Dante looked at each other with radiant smiles and then back at their mate. They watched the elation on her face and the bounce in her step as they twirled her around in their arms; her joy and happiness were theirs.

Dante gazed at his beautiful mate. *I love everything about her; the way she smells of jasmine wrapped in early morning dew, the way I see her love at a glance, a subtle touch, or the passion in her kiss.*

Silas held her hand, lifted it up, and moved gracefully around her. He slowed when someone bumped into his shoulder.

"Excuse me, milord," Eden stated. "I was wondering if I may switch partners."

"You sure your mate can handle us both?" Silas stated as he winked at Maddie.

Eden squeezed Maddie's hand. "I think she can hold her own."

"In that case, milady—may we have this dance?" Dante asked as they held their hands out to Maddie.

Maddie chuckled at the enhanced accent Dante was speaking with. "It would honor me, milords." She strode away, hand in hand with Dante and Silas.

"Milady," Eden said as he bowed.

"Milord," she replied, with an overemphasized curtsy, which cracked him up.

"Has hell lost their demon?" he joked.

Other than being in Fréyonne with him, I've never seen him release his stresses and preoccupations with business matters. I love it. "So now you're a funny vampire instead of one with a headache?"

Eden again laughed at her quip. "So far you haven't given me one. I haven't seen one mummified body."

Jadis patted his chest. "The night's still young."

"I think I have plenty of backup tonight." He winked.

She gave him an overdramatic eye roll, causing another round of laughter between them.

Eden held her hand in his and had his other on her lower back. He pulled her into his body and spun in circles. Her lighthearted laughter and confident charm warmed his heart.

Jadis felt Eden pull her in close and twirl them around, feet from where they had been. She was enjoying Eden's company so much, so she hadn't noticed how close the crowd had moved in around them.

She looked around and the males within a few feet had her pinned in their sights. *The way they glance in my direction and nod when our eyes meet is uncomfortable.* Luciana's words of warning went off like alarm bells. *They are noticing me.*

"It's fine, baby girl, I got you." Eden smiled, calming her nerves.

She returned the smile, knowing he wouldn't let anyone near her.

"Milady, all is well." Sigurd was suddenly next to her and Eden with a beautiful partner of his own.

Jadis's eyes went wide, seeing Sigurd dancing. "Not only does he joke, he dances!"

"Aye, milady, quite well," he replied.

The music changed, and Silas and Dante moved back in. "I believe a slow dance is in order," Dante suggested.

"I believe I owe that to my mate." Eden smiled at Maddie and took her hand.

"I'll let our new lord have the first dance." Silas's soft lips met hers, as well as the heat of his tongue, before he handed her over to Dante.

Dante picked her up in his arms and twirled around. She rested her face in the crook of his neck.

He held her tightly as he glided around the floor with her in his arms. The simple gestures of their hands, the way they looked into each other's eyes, and the unannounced eroticism of their bodies swaying together, made her deaf to envious whispers and unwanted glances.

Dante's mouth fell to hers as he held the back of her neck. After a long, passion-filled kiss, she felt the intimate warmth of his breath in her ear.

"Mon amour, the last time I danced with you, I could only imagine what I desired to do with you—tonight, I will do what I desired to imagine," he whispered.

"The entire world could disappear as long as I am in your arms." She pulled back and kissed him again. "I'm hungry," she whispered.

Dante bent his head and the sharp pierce of her canines into his vein sent a lust-filled hunger through his body. After she took her fill, he pulled her head back and peered into her swirling amber eyes.

"My turn." He pulled the choker down with his finger and sank his canines into her tender flesh.

Between feeding from Dante, the music playing in the background, and the fact they were still dancing sent her mind spiraling and her veins humming.

"You intoxicate me," she whispered.

"I can feel the flow of passion in your blood, mon amour. I love you with all that I am."

"And I you, milord."

"I like how that sounds on your tongue."

"And I like the taste of yours," she growled.

He set her down and spun her in circles. He stretched their arms their full length before letting go of her hand. The momentum sent her backward, and she bumped into someone else.

Silas grabbed her shoulders and spun her around so she was facing him.

"Shall we, mon chéri?"

"We shall. Now kiss me, milord."

He swept her into his arms and his tongue danced with hers to the same tune as their bodies. She pulled back and sank her canines into his musky skin, letting his blood pool into her mouth.

Silas moaned and squeezed her butt cheek in his hand. As soon as she finished, she offered her vein to him.

Once he took his fill, his canines receded, and licked the little trickles of blood from her neck and took her mouth again.

"I love you, vampire, and I love the way you send shivers up my spine, and the way you growl—you are mine," she whispered.

"Let me hear you say it, mon chéri."

"I am yours, vampire. Body, blood, and heart."

"Have I ever mentioned that you take my breath away?"

"And you, assassin, have my heart buried within yours."

The music changed again, and Silas set her down. Dante moved in, and the three of them fell back into step with each other.

Sigurd spun a new lady in their direction and met Silas, Dante, and Jadis, shoulder to shoulder.

"Milords." He nodded.

"A brunet this time?" Jadis joked telepathically, so his partner wouldn't take offense. *"Under all that stoicism you're quite the lady's man. Who would have thought?"*

"He's never had a problem with the ladies," Silas replied.

"So all it takes to disappear on you is to have a couple of beauties on hand?"

"Nye, milady, nothing comes before our duty and fealty to our lords, not even the ladies. I will stop you." He furrowed his brows in jest, and his unfamiliar humor forced her to laugh aloud.

Bain made his way around the dance floor to where Jadis, Silas, and Dante were with the rest of their clan. "Now that you're married to two lords, do you think you can dance with a mere wizard?" Bain asked as he held out his hand.

"I think I can dance with my nanny," she joked.

Bain cocked his head at her. "So I'm still *your nanny*?"

"No one has said otherwise."

Bain took Jadis's hand and escorted his lady off the floor before spinning Jadis around so quickly she almost lost her balance, making him laugh as he caught her.

"Silas, Dante, will you retrieve the bruja named Amsi and bring her to the floor?" Jadis asked privately.

"What are you up to now, darling?" Dante asked.

"Nothing, baby."

"You're never up to nothing, my dear," Silas replied.

Silas and Dante headed off to find Amsi.

"Amsi, I presume?" Silas asked.

"Yes—yes, I am, milords," she stuttered, shocked they were approaching her.

"Care to dance?" Dante asked.

"It would be my honor, milords," she said, along with a polite curtsy. As they escorted her to the floor, the ostentatious looks of jealousy she noticed were only increasing her anxiety.

"No need to worry. Our mate asked us to retrieve you," Silas admitted, letting her know she was not for them for more than one reason. Betraying Jadis would be tantamount to a snowflake surviving in hell.

They escorted her to the floor for Jadis. *"Bain?"* Dante chuckled to Silas privately.

"I'm afraid so."

CHAPTER 4

The girls had met Amsi when she accompanied her father, Adelrik, to the oasis a month ago. He was another aristocratic vampire who had close ties to Jabari and his clan. He had offered his clan's help to locate Evanora after word had spread about her disappearance.

The girls enjoyed Amsi's company, even though they had only hung out with her on a few occasions. She was pleasant, refined, not to mention beautiful, and a powerful bruja in her own right. She, too, was a descendant of the original coven that fought during the Great War. They had all become friends, and she was one of the few girls to be allowed free access to the temple.

Dante and Silas danced their way toward Jadis and Bain with Amsi and moved in next to them.

"Jadis, how are you? You look stunning." Amsi smiled.

"As do you, and have you met Bain?"

"No, I haven't."

"Well, this is Bain. Bain, I'd like you to meet Amsi. She's a friend of ours and Adelrik's daughter."

"What are you doing, darling?" Bain questioned silently.

"I thought you should meet a nice girl rather than hanging with the 'feeders' all the time," she admitted.

"You do—do you?" He nodded to Amsi and smiled. *"She is stunning, Jadis."*

"I think so," she replied before addressing Amsi. "I believe I want my mates back. How about you dance with Bain?"

"I would be honored." Amsi smiled at Bain and Jadis watched as her face became rosy. *Her shyness is adorable,* Jadis thought.

"Amsi," Bain stated, as he held his hand out to her. She smiled and took his hand in hers.

"Well done, baby." Dante winked.

"Amsi's a step up." She chuckled.

"Yes, she is," Silas agreed.

Aiden and Aria moved in next to them. "Did you just set Bain up with Amsi?" Aria asked.

"I did. I like her."

"As do I. Excellent choice."

"Jadis, will do me the honor?" Aiden asked.

"Absolutely!"

"You going to be okay with those two?" Aiden asked as he handed Aria off to Silas and Dante.

"I believe I can manage. As long as they can handle you dancing with Jadis. You're all a little possessive," she teased.

Dante looked at Jadis and Aria. "We're *possessive*? Didn't the two of you have a couple witches banished?"

"Better to banish them than let Jadis do it." Aria laughed.

"You're not wrong." Silas chuckled.

Aiden spun Jadis onto the floor and held her close.

"I'm so proud of you, Aiden. You more than deserved the recognition, and you look gorgeous, by the way."

"Thank you, darling, and have I mentioned you are stunning?" He held her against his body, transfixed with the whites of her canines when her mouth parted with laughter, and how her eyes reflected the flickering candlelight. His heart and mind were a battlefield, and she was the puppet master pulling his strings. He couldn't help but wonder how different things had ended up over the last few years. Back were his eyes of betrayal as quickly as he had closed them.

He noticed the way she tilted her head, as if trying to capture his thoughts. He twirled them around, trying to mask his feelings. *I will not interfere with her happiness, nor let her feel my chaos,* he told himself.

"I see Bain is dancing with Amsi. It's safe to assume that was you're doing?"

"Yes, we think she's wonderful, not to mention beautiful."

"Well, if she has your approval, far be it for me to say anything. Just try not to pull her down the rabbit's hole. She's quite reserved. Let's keep it that way for Bain's sake." He laughed.

"Still a funny vampire, I see, and I believe you followed us down the hole willingly."

"Darling, I believe that was all the 'Bewitching Queen of Blackened Hearts' doing'."

She let out a larger-than-life laugh as they took a few more graceful steps before he twirled the two of them around again in unison with the large crown.

Jadis nodded in their direction. "Look at Bain. He seems to be enjoying her company."

"Yes, he is. You did him justice."

"Aria and I already invited her to stay in the temple with us. It'll give them plenty of time to get acquainted."

Aiden looked at her with an amused expression. "May your gods help her."

"Help her? She's a little more spirited than you think."

"Great—so we've got another hellion on our hands?"

"Aren't you a lord now? You all should be able to handle it."

"Our titles have nothing to do with you and Aria being a pain in the ass."

"I would call you an idiot, but I don't want to disrespect a lord," she teased.

He let out a belly laugh in response. "Well, hell, who would have thought a title would get you to hold your tongue, although I don't expect it to last, IF—I'm being honest."

"By the way, the cuff is beautiful, and I understand you had a little something to do with it?"

"I did." He winked.

"It means more to me than you will ever know. I will cherish it always."

"I know the feeling," Aiden replied.

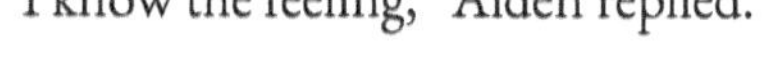

"You look exquisite tonight." Bain smiled.

"Thank you, milord." Amsi felt the warmth of her cheeks once again. She tried to avoid the green-eyed glances from the blood hosts, not to mention the unmated brujas, most of whom saw Bain as one of the most sought-after warriors in the temple.

"I understand the girls have invited you to stay in the temple—yes?" Bain looked at the rosiness in her cheeks that complemented her sea-green eyes and delicate shyness. He admired her velvety auburn hair flowing over her shoulders and down her back. *She's intoxicating.* Her gentle nature reminded him of Maddie. However, he felt a supernatural force enshrouded beneath her vulnerable appearance. The unexpected allure caught him off guard, as did his desire to shield and possess her.

"Yes, they have and they've been wonderful."

"Be careful with them. Jadis becomes a flame before a spark." He chuckled.

Amsi chuckled as well. "Yes, I am aware. They have told me a few stories."

The music transitioned, and the crowd slowed, shifting positions and partners. "Would you join me for a drink?" Bain asked.

"I would love to." She smiled.

Bain escorted them off the floor and joined his clan, who had gathered near the bar.

"Is there room for two more?" Bain asked as he nodded to the bartender, who handed over two glasses. Bain handed one to Amsi and tilted his glass toward her. She responded in kind and took a sip with a radiating smile.

As soon as Bain appeared with Amsi in tow, the girls moved in and surrounded Amsi with a warm greeting.

"I see you have captured Bain's attention," Maddie whispered.

"I don't know about that. It's just a couple of dances," Amsi replied modestly.

"It's more than that. He likes you." Jadis winked.

Amsi tilted her glass to Jadis. "I assume you have ulterior motives?"

"Yes, he needs a mate."

"Jadis!" she stated, feeling somewhat embarrassed. "There are many ladies here tonight who would be more suitable."

Aria looked around at the women with a glare. "Most of whom are ambitious worms."

"I'm sure some of them are very nice," Amsi replied.

Skye laughed aloud. "Nice? Just wait and see how *nice* they are when they see you on Bain's arm."

"We're just watching out for you. We know what's coming your way," Ivory offered.

"You don't have to do that. I'm comfortable going back to the guest-house. I don't want to intrude."

"Nonsense, we have each other's backs. Plus, it will give us all time to get better acquainted," Maddie added.

"You don't know how devious those girls can be," Jadis rumbled. "Just look around. They are all desperately vying for his attention. They whisper of new lords rising, while the tips of their tongues are covered in thorns."

Amsi was taken aback by Jadis's searing words of warning. She looked around the expansive room and caught the glares and eye rolls.

Aria reached for Amsi's hand and gave it a gentle squeeze. "Don't let them bother you. We deal with it every day. Just stick with us and you'll be fine."

Their sincerity was heartwarming; she enjoyed Bain's company and was grateful to have them watching out for her. If Bain indeed courted her, she wasn't sure she could deal with what appeared to be an envious crowd with ulterior motives.

"Jadis?" a voice stated.

She turned around, only to see Giovanna Mercado standing there.

"Giovanna! Well, hell I didn't know you would be here."

They grabbed each other in a tight embrace, happy to see each other again.

"I was going to reach out, but I figured you were pretty busy with everything going on," Giovanna admitted.

"Skye—Ivory," Jadis called. They turned around and squealed in delight.

"Giovanna!" they stated in unison, along with an endearing hug.

"Why didn't you get in touch with us when you arrived?" Ivory asked.

"As I told Jadis, I was going to, but I assumed you all would have more important matters to attend to."

"We are never too busy for friends," Skye offered. "Next time you will reach out regardless of the situation."

"Dante, Silas," Jadis called.

"What's up, darling?" Silas asked as he and Dante walked over.

"I want you to meet a close friend of ours. This is Giovanna Mercado, and these are my mates Silas and Dante."

"Mercado? Are you Agustos's daughter?" Silas asked.

"I am, milord," she answered with a polite curtsy.

"It's a pleasure to make your acquaintance. Your father is well-known to us," Dante offered.

"Thank you, milord, it's nice to meet you as well." She smiled.

"I didn't know when you mentioned Giovanna she was Agustos's daughter," Silas added.

"I never thought about it," Jadis admitted.

"You are welcome to stay in the temple with the girls anytime you visit," Silas offered.

"Thank you, milord, that's very generous."

"If you will excuse us, we are going to find your father." Silas nodded.

"We'll be back, darling," Dante added as he gave Jadis a gentle kiss on the forehead.

Silas lifted her chin with his fingers and kissed her cheek before leaving with Dante to find Agustos.

Jadis, Skye, and Ivory had met Giovanna years ago; she was also a powerful bruja with a flair for adventure. She was beautiful, a bit on the taller side, five-foot-seven with a slim frame, muscular build and long, wavy, auburn hair that reached the middle of her back and deep, soul-stealing, umber-brown eyes.

Her family had moved to Sagvon from Montefeltro for a short period when her father, a well-respected warrior, was there on business. Her mother was also a powerful bruja and one of the originals. Giovanna and her family moved around, never staying in one place for long. She was a well-trained equestrian since her father owned a stable of pure-bred Arabians. She was well-traveled, educated, and wild; there were many nights and weekends she spent with Jadis, Skye, and Ivory raising hell. She was also quick-witted with a sharp tongue and not afraid of confrontation.

Giovanna, Skye, Ivory, and Jadis were catching up with each other and introducing her to Maddie, Aria, and Amsi when someone bumped into Jadis, making her spill her drink.

"My apologies, milady, I didn't see you standing there." He took a few steps forward and stood chest to chest with her. "Since we're standing here, how about a drink or maybe a dance elsewhere?" There was a burning intensity pooling in his eyes as he glanced down at her chest and scanned her body before running his hand over her shoulder.

Sigurd grabbed him by the shoulder and spun him around. "Milady is not open for invitations."

As he faced Sigurd, he shot him a challenging look and tried to knock Sigurd's hand off his shoulder.

Dante and Silas didn't have time to greet Agustos before feeling the threat to Jadis. The crowd noticed the error in his judgment and moved back the moment Silas and Dante appeared.

"I offered her a drink and a dance, milords. I didn't offer to bed her. Not yet anyway," he drunkenly snarled, also having 'turned' at the looming threat.

Silas snarled and cocked his head. "You should have thought twice before speaking."

He and Dante latched onto either side of his neck and drained him. Silas then waved his hand over the mess, leaving only his ashes at their feet.

The ladies gasped, some of whom had covered their mouths. The warriors, however, cheered and chanted.

"One who succumbs to ignorance finds death!" a voice rang out from the boisterous crowd.

"He who cannot control his drink cannot control his life!" another announced.

"Aru—Aru—Aru!" the rest chanted.

"Oh my gods," Amsi whispered, having grabbed Maddie's hand.

"Our mates don't take kindly to someone touching or speaking to us so brazenly." Maddie smiled at her and gave her hand a gentle squeeze.

Amsi's father, Adelrik, walked over and stood behind her. "Their reputation precedes them. I'm not sure you understand who Silas is. I think it's best if you keep your distance from their clan, my love."

"Father, Bain has been a perfect gentleman."

"Are you interested in him?"

"Oh, Father, it's too early to judge. I'm simply enjoying his company."

"Just so you know, I too will stay in the temple."

Amsi looked back at the girls and rolled her eyes out of her father's line of sight.

Silas and Dante stepped toward Jadis. "I believe we'll have to keep a closer eye on you," Dante said.

"I believe our mate needs a fresh drink," Silas added.

Her spilled drink was already being cleaned up, and the maître d' handed her a warm, wet rag to clean her hands. "Did the drink soil your dress, milady?" he asked, looking her up and down.

"No, it's fine, thank you for asking."

As soon as she had finished wiping her hands, he took the rag from her and handed her a fresh drink.

Dante then glanced at her gown, waived his hand and the crimson stain disappeared.

"Thank you, baby."

Dante smiled and placed a gentle kiss on her lips. "We can't have you walking around in a soilded gown, now can we?"

"No, no we can't." She smiled. "By the way, have I thanked you two for the cuff? You don't know how much it means to me."

"No need. We heard you and Luciana speaking," Silas admitted.

Jadis smiled, not being a bit surprised. "A couple little eavesdroppers?"

"For you, yes," Dante replied.

"I will cherish it always."

"As we do you," Silas answered.

"I expected Jadis to be the one to drain someone tonight," Eden said as he and Maddie joined them.

"You're ridiculous," Jadis replied.

Amsi politely acknowledged Silas and Dante. "Milords." Their intimidating presence sent her body into a heap of nerves again, especially after what she had just witnessed; not to mention what her father said about Silas. She had to cup her hands together to stop them from trembling.

"No need to address us so formally, Amsi. A friend of our mate's is a friend of ours," Dante said.

"Adelrik." Dante took his forearm.

"Milord, I believe congratulations are in order."

"Thank you."

"Adelrik." Silas grasped his forearm.

"Milord," Adelrik replied.

Bain looked at Adelrik, who was standing behind his daughter. "Good to see you again."

"Aye, and you as well," Adelrik replied.

As soon as Bain walked away from Adelrik, Jadis took a moment to introduce him to Giovanna. "Bain, I'd like you to meet our friend, Giovanna. She is Agustos's daughter."

"Nice to me you." Bain smiled.

"It's my pleasure," Giovanna replied.

Bain handed Amsi another drink. "Enjoying yourself?"

"Very much so and thank you."

Amsi noticed a group of girls headed their way and she nervously shifted her stance, knowing they were heading for Bain.

"Jadis, Aria, mind if we join you?" one of them asked.

Aria and Jadis side-eyed each other; their annoyance clear to their group. Jadis gave her girls an overdramatic eye roll, causing them all to chuckle.

"Oh, the desperation," Giovanna coughed under her breath.

Jadis pulled the girls' thoughts. *They are indeed jealous and trying to get close to us in order to get to Bain. They are also hoping to push Amsi out of their way.*

Mensi nodded at Bain with a curtsy and fluttered her eyelashes. "Maybe you would do me the honor and join me for a dance later?" Mensi ignored the girls snickering at her, not wanting to offend Bain.

Bain looked at Amsi and winked. He placed his arm around her waist and pulled her in tight. "I have promised the night to Amsi." He nodded in the direction they came from, letting them know it was time to leave.

"Tonight is for family," Silas stated, also gesturing for them to leave.

Amsi looked at Bain, smiled, and placed her arm around his back.

"I'll leave the two of you to get better acquainted." Adelrik kissed Amsi on either cheek and nodded at Bain as he walked away. The girls curtseyed, leaving angry and embarrassed, from being dismissed by them all.

"Who do they think they are?" Mensi grumbled.

"They are the Montiago and Cirillo mates, that's who," Elanora stated angrily.

"So, who's the new bitch with Bain?" another questioned.

"Who the hell knows, just a lord digger," she answered, laughing at her own pun.

Jadis and the girls could still hear their thoughts as they walked away; Maddie looked at Amsi. "Get used to it. Hence the reason we keep our circle small."

"Want me to take them out back?" Giovanna joked.

"Maybe later." Ivory chuckled.

Aria waved her hand dismissively. "They aren't even worth our time."

"Who is the warrior who spun that jerk around?" Giovanna asked.

"Sigurd. He's Silas's first-in-command and not to be taken lightly," Jadis explained.

Giovanna took a sip of her drink and peered at Sigurd over the rim of her glass. "He's hot as hell!"

"Maybe I can get you a dance with him?" Jadis offered.

"I would owe you big time."

As the sun began to rise, the crowd dispersed. Bain walked arm in arm with Amsi as he escorted her to her room.

"I have enjoyed your company tonight." Bain smiled.

"And I yours. Thank you for seeing me to my room."

"My pleasure. We will sleep through the day. Would you join me for a late lunch?"

"I would love to."

"I will come for you. Until tomorrow then." Bain kissed the back of her hand and she shut the door behind her once she was safely in her room.

Amsi fell onto her back on the bed, smiling from ear to ear, her anxious heart pounding. She cupped her hands together and held them to her mouth, thinking about Bain. The way he smelled, how polite he had been, and his tender kiss. She was grateful to Jadis for setting her up. *He seems wonderful. I can't wait for tomorrow to come.* She also thought about how easily Silas and Dante killed the warrior. *I wonder if Bain would react the same way?*

As soon as Silas, Dante, and Jadis made it to their room, they headed straight for the shower. Silas and Dante shucked their tunics and tossed them onto a chair before pulling off their boots mid-stride.

Silas turned Jadis around and untied the laces on the back of her dress, freeing each crisscross with his fingers. He swept the hair off her neck and over her other shoulder, then ran the back of his fingers down her slim neckline and over her shoulders. He trailed his hands along her arms, pushing her dress down to her waist.

She leaned her head against his chest, reached up, and cupped her hand around the back of his neck, pulling him down for a heated kiss. He cupped her breast in his hand before pushing the dress off her hips into a soft pile at her feet.

"After waiting for this all night, we are going to take you all morning." Silas moaned into her mouth before pulling back.

He slid his hands over her shoulders and down her arms, and brushed the sides of her breasts. Small bumps rose on her skin as he traced his fingers over her naked body.

Dante stood in front of her, and she began pulling his shirt up and untucked it from his pants. He grabbed the bottom of it and pulled it the rest of the way off, then tossed it onto the floor.

She ran her hands over his perfect chest and his muscular shoulders, admiring his intricate tattoos and battle scars, kissing each one as she traced them with her fingers.

"Damn, I want you," Dante moaned before pulling her mouth to his.

The sensations of his mouth on hers and Silas behind her, kissing her shoulders, swept her into a heated current, the desperation filling the core between her legs.

Silas pulled his shirt off and ran his hands down her waist and over her toned, taut ass while Dante took a slight step back as she untied his laces. He was already hard and uncomfortable from the tightness of the leather holding back his erection.

Jadis pushed his pants down and ran her hand over his large swell as she pulled his mouth to hers again. She pulled away and turned around to face Silas. She untied his pants and let her hands tease his hardened groin as she pulled on the laces.

They headed into the shower, and the hot water rushed over their bodies.

"We are going to take all of you, mon amour," Dante growled.

"My dick haas been hard as a rock all night," Silas moaned.

The anticipation of having sex with them the entire evening sent a fresh rush of wetness between her legs.

Dante moved behind her, cupped her breasts in his hands, and massaged them. He pinched her plump, hardened nipples between his fingers, causing her to moan softly.

Silas stood in front of her and placed his hand between her legs, letting his fingers slip into her wet core, titillating her nub with his thumb. She let out a gasp and grabbed the back of his head, her soft, warm tongue tasting his.

"You made us an offer earlier," Silas whispered into her mouth.

She pulled back and her eyes widened.

Dante pulled her head back, and his mouth met hers. "We are going to show you what it's like for us to feed from each other—at the same time," Dante moaned.

They heard her heart skip a beat and her heightened pulse began pushing her blood through her veins at a feverish pace. They sank their canines into her tender flesh on either side of her neck and pulled her blood in opposite directions.

She could feel everything they did. *It's like having triple sensations rushing through my veins and mind.*

"I told you it would be fucking amazing," Dante stated telepathically.

Silas and Dante slit their wrists and held them up with their fists cupped together. They let their blood pool into her mouth at the same time they drank from her.

"Take it all in, mon chéri," Silas stated.

As she drank their blood, it was as if she was being pulled into an ethereal realm. *It's as if all of our lives are flowing together.* Silas, shoving his fingers in, nearly undid her. They had her turned on all night and now, playing with their naked bodies while they played with hers, not to mention feeding from her at the same time she drank from them, sent her mind spiraling in a hundred different directions.

She reached behind her and grabbed Dante's shaft in a tight grip and rubbed the length of his erection as he stood behind her.

As soon as Dante felt her firm grip, he let go of her neck with a guttural groan and massaged her breasts harder. The warmth of her hand, the soft flesh rubbing his, brought about a desperate need to come in her, and now. He leaned against the shower wall, grabbed a fistful of her hair, pulled her head backward toward his chest, and shoved his tongue into her mouth.

She had to pull away from Dante in order to gasp for a breath. Silas was relentless between her legs. His fingers sliding in and out, his thumb moving in rough circles over her sex, was calling her orgasm to the surface. As soon as the wave of pleasure rose, Silas slipped them out.

"Not yet, mon chéri, I want you begging."

"Silas—" she groaned.

He leaned against the wall and pushed her head down, wanting her to take him into her mouth.

As soon as she was on her knees, Dante kneeled behind her, reached around, slipped his fingers in, and teased her swollen, sensitive nub. Her whispered moans were only ratcheting up his own arousal.

She took Silas's shaft into the slickness of her mouth, sucking and licking her way around his vein. He wrapped her hair around his fist and leaned the back of his head into the shower wall. "Goddamn, that's amazing," he groaned.

He took a deep breath when the tips of her canines scraped his skin as she slid his shaft from her mouth. She then nipped his tip with her canines, making him flinch.

"Fuck!" He had to place his other palm on the wall in order to hold himself steady as he watched her; the painful pricks of pleasure brought about his need to release.

Another wave of pleasure rose when Dante lifted her hips and lowered her body onto his rigid shaft. They were all succumbing to the orgasms they had been chasing all night.

Silas groaned as he released himself into her mouth.

"Ahhh—hell," Dante rumbled. He gave another hard shove followed by another, bringing about both his and Jadis's orgasms.

"Dante—shit," she moaned, as the pleasure bordered on pain. She reached around to hold his hips back, but he grabbed her hand.

"We are not going to be gentle," Dante mumbled. With a few more hard shoves and a guttural groan, he let his fluid fill her body.

After a few minutes of gathering themselves together, Silas slid down the wall, and Dante and Jadis moved onto the bench.

She lay across their laps as they let their bodies relax. She reveled in the spray's warmth and the way their hands slid across her body.

Silas glanced at Dante. "Not sure about you, but I'm not done."

Dante pulled her wet hair to the side, exposing her face. "We are just getting started, mon amour."

Silas ran his hand down her back and slapped her ass. "Oww—dammit!"

"Time for bed," Dante stated.

They stood up, and Dante tossed her over his shoulder and carried her to their bed. He tossed her onto her back and slid in next to her.

"Can I at least have ten minutes?" She chuckled.

"No can do, love," Dante replied.

He moved his body over hers and parted her mouth with his. He rubbed his already hard shaft between her legs before moving to the side.

Silas flipped her onto her stomach, and the two of them massaged her body.

Their powerful hands feel amazing massaging me, she thought.

She felt the warmth of Silas's breath in her ear. "This is the only moment of relaxation we are going to give you."

They massaged their way around her entire body, making her squirm beneath their touch.

Dante massaged her thighs and spread them apart; he ran his hand over her cheeks and moved his thumbs alongside her sex. Every time he moved from her thighs to her butt, she raised it a little, desperate for him to move further between her legs.

"Dante—" she moaned, begging for him to touch her elsewhere.

She tried to roll over, but Silas pinned her down while Dante held her legs.

Silas turned her head to the side to face him. "We didn't ask you to move," he stated as he stole a kiss.

"Silas—" she whispered.

"Be still," he growled.

Dante moved his hand between her legs and cupped her sex, his palm moving in a hard circle. "Is this what you want, darling?"

"Yes—" she whispered.

Silas slipped his hands beneath her body and massaged her breasts and nipples.

She let out a guttural moan when Dante slid his fingers into her core. Her body trembled, aching to release again. As soon as her orgasm settled, they flipped her over and switched places.

She looked down, and Silas had lowered his head between her legs and pushed her thighs apart. He began teasing her with the warmth of his mouth and flickering tongue. She shoved her head into the pillows and looked up at Dante and cupped the side of his face in her hand.

Dante bent over and took her mouth to his, wanting to replace his tongue with his shaft. He straddled her, and she slid her tongue up and down his vein, scraping her canines along the sides.

He placed one hand on the headboard and grabbed her head with the other. "Take it, baby," he moaned.

Silas sucked her sex into his mouth and slid his fingers into her core. He could feel her body clench his fingers and he watched as she bunched the sheet up in her free hand.

Her mind danced between dizzying thoughts and pleasure; she was soaking in their ecstasy and they hers. Her body released as another heated swell rose.

As soon as her convulsions slowed, Silas forcefully slid himself in.

Her body didn't come down before Silas gave a hard shove. The sharp pains succumbed to pleasure as she relaxed enough to take him all in.

"Mon amour—" Dante rumbled.

She could feel his vein pulse and he let out a guttural moan and released himself. After a few breathless minutes, he pulled his shaft from her mouth and fell onto his back next to her.

"Irrumabo mi hi," Silas moaned as he moved up her body and flipped her over.

She wrapped her legs around his waist and her arms around his neck. He thrust himself in a few more times, bringing them both the pleasure of another release.

Silas fell on top of her body, his breathing heavy. He lifted his head and peered into her eyes. "You belong to us—say it."

"I am yours, milords."

Silas rolled off and lay next to her. She looked at Dante, who rolled over and slipped her a little tongue. He moved his body against her backside and she tucked his arm under her breasts. She laid her head on Silas's shoulder and bent her leg over his crotch.

CHAPTER 5

J adis awoke the following afternoon with her head on Dante's shoulder, and he and Silas were already awake as usual.

"It's about time you joined us, baby." Dante stroked her hair and kissed her forehead.

"You slept well. We thought we might have to wake you." Silas pulled her head toward him and parted her mouth.

"After all the two of you did to me for hours, I don't think I can get out of bed." She chuckled.

"Maybe we should wake you properly," Dante teased.

"Don't even think about it."

"Then I suggest you get up. We have somewhere we need to be."

"Where? I'm tired, not to mention sore. Can't we just stay in bed and sleep?" She nestled into the crook of Dante's neck, reached for Silas's arm, and pulled him against her back.

Silas kissed her shoulder and neck, and she let out a soft, sleepy moan.

"Mon amour, you need to wake up. We have a few stallions to take care of."

How Dante said it warmed her heart. "Yes—we do!"

"Well, that seemed to wake you." Silas chuckled.

She sat straight up and bounced onto her knees and faced them both. "Well? Are we going or not?" She laughed as she pulled their arms.

They sat up and pushed her onto her back and plopped on either side of her.

"Come on, get up." She pushed their bodies, but they held steady.

"Someone's frisky all of a sudden. Maybe we should oblige, milady." Dante winked.

"I thought you wanted to see our stallions?"

"I thought you wanted to stay in bed?" Silas asked.

They grabbed her arms and pinned them above her head. "If you can't take us again, how about we have breakfast together?" Dante suggested.

"As in ONLY feed together?" she questioned.

"Yes, mon amour, blood only. We'll take your body later." Dante smiled coyly.

"Okay," she replied, not sure they would be able to control themselves.

"Only blood for now," Silas replied.

They repositioned her body between theirs and sank their canines into their wrists and grasped each other's fist. She cupped her hands around theirs and held their wrists over her mouth and let the blood pool into her mouth.

They bent down on either side of her neck and sank their canines into her flesh. She tasted her own blood flowing through Dante's and Silas's veins as they fed together. *It's incredible,* she thought.

They walked arm in arm together as they headed for the stables. As soon as the stables were in view, a group of girls were leaning over the iron railings, trying to feed their stallions.

"What the hell are they doing?" Jadis snarled.

"We shall find out," Dante rumbled.

The girls jumped off the rail when they noticed Jadis, Silas, and Dante walk up behind them.

"Milords," they stated in unison, with a nervous curtsy.

"You will address our mate as milady," Silas demanded.

They nodded and addressed Jadis formally. "Milady."

"What are you doing here?" Jadis snarled as she let go of her mates.

"We were just looking at the horses. They are beautiful, milady." The young gal side-eyed her friends and Jadis knew they were annoyed she showed up with Silas and Dante.

"They're stallions and I don't remember any of us giving you permission to be here and what the hell are you trying to feed them?" she demanded as she took one slow step after the other toward them.

"Milady—we—we are sorry, we didn't think—"

Jadis cut her off mid-sentence. "You're right, you didn't," she replied as she circled them before grabbing the food from the gal's hand. "Grass—you're trying to feed them grass?" She tossed the grass down and snatched two of them by the throat.

Their friends yelped and tried to run. However, Silas and Dante materialized in front of them.

Dante held his hand up, stopping them from leaving. "Going somewhere?"

"You haven't answered our mate's questions. We would also like to know what you are doing here," Silas demanded.

Jadis released her grip just enough to let them speak.

"We—we were just admiring them," another stuttered.

"You forget who I am. I've pulled your thoughts and you speak bullshit and your intentions are devious."

"Milady, we—"

Again, Jadis cut her off. "You choose to lie to me?"

Jadis looked at Silas and Dante. "Should I drain them now? It seems they were hoping to catch one or both of you here alone. They're also hoping to find Bain."

Sigurd appeared as if out of nowhere. "Milords." He nodded. "It appears you have an issue?"

The girls' eyes went wide and their faces turned ashen at the looks on Silas's, Dante's, and Sigurd's faces.

"It appears so," Silas replied.

Dante looked at Silas and Sigurd. "We should intervene before we have five mummified bodies in our hands."

"Jadis, let them go. They will be dealt with appropriately," Silas stated.

Jadis looked at them and squinted her eyes. She wanted to drain them for the mere thought of what they wanted to do with her mates.

"Mon amour, let them go," Dante added.

She turned back to the girls in her grasp. "They are my mates, and those are our stallions. I ever see you back here again, I promise you'll see your last days." She tossed them to the side, and they stumbled and fell to the ground.

Sigurd stood over them. "Get up."

They gathered themselves off the ground and stood in a petrified group.

"Enjoy your ride. I'll handle the offenders," Sigurd offered.

"Take them to the cells for a week. Let them have a taste of what ill intentions will get them," Silas ordered.

"A week in the cells?" one of them cried. "You can't do that!"

Silas tilted his head with raised his eyebrows. "I assure you I can."

Sigurd motioned for the girls to move, not letting them argue any further.

"A week?" Jadis questioned.

"You're displeased," Silas said.

Dante looked at Silas before addressing Jadis. "I'm almost afraid to ask. What would you like to see happen?"

"How about a week for each stallion and another two for having desires for my mates?"

Silas and Dante looked at each other and then back at Jadis. "Have we ever denied you anything?" Silas smiled.

"Five weeks is appropriate. Better than death. Had it been a male having such thoughts about you, there would be no need for a cell," Dante said.

"Five it is then," Silas agreed. "Now that we have put the issue to rest, shall we ride?"

"Yes, but you still should have let me drain them."

"Sigurd will give them a lashing," Silas replied, chuckling.

She looked around. "Who the hell left them unattended?"

"We will find out and handle it," Dante said as held out his hand. "Come, love."

Silas and Dante put the reins on their stallions and watched Jadis levitating to get her stallion's reins on.

"Am I amusing you?" she asked.

"Yes, let me put those on for you." Silas pulled her into his arms, took the reins from her hands, and set her down.

"Here's your saddle. I'm assuming we'll have to put that on as well?" Dante teased.

"Yes, but bareback is better." She winked.

"I agree," Silas replied with a half turned up smile.

Dante walked over and wrapped Jadis in his arms. "Something's missing."

She rested her head against his chest and thought momentarily. "Their names?"

"Yes, any ideas?" Dante asked.

"Saga, Lucidus, and Helios?" she offered.

Silas stepped behind them and placed a hand on Dante's shoulder and the other on Jadis's, and she reached up and held his forearm.

"I love the names, darling." Silas smiled.

"As do I," Dante agreed.

Silas picked her up and sat her on Saga.

"I can manage, you know."

"An excuse to sweep you off your feet," Silas joked.

Dante and Silas backed up, admiring how beautiful she looked, sitting confidently on such a large stallion. Saga began digging her front hoof into the dirt before rising up on her hind legs.

She laughed at the looks on Silas's and Dante's faces as they rushed next to Saga, each having grabbed her reins. "You don't think I can handle her?"

"Darling, she is ten times your size. If you get thrown off," Dante mumbled.

"Trust me, if I can handle the two of you, I can handle Saga."

They let go of her reins and stepped back. Saga rose on her hind legs again and Jadis squeezed her thighs. "I'm fine and I know not to underestimate her. I'll be careful. Now let's go," she stated as she patted Saga on the neck.

Silas and Dante mounted their stallions in one smooth movement, and they headed out of the stables. They rode on either side of Jadis, and she felt their trepidation, forcing her to chuckle to herself.

Jadis looked at Silas and Dante, admiring how amazing they looked. *They control Lucidus and Helios with such ease it's as if they were born to ride.* She envisioned them hundreds of years ago and wished she would have been there in their early years.

They came to a clearing, and Jadis pulled back on Saga's reins. Saga stood in place, prancing and moving in half circles, while Lucidus and Helios were anxiously sidestepping and bouncing their heads up and down. In response to Lucidus and Helios, Saga dug her front hooves into the dirt.

They're unbroken for the most part and their movements are restless; they need to unleash some of their pent-up energy, Jadis thought. "It seems someone wants to run." Jadis ran her hand under her full mane and patted the side of her neck. "Shall we, my beautiful girl?"

"Jadis, do not let her take off," Silas demanded.

"It's fine. Let them run," she replied.

"Darling?" Dante tilted his head toward her. "If she gets out of control, use your powers."

"I'll be fine." She smiled as she tightened her hands around the reins and leaned forward, making a clicking sound. She then kicked her heels into Saga's hindquarters, and she leapt forward and broke into a powerful stride. Jadis looked over, and Silas and Dante were right next to her.

"Seems you know what you're doing, after all," Dante stated.

"Shall we race to the edge of the valley?" Silas offered.

Jadis smiled back and kicked at her hips again. "Saga, ire!"

They thundered through the valley, their powerful hooves tearing into the dirt. Jadis knew Silas and Dante would outride her any day and knew they were holding Lucidus and Helios back.

They looked at Jadis, then at each other with a challenging grin. Silas and Dante nodded to each other and kicked their heels, encouraging

Lucidus and Helios to pick up the pace, and they moved ahead of Jadis and Saga. By the time they made it to the edge of the valley, Silas had moved ahead of Dante, and Jadis could see them laughing as they turned to face her, having stopped just short of the edge of the Nakele river.

As soon as Saga made it to her companions, she came to an immediate halt, lowered her butt, and planted her hooves on the solid ground.

Dante and Silas were watching as Jadis lost her balance, not ready for Saga's sudden change in pace. "Oh, shit!" Dante yelled.

Jadis flew over Saga's head and landed with a solid thump on her back, and they heard the air being released from her lungs.

"Jadis!" Silas called out. They tossed their legs over their stallions' hind quarters and dropped to their knees over her.

"Darling, are you okay?" Dante asked.

After getting her breath back, she started laughing hysterically at how stupid she must have looked. "I'm fine."

They grabbed her arms and pulled her to her feet. "Baby, are you sure you're okay?" Silas asked again.

"I'm more embarrassed than hurt."

They, too, began laughing. "Well, that was a sight," Dante stated. He brushed the dirt off her back and butt.

"You need a few more riding lessons," Silas teased.

"I agree." Jadis chuckled.

"You are Nosferatu. You should try to be more graceful," Dante joked.

"You have always been clumsy on your feet, but this—that was something to witness," Silas added.

"You couldn't even land on your feet." Dante laughed.

She scrunched her face at them in a joking manner, unable to find a suitable comeback; they weren't wrong and her laughter only grew with their continued amusement and humorous jabs.

Dante picked her up and sat her back down on Saga. "We'll take it slower this time." He winked.

They walked along the edge of the Nakele river, enjoying each other's company as they headed back to the stables.

Silas, Dante, and Jadis joined everyone in the garden, everyone but Bain and Amsi. They took a seat on one of the half-round stone benches that were lined with plush velvet cushions. Jadis reached up to fix her windblown ponytail, and Silas and Dante placed their boots on the footrest and crossed their legs.

"You look like you've been rolling around in the dirt. I thought you were going riding," Maddie asked.

"Jadis took a bit of a tumble," Dante replied.

"More like head over heels," Silas added.

"I'm never going to hear the end of this, am I?"

Dante tugged Jadis's ponytail. "Not unless our memories fail us."

"What happened?" Aria asked, amused by Silas and Dante's humor.

"Jadis being tossed off Saga flat onto her back," Silas replied, laughing all the more.

"Oh my, are you okay?" Maddie chuckled.

"It's only my ego that hurts."

"I would have loved to have seen that," Skye stated.

"Jadis has a tendency to fall on her ass regardless of what she's doing," Aiden joked.

Jadis smiled when Bain appeared arm in arm with Amsi, which pulled everyone's attention away from her. Bain adjusted the cushions on another stone bench before they took a seat.

"Wow, from nanny to maître d'," Jadis joked.

"Oh snap," Bain replied. "What happened to you?"

She rolled her eyes at him for having brought up her minor mishap. Of course, Dante and Silas told them what happened, as well as showing them the entire scene telepathically.

"How can you be so clumsy?" Bain asked as he laughed.

"I've never seen a vampire land flat on her back, at least not without being tossed onto a bed." Eden laughed all the more when Maddie and Amsi choked on their drinks.

"Eden!" Maddie scolded, trying to sound serious.

"Really, Eden?" Jadis said.

Santiago and Luciana walked in with Jabari and took a seat. "What has you all so entertained?" Luciana asked.

Silas didn't speak. He relayed the entire scene telepathically.

"Oh my lord," Luciana exclaimed. "Darling, are you okay?" She tried her best to hide her amusement.

"Yes, I'm fine." Jadis brushed some of the dirt off her pant leg, which only added to their hilarity.

Silas grabbed her ponytail, pulled her head back, and planted a few hard, playful kisses on her lips. "You never fail to amuse us."

"I'd rather amuse you than piss you off." She winked.

"Agreed," Silas stated.

One of their keepers showed with Mag, Limi, Badru, and Sindri in tow; the staff members and temple guardians began referring to them as 'Milady's Posse'. They ran over and jumped into Jadis's lap before leaping off to explore the gardens and tussle around.

"Once they're bigger, we will have to take them with us when we ride," Silas stated.

"I'm curious who will outrun who," Dante added.

Jadis looked at the cubs. "It'll be a close race between the cubs and the stallions. I'm not sure who would win."

"Maybe we should have a stable full of stallions. After seeing you all today, it brought about some very fond memories," Aiden admitted.

Eden looked at Maddie and squeezed her thigh. "I couldn't agree more."

"If you think you are getting me on a stallion like theirs, it's not happening," Maddie replied.

"We'll get you a pony," Aria teased. "Amsi, can you ride or do you need a pony also?"

Amsi sipped her drink and tilted it toward Maddie. "I can ride, but I'm with Maddie on this one."

"Two ponies it is," Bain joked.

Santiago spun his glass around, thinking about the girls who were locked up. "Since we are on the subject, I hear there was a minor incident at the stables earlier."

Jadis diverted her eyes and looked at Silas and Dante.

Santiago took a drink and looked their way, waiting for an answer. "I see there are five brujas in the cells for five weeks?"

Everyone remained silent, waiting to see how Jadis, who was a master of sidestepping questions, would handle Santiago.

Luciana was holding her cup to her lips, peering over the rim. Jadis looked over and Luciana winked.

Based on her winking, Jadis knew Santiago would not be pressing the issue. So she hoped Silas and Dante would speak.

"Silas, tell him," she demanded telepathically.

Silas let her squirm for another minute before answering. "We have handled it, Father."

"I assume there was reason other than Jadis's lack of empathy?"

"Yes, and Jadis had a say in the matter." Dante chuckled.

She squinted her eyes at Dante for how he was smirking at her.

"I assume the punishment is fitting the crime?" Santiago asked.

"Jadis?" Silas stated for no other reason than his own entertainment.

"You'll pay for this later," Jadis threatened before answering. "Yes, Father,"

"Care to explain?"

"Here comes the deflection," Eden joked telepathically.

"They disregarded Silas's and Dante's authority," Jadis answered.

"Our authority?" Silas asked.

"That's a serious matter indeed." Santiago chuckled.

"Leave the poor girl alone," Luciana stated.

The servants brought food for the girls and a fresh supply of whiskey for everyone else. Jadis and the girls moved to the table while their mates sat with each other.

"Amsi, how was last night?" Jadis asked.

"Bain was a perfect gentleman. He escorted me to my room and left after inviting me to join him for a late lunch." Her smile was radiant. It was clear she was mesmerized by him.

"Soo—he didn't even try?" Aria asked.

"Aria!" Maddie snapped.

"We want all the dirty details," Ivory demanded.

"There are no *dirty details*. He didn't try a thing." The more Amsi spoke about him, the more she felt the flush of her cheeks.

"You like him," Jadis stated.

"Very much so," she admitted.

"Bain, a gentleman. Who would have thought? The only time I've seen him is when he's locking us up and it's not a pretty sight," Ivory said.

Amsi looked at the girls and then at Bain. "He doesn't seem to be possessive or easily angered."

Jadis laughed aloud. "You better look a little deeper."

"Well, enlighten me then," Amsi chuckled.

"We've been face to face with him when he's infuriated, and it's not something you want to see," Jadis admitted.

"Jadis has a tendency to try their patience. Bain and Dante had to babysit us for weeks because of her shenanigans before she and Silas mated," Skye explained.

"My fault? The two of you had a lot to do with it. I didn't create that portal myself."

It stunned Amsi they had that kind of power. "A portal?"

Maddie waved her hand toward the girls. "It's a long story."

"I have plenty of time. You must tell me," Amsi stated.

"Jadis, it was your idea. You tell her," Ivory suggested.

"I see things went well with Amsi last night," Aiden asked, not waiting to put Bain on the burner.

"Jadis knows her girls," Bain replied.

"She does. However, I suggest you move with caution. Jadis is attracted to those that wouldn't bend to the winds. We all know she craves the chaos within the darkness." Aiden chuckled.

"Except for Maddie, those girls were born under a dark moon," Eden added.

"I can promise you she won't pull Amsi into any of their fuckery," Bain replied.

"Between Jadis, Skye, and Ivory, not to mention Aria, you better find a golden anklet," Dante retorted.

"If need be, I have a little experience," Bain joked.

"You're serious about her after only a night?" Eden questioned.

"The pull has me, and there is more behind her demure veil than she lets on."

"Shit, you're swooning over a soon-to-be mate." Aiden laughed.

"Bain, you're smitten," Eden joked. "Can I offer a word of advice, brother?"

Bain motioned for Eden to continue. "Well, this ought to be good."

"As long as she's around the girls, keep a bottle of little white pills in your pocket."

"I'm also going to give you a piece of advice. Adelrik is very possessive with his daughter. If those girls pull her into a situation, there'll be hell to pay," Jabari added.

Santiago crossed his leg over his knee and looked at Bain. "The girls get along well. Proceed with caution. Adelrik has shared a few stories about his struggles to contain her."

"All the shit you've given us, it appears you will soon know the struggle," Dante added.

"You don't think I don't know the struggles with Jadis on a personal level?"

Silas placed his hand on Bain's shoulder in a joking manner. "Just wait until it's your mate pulling the shit."

As the sun fell into the horizon, an endless array of prismatic colors painted the darkening sky with spilled wine and cerise pomegranate.

Dante found himself as mesmerized by Jadis's thoughts as she was with the setting sun; he squeezed her hand. "It's beautiful, mon amour."

"It is." She smiled.

"Let's take the stallions out before sunset tomorrow. We will watch from the edge of the Nakele" Silas offered.

"I would love to," Jadis replied.

"Amsi, would you like to join me for a walk?" Bain suggested as he stood and scooted his chair back.

"Of course." She smiled, embarrassed by the amused looks shot her way and Jadis winking at her.

"The sunset is beautiful tonight," Bain offered as they walked along the original limestone path winding its way through the exotic botanical garden.

"It is. How long have you all lived here?"

"Not long. We don't live here. It's a complicated story." Bain let out a sigh, remembering back to the reasons they ended up staying in the oasis.

"I'm sorry. By the look on your face, it doesn't seem to be a fond memory," Amsi smiled.

"No need to apologize. It seems like a lifetime ago."

"You don't have to talk about it," Amsi stated.

"I don't mind. I'm sure you've heard the story about Silas, Dante, and Jadis being captured by Abigor—yes?"

"Yes, Father has shared some of it. Not to mention I've heard the rumors that have spread within the clans."

"We stayed here for Jadis's protection after we rescued them from Abigor's lair." Bain explained most of what had happened during the Bergelême war. "There's not much more to it and until we deal with Evanora, this is the safest place for her to be."

"That is unbelievable. I didn't know Jadis has suffered so much, not to mention Silas and Dante. It explains a lot," she stated as they took a seat on the bank of the Nakele.

"Jadis is the most resilient woman I have ever met," Bain said.

"You're very fond of her."

"Very much so, even though she's a serious pain in our ass," he joked.

"She and the girls have been wonderful."

Bain chuckled at Amsi's naivety; *she doesn't have a clue how much trouble the girls get into.* "Be careful around them. They tend to walk beyond the shadows and play in the darkness with all that resides there."

"I'm not sure I will be here long enough to find out." She sighed. "Father wants to head home in two days. Business awaits." She picked up a small stick and ran it through her fingers, feeling heavy-hearted.

"Two days?" Bain questioned.

"Yes." She tried to hide her disappointment; she wanted nothing more than to stay there with him.

She turned her attention to the glowing yellowy-orange colors of the half crescent moon glinting off the top of the calm waters and creeping up the bank before them. "The beauty here is like nothing I have ever seen. It's as if time has ceased to exist and remains unmarred by mortal souls."

Bain contemplated her leaving and decided he wouldn't let her go. "Would you be happy here, for the long term?"

"I would," she replied, not realizing what he was hinting at.

"I will speak to your father in the morning then."

"Wait—what are you saying?"

"I would like for you to remain here with me if it pleases you."

"*If it pleases me*? I am not sure what to say other than I would love nothing more, and would it *please you*?" she asked nervously.

"I'm asking, so yes, it *would please me* if you stayed," he replied with a demure grin.

"Where would I stay and will everyone else be okay with this, especially Jabari?"

"Of course they will be, and you can either stay in the room you have now, or you can move into mine. The choice is yours."

Her heart skipped a couple beats, and the nerves danced in her stomach like a swarm of fluttering birds. Staying in his room also meant sleeping in his bed and all that it would entail.

He picked up on her trepidation and had to hide his amusement, not wanting to embarrass or offend her, having read her thoughts. He reached over and placed his fist under her chin and turned her head toward his, then placed his mouth against hers.

Within the passion of his kiss was the promise of a lifetime. A rush of helplessness and a surging tide of desire left her limp. Her heart leapt and her pulse raced with both fear, excitement, and an entanglement of nervous anticipation.

He laid her on her back on the soft ground and she wrapped her arms around his muscular back and pulled him in.

He slid his hand under her shirt, gliding it up her thin waist before moving around to her back and unlatching her bra.

"I'm going to show you how much it pleases me," he whispered.

She reached for the bottom of his tight T-shirt and began pulling it over his head; he sat up and pulled it the rest of the way off before removing hers.

He kneeled above her, admiring how beautiful she looked and how perfect her toned body was. Her wavy chestnut hair, with strands of gold and auburn, glistened under the soft light of the moon. *Beneath her calm demeanor, there's a dangerous complexity to her swirling behind her serene, green eyes.* "You are stunning."

He pulled both their jeans off before he laid his bare chest on hers, taking her mouth with his again.

She pulled back slightly. "Here?" she whispered.

He sat up on his elbows and moved her hair off her forehead. "It's fine, darling, we're alone."

She ran her hands over his large biceps and up his shoulders, admiring how perfect his body was. His intricate tattoos mesmerized her as she ran her fingers over his arms, tracing the colorful lines.

Bain lay on her body, and his lips fell to hers again. He spread her legs apart with his knees and repositioned himself between them; he felt the heavy thumping of her heart beating against his chest. "May I ask a question?"

"Yes."

"You are a virgin—yes?"

She felt the warmth radiate across her cheeks and the flush of color she couldn't hide. "I am," she whispered, not sure how he would react.

"If you would like me to stop or slow things down, tell me."

"No—I don't want you to stop." She grabbed the back of his head and pulled him in for another heated kiss. The waves of desire rolled through her body like a swelling tide.

There's a hint of honeysuckle within her kiss and she tastes as pure as the blood of a beyorn, he thought.

He ran his hand down her stomach and between her legs. He rubbed her sex with his fingers before sliding them into her tight, wet core.

As soon as his fingers slid inside, she let out a moan and arched her back. She slid her hand over his taut ass and pulled him closer. The desire for him to be inside her was overwhelming.

"Bain," she groaned. "I want you inside me."

He removed his fingers and placed his tip against her opening and began sliding his shaft into her, knowing he was about to claim her, as well as her virtue.

"Oh shittt," she moaned as she pressed the back of her head into the soft dirt beneath them.

"Damn, you are so tight." He squeezed the flesh on her thigh and pulled her leg higher over his hip and slid himself farther in.

Her moans and the way the movements of her hips matched his brought about a rush of pleasure. "Holy shit, I want to come inside you."

"I want you—all the way in," she moaned.

He thrust his hips and slid all of himself into the slick warmth of her body; her core tightly enveloping his shaft.

"Ahh—shit, it hurts," she whispered.

"Need me to stop?" he asked with a moan-filled whisper.

"No, it feels amazing. Don't stop. I think I'm going to—"

He thrust his hips, driving himself farther in; he began gently at first, allowing her body to stretch to his size before he became more forceful. "Fuck," he mumbled.

She let out a groan that sounded like a mixture of pleasure and pain, pulling her orgasm to the surface. She grabbed the back of his head, holding his face next to hers as the orgasm swept her body into an intoxicating release.

As soon as her swollen core throbbed against his shaft, he succumbed to his own release.

He rested on top of her body, allowing their racing hearts and heavy breathing to return to normal. He rolled onto his back and pulled her next to him.

"I assume you will stay in my room now?" he said as he pulled her leg over his crotch and cradled her thigh in his hand.

"I assume so." She chuckled.

After a few moments of silence, she asked an embarrassing question. "You don't think I could get—you know—pregnant?"

Bain let out a hearty chuckle. "No, baby, in order for that to happen, I would need to will it."

She responded with a sigh of relief, amusing him all the more. "So, feeding from me, will you do that as well?"

"Only after we are mated. Your vein is safe for now, unless you decide otherwise."

"Mated?" she questioned.

"Yes, if you agree."

"I agree," she replied.

"Then we shall be mated under the next full Moon in two months."

"You'll feed from no one else?"

"Never," he stated firmly.

"Don't you need to feed?"

"Yes, however, we can go weeks without feeding, but we can also feed from family should the need arise."

"You can feed from me. I'm okay with that."

"If you are comfortable with it, then yes, I would rather feed from you. A little honeysuckle to tempt the taste buds."

"Such a joker." She laughed.

He rolled on top of her and ran his thumb across her bottom lip. "What say we finish this in my bed?"

"*What say* we do." She winked as she pulled his mouth to hers again.

CHAPTER 6

It had been a few weeks since the ceremony and the girls' mates reluctantly agreed to let them go back to the cenote residing within the pyramid. Sigurd and a few of his warriors had agreed to accompany the girls so they were free to spend the day there while their mates were tied up with Santiago and Jabari.

They were relieved to be somewhere other than the oasis for once. It was a hidden gem of rejuvenation. But for the lack of any eerie feels they experienced; the waters of the cenote were far more magical than one would think. The Mediterranean-blue water was as clear as glass and the sand glinted at the bottom like crushed emeralds. The light coming from the opening in the pyramid's top was refracted off the water, onto the stone walls, and looked like rippling waves of stained glass.

Aria, Amsi, and Jadis were in the water while Skye, Ivory, and Maddie sat at the edge, dangling their feet in the cool water, sipping their drinks.

Jadis splashed Aria in the face and dove to the bottom; Aria followed and met her face to face. They looked at each other before Jadis pointed toward the top. They rose to the surface and grabbed Amsi's legs and pulled her beneath the surface.

Amsi rose from the water and took a deep breath of air. "What the hell?" She laughed as she splashed Aria and Jadis, who had risen next to her.

Sigurd was standing with his back against the gray stone wall near the entrance, watching the girls enjoying themselves. He picked up on a subtle tension and energetic shift swirling around the cenote. After four hundred plus years of experience on the battlefield, he didn't operate on default and ordered his warriors to make another round outside the main pyramid.

Jadis saw her cubs cock their heads with pointed ears before darting up the stone steps. "Badru, Sindri, veni!" she yelled.

Maddie, Skye, and Ivory jumped to their feet and tried to grab them. Sigurd looked at the cubs as they leapt up the stairs. He uncrossed his arms and held up his hand toward the girls.

Something's amiss. I don't want them running out of the pyramid until I check it out. "I'll retrieve them, lass," Sigurd stated.

Once he was out of the girls' sight, he pulled his sword from the sheath on his back and ordered his warriors to meet him outside the entrance. He then let Silas know he was uncomfortable with the cubs' sudden disappearance. As benign as it appeared to be on the surface, he wasn't about to take a chance. He took one slow, cautious step after the other up the time worn stone steps.

"Milord."

"Sigurd, is everything okay?" Silas asked.

"Aye, the cubs took off. I'm retrieving them now. Something's off with the entire situation."

"Say no more." Silas looked at Dante, Bain, Aiden, and Eden. "We need to go. Sigurd sounds concerned."

Maddie noticed how Mag and Limi stepped toward the edge of the cenote. Their hackles were raised along their backs and they let out deep-throated snarls. "What's up with them?"

"I'm not sure." Jadis swam over and began rubbing their faces. "Calm," she urged, and they appeared to settle down. She splashed their faces, and they playfully snapped at the water.

"They're fine," Jadis stated as she swam back to Aria and Amsi.

Maddie looked around and the chamber was getting dark. It seemed as if the sun had set and was casting shadows against the stone walls.

"Why is it getting dark?" Maddie asked, looking around.

Skye and Ivory looked around as well. The three of them stood near the edge and looked at Jadis, Aria, and Amsi as they played around in the water, clueless to what was happening. The water began bubbling around the edges like a slow boil.

"You need to get out of the water," Skye stated.

Aria, Amsi, and Jadis looked at each other and the once calm water was now a swirling whirlpool.

"What the fuck?" Aria yelled.

The suction under Jadis's legs began pulling her underwater like a powerful rip current. "We need out and now!" she yelled.

They tried to swim to the edge, but the water swirled with such an intensity, they began spinning in circles and grabbed a hold of each other's forearms.

"Jadis, get us the fuck out of here!" Aria yelled.

"What the hell is happening?" Amsi demanded.

Jadis tried to disappear like she had many times before, but the pull of the whirlpool beneath them was stronger than her ability to dissipate with the girls; something was controlling the surrounding energy.

Mag and Limi jumped into the water, and the girls grabbed the napes of their necks and hung on. Mag and Limi tried to swim out, but they also succumbed to the treacherous suction.

Maddie, Skye, and Ivory were yelling at the girls to get out. They dropped to their knees and stretched their arms out, but were unable to reach them. The center opened and pulled them farther beneath the surface. What seemed like minutes was only seconds before they were submerged beneath the turbulent water.

Sigurd felt the threat and materialized behind the girls. He scanned the swirling water and dove in and hit what seemed to be some sort of otherworldly barrier. He could see the girls reaching up, but wasn't able to grab them.

His men had also jumped in, following his lead. Every attempt they made to grab the girls was in vain.

The girls' hair floated upward, and the light from the pyramid faded into the distance.

Jadis looked up and saw Sigurd and his warriors in the water above their heads reaching out. She kept her eyes pinned on Sigurd's and was powerless to do anything other than watch as he disappeared.

"Sigurd!" Maddie screamed as she looked at the water, watching the chaos.

Silas, Dante, and Bain appeared along with the rest of their clan and found themselves in the middle of a shit storm.

Sigurd and his warriors were at the bottom of the cenote, the girls were kneeling at the edge screaming Jadis's, Aria's, and Amsi's names and Jadis, Aria, and Amsi were nowhere in sight.

Silas, Dante, Aiden, and Bain dove into the water, only to be stopped by the same energetic barrier.

Dante rose out of the water. "What the fuck happened? Where are they?"

"One minute they were swimming and the next they had disappeared," Ivory cried.

Bain jumped out of the cenote and pinched the bridge of his nose, trying to contain his outrage as he paced back and forth.

Silas swept the wet hair off his forehead and looked at the girls. "Mag and Limi, were they with Jadis?"

Skye wrapped her arms around her body and stood trembling. "Yes, they jumped in after them."

Maddie ran toward Eden and he grasped her shoulders. "Maddie, what the hell is going on?"

"We tried to reach for them, but the water sucked them into some type of whirlpool."

Silas looked at Sigurd, demanding an answer without speaking.

"Milord, by the time we were back, they were already below the surface. The magic, we have felt it before while in Bergelême. I'm afraid the Enchantress has taken them."

Dante kneeled and swirled his fingers through the water, trying to pick up on an energetic trail. "Bain, we need to recreate that fucking whirlpool!"

They stood side by side and swirled their hands; the water churned and spun in the same direction. As the whirlpool formed, it sank beneath the surface before thundering from the center of the cenote. It splashed against the pyramid's ceiling, spanning out in every direction before falling from the ceiling like a torrential rain storm.

The girls screamed and ducked, not expecting the thunderous sounds that followed.

"Fuck, it's been reversed," Bain snapped as he wiped the water from his face.

They stood at the edge of the cenote, enraged and confused, trying to figure out what to do next.

"Milord." Sigurd nodded to Silas.

Silas gave him a hard pat on the shoulder; regardless of his personal feelings, there was no room for emotion. "You were following orders and you have never failed me. We're all aware of what Evanora is capable of. I should have never agreed to let them come here."

Aiden paced back and forth, staring into the cenote. *Evanora is out to assassinate Jadis. Aria and Amsi will be nothing more than collateral damage.* He looked at no one in particular as he spoke. "Jadis has faced her before, which means Evanora knows the powers she yields. She won't underestimate her again. They're in serious trouble."

Bain looked at Dante and then back at the cenote. "She's created a fucking prismatic wall."

Dante stood next to Bain with the same transfixed expression. "We need the orb Aiden took from Abigor's egregore."

"Search the grounds. We need to find anything, something that would indicate this was a trap. Those cubs did not run on their own," Silas stated.

They rushed from the temple and spanned out, searching the entire area.

It wasn't long before Sigurd called out, "I found something."

"What is it?" Silas questioned as they appeared.

"When I caught the cubs, they were heading in this direction." He kneeled down and picked up a piece of the carcass before tossing it down. "Fresh kill, and they didn't do it, milord."

Silas, Dante, and Bain also kneeled down, studying the remains. Dante picked up a piece and rubbed it between his fingers. "Smell that. It's fucking sorcery."

The rest followed suit and they too picked up the subtle scent of amaranth, which was used for summoning the forces of darkness and cosmic invisibility.

"Evanora did not locate the girls on her own." Silas stared at the carcass when the realization hit him.

"It appears we are all thinking the same thing," Dante growled.

"Mercia and Aisley?" Bain snarled. "They were the two brujas Aria and Jadis had Jabari banish. I can smell them."

"And the five who were locked up?" Silas asked.

"No trace of Kekat, Kali, Lizean, Melean, or Zinra," Bain replied.

"Sigurd, I want Mercia and Aisley in the temple and now." Silas ordered. "After which, find out where the other five disappeared to."

"Aye, milord, I'll take Lars with us."

"Lars stood and tossed a bone to the ground. "Whatever you need, let's go."

"Inform me the moment you locate them," Silas demanded.

"Aye, milord." Sigurd nodded.

Jadis, Aria, and Amsi dropped from the portal's opening and plunged to the ground in a tangled heap. The girls rolled onto their stomachs, gasping for breath as they coughed up the water they had inhaled, as did Mag and Limi. After a few moments, they sat on their knees, terrified and lightheaded. They were stunned when they looked at the vast, unknown, fertile landscape before them, which appeared to be a place far away from the world they knew. They were struck with a waft of sweltering, humid air that took their breath away.

"Where the hell are we?" Aria asked.

"No fucking idea," Jadis replied.

They stood, looked into the trees, and walked a short distance. The strangest birds fluttered overhead and rested in the canopy, and the calls and grunts of the creatures off in the distance were as unfamiliar as the landscape itself.

Amsi screamed and began flailing her arms, jumping around, and slapping her body; Jadis and Aria stared at her as if she'd gone crazy.

"Get them off!" Amsi screamed.

Jadis and Aria looked down and what appeared to be oversized leaf cutters also covered their feet and legs. They pranced in place and slapped at their legs.

Aria looked down and the ground seemed to move like a gentle wave. "Holy hell!"

The girls took off running and as soon as Jadis realized they were out of the living tide, she called to the girls. "Stop! Anything could be out there!" She grabbed the back of Amsi's and Aria's shoulders and pulled them to an immediate halt.

"This shit hurts so bad." Amsi looked at the swollen red lumps all over her lower body and rubbed her hands over the welts, trying to soothe the stinging sensations.

"Those goddamn things were the size of fucking crickets," Aria stated.

"We're in sooo much trouble," Jadis rumbled.

Mag and Limi cocked their heads before taking one choreographed step at a time, as if they had picked up a scent. Their hackles rose along their backs and their guttural growls and canine bearing snarls spooked the girls. Jadis used her keen eyesight and could see a reddish-hued aura surrounding what appeared to be a small creature off in the distance.

"Mag and Limi are big enough now to take out almost any threat," Jadis whispered, trying to give Aria, Amsi, and herself some sense of relief. "We have some protection with us."

The wolves were grown now, and their backs were as high as the girls' waists and easily outweighed them by about a hundred pounds.

"Whatever they are focused on is making me nervous. Do you see anything?" Aria asked.

"Whatever it is, they don't like it. I can only make out its form, but it doesn't appear to be that big—it sort of looks like a monkey," Jadis explained.

Amsi looked around and there was not a trace of anything familiar. "Where the fuck are we?"

"Can you get us back into the portal?" Aria asked, trying to stop the panic from setting in.

"No, not without my sisters seeing how I didn't create it." Jadis was having the same unrelenting feeling creeping up; one she knew all too well. She watched the fear radiate across Amsi's and Aria's faces as they scanned the ominous-looking landscape once again.

Evanora sat on the ledge just outside the small entrance of the cave, staring off in the distance. The prismatic rays of the early morning sun pierced the vastness of the jungle thicket and the heavy sulfuric stench and sweltering, muggy air never seemed to go away. *It won't be long now. Soon enough I will have my vengeance,* she thought.

She hadn't realized she had dozed off until a voice startled her. "The Dhamphyr is here, but she is not alone. Two females and two enormous creatures are with her." The Mundung, whom she called Mun, informed her.

Evanora let out a decrepit laugh. "That is good news. Follow me, I want to see the beiskaldis' for myself." She stood and headed for her egregore, with Mun in tow.

Mun was a powerful shaman who lived among the tribe of indigenous creatures known as Graftons. They lived in primitive villages at the base of the mountain below Evanora's makeshift lair. Mun's vast knowledge about the strange world and its inhabitants was invaluable. Evanora kept her at her side and covertly abused her beliefs in order to maintain control over the tribe's aboriginal-like beings. She had also implanted the knowledge of her language into Mun's and Dolog's heads in order to communicate with them.

Not only did she enslave the Mun, she also took control of Dolog, their tribal leader. Once she drew them into her lair with her enchanting beauty and deception, she used her sorcery to control their every thought, every move; either they did as she said or they suffered beneath her wrath.

The Graftons were dour, ugly, and had grotesque physical features. Their human characteristics gave way to animalistic, elf-like bodies. They stood about four feet tall but were nonetheless evil and physically adept. The creatures were destructive, dangerous, and quite capable of taking down any beast as a tribe. They were armed with primitive spears, knives, clubs, and various other weapons forged from plant fibers, stones, and wood.

The Graftons were well aware of what else the Enchantress controlled; the flying creatures that could destroy anything in their path. Evanora twisted their stories and retold them in order to convince them there was honor in their suffering rather than seeing their cowardice. They had no choice but to surrender to her malevolence; they now lived under her malicious rule as nothing more than depraved minions.

"Wherever we are, at first glance, it's beautiful," Aria stated, hoping the enchanted splendor surrounding them was benign.

"Don't be a fool, Aria. You know as well as I do appearance is fallible. Beauty can draw you into its snare of deception before you even realize what's happened," Jadis replied.

"Like a breath of unanticipated poison," Amsi mumbled.

"I don't know about you, but I think we should move and find some-place safe to stay. Who knows how long it's going to take for our mates to find us," Aria added.

"I don't understand, how did this happen?" Amsi took a few deep breaths, trying to calm the unrelenting dread creeping up. In this moment, she was having trouble coming to terms with their current predicament.

They scanned the surrounding landscape again to see in which direction they should head. Aria pointed to the right. "There seems to be a mountain range over there. Maybe we can find a cave that will provide some sort of protection?"

They stared at the primeval, jagged mountain range looming above the jungle canopy. It appeared to be as obstinate and dangerous as Hades's backbone. However, their biggest concern, standing between it and them, was a vast landscape of unknown dangers.

"Not sure we should do this barefooted and in swimsuits. Can you dress us in something more appropriate?" Aria chuckled nervously.

"Sure." Jadis snapped her wrist and waved it over Aria, Amsi, and herself, but nothing happened. She did it again and barely felt her own energy, their concern growing by the minute.

The girls looked at each other, shocked she was having so much trouble conjuring the simplest of spells.

Jadis knew her powers were waning, and it scared her all the more. She tried again, adding more effort, and they were in jeans, T-shits, and hiking boots.

"What took so long? Were you deciding what we should wear?" Aria said sarcastically.

"What was that about?" Amsi asked.

Jadis faintly heard Amsi and Aria before her sight became glinting, speckles of light flickering before her. Her head throbbed and a haze of darkness crossed her mind before she fell to her knees.

"Jadis! What's wrong?" Aria asked as she and Amsi kneeled beside her.

Aria placed her hand on Jadis's back. "Are you okay?"

"Jadis—can you hear us?" Amsi asked.

"Yes, I hear you. It's as if I have no attachment to my powers." She took a few heavy breaths and let the dizziness subside.

"What the fuck?" Aria stated, her voice shaky.

"This is terrible." Amsi closed her eyes to see if she could grasp her powers and after a few minutes, she opened her eyes, revealing her panic. "Shit, I can't connect with mine either."

"There seems to be a powerful energy surrounding us. I can't penetrate it," Jadis admitted.

"If that's the case, we need to move and hide," Aria reasoned.

"You're right. Being out in the open is a bad idea. We have no idea what may be out there. I've experienced enough monsters lurking in the shadows to know if I'm powerless here, we're screwed," Jadis replied.

They walked in the mountain's direction, which, from their vantage point, didn't appear to be far. The ancient, gnarled trees and exotic plants were like nothing they had ever seen before. The plethora of vegetation looked like a botanical wonderland and the trumpet-like vines seemed to be living beings based on the bee-like humming sounds they made as they swayed around the girls.

Mag and Limi lifted their heads to the air, smelled the vegetation, and dragged their noses along the ground, absorbing the unfamiliar scents.

The jungle reeked of age. The composing, organic smell, along with the effervescent scent of the flowers and rotten foliage beneath their feet, swept over them like an aromatic phantom. They were indeed walking through some sort of mythical world.

A thought hit Jadis and she stopped mid-stride. "Holy shit!"

Aria shot a look of fear in Jadis's direction. "Nooo—please don't think that!"

Amsi replied as well. "Please say it isn't so."

"This place reminds me of Evanora's garden in Abigor's world." Jadis could feel the slow, dragging beat of her heart as soon as the realization washed over her. "It's her! She fucking transported us here."

"We need to keep moving," Aria stated. After everything Jadis had told her about how powerful and evil Evanora was, not to mention how much she had enraged her, that was the last thing she wanted to hear.

Amsi placed a hand across her stomach, feeling sick at the mere thought this was all Evanora's doing. "Are you saying we're here because of Evanora? The same Evanora from Abigor's lair you told me about?"

"Yes," Jadis replied.

"Oh shit, what are we going to do?" Amsi asked.

"Find a place to hide right now," Aria replied.

Trees towered over them and creatures they had never seen before jumped amongst the canopies and seemed to follow them. The trunks of the trees were tall enough off the ground the girls walked under their twisted roots. The ground was gnarled and uneven from the ancient roots, ruts and vines, making their trek slow and difficult as they traversed their way through the dense, unforgiving entanglement. Enormous boulders and rocks covered in green and brown mosses were scattered throughout the landscape and were barely visible amongst the thick tangle of brush. An abundance of strange, colorful birds sat on the long, twisted vines hanging loosely in the trees. Eerie shadows appeared under the negligible amount of light penetrating the canopy, and it became suspiciously quiet. With each step, they walked between the seen and unseen, lost in a trackless, hostile world beyond the veil.

"Holy shit," Amsi whispered. "What is this?"

"I'm afraid to say it out loud," Jadis replied.

They moved through what appeared to be a labyrinthine of enormous, black, intricately woven, three-dimensional shapes. Oversized bugs trapped within them were fighting to escape.

"Jadis, why does everything seem so big?" Amsi asked as she stared at the menacing black webs.

The more they looked around, the more webs they saw weaved amongst the trees and hollows.

As the adrenaline pumped through Aria's body, she reached down and picked up a large stick. "Let's get the fuck out of here."

They continued walking, and after a few anxious moments, Jadis heard what sounded like flapping wings, so she looked up and saw a large bird hanging by her wing, too entangled to fly. The bird fluttered her free wing about a dozen times, and the intensity of her shivering increased with each failed attempt.

Jadis held her hand out to Aria. "Give me the stick."

Aria and Amsi looked at the struggling creature and Aria handed it over. "Be careful, Jadis."

She swung the stick through the thick silken thread and the bird fell at her feet before flying off.

"No more distractions. We need to get out of here," Amsi demanded, her face ashen.

"I'm afraid we've walked into some sort of giant nesting area," Jadis stated.

Aria glanced at Jadis and Amsi. "As big as those bugs are, I would hate to see the size of the spider itself."

Amsi's hands trembled and beads of sweat dripped down her brow. She grabbed the bottom of her T-shirt and wiped the moisture from her face. "I fucking hate spiders!"

Large banana-like leaves hanging above their heads rustled and a monstrous, black, jointed leg dropped from the entanglement of the branches. The rustling sound was now coming from every direction. The girls let out a deafening scream and took off running.

Amsi was so terrified her body moved faster than her legs and she tripped and fell. Aria and Jadis heard the air being released from her lungs as she hit the ground chest first.

"Get up," Jadis yelled as she and Aria grabbed her arms and pulled her to her feet.

Even though the webs had disappeared behind them, they continued on until they felt they had put enough distance between themselves and what would be an agonizing death.

Jadis leaned against a large boulder and bent over, holding her waist. She looked at Amsi and she was wiping the tears from her eyes.

"Amsi, it's going to be okay," Jadis offered, although she, too, wanted nothing more than to cry with her.

"Do you know what it's like to be wrapped in a spider's web?" Amsi asked.

Aria and Jadis looked at her, a bit confused, wondering how she would know.

"No—do you?" Aria asked inquisitively.

"Hell no, and I don't want to find out!"

"Well, shit, we thought you did." Aria chuckled.

"It's not funny!" Amsi said firmly. However, Jadis's and Aria's laughter was contagious.

They made sure not to touch the unfamiliar foliage as best as they could. Based on their skills and vast knowledge of plants, they knew a simple sting or the sap from the trees may be toxic and they didn't recognize a single leaf or flower.

The girls spoke on using a private, energetic veil Jadis managed to create, assuming the Enchantress was listening to everything they said aloud.

"If either of you feels even the slightest pull in any direction, tell me. I've been there, done that. We will need to move in the opposite direction. I am going to err on the side of caution and not walk into another trap!" Jadis stated.

"Believe me, you will be the first to know," Amsi replied.

As they headed for the mountain range, the animals, plants, and creatures all seemed to grow in size. The rustling of the brush startled the girls and as they looked in the sounds direction something was peering at them from behind a tree.

Mag and Limi snarled in its direction. "Jadis—can you control Mag and Limi? I know for a fact if they take off, you're going after them," Aria stated.

"Yes, I can, but just in case." She flicked her wrist and nothing happened. She tried again, and then two more times before a chain appeared around each of their necks.

Aria and Jadis grabbed a hold of the chains and wrapped them around their hands. "Just know if Mag takes off, you're going to be dragged behind him." Jadis couldn't help but chuckle to herself at the thought of Aria being dragged on her stomach across the rugged terrain.

"That would be a sight to see," Amsi stated, sounding somewhat amused.

"I wouldn't find anything funny about it," Aria scolded.

The thing that had been watching them crawled around the tree and onto the ground, hiding in the dense underbrush. It looked like a little humanoid creature that appeared harmless enough from what little they could see of it.

It let out a clicking, hissing noise and tilted its pointed ears in their direction. It appeared to be studying the girls as much as the girls were studying it. As it rose on its back feet, it grew in size and now stood about three feet tall.

"Jadis—" Aria whispered.

"Don't move," she replied.

Amsi grabbed a hold of Aria's and Jadis's forearms and stood frozen between them.

The little creature had long arms and legs, a fat, hairless body, and skin like that of a lizard. Its face looked like an unknown monkey and its colors morphed, matching its surroundings.

Mag and Limi walked forward and stood between the girls and the little creature. They let out a low, guttural snarl and bared their enormous canines.

The thing let out a deafening screech and its mouth was full of blackened, razor-like teeth in multiple rows.

It lunged for the girls, and they screamed and jumped, trying to dodge the attack. Mag and Limi also lunged and their chains yanked Aria and Jadis toward it.

Mag snatched it out of the air and began shaking it violently. Limi grabbed the other end and shook and tugged its body like a toy rope before dropping its dismembered body onto the ground.

"Holy shit, what the hell was that?" Aria yelled.

Jadis stared at Aria and Amsi in disbelief. "We need to assume everything here is going to pose a threat."

Amsi wrapped her arms around her body and rubbed her shoulders. "I can't deal with all of this," she admitted.

"Fuck the walking, Jadis. Do your thing and get us to the mountain. If you have anything left, use it now," Aria demanded.

"I don't think I can," Jadis admitted.

They held hands and Jadis closed her eyes, but nothing happened. "Fuck me!" She tried again and they hadn't moved an inch.

"Jadis, come on, get us out of here," Aria demanded again.

"I can't. It's not fucking working!" she snapped back.

"Well, why the hell not?" Aria barked.

"I don't know, it's not like I'm not trying!" *The last time I felt like this I was being controlled by Abigor.* "This is all too familiar," Jadis said.

"Evanora knows what she's doing. She studied my abilities enough to know almost everything about me."

"Shit!" Aria stated.

"I don't know what to do or say right now. Do you think Bain and your mates are trying to come for us?" Amsi asked.

"Yes!" Jadis and Aria stated in unison, to Amsi's relief.

They walked a little faster, trying to make it to their destination and out of the lush vegetation that could conceal anything. The strange calls, grunts, shrieks, and bird songs were like an orchestra of death. The jungle became denser, steeper, and rockier. Jadis could traverse the terrain with little effort. However, Amsi and Aria seemed to struggle more the farther they went. After what seemed like hours, the higher they trekked, the less dense the foliage became.

Aria tripped and barely caught herself. "Dammit!" She glanced at Jadis and noticed the look that crossed her face. "It's not funny! I can't get through this shit as easily as you can. I'm not a fucking vampire, so slow down," she demanded.

"Sorry, I'm used to being the slow, clumsy one around Silas and Dante," Jadis replied.

"Slow, clumsy? Well, snap—sorry if I'm slowing you down," Aria said.

"I agree with Aria. I can't keep up with you. Mind if we catch our breaths for a minute?" Amsi requested.

"Fine, I'll take baby steps for the two of you," Jadis said in jest.

Once they had the strength, they climbed up the rocky slope and Jadis had to help pull them up the boulders more than once. They stopped after making it halfway up and looked behind them, having a better view of the jungle below, which stretched as far as the eye could see.

Jadis looked around and pointed at a pile of large boulders. "There, it's high enough up we should have a better view of everything."

"Seriously?" Aria asked. "How the hell do you think we can climb up there?"

Amsi stared at the weather-worn stones. "Jadis, I don't think I can make it."

Jadis rolled her eyes. "It's not that big a deal. I'll help you both up."

Jadis went first and showed them where to place their hands and feet while Mag and Limi climbed ahead of them. She had to climb up a couple of feet and then reach down to help pull the girls up. As soon as they made it to the top and took the time to look around, it was clear they were in a different realm altogether. The stifling atmosphere, dense foliage, and dark shadows seemed to favor those worshipping the darkness.

Before them lay the jungle they had just come from and behind them was a large, raging river. They were trapped in the middle and neither choice looked promising.

They took a seat so Aria and Amsi could catch their breaths while they decided what to do. A rumble rose from below the girls and branches snapped and the canopy swayed. What appeared to be the tip of leathery wing rose above the tress before disappearing.

"Holy fuck!" Aria stated.

"Thank the gods we got out of there," Amsi whispered.

Jadis lay down on the rock on her stomach and moved back. "Scoot back."

Amsi and Aria scooted back and lay down, doing their best to conceal themselves. Mag's and Limi's snarling would undoubtedly alert whatever it was to their presence.

"Jadis, shut them up," Aria demanded.

"Descendit!" Jadis stated as she held up her palm toward them; they lay on either side of the girls and growled under their breath.

The thing roared with such ferocity; the birds flew from the treetops in thick, choreographed flocks, so large they stretched for a block and an abundance of winged creatures flew over their heads. Some had quirky feathers, odd-shaped bills, and multicolored fur covering their bodies. Others had long beaks with a row of razor-sharp teeth; their tails and tips of their wings had long feathers that appeared to be about three feet long.

"I don't want to know what that was," Jadis whispered.

"You and me both. Not even Mag or Limi would be able to take that thing," Aria replied.

"All the more reason we need a cave. At least we will only have one opening to deal with," Amsi added.

Aria slid down the back of the rock on her butt. "Let's go. I don't want to be in the open at night."

CHAPTER 7

"**I** need to observe for myself what happened," Santiago stated.

Maddie, Skye, and Ivory were sitting in the parlor, while everyone tried to figure out what to do next. Skye and Ivory were crying, too distraught to explain anything in greater detail, and Maddie was not sharing much more.

"We need to see if we can get a glimpse of anything," Dante stated.

Santiago nodded in agreement. "Maddie, it's not comfortable, but Dante and Bain are going to have to take the information."

"I don't care. Do whatever it takes."

"Been there, done that. Take it," Skye added, along with a nod of agreement from Ivory.

Dante and Bain took what they needed and projected it to everyone, and it was clear Evanora had indeed taken them.

"We should have killed that bitch when we had the chance," Silas raged.

Dante rubbed his chin with his hand. "As soon as the chains released themselves, I should have fucking ended her."

"Second-guessing our decisions is not how we operate. You handled the situation the way you needed to." Santiago had been around far too long to look back and regret any decision made in a time of battle or war.

"Some battles are won, others lost. Unless you are put to death, there is always time to make another plan of attack."

"They're lost to us and within Evanora's reach. The threats to Jadis, Aria, and Amsi are unspeakable." Silas was pacing the room once again, feeling like he had failed his mate.

"All that matters is opening her portal and going after them." Bain, too, was feeling helpless and more than angry with himself with each passing minute. "I'm not confident Amsi can handle an encounter with Evanora."

"Standing around talking about the situation isn't going to help our mates. Bain, let's go. We are going to get there no matter what it takes," Dante stated.

Dante and Bain ripped open large cabinets that contained all they would need to yield powerful, archaic sorcery. Various-sized round stones, concave orbs, and a multitude of ancient instruments, along with potions, scrolls, and an assortment of mystical stones, lined the shelves. Dante pulled out a large, crystalline orb and carried it over to a wooden desk and placed it on a large three-footed stone stand, whose feet resembled that of a demon. As he set the orb onto the hands, the claws stretched outward and the sides wrapped themselves around the orb as if the stand itself was a living creature.

"We both know what happens in one world echoes in the other. If we can get a good image of the girls, we can use the orb Aiden took from Abigor and combine it with the energy our orb carries. Together they should open the portal back up," Dante said, thinking aloud.

Bain motioned his hand over the crystalline orb and a mystic, smoky haze began swirling within the center. "If we can create a rift between the veils, we can take control of her portal."

Dante nodded and swirled his hand over the top of Bain's, and the somber mist within the orb morphed in and out before the pool in the pyramid was visible.

They concentrated on getting a picture beyond the swirling waters; the water went deep beneath the base of the pyramid and sweeping desert sands. After a moment or two, a blurry image of a jungle canopy appeared.

Dante and Bain studied the image intently before the swirling, twisting image disappeared into the thick haze within the crystalline orb. The realization hit them at the same time.

"Avenolon!" Dante picked up a round, black obsidian shew stone and hurled it across the room; it collided with the wall, shattering into pieces. "So that's where the bitch disappeared to."

Mercia and Aisley were packing what little they had after having made a deal with an unknown Nosferatu warrior who said he had a connection to Evanora and heard their pleas. Mercia grabbed the bag of gold coins he had given them in exchange for their help in trapping Jadis, and shoved them into the bottom of her duffle bag.

They had been hiding out in a brothel in the inner ghetto of Talia. It was a small shantytown on the outskirts of the Valley of the Old Gods.

"We need to disappear, and the sooner the better. The coins should be enough to get us far away from this hellhole," Aisley stated.

"We shouldn't have come back here." Mercia took a large drink from the new bottle vodka bottle she had purchased before handing it to Aisley.

After taking a drink to quell her nerves, Aisley placed the cork back into the bottle and shoved it into her bag. "Let's get the fuck out of here before they realize what we did."

Mercia looked at Aisley and picked up her bag. "Let's go. I've got a terrible feeling about this entire situation."

"Me too," Aisley replied as she headed for the door.

Before they made it three steps, the door exploded into pieces, knocking them both off their feet.

Sigurd stood before the terrified girls, who were trying to gather their senses. "Going somewhere?" he snarled.

Mercia and Aisley scrambled to their feet and headed for the window in order to climb down the fire escape.

Lars grabbed Mercia's and Aisley's shirts in a tight grip. "Mmm, I don't think so!" He shoved them forward to face Sigurd and the other warriors.

"It appears your reactions confirm our suspicions," Sigurd stated.

"Whh-what are you—t-talking about?" Mercia asked, stuttering her words and trying to sound innocent.

"Whatever you think we did, we had nothing to do with it!" Aisley cried.

"Sir." One of Sigurd's warriors tossed him the bag of gold coins he found in their duffle bag.

Sigurd opened the small bag and dumped some coins into his hand. "Care to explain how you acquired these, lass?"

"I don't have to explain anything to you!" Mercia yelled.

"I would be careful with your words. There's a lingering trace of the two of you, as well as your magic near the cenote," Lars growled.

"Aye, the two of you have made a grave mistake. Take them!" Sigurd ordered.

"W-wait—where are you taking us?" Aisley tried to fight back against the warrior's unrelenting grip, but Sigurd stepped forward and grabbed her by the throat. "I would fucking walk if I were you," he threatened.

"You can't do this!" Mercia cried.

Lars grabbed Mercia by the jaw. "We will extract the information one way or another and it's up to you how this plays out."

Dante and Bain materialized in the main temple. "We found them. They're in Avenolon," Bain stated.

"*Avenolon*?" Santiago repeated.

"Yes, tell us everything you know about that fucking place," Dante demanded.

Santiago rubbed his hand over his jaw and paced back and forth. "I'll admit this is a problem, a big problem."

"Speak, Father," Silas urged.

Santiago walked to the bar and filled his glass. He then turned to his clan and stood, contemplating the dire situation the girls were in.

"Come." He motioned for them to follow as he took a seat. "You have all heard the stories of Avenolon, but you don't know its genuine history. The energy in Avenolon ebbs and flows. It's a place of creation. Dante, Bain, as you know, initially your powers are not your own. They come from the universe itself. Avenolon is a matrix within itself. Anyone who enters will be barren of their innate powers. That's the reason all wizards were sent to train at one time. If they couldn't control their own sorcery, they would have to learn to control and harness it from the world around them. It took years for them to learn to control that which they had no control over."

"What you're saying is that Jadis, Amsi, and Aria will be powerless," Silas stated.

"Yes," Santiago answered.

"Holy shit," Dante stated.

"Our ancestors sealed Avenolon just as the Original War began in order to protect it. All clans came to a mutual agreement the best course of action was to keep it hidden. If the Baskales who rose up from the underworld would have found the portal's entrance, it would have been disastrous. Should they were to harness the powers of Avenolon, theoretically, they would have complete control over the entire planet."

"It's been over a thousand years now. Why did our ancestors abandon it for so long?" Bain asked.

"After the chaos of the war and the years following, it disappeared from everyone's minds. The elders who controlled the portals have since passed and the younger generations never gave it another thought. Sometimes the old ways die and fade from memory."

"Then there is a way in?" Silas asked.

"Yes, however, the original entrance has long disappeared."

Dante looked at Bain and Silas. "So we create a new one."

Santiago tilted his glass at them. "Easier said than done. My biggest concern is getting word to the girls. There is no way for them to know about the creatures lurking beyond the shadows. Even if the girls could use thier powers, they are no match for Avenolon."

"Well, I've heard enough. Now that we know where they are, we need to get to work," Silas stated.

The girls climbed down the other side of the boulder, deciding the jungle was far too dangerous. After their single encounter, not to mention the thing that crashed through the trees, there was no way in hell they were going to stay there in the blanket of night.

They made it down to the edge of the raging river and stood watching the powerful, turbulent waters crash into, and rush over large, moss-laden boulders.

Any one of us gets caught in that current, it will carry us downstream, not to mention the dangers we will face from the undertow, Jadis thought.

They didn't venture too close to the edge. If the creatures they saw on land were any sign of the dangers this unknown world possessed, who the hell knew what might lie in wait below the water's surface. The girls followed the river for about an hour as it snaked its way through the jungle before it grew in width and the brutal waves and swells subsided.

They studied the river to figure out the safest way to cross so they could make their way up the rocky foothills on the other side. They continued along the river's edge until the water calmed enough they thought they could cross it.

"It's slowed but don't be fooled, the current beneath the surface will be powerful," Jadis cautioned.

"We should go farther down. The wider it gets, the shallower it will become. Maybe we can find a better crossing point," Amsi offered.

They walked about another mile before it looked relatively shallow. "I think this is as good as we are going to get. At least if we slip on a rock and fall in, we can swim to the other side," Jadis stated.

Amsi looked up and down the river. "I agree—it will be dark soon. We need to get across."

Aria walked toward the water. "Well, shit, let's do this,"

Jadis grabbed her forearm. "Wait."

"Wait for what?" Aria asked.

"Grab some rocks and toss them into the water. If something is there, the rocks should disturb it."

"What are we going to do? Scare a bunch of fish?" Amsi chuckled.

"I don't see any signs of a river monster," Aria joked as she looked up and down the river bank to see if there were tracks in the dirt.

"Better to be safe than dead," Jadis replied.

They grabbed a couple of large rocks and began throwing them into the river, and waited. After the initial splash, the water became calm once the rocks sank to the bottom; they threw a couple more and nothing stirred.

Aria waited for a few more minutes. "I don't so much as see a fish moving."

Jadis grabbed one more heavy rock and threw it as far up the river as she could, and it came down with a heavy splash. "I guess we should cross. It's now or never."

They only made it a few steps toward the water before Mag and Limi let out a long, guttural growl. They stopped mid-stride and looked in the direction the wolves were snarling.

The water swirled at the surface and they moved as far back as they could and waited. What looked like the back of a giant, fin-laden snake broke the surface of the water, followed by another breach and then another.

"Shit! What kind of huge-ass snake is that?" Aria questioned.

Jadis grabbed another rock and threw it at the creature; it dipped below the surface and they stood watching in horror.

The water rippled before them once again and the snake-like creature breached the surface once again. They gasped as it rose up about eight feet above the surface and that didn't include what they couldn't see. It hissed in their direction, revealing a mouthful of razor-edged daggers. Large, pointed fins ran down its backside, and its face was bestial. It was as thick as a tree trunk and mossy, brown scales covered its entire body. Its eyes were fixated on the girls like an executioner, merciless and cold. The girls ran and it disappeared back into the water, creating gentle waves at the surface, following its slithering movements as it gave chase.

The girls couldn't get far enough away from the edge of the river or the looming threat due to steep canyons that rose up along the river bed, blocking any quick escape.

Aria, Amsi, Mag, and Limi have no chance of climbing fast enough if that thing can slither on land as quickly as it does in the water. I can only pull them up one at a time and that's not an option, Jadis thought as she looked around for an escape.

The ground was littered with debris and the large branches, rocks, and boulders made it difficult for them to gain any real momentum. Ahead in the distance, it was clear they were going to end up trapped. The girls stood, feeling helpless as the steep cliffs following the river jutted out farther toward the water's edge, giving them no choice but to run into the water and swim around the cliffs.

"We're fucking trapped!" Amsi yelled as she and Aria stood with their backs against the canyon wall.

Jadis moved in front of the girls and waited for the creature to appear.

The creature swam in circles in the water before rising again. It hissed, flicked its forked tongue and its merciless, viridian green, reptilian eyes were fixed on them. It swayed its head in subtle sideways motions as it slithered its way out of the water.

They held their breaths, released the chains from Mag and Limi, and waited; they had no choice but to stand their ground. Once it made on the land, it dropped and thrust its body forward. Mag and Limi lunged and attacked the oncoming threat and the creature snapped in Mag's direction, taking its focus off the girls. Limi continued tearing at its body before ripping a sizeable chunk of its flesh off. Mag jumped out of the way, avoiding the snapping jaws, and lunged again. He lunged for the creatures head and his large canines lacerated its flesh. The creature swung the tail of its body, striking Limi and sending her tumbling to the ground.

Jadis sized it up and lowered her stance, getting ready to attack.

Aria grabbed Jadis's arm and pulled her back. "Jadis, don't!"

Jadis wrenched her arm from Aria's grip. "Stay the fuck back!" she yelled as she grabbed a large rock and launched herself above it. She raised both her arms over her head and brought the rock crashing down on its skull. It flung its head and sent her tumbling onto the rocky riverbed. She rolled head over heels before stopping in a crouched position, ready to attack again. She ran to its side, swung her arm, and the force of the blow to the side of its face drove its head into the riverbed. It let out a deafening, hissing sound, and convulsed its head back and forth. It spun its body and snapped in Jadis's direction. She lunged to the side and landed another powerful blow, dislodging its lower jaw.

Mag and Lime attacked the creature again, tearing sizeable chunks of flesh from it head and neck.

As the blood spewed from its gaping wounds, its violent movements subsided.

Jadis stood breathless as the beads of sweat ran down her face.

"How did you manage that?" Aria asked.

"I'm Nosferatu. Evanora can't control that."

"Thank the gods something's working in our favor." Amsi sighed.

They waited a few heart-pounding moments as it lay motionless to make sure it was indeed dead.

"Let's get the hell across the river," Amsi demanded.

They jumped onto the multiple boulders and crossed the river before they had to face another creature. *This time we were lucky. The next time might not turn out so well should we meet a larger one,* Aria thought.

They climbed the rocky cliff side to get as far away from the river as possible. Mag and Limi jumped and climbed the rocks and boulders, helping to pull Aria and Amsi up the steep cliffs. By the time they made it halfway up, the sun was setting beneath the horizon, shadows replacing the bright sunlight. Jadis closed her eyes, took a deep breath, and followed the ledge they stood on.

"Jadis, where are we going?" Amsi asked.

"I don't know. Just a feeling."

As they rounded the corner, there was an opening, and they reluctantly peered in. The air was musty, and the back of the weathered cave was eerily dark and dank. After all they had been through, they wanted to make sure nothing else was lurking in the dark. Jadis stepped in with Mag and Limi. They cocked her heads, and listened for any sounds. Jadis lifted her nose to the air, and the musty smell drifted toward her nostrils.

"I think it's okay. I don't think anything's been in here in a long time.

Mag and Limi casually walked around smelling the unfamiliar area.

Amsi and Aria followed Jadis and looked around. It wasn't large, but they could fit comfortably. They checked the small cave, making sure the only entrance was from that of the ledge where the entered. They decided it was safe and sat down, trying to calm the adrenaline coursing through their veins.

Mag and Limi plopped down, and their heavy panting returned to normal. It was pitch-black and the only light in the cave came from the glowing eyes of Jadis's wolves. They appeared to be relaxed, so the girls leaned against the uneven wall and sat shoulder to shoulder.

"This entire situation is fucked up. Jadis, had you not had Mag and Limi, we would have been its next meal," Aria stated.

Amsi sat quietly and rubbed the top of Limi's head.

Jadis didn't speak. She looked at Mag, who had laid his head in her lap, grateful they were okay after having attacked the creature.

As the night crept in, the temperature dropped and the cold air wrapped itself around their bodies, chilling them to the bone. At least they had shelter, but they were too exhausted to light a fire. They lay next to each other on the cold, damp ground with Mag and Limi curled up on either side. Their warm bodies and thick fur added a layer of protection from the chilly night air.

The light from the early morning sun penetrated the cave, waking the girls. They were sore, tired,, and did not know what they were going to do. They gathered themselves together, ready to face whatever impending doom the day may bring.

Mag and Limi lifted their heads into the air before sitting next to where the girls stood on the ledge in order to get a better view of their current surroundings.

"What now? I don't even know where to begin." Aria rubbed her face, not wanting to face another day there.

"I don't know. I'm as lost as you. Wherever we are, I can feel her—Evanora is waiting for us." Jadis sighed.

"That's not what I needed to hear," Amsi stated as she folded her arms across her chest, trying to warm herself.

"Right now, we're protected on all sides, and this is the only entrance. I say we stay put. You know as well as I do our mates will come for us," Jadis stated, trying to give Aria and Amsi a sense of relief, as well as herself.

"Hell, it could take a day, a week—who knows?" Aria rumbled.

Amsi shrugged her shoulders, feeling as unsure as Aria and Jadis. They took a seat on the edge, not sure what to do.

"What if they don't know where we are?" Amsi asked.

We have no chance of getting out of this godforsaken place without our mates, Jadis thought. "They'll find us, Amsi, I promise."

"Jadis, let's see if you can do something. You are a Dhamphyr, after all."

"Yes, but from painful experience, I know my abilities can be controlled. I had no powers in Abigor's world unless he allowed it. This feels different but the same, if that makes any sense."

"It can't hurt to try," Amsi replied.

"Well, here goes nothing. I'll start with something small and go from there. Let me see if I can conjure a fire."

They stood and walked back into the cave. Jadis kneeled down and closed her eyes. She took a few deep breaths before waving her hand over the ground, but nothing happened. She tried a couple more times and conjured nothing more than a small spark, which dissipated beneath the humid air.

"Fuck me." Jadis grabbed a rock and threw it against the wall. It bounced off and rolled over to where Aria and Amsi were standing. *We are screwed,* she thought.

"Someone's testy." Aria chuckled, trying to make light of the situation.

"*Testy?* I'm a bit more than *testy.*"

"Jadis, what's that?" Amsi asked.

Jadis and Aria looked at Amsi, who was holding the rock in her hand.

Jadis took the rock from her and it was covered with a black, tar-like substance. "Holy shit! It's cimruta."

"*Cimruta?*" Amsi questioned.

"Yes, it's a long story I'll tell you later, but right now, this is a good thing," Jadis said.

"Well, maybe I need to piss you off. It seems your emotions can do something," Aria teased.

"At least we can have fire." Jadis smiled.

"Fire? How?" Amsi questioned.

"I'll show you." Jadis placed the rock in the center of the cave toward the entrance. She grabbed a couple of stones and struck them together multiple times before a spark hit the substance, lighting it on fire.

"Shit!" Aria stated. "If you can do that to the tip of sticks, we can make a few torches and light this place up at night."

Jadis smiled, feeling for the first time she did indeed have some control.

"What now?" Amsi asked.

"We need rocks, logs, and, most of all, water. I don't know about you all, but I'm dying of thirst," Aria replied.

They each felt the other's trepidation, knowing they would have to venture out of the cave in order to find what they needed, and only the gods knew what they might come across.

CHAPTER 8

They stayed up all night while Dante and Bain did all they could to capture whatever images the orb conveyed. They had also ruthlessly questioned Mercia and Aisley and had them locked in a temple cell under guard.

"I never understood how you or Silas dealt with the situation when Abigor had Jadis. I'm not sure I know what to do?" Bain rumbled.

"Jadis faced Abigor for months and stood toe to toe with Evanora as well. She will watch out for Amsi and Aria, although I'm hoping it doesn't come to that," Dante answered.

"You trying to convince me or yourself they can handle Evanora in their current situation?" Bain questioned.

"Both, which means we need to get there before they face off. We need to take the orb to the cenote and recreate the portal from there. Regardless of what Evanora did, the sorcery should still linger around the cenote," Dante explained.

"The orb should connect us with whatever she's done. After all, we know the orb belongs to Evanora, not Abigor," Bain agreed.

Santiago placed his palms on the table and leaned over the orb. "See if you can gather anything else before we disturb it."

Dante and Bain began chanting their own mantras as they stared deep into Evanora's orb, mesmerized by the swirling, multicolored fog. A seamless, black sheen replaced the colors, and a slight spot of iridescent red appeared.

"What's that?" Bain looked at Dante, noticing something else appearing from within a tiny red haze.

"It looks like symbols?" Dante answered.

They memorized every symbol as they took shape. The symbols vanished into a small puff of smoke before the fog morphed and swirled, revealing another set of symbols. They mumbled another hushed chant, looking for any sign of weakness in the portal they could exploit. The pattern twisted and morphed, this time revealing a large, blurry image of an interwoven, black web that appeared to be a map of sorts.

"The girls, they were there," Dante announced.

Everyone in the room stood with nervous anticipation, hoping to catch even the slightest glimpse of the girls as Dante and Bain chanted another complex incantation. The black web twisted, morphed, and swirled, revealing another faint image that appeared as turbulent, rushing waters.

"What the hell is that?" Bain asked.

Dante peered deeper and could see the faint image of something lying lifeless at the water's edge. His heart leapt into his throat, fearing the worst. As the image grew, they realized it was some type of snake that appeared to have been torn apart.

"It's not a snake, it's a Scylla, and it's shredded in places," Santiago stated.

"Mag and Limi," Dante announced.

Silas rubbed his stubble-laden chin riddled with guilt and worry. "Well, shit, at least they have those two. Mag and Limi won't let anything within a foot of Jadis."

"From the looks of it, that Scylla was just a baby," Santiago said.

As they peered back into the orb, the colors morphed again before dissipating.

Santiago stepped forward and placed his hand on Dante's shoulder. "We need to remain calm. They are alive and we know where they are. They also have her wolves, who will be a formidable challenge to anyone or anything that poses a threat. Now we need to put all our energy into opening the portal within the pyramid."

"Let's do this. We don't have time to just stare into a fucking ball," Silas rumbled.

"I think we should climb up the mountain rather than back down. I don't want to get stuck within the canyon walls again, so close to the river. That thing we faced was huge. If there are bigger ones, even Mag and Limi will be in trouble." Jadis waited for Aria or Amsi to answer.

Amsi replied, "I'm with you. I don't want to be near the water either."

They left the cave and followed the ledge until they found an area that looked like they could climb farther up the cliff. They came across a gully where the heavy rains had washed down the side of the mountain. It was wide and more of a slope than a sheer cliff. There were plenty of rocks, brush, and roots they could grab a hold of and step on in order the climb to the top.

"I'll go first, but pay close attention. The ground will be loose underfoot and I can easily send rocks falling your way," Jadis stated.

Aria looked less than enthused. This was all foreign to her. "Just watch where you step. The last thing I need is to get hit in the head with a boulder."

"Jadis, are you sure this is safe?" Amsi asked.

"Yes, just follow me—slowly."

Jadis climbed the steep path, and Mag jumped ahead. His enormous nails dug into the dirt, keeping himself from slipping on the loose gravel. Jadis checked each foot and handhold for stability before letting it carry her weight.

"Aria, come on up, but watch where I place my hands and feet and follow me. Before you step or pull yourself up, make sure whatever you grab or step on is stable. Amsi, follow Aria."

Aria and Amsi held on to Limi's long chain and made their way up the gully with Limi in front, helping to pull them up the steep incline.

The higher up they ascended, large, knotted roots cut the ground in places, forming natural footholds, making climbing a little easier. After what must have been a few hours, they reached the top, only to find another vast jungle lying before them. They walked a few steps away from the ledge and sat down; the sweltering heat and humidity were taking their toll.

"Holy shit, if you think I'm doing that again, you're out of your mind. Getting up was hard enough. How do you think we are going to get back down?" Aria's breathing was heavy and her face dripped with beads of sweat from the exertion of climbing for the last few hours.

Amsi wiped the sweat from her forehead as she stared down the steep cliffs and rubbed her hands together, trying to get the debris out of her skin. The mere thought of being stuck in such an unforgiving place was sending her mind into an abysmal spiral. "Are you sure they will be able to come for us?"

"Without a doubt." Jadis smiled warmly.

"I'm so thirsty my tongue feels like sandpaper," Aria rumbled.

"I know for a fact Mag and Limi need water," Jadis replied.

"That goes for all of us. My throat is so dry and sore it hurts to talk. It feels like I'm swallowing shards of glass," Amsi stated.

"Jadis, do you think they can sniff out a water source?" Aria asked.

"We will soon find out. Let them lead the way. Their thirst will find it," Jadis offered, as she ushered Mag and Limi forward, letting their senses lead the way. The girls paid close attention to every noise and every movement they heard or saw. Mag and Limi were always on high alert. Many times, they would let out a deep growl, their ears pointing toward the sounds they picked up on.

The farther across the plateau they walked, the denser the surrounding jungle became and the trees once again loomed overhead.

"I don't feel right venturing so far into the brush. Only the gods know what's in there," Aria said.

Mag and Limi stopped, cocked their heads, pointed their ears, and looked straight ahead. The girls stood motionless, trying to decipher what they were sensing.

Jadis looked around and noticed small piles of dirt at the base of almost every tree trunk. "Aria, Amsi," she whispered, pointing toward the base of the trees. "Look, do you see those piles?"

Aria and Amsi looked at the dirt piles and then back at Jadis. "They look like snake holes, maybe?" Aria suggested.

Amsi grabbed Jadis's forearm. "You're freaking me out. They're just anthills."

"From painful experience, a pile of dirt is not a good thing," Jadis argued, remembering back to the piles of dirt the Dragurs clawed their way out of. "Let's get the hell out of here."

They moved as quickly as they could when they heard little yelp-like calls that sounded like minuscule dogs barking. All around the girls, the tree branches shook, leaves rained down overhead, and the sounds grew in intensity.

Something hit Jadis on the back of the head. "Ow—what the hell?"

"What?" Aria yelled.

Jadis was rubbing the back of her head and felt a small, swollen lump. "Something just hit me in the goddamn head!"

"Owww—damn," Amsi yelled. "Something just hit me in the back!"

Without hesitation, they ran, not wanting to find out what or who was throwing rocks at them. The brush behind them, as well as the branches in the trees all around them, convulsed, and it was apparent they were being chased.

Aria let out a yelp as something stabbed her bicep. She looked down, and an arrow made from a large thorn about six inches long was sticking out of her arm. She pulled it out and threw it on the ground. "They're fucking shooting at us!"

They could hear the brush behind them crunching and snapping, and they stopped momentarily to see what was chasing them. Mag and Limi surrounded them and positioned themselves between the girls and whatever was heading in their direction.

Once they stopped moving, so did the sounds that followed, and the jungle became eerily silent. The girls could see something peering at them before it leapt from a branch onto the trunk of a tree. It looked like a humanoid creature and dressed like an Aboriginal warrior.

"Grab something!" Aria looked over and grabbed a large log about the size of her arm. Amsi and Jadis did the same, and they backed up one slow step at a time.

As soon as the thing disappeared, the girls side-eyed each other and waited with bated breath.

What sounded like a swarm of rats headed their way and a stampede of fury-driven, rabid creatures swarmed before the girls. They rained down from the trees and appeared from under the brush on either side of them and attacked.

The girls screamed and started swatting the creatures out of mid-air with their logs. Mag and Limi were snatching them off the ground and leaping into the air, catching them in their mouths. They tore through the little bodies and the lifeless creatures flew from their mouths, crashing to the ground and into the trees and brush.

The girls felt the stings of their arrows again. "Run!" Jadis screamed.

They took off running in the opposite direction and Jadis jumped over the rocks, logs, and dense brush; Aria and Amsi, however, tripped multiple times.

The farther they ran, the more the land began sloping downward and they found themselves running downhill.

Amsi tripped over a large log and landed face down on the harsh terrain, and Jadis stopped mid-stride and slipped on the moist, decaying foliage and landed on her ass.

Mag and Limi jumped to their sides, spun around, and faced the creatures that followed while Jadis got to her feet. She grabbed Amsi's arm and pulled her off the ground. "Go! I'll be right behind you," Jadis said.

"Jadis, no!" Amsi yelled.

"Just go!" She shoved Amsi into Aria, and Aria grabbed her arm and ran.

Jadis *turned*, her canines slid from her gums, and she, Mag, and Limi killed at least two dozen of the little creatures, allowing Aria and Amsi to gain some distance. The things retreated and disappeared back into the entanglement of the brush.

Jadis caught up with Aria and Amsi, and Mag and Limi came to an abrupt halt, sliding to a stop. However, Aria wasn't able to stop as quickly as the wolves and she tumbled down a steep embankment while Amsi slipped and landed flat on her back. The root Aria had grabbed kept her from tumbling down the embankment head over heels.

"Aria," Amsi screamed.

Limi yelped and Jadis spun around and the ravenous creatures began shooting at them, having resumed the attack.

They leapt down the embankment and had to slide on their asses partway down the steep incline.

Once they made it to the bottom, Amsi stopped, turned around, and flung her hands out to the side of her body. The vegetation bent and swayed from the intensity of the energy and the creatures scrambled for cover as if she had conjured the winds.

"What the hell was that?" Aria asked.

Jadis looked at Aria, wide-eyed, not realizing Amsi had such powers.

"Go!" Amsi yelled.

They ran as far as they could until Amsi couldn't run any further and had to stop to catch her breath; she placed her palm against a tree to hold herself up and held her stomach with the other.

"Wait, I need a minute," Amsi admitted.

Their breathing was labored and their hands trembled as they pulled the arrows from their bodies.

Jadis placed her hand on Amsi's back as she was bending over. "Are you okay?"

"Yes, it took a lot to do that and it was weak compared to what I can usually do," she replied.

"Amsi, I didn't know you yielded that kind of power," Aria stated.

"Well, now you know. Father likes to keep it a secret for fear of someone wanting to exploit them or me."

"Well, shit, does Bain know?" Jadis asked, genuinely curious.

"Yes, he knows everything and offered to give me a few lessons on how to better control and use the power," Amsi replied.

The girls ran their hands over Mag and Limi to see if they had anything stuck in them, but their thick fur had acted as a barrier. They had only found a couple projectiles that had penetrated their legs and the back of their heads. The girls, however, looked like they had fallen into a cactus patch. As they continued to pull the arrows from themselves, Mag and Limi whined and anxiously pranced in place.

"What the hell now?" Jadis rumbled.

"Shhh—listen." Aria was looking in the same direction as the wolves. "You hear that?"

Jadis listened intently and tilted her head toward the sounds, and could hear a gentle trickle and smell the water. She looked at Aria and Amsi and smiled.

"Water?" Aria asked.

"Yes," Jadis replied.

The girls walked toward the sounds of the rushing water and the closer they got, the louder it became. They hiked for a few more minutes and the jungle opened up, revealing a waterfall tumbling down a steep cliff. They stepped out of the tree line and stood a few feet above the stream. Despite its serenity, they remained cautious.

"At least it's shallow," Aria stated.

The crystal clear water flowed over the pebbled river bed while the waterfall tumbled down the cliffs from about thirty feet above their heads. It gushed over the rocks, churning the aquamarine, blue water below. A gentle stream, rather than a raging river lazily snaked its way through the dense landscape.

"Take it slow," Jadis cautioned as she jumped down the embankment.

Aria and Amsi slid down the embankment on their butts and walked to the edge of the river bed.

Mag and Limi lifted their noses, taking nervous steps toward the water, unable to resist the moist, aromatic scent. They leapt into the shallows and began lapping up the cool liquid. The girls kneeled down and took handfuls of the thirst-quenching water; it was the first proper drink they had in two days.

"You know drinking from unknown waters can be dangerous," Jadis said as she splashed the water on her face and arms, reveling in its soothing, refreshing feeling.

"Maybe so, but if we don't drink, we die from dehydration." Aria was also washing the dirt and grime off her face and neck.

"I don't give a shit right now." Amsi chuckled.

Mag and Limi were standing in the middle of the stream, pawing and splashing with robust, wagging tails.

"I assume if something was threatening, they wouldn't be so casual." Amsi sat crouched down, watching the wolves lie down and roll over in the water.

Aria reached around her back and pulled a small thorn from her shoulder. "I need these things out of my back."

"Me too. Let's look around before we get too comfortable," Amsi suggested.

They walked up and down the river's edge for about half a mile before making their way back to the waterfall where they waded into the shallow pool beneath the flowing falls, letting it wash the sweat, dirt, and stench from their bodies. The girls removed their shirts and pulled the arrows from each other's backs, then let the cold water soothe the stinging welts.

"This water feels amazing," Aria stated.

"Yes, it does. I feel like we looked and smelled like jungle rot." Amsi chuckled.

"You did kind of look like it," Jadis joked as she splashed the water in their faces with a chuckle. "Let's go sit and figure out what to do next."

They sat on a flat, river-worn boulder in the middle of the stream, enjoying a moment of refreshing calmness.

Jadis's body began healing and her body pushed out whatever bits of thorns remained. She was looking at the welts covering most of Aria's and Amsi's arms and back when it dawned on her.

"I can heal those for you, if you say please," she joked.

"Say please? You're ridiculous," Aria chuckled.

"How can you do that?" Amsi asked.

"You okay drinking my blood?"

"Jadis, right now I would drink almost anything to stop the pain," Amsi admitted.

"Drink your blood—you're just now suggesting this?" Aria asked.

"I hadn't thought about it until now." She bit her wrist and held it out to Aria, who tilted her head back and let the drops drip into her mouth. As soon as she swallowed, the scrapes, scratches, and punctures began healing.

Jadis did the same for Amsi, and her injuries also healed.

"Holy shit, I can feel my body responding. That's crazy." Aria laughed.

"I hadn't even thought about taking your blood," Amsi stated.

"Now that the two of you feel better, what are we going to do?" Jadis asked.

"I don't know, but the hell if I'm going back to the original cave after all that," Aria stated.

Jadis looked at Aria. "I have no desire to be chased by those little demons again either."

"Then we need to find another place before nightfall," Amsi agreed.

Aria was already standing. "Amsi's right—it's going to be dark in a few hours. We can't sleep out in the open."

Jadis reaached for her shirt, lying on a flat rock. "What are we waiting for?"

They weren't sure which direction they should head in order to find shelter. They couldn't go back the way they had just come from and who knew what might lurk on the other side of them. Jadis looked at the beautiful, cascading waters and it hit her. "Evanora's gardens."

"What?" Aria asked.

Amsi looked between Jadis and Aria, not understanding what she was talking about, either.

"The waterfall—it's dark behind the water. It looks just like it did in her gardens, not to mention the large ledge behind the water. It can't hurt to look."

"I don't know what you're talking about, but what the hell. You lead, we'll follow," Amsi agreed.

It was a pretty easy climb up to the ledge, which was about four feet wide and stretched from one side of the river to the other. And sure enough, there was a cave behind the flowing water that appeared to be bigger than the one they stayed in the night before.

The girls gathered up some rocks and made a firepit near the entrance to keep out any potential intruders during the night. They filled the circular pit with dry brush and made another pile in the back of the cave in case it rained, hoping they wouldn't need it, but they weren't about to take any chances.

They also used large, long logs and vines to create a door of sorts at the entrance; not that it would keep anything from tearing it down, but it made them feel better. They fastened the ends of the makeshift door to the large tree roots lining the sides of the cliff in order to keep it closed at night.

Aria nodded. "It's now or never, Jadis."

It ended up taking Jadis about fifteen minutes to generate enough of the substance from her palms to light a fire which would last through the night. As soon as she finished, she plopped onto her back, shocked at how anything she did seemed to cause a bout of dizzying nausea.

Aria and Amsi let her rest and grabbed a couple of rocks and knocked them together. A spark hit the substance and a flame sprang to life.

"Hell yes," Aria shouted with a hearty laugh.

Amsi laughed with Aria. "Yesss!"

Living her entire life in the oasis, Aria was a master at creating things from the environment. She weaved together watertight bowls, so they didn't have to venture out at night if they got thirsty. She had also woven belts made of a thick vine to hold the multiple makeshift knives they created. They rubbed the tips of the stones into sharp points, using the boulders as a sharpening tool. They then inserted the blunt end of the tips into the ends of sticks and wound vines around the ends to hold the tips. While they were sitting at the edge of the river creating their weapons, they were also trying to figure out what they were going to do about Evanora.

"I don't know about you, but I'm starving," Aria announced.

Jadis could hear Aria's stomach growling, and it hadn't even dawned on her they would need to eat. She had enough of Silas's and Dante's blood it should last her at least a couple of weeks. "Where there's water, there's food." She shrugged.

"I'm not sure I want to eat anything here." Amsi chuckled as she stood and wiped the dirt from her butt.

"It's better than starving to death," Aria replied.

"I figure if anything makes either of you sick, my blood will be able to heal you," Jadis replied.

They walked downstream, following the river bed and scourging for anything that might be edible. The river became wider and deeper, and the current swifter; they failed in finding anything edible, so they headed back, not wanting to venture too far from the safety of their cave.

"Well, shit, it looks like we're out of luck. There's nothing here." Amsi sighed.

"It's going to be dark in a couple of hours. We should get back to the cave," Aria reasoned.

Jadis looked one more time before deciding it was futile. "I agree, we'll find something tomorrow."

As they headed back, Mag's and Limi's ears perked up, and they stood frozen with pointed tails and tilted heads. Jadis and Aria grabbed the napes of their necks to hold them back, but they lunged forward.

"Mag—Limi—veni!" Jadis stated firmly. However, they disappeared into the dense foliage and Jadis leapt up the embankment to go after them.

"Jadis!" Aria yelled as she scrambled to climb up the edge.

"Jadis, wait!" Amsi called.

She reached down and grabbed Aria's and Amsi's hands and pulled them up.

They searched for about fifteen minutes and couldn't find them. Jadis looked at Aria and Amsi. They could see the worry on her face.

"Jadis, they are Dire Wolves. There isn't much that is a threat to them," Aria stated.

Jadis tilted her head in their direction and listened intently, and after a few minutes, she caught the sounds of their heavy panting off in the distance.

She grabbed Amsi's arm. "Wait, I hear them."

They heard loud squeals and growling and stood frozen as they waited a few heart-pounding moments before Mag and Limi bounded through the trees and brush before them.

Limi dropped what appeared to be a rabbit-like creature at Aria's feet and Mag had another large one in his mouth.

"Holy shit, they brought us dinner," Aria stated as she picked up the animal.

"This is amazing," Amsi agreed as she stroked their thick fur along their backs.

They made it back to the cave, and Aria and Amsi had dinner at the edge of the river. They had skinned, cleaned, and cooked the strange-looking animal.

Mag and Limi shared the other, consuming it in its entirety, and were now lying at the girls' side, contently chewing on a couple of bones.

The girls sat quietly, watching the colors of the sky morph as the sun set beyond the canopy. As beautiful as it appeared, it was just a prelude to the hauntingly eerie sounds of the night that would soon bring about their paranoid imaginations. They tied the ends of the door to the roots that had grown into the crevices as best as they could and sat in the back of the cave, waiting for the darkness to fall over the jungle.

"Think you can conjure up a bottle of something—anything?" Aria chuckled.

"I'll take moonshine at this point." Amsi winked.

"I'll try," Jadis replied as she shrugged her shoulders.

"Seems you're pretty useless," Aria joked.

"Give me a minute," Jadis snapped.

"It's been ten already," Amsi teased.

"Shit, Aria, you couldn't even light a simple fire." Jadis chuckled.

"Everything's wet," Aria replied, making excuses for their earlier failures.

"We should combine our powers and see if we can attach to each other," Jadis suggested.

"True, we need to know what we can do anyway," Amsi agreed.

They sat in a circle and concentrated together, and it wasn't long before they conjured a bottle of whiskey.

"Yesss!" Aria laughed.

"Holy shit, it worked," Amsi squealed with delight.

"It may be a minor feat, but at least we can do something together," Jadis stated.

They rested next to each other and talked about what they were going to do tomorrow while they sipped from the bottle.

Aria had been thinking about Aiden and all that had transpired over the last few years. "Jadis, can I ask you something?"

"Of course."

"Are you in love with Aiden?"

The unexpected question was a bit of a shock. Jadis wasn't sure what to say. *If I admit the truth, it'll feel like a betrayal to Silas and Dante, and if I lie, I'm betraying Aria,* she thought.

"The truth, whatever it is—you and I have never lied to each other." Aria could feel her hesitation, which said more than her words.

"Honestly, I don't know and I don't have a simple answer." She reached for the bottle and took a drink before continuing, trying to be cautious with her words.

"I assume that would be a yes in a roundabout way." Aria chuckled as she handed the bottle to Amsi.

"I mean, yes, I love him, I won't deny that, but I am wholeheartedly in love with Silas and Dante and would never betray them or you. It's not that simple. Aiden and I have a history and there was a time when I thought he was all I wanted." She paused, trying to decipher the complexity of her and Aiden's relationship.

"If it makes it any easier, I know he's still in love with you. I know he loves me and we are mated, but deep down I can feel his conflicting emotions whenever he's near you." Aria took another drink, trying to come to terms with what she never wanted to say out loud. *Thinking about it and saying it are two different things.*

Amsi took the bottle from Aria, not realizing Jadis and Aiden had such a long history. "Oie Vey," she mumbled as the conversation brought her own fears to the surface.

"Aria, he loves you and too much time has passed for us to be anything more." Jadis smiled.

"I know he loves me. It's just been weighing heavy on my mind since the Titling Ceremony, not to mention the way he went stone-cold the night we found out you and Dante had mated."

"I believe everyone was in shock when they found out about me and Dante." Jadis chuckled.

"It's not about him being shocked in the literal sense. I guess I wanted to hear it, so I knew I wasn't crazy." Aria sighed.

"You're not crazy, but the love we have for each other differs from what we feel for our mates." Jadis tried to explain but felt as if she was only making it worse and she felt terrible.

"Jadis, it's okay."

"Is it always this complicated?" Amsi asked, wondering if she could end up in the same situation with Bain.

"Put it like this—you and Amsi are half mortal, so you find one partner. We are Nosferatu and run in packs. Taking more than one mate seems to be the norm for the most part. I haven't been a vampire long enough to understand it myself," Jadis explained.

"That's probably the most sense you've made. When you put it like that, I understand," Aria replied.

"I get it. My father is Nosferatu and my mother is a bruja. I don't think I have ever seen my father without more than one of his breed with him. I never even thought about it until you said it." Amsi took a drink and thought about Bain, how she felt about him, and wondered if he felt the same way or if she was just going to end up having to deal with him mating another.

Jadis could hear Amsi's thoughts. *I know Bain well enough to know she is much more than just another lover.* "Amsi, Bain asked you to agree to become his mate, so do not underestimate the loyalty he has for you already. He would never stray and I can assure you, he would never betray you with another lover. I also know he hasn't been with anyone since the night you met." Jadis smiled at her and felt the sense of relief that crossed her mind.

"Thanks for saying that." Amsi felt better knowing Jadis wouldn't lie to comfort her.

They lay down for the night to get some sleep, but each of them felt tormented by conflicting emotions.

The sounds during the night were by far the worst. Unknown howling, grunting, and screeching filled the night air as creatures were being both hunted and hunting. They didn't sleep well all night, as soon as they would fall asleep, something would startle them awake.

CHAPTER 9

"**Y**ou know Jadis has gone a week now without feeding," Silas rumbled.

"I know, and she's going to get sick. This is the first time she has had to deal with the hunger."

Aiden looked at Dante and Silas, knowing what they were saying. "If the hunger consumes her—"

Eden was also concerned, but wouldn't let on. "Look, Jadis won't hurt Aria or Amsi. I would assume if it came to that, they would let Jadis feed from them. They aren't naïve and from what we have all witnessed so far they can adapt to most situations."

"And if Aria and Amsi haven't eaten enough for their bodies to replenish themselves—then what?" Aiden questioned.

"It's clear they have found food. We saw a vision of them two nights ago. They didn't look like they were sick or starving from the little we could see." Santiago was always calm and logical, so they dropped the subject for the time being and went back to work.

Dante and Bain had gathered enough from the orb to know Evanora had another, more powerful one with her. They assumed if they could somehow communicate with Jadis, they could tell her to get to it. If they could connect the power of the orbs together, they could recreate the portal and slip in.

They worked day and night, trying to create a cosmic alliance between the realms. The chaos of the universe also has a synchronicity Dante and Bain were using to try and communicate with Jadis.

Silas, Dante, Bain, and Aiden were beside themselves. Evanora had their mates, they were lost in a dangerous world, and Evanora wanted nothing more than to execute Jadis; and they knew she would not hesitate to kill Aria and Amsi as well.

"We both know why Evanora took her." Silas looked at Dante and rumbled what they were both fearing most.

"At least Jadis has dealt with her before. The mystic energy of Avenolon will also render Evanora powerless," Dante replied half-heartedly.

"Which means she will need Jadis in her lair in order to use her own powers against them." Bain sighed.

"Evanora will be waiting and that's the direction they are heading now," Dante rumbled.

Santiago had been listening to them speaking, and he too was fearing the worst. However, he also knew how powerful Jadis was. "Jadis fought Evanora before and came out relatively unscathed. She can match her wit for wit, power for power, and we need them to get to the orb. We cannot let our emotions interfere with our plan—it's the only way."

"Father, you know damn good and well Jadis was under Abigor's protection when it came to Evanora," Dante snapped.

"Not only did Jadis fight her, she brought out the fury in her," Silas added.

Dante and Silas stared at each other, remembering the last words Evanora spoke. *'Should I get to the bitch first, I will kill her',* they thought in unison.

Dante and Bain combined the symbols and the powers of the orb, using an ancient cantrip to connect with Jadis; failure was not an option. The milky mixture swirled and the mysterious symbols morphed and twisted; a wavy image appeared before them. They could make out an image of the girls, so they opened their minds and moved into a higher realm of consciousness.

The girls had remained in the cave's safety for a week and they ventured out only during the day and retreated to the cave before the sun set. Once they felt an ethereal pull, they knew Evanora was summoning them; there wasn't a doubt in their minds.

Jadis was having a hard time waking up, while Aria messed with the fire, keeping it burning. "Jadis, we should head out for a while."

"I just need a minute." She rubbed her face, knowing how desperately she needed to feed. "I'm feeling sick," she admitted.

"Jadis, what's wrong?" Amsi asked.

"I haven't fed, and I don't have any of Silas's and Dante's blood in my veins. I knew it would only last a few weeks."

Aria and Amsi looked at each other and felt terrible. They hadn't even thought about her needing blood.

"Look, it's not a big deal. Just feed from me," Aria offered.

"You can feed from me as well. I have no problem with it," Amsi agreed.

Jadis looked at them and realized she should have brought it up earlier. Her biggest fear was if the hunger grew in intensity, she might drain them.

"Are you sure?" Jadis asked.

"It's not a big deal. Aiden feeds from me all the time. Just don't think I'm going to let you have sex with me after," Aria joked.

"Okay, but if I get 'the look' get the hell out of here."

Aria rolled her eyes and held out her wrist. "Feed, Jadis."

Jadis bit down, and she felt her body absorb every nourishing drop. After she took enough to feel the difference, she released her grip and sealed the punctures.

"Aria, you have no idea how much I needed that."

"Jadis, your wolves have been bringing us food for a week. It's the least I can do." Aria looked into Jadis's eyes, mesmerized by their swirling colors after having fed. *She looks exactly like Silas.*

Jadis tilted her head, looking like she had something else to say. "Why are you looking like that?" Amsi asked.

"I need my mates." She chuckled.

Aria laughed aloud again. "I don't know what to tell you. I'm not taking care of *that* need."

"Neither will I, but I'll give you lunch or dinner." Amsi chuckled.

"Well, the sooner we figure out how the hell to get out of this hellhole, the better. We can't just sit here and continue to do nothing," Jadis replied.

"I would have thought they would be here by now." Aria also let out a heavy sigh as they lay back down and dozed off for a while.

Jadis sat up when she heard a voice in her head calling her name. *"Jadis,"* the voice called.

"Holy shit," she exclaimed as she smacked Amsi's and Aria's thighs.

"What the fuck!" Aria exclaimed, having been startled.

"Shhh—" She held up her hand and listened. "It's Dante!"

"No shit?" Aria whispered before it hit her. "Tell Aiden to get his ass here."

"Shut up," Jadis demanded. "I'm trying to listen."

"Tell Bain to hurry the hell up!" Amsi demanded.

"Just tell him," Aria demanded again.

"I will! Now will the two of you shut the fuck up."

"Jadis—" Dante called. After he called her name a dozen times, she sat up.

"Now. Tell her, Dante," Bain demanded.

"Jadis, if you can hear me, get to Evanora. There is another orb. We need a connection to where are."

It appeared as if she was listening from what little they made out of the churning image.

"Dante?" Jadis questioned telepathically.

"Yes, baby, it's us. Can you hear me okay?"

"Barely. Where the hell are you?" Jadis snapped.

"We're coming, baby. Evanora—she has another orb. You need to get to it, darling. Head for the volcanic mountain range," Dante spoke quickly and clearly, knowing time was limited.

"The Enchantress, a volcano and an orb, got it! Sure—no problem, we'll just knock on her door. Hi, Evanora, I hear you have an orb. Can we have it!"

Dante chuckled before getting serious again. *"Jadis, be careful, baby, get the orb."*

"I love you, Dante, and tell Silas I love him and just get your asses here. And before Aria and Amsi annoy the hell out of me, tell Aiden Aria said to get his ass here and Amsi said tell Bain to hurry the hell up."

Before Jadis could finish, her voice dissipated, as did their connection to her.

"Goddamn! You got to her? Are you sure she heard you?" Silas questioned.

"Yes," Dante replied. "She heard. She said we need to get our asses there and now. She had a few more words as well."

"I bet she did." Silas patted Dante on the back.

"You sure they're okay?" Aiden asked.

"Yes, I could faintly hear Aria and Amsi demanding Jadis to give you the messages and Jadis was telling them to shut the fuck up."

Everyone let out a sigh of relief before the heaviness and worry resumed.

"Dante?" Jadis questioned. *"Dante—Dante?"*

"What was all that about?" Aria asked.

"He told me Evanora has another orb and we need to get to it."

Aria and Amsi didn't know what to say or think.

"What the hell?" Aria rumbled. "We are to get to Evanora and just like that, steal a fucking orb?"

"There is no way I am going after the Enchantress," Amsi protested.

Jadis didn't know what to think, either. "If we get to Evanora, there will most definitely be a way for our mates to get here. Hell, she got us here."

"Jadis! Is that the pull talking, or are you thinking rationally? After everything you told me about her, what makes you think the three of us can fight her?" Aria reasoned.

"Our powers are useless out here, so I assume hers are as well. We haven't seen hide nor hair of her," Jadis speculated.

"I don't think we can assume anything after all I have heard," Amsi snapped.

"I'm not so confident. It's better to stay put and let our mates figure this one out." Aria stood and walked to the entrance of the cave and stared into the jungle.

"Aria, since when have you ever been afraid of anything?" Jadis asked.

"Since you told me what an evil bitch she is," Aria replied.

"We have to decide together. I'll let the two of you decide, but I, for one, am tired of waiting. Dante would have never told us to go if they didn't have a plan."

"I can't argue with that. Aiden would never agree if they weren't up to something—fuck it, let's go," Aria said.

"Wait, are the two of you serious right now?" Amsi questioned.

"Jadis is right. I don't think we have much of a choice and Bain would have never agreed to this if they hadn't discussed this in detail," Aria replied.

They looked at each other, knowing how unpredictable and dangerous the primeval jungle was.

"I'm second-guessing this already," Amsi admitted.

"The longer we stand here contemplating our decision, the less likely it is we are going back out there. Either we go now or we stay put," Aria replied.

I don't want to leave either, but it might be better to go by myself, Jadis thought. "I'll go alone and take Mag. I might move faster."

"The hell you will. There's no way we're splitting up!" Amsi scolded.

"Absolutely not. We all go or no one goes," Aria added.

Evanora sat back, knowing Petra was on her way and she had more than one surprise in store for them.

"Dolog, go to the valley and bring me the ones that look like me as well as the creatures you refer to." *I will keep those beautiful wolves for myself,* she thought.

"Sprigga Dama," Dolog answered before leaving with a dozen of his tribesmen.

Evanora was fascinated with the Dire Wolves, their size, their strength, not to mention their beauty, and she wanted them. *They will be more than useful once I turn them against Petra.* She laughed, thinking how much she would enjoy watching her die at the mouths of her own wolves.

The girls stood on the ledge, looking toward the mountain, and could see a faint glow and a gentle plume of smoke. "That's it. I assume the glow would be lava," Jadis offered.

Amsi kicked a rock off the ledge and watched it splash into the stream below. "Well, shit."

"Evanora's there." Jadis looked at Aria and Amsi, and they too looked as scared as she felt.

Amsi pointed to the top of the large smoke-filled peak. "What are those things flying over the top of the peak? If we can see them from here, they must be enormous."

Jadis could also see the large birds, or so they hoped they were birds. Each of them was barely a discernible silhouette against the milky wash of the sky. Jadis spun the makeshift spear in her hand, trying to comfort herself.

"Shit," was all Aria mumbled.

They reluctantly hiked down the steep embankment and into the entanglement of the valley brush. The heat and humidity hung in the air like a wet blanket, and the smells were as sweet as they were deadly. Infused within the aroma of the vegetation, there was always a nefarious pungency to it. Trees towered above them, and once again, the contorted branches stretched toward the sky, blocking most of the sunlight.

Whatever lived in the canopy seemed to follow them. The girls had become used to it, but it was nonetheless menacing. They felt as if they were insignificant beings lost in an alien world. *Without my powers, I am no longer the threat, and nothing is as benign as it appears to be,* Jadis thought, as she watched the shadows morph in and out of the tree trunks and branches as if they were living creatures.

They had been hiking for what seemed like an eternity; an hour passed and then another, followed by another. They stopped multiple times to catch their breaths and take a small drink of water from the makeshift containers they carried.

"How far do you think we still have to go?" Aria asked, breathless.

"All I know is that I'm scared shitless right now. This doesn't feel right," Amsi replied.

The dense brush ahead of them snapped, and they froze. A loud hiss put an end to their progress as the thing rose from the underbrush and raised about five feet above the foliage. They were face to face with its wide jaw and black, elliptical pupils and a fantasy of death flashed before their eyes.

"Jadis—" Aria pulled on Limi's chain and took one step back.

Amsi and Jadis followed, but her wolves had other ideas and they went rabid. Aria didn't have the strength to pull Limi back, so Jadis grabbed her chain as well.

"Discendant!" Jadis yelled.

The girls backed up with Mag and Limi and watched its flickering, forked tongue dart in and out of its enormous, triangular mouth.

It lowered its head and slithered toward them. They screamed and lunged to the side, and it reared up on its body and hovered over Jadis and Mag. She had no choice but to release the chains.

"Jadis!" Aria and Amsi screamed as Mag and Limi lunged for the massive reptile.

It opened its jaw and snapped at Mag, who leapt to the side, avoiding the deadly bite. Jadis jumped to her feet and ran to the side of it, meeting Aria and Amsi.

Limi jumped on the back of its head and tore at its flesh as Mag lunged again and had a grip on its body.

It shook its head and long body back and forth with such ferocity the wolves lost their grip and tumbled through the brush.

It was bleeding profusely from the gaping wounds the wolves had created, slowing its movements; even so, it was still intent on taking the girls as its next meal.

They called Mag and Limi and ran, hoping the grievous wounds would slow it down long enough for them to get away. However, it spun around and slithered after them, and they could hear the brush breaking and crunching as it gave chase. Jadis had to stop herself from moving too swiftly. She stayed with Amsi and Aria, and could hear it gaining momentum and knew at any minute it would be on top of them. She stopped and grabbed Aria's arm, spun her around, and tossed her to the side before she shoved Amsi out of the way.

"Jadis, move!" Aria shouted.

"Jadis—don't!" Amsi demanded.

"Stay back!" Jadis held her hand toward them, trying to keep them from joining her.

As soon as it broke through the brush and saw Jadis, it coiled up and veered its enormous head and faced her. Its tongue flicked in and out, tasting the air. *It's tasting us,* Jadis thought.

Aria and Amsi ran to her side and its massive body now loomed before them, ready to strike.

"I told you to stay back!" Jadis yelled.

"I'm not letting you face this thing alone!" Amsi snapped.

"I'm a fucking vampire. You're just a powerless bruja," Jadis scolded.

"Well, that's a jab I wasn't expecting, especially since you are fucking powerless as well!" Aria snapped back.

"Do you ever fucking listen?" Jadis barked.

"About as well as you fucking do," Aria fumed.

"Screw the arguing. We can do this together," Amsi stated.

They stood holding their primitively made daggers and their breaths, waiting for it to make its move. It dipped its head and came right at them.

Without warning, its severed head fell to the ground and rolled to their feet, while its body continued to twist and contort.

They stood shaking, breathless, and petrified.

"What the hell just happened?" Jadis questioned.

Amsi stared at the wide jaw and stepped back. "What the fuck?"

"Our mates?" Jadis questioned.

"How?" Amsi asked.

"No idea," Jadis replied.

"I'm done. Fuck this place!" Aria bellowed.

"I've had my fair share of run-ins with snakes in the Coastal areas, but nothing has ever been big enough to eat me," Amsi said.

"Let's just go. I can't face any more goddamn monsters," Jadis snarled.

They again walked for hours, and the density of the jungle gave way and appeared to be opening up. The sunlight was disappearing and the darkness consumed the landscape, casting eerie shadows as the sun dipped beyond the horizon.

"It's getting dark. We need to find a place to stay for the night." Aria was looking all around, but there wasn't a safe place to hide.

"I wish we had never left the cave. At least in there we were safe at night—mostly," Amsi stated.

"We don't have time to second-guess anything right now," Jadis replied.

They sat against a few trees that would provide a partial barrier and protect their backs. They made a large fire and lit makeshift torches in a circle around them, hoping the fire would keep whatever was lurking in the night at bay.

It was ominously dark, and the sounds were unrelenting. *At least I can see in the dark. If it weren't for the soft glow of the flames, Aria and Amsi would be blind.*

The girls were exhausted and overcome with the perils they faced day and night, and were tired of fighting for their lives every time they turned a corner; they spent the majority of their time worrying about what they would have to face next.

As soon as the sun rose, they began their trek without haste. They walked for about an hour and their surroundings seemed unusually quiet. Even though the canopy was dense, the sunlight pierced through in places, dotting the jungle floor. The vines twisted, turned, and tangled into fantastic shapes and hung loosely from the trees overhead.

They noticed the shadows had once again began to shape-shift within the branches. As soon as the sound of their footsteps fell silent, the trees seemed to whisper.

Creatures morphed from every trunk. They were thin and about half the girl's size and looked like the trees themselves.

A thought crossed Jadis's mind. "Dryads," she stated.

"Dri—what?" Aria asked.

"I think we better run!" Amsi whispered harshly.

They sprinted forward, but the creatures morphing from the trees were not only following them, but appearing before them as well.

Aria let out a deafening scream and Jadis stopped mid-stride, slipped on the rotten foliage, and landed on her hip. She looked over and Aria was hanging upside down from a tree. She was bound with vines and her arms were pinned at her sides.

"Aria!" Amsi yelled as she ran toward her.

Jadis jumped to her feet and ran over to Aria and leapt toward her, only to have vines coil around her body so tightly she was having a hard time breathing, as they hoisted her about ten feet off the ground.

"Jadis—Aria!" Amsi outstretched her arms and screamed. Nothing more than a slight breeze blew before they wrapped her in vine and hoisted her into the tree.

Mag and Limi were below the hanging girls, moving in slow, protective circles and snarling in every direction. The tribesmen tossed a long lasso made of vines toward Mag and Limi and yanked their legs out from under them.

One Dryad appeared a few feet away from where the girls dangled from the tree. He wore many necklaces made of seeds and stones, and a crown of thorns. His clothes, or lack thereof, were made from skins and he carried a thick net that covered most of his body and dragged on the ground behind him.

Dozens of the Dryads, all holding long spears and other weapons, surrounded the girls. They thumped the ends of the spears against the dirt and began chanting. Well, more like grunting in a foreign language.

Just as the grunting and activity seemed to reach a feverish pitch, an inhuman call erupted.

The Dryads froze and fell deathly silent; the call seemed to cause a frenzy of panicked fear amongst them and all their eyes filled with a dark, foreboding look.

Before them stood a line of the ugliest little creatures the girls had ever seen. They were raising their weapons and making threatening gestures and there was a harshness in their grunting and movements, an inner evil that matched that of Avenolon itself.

Dolog sat with his dirty, bare toes gripping the brown branches of the ancient tree as he watched the odd creatures struggling to free themselves.

His tribesmen billowed and spun within the hidden winds and attacked the Dryads, sending them scurrying deep into the shadows of the surrounding jungle.

Aria, Amsi, and Jadis landed with a hard thump as the creatures cut them from the trees. Jadis tried to break the vines, which should have been a simple task, but she failed miserably.

They carried the girls for an entire day before a primitive village appeared in a valley resting below the steep volcanic cliffs of the mountains. By the time they reached the village, the sun had sunk below the horizon, allowing Avenolon's darkened vesper to commence. The only light, other than the bright moon, was the glow from multiple fires scattered throughout the valley.

They forced the girls to their knees, and they kneeled on the ground with their hands and legs bound behind them. Mag and Limi had been tossed into a cage and were chewing at the vines binding their legs.

The entire tribe came to peer at the strange creatures that had been captured, after which they chanted and danced around what appeared to be a rock altar in the center of the village. The girls were surrounded by the tribesmen and their grunting and rage-filled words were spoken in a foreign language.

More than one of them raised their heads and looked in the girls' direction, having a bestial expression as they picked up their spears and pointed and shook them in their direction.

Aria, Amsi, and Jadis side-eyed each other, not knowing what was about to happen, but feared the worst.

The spears were each a yard-long shaft bound with vine to an arrowhead. Based on the difference in the tips, they appeared to have been designed for specific prey.

"They are going to eat us," Aria whispered.

"Either that or sacrifice us," Jadis replied.

"This can't be happening," Amsi rumbled.

Their hearts beat, pulses raced, and they trembled uncontrollably. They didn't know if the tribe was sent by Evanora or if they had captured them for themselves. The tribe's people were so primitive they mostly communicated with grunts and gestures.

The girls looked around to find a way out of their precarious situation.

Four of the tribesmen approached the girls and began grunting and pushing them around as if trying to communicate. When they failed to reply, they were dragged toward the altar, forced to their knees, and their arms were tied above their heads. All the while, Dolog stood in the small thatched opening of his hut, listening to the whispers of Evanora. *"Sprigga Dama,"* he replied telepathically.

He approached the girls and began grunting and chanting and waving his spear before standing behind them.

Another grabbed a handful of Aria's hair and wrenched her head back, forcing her to drink a pungent liquid. They then did the same to Aria and Jadis, and it wasn't long before Aria and Amsi began feeling disoriented. However, it seemed to have little effect on Jadis, unbeknownst to the tribesmen.

As disoriented as Aria and Amsi felt, they were peculiarly alert enough to hear the sounds of the ritual and see the visions wafting in and out of their minds, feeling as if they were being condemned to death.

Aria's refusal to take another drink of the noxious liquid by pursing her lips together did nothing more than enrage the one who appeared to be in charge. She let out a belt of air and muffled scream as soon as the blunt end of his spear crossed her body. Two more approached and beat her relentlessly, knocking her unconscious.

"I will fucking kill you all!" Jadis roared as she *turned*.

The tribesmen jumped back, having never seen such a dangerous creature. Dolog hastily waved his spear and began shoving the tribesmen back toward the girls and beating the ones who refused.

Jadis noticed the one that appeared to be in charge glance toward the tree line and then back at Amsi. He let out a few fetid grunts and slid his hand under her shirt and cupped her breasts in his dirty, weather-worn hands.

Amsi spun her body, doing her best to stop him from touching her. "G-get the fuck off me—sick piece of shit!" she demanded, slurring her words.

Three other tribesmen cautiously approached Aria, doing their best to avoid stepping too close to the one they feared, and began feeling their way around her body, grabbing her breasts and running their fingers over her face and mouth.

Aria shifted her legs out from under herself and threw them forward, knocking one of them head over heels. He jumped to his feet, screamed words she couldn't understand, and stared at her with eyes as lifeless as a gravestone. He walked behind her and began striking her back with a club-like object.

Aria let out a deafening scream when she felt the searing sensation cross her waist and a gush of warm liquid saturate her T-shirt. One of the tribesman grabbed a fistful of her hair, slid his hand down the front of her pants, and began feeling his way around and fondling her sex.

"Stop!" Jadis thundered. "You fucking bastard, get the fuck off her!" She watched the entire situation unfolding, feeling utterly helpless.

The tribesman suddenly pulled his hand from Aria's pants and glanced at the tree line again.

Someone's out there, Jadis told herself. She took a closer look and noticed what appeared to be the silhouette of a man leaning against a tree hidden within the shadows. "If you're doing this, I will fucking kill you!" Jadis yelled to him.

"Ahh, Petra, you still have an uncanny inability to keep your fucking mouth shut," Jadis heard telepathically.

"Who the fuck are you?"

"Well, hell, you really don't know?"

"Do something!"

"I just did, and I think an old-fashioned beating will suffice."

His voice? Jadis thought before it hit her. "It's you! You motherfucker!" Her heart rate increased, she began sweating, and a sense of overwhelming fear and anxiety brought her back to Bergelême.

"'Motherfucker'?" he repeated with a chuckle. *"I believe I've not only saved your lives once already, but I've stopped the males from fucking your girls."*

"Arkyn! All this time we thought it was that bitch Evanora!"

"This is all Evanora's doing. I'm just enjoying the show." He laughed.

Shit! That's tantamount to him saying you owe me, Jadis thought *"Silas and Dante will never let the two of you get away with this!"*

"By the time they get here, you and I will be long gone."

Before she could reply, a blow struck the side of her head, causing her vision to blur. She slumped to the ground, and the last sound she heard was the sadistic laughter of Abigor, Vidar, and Arkyn echoing in her mind as the darkness consumed her.

The girls were being held in a tiny, heavily guarded corral and after what seemed like hours of lying on the damp ground fading in and out before they were dragged to a makeshift cage and tossed onto the thatched floor.

Jadis finally regained consciousness, and she lay there watching the streaks of lightning snaking their way through the turbulent night sky. She assumed the only reason the ritualistic beatings ended was because of the torrential rains that followed the claps of thunder. She realized her hands were now bound in front of her rather than behind her back as she rolled over. She looked at Aria and Amsi, and it was clear they were in dire straits. "You need to feed from me," she whispered.

Amsi replied with nothing more than a pain-filled moan and the tears flowed from her bloody, discolored eyes, one of which was swollen shut, and Aria failed to respond at all.

Jadis rolled Amsi onto her back and bit her wrist, allowing the trickles of blood to flow into her mouth as she held open. She then turned to Aria. "Aria—Aria, wake up," Jadis said as she ran her hand over her forehead. "I need you to drink."

Aria's eyelashes fluttered and her eyes opened.

"Take my blood," Jadis urged.

Aria opened her mouth as best as she could and looked up at Jadis.

"You're going to be okay. My blood will heal you."

The girls woke a day later, having felt the warmth from the early morning rays, which brought some sense of relief. However, they would soon be at the mercy of the sweltering heat of the midday sun; they didn't know which was worse. They sat up against the bamboo poles, trying to get comfortable, having been bound for three days now. Their bodies ached and their hands and feet were numb. Sitting hurt, lying down hurt. Hell, it all hurt. They hated to face another day in captivity, not to mention the constant beatings. They were always stuck between extremes: boredom, pain, and the anxiety of not knowing what was going to happen.

Two females approached, and they seemed to pity the girls based on the looks on their oddly shaped faces. They climbed onto the roof of their cage and wove some large leaves between the bamboo, allowing the girls some shelter from the searing heat of the sun; it wasn't much, but it provided some shade. Other than that small act of kindness the females showed the girls, they appeared to be totally feral. They had also brought them a meager amount of food and fresh water. What little of it there was, the girls were grateful, even though Jadis didn't need to eat. They also fed Mag and Limi, who had chewed through the vines on the first night and paced back and forth, whining, digging, and chewing at the cage.

"At least you each get a ration and a half," Jadis whispered.

"If I didn't have this, I'd be too weak to feed you," Aria replied in a hushed tone.

"How are the two of you feeling?" Jadis asked.

"Better. My body has healed, but I can't take another beating—mentally or physically," Amsi said.

"I can't stop them, but just know I will heal you," Jadis replied.

Aria sat back and leaned against the poles. "Jadis, I can't take much more, either. Every time one of them approaches us I feel like I'm going to throw up."

"I'm so sorry," Jadis said, feeling as though she brought this upon them.

"It's not your fault. Stop apologizing," Aria rumbled.

The heat was unrelenting, and the gentle breeze felt like the breath of hell was blowing on the girls. Every day became less bearable, and they counted down the hours until the setting sun brought the sweet relief of the cool evening air. Mag and Limi were incessantly chewing and digging at the bars attached to the bottom of their makeshift cage and Jadis noticed they had become loose and Mag and Limi were pushing them outward.

Jadis looked at Aria and Amsi. "Those things didn't forge those cages."

Aria looked at Jadis with the same dreadful feeling. "No, they did not."

They sat on the thatched floor, planning their escape.

"The tribesmen aren't as intent on guarding us anymore. They seem to be losing interest," Amsi whispered.

"I've noticed that too," Jadis agreed.

"We'll leave under the cover of night the first chance we get," Aria stated.

Another tortuous day came and went and as the evening arrived, the tribesmen sat deceptively quietly in a large circle around the unglamorous altar.

"Something's off tonight. It doesn't feel right," Jadis whispered.

"I feel it too, and what's up with all the new spears?" Aria asked.

"The altar, it looks different somehow," Amsi replied.

"I don't know, but it's new. They have never set it up like that before," Jadis said.

Spears with strange skulls sitting on top of them surrounded the tribesmen and the altar. The heads looked old and dusty, but there were still bits of what appeared to be flesh on their shriveled skeletons. A jagged hole marred the forehead of more than one skull, while various hardened, black nuts, small bones and what looked like hag stones hung from the spears beneath the skulls and rattled in the winds.

"I need to tell you all something," Jadis admitted, having decided Aria and Amsi had healed enough to hear the truth.

Aria and Amsi glanced at each other, not sure they wanted to hear it.

"What is it?" Aria asked.

"Arkyn is here with Evanora."

"Arkyn? How the fuck do you know that?" Aria asked.

"Arkyn was watching us being tortured. The shadow they kept turning to and looking at was him."

"It was a shadow, Jadis. What makes you think it was Arkyn?" Amsi asked.

"We had a conversation, if you can call it that."

Aria squinted her eyes at Jadis. "Why are you just now telling us?"

"Neither of you was in any shape to hear it. I didn't want to put anything else on you."

Aria recalled all that Jadis had told her about Abigor, Arkyn, and Vidar. "He's coming for you, isn't he?"

"I'm afraid so." Jadis sighed.

Evanora ripped the tattered piece of material from the front of the cave, about a mile from the volcanic mountain, tossed it aside and rushed in. "You kopele! Why the hell are you interfering with that kuchko Petra?"

Arkyn leapt from the makeshift bed. "You stupid bitch, you're going to kill them before you get your hands on them," he roared, along with a swift backhand.

Evanora stumbled on her feet and grabbed the rock wall to hold herself up. "Stay the fuck out of my business!"

He grasped her by the throat and ripped her away from the wall. "Petra is my business and I should fucking kill you right now," he snarled.

"Kill me and you will never get out of Avenolon!" Evanora threatened, her words barely audible beneath his grip.

"Threatening me is not in your best interest. As for Petra, should you fail to open the portal, we can use the fucking Dhamphyr! If she's devoured by a fucking snake or beaten to death, what good is she?" he roared as he released his grip, tossing her aside.

"You fucking traitor! I know you want Petra for yourself, but what about the other two?"

"My plans for Petra are not your concern. As for the other two, they're fucking brujas and those vermin mean less to me than the scant from a rat's ass."

Evanora laughed in his face in a mocking tone. "You have forged your cock between more legs than anyone I know and now you have a fucking conscience—or should I say preference?"

He landed a hard front kick to her abdomen, which sent her spiraling out of the entrance. "They were all mine to take, you fucking kuchka!"

On the fourth evening, as dusk set in, the girls were unguarded. They were making a plan of escape when there was a frenzy of commotion. The tribesmen chanted and pounded the end of their spears on the ground, which came to an abrupt halt when a voice broke the air from behind the girls.

"Welcome to a new world, Petra. It seems you and I have unfinished business," Evanora said as she morphed into view.

The bitch has changed since I last saw her, Jadis thought.

A black-haired devil with roguish eyes was standing before them. "I have big plans for you. It seems you also brought friends, which will be even more entertaining."

The same seething hatred Jadis had felt for her rose to the surface. "I see the color of your hair now matches that of your rotten heart," Jadis growled.

"You will rot beneath the madness of your own mind when I'm finished," Evanora shot back.

"You are nothing more than a coward hiding within your stone walls," Jadis snarled.

Evanora kneeled down and grabbed a fistful of her hair, then wrenched her face into the bamboo poles and held her there. "When dawn comes, you will have your wish, only you will face me on your knees." She tossed Jadis's head back and released her grip as she stood.

"Based on the bruises around your throat, it looks like Arkyn has already put you on yours. I'm curious, though, do you whore for him as well as you did Abigor?" Jadis smirked.

Evanora glanced at Mag and Limi. "There will be no solace for the pain I'm going to inflict upon you."

"Your world is nothing but a hollow echo of your own misery," Jadis snapped back.

"Enjoy what little time you have left, Petra," Evanora said as she faded from sight.

"Mouthing off to her is a terrible idea!" Aria scolded.

"Jadis! All you're doing is baiting her," Amsi interjected.

Jadis looked away from Aria and Amsi and stared at the altar. *All we have to do is get the orb and this will all be over*, Jadis thought, as her determination to get away from Evanora and Arkyn took ahold of her.

They had all remained positioned around the orb, having picked up another blurry image of the girls, who were caged and bound.

Dante looked over at Bain. "Seems the last spell we cast has penetrated the barrier. The Graftons are no longer guarding them."

"Let's cast a simulacrum and see if we can weaken the sorcery surrounding the bars and bamboo."

"It's worth—" Dante began.

"Is that bruising around their faces?" Aiden blurted out, stopping Dante mid-sentence.

Silas, Dante, Bain, and Aiden leaned over the orb to take a closer look while the rest of their clan moved aside.

"Evanora!" Bain snarled.

None of them had the words to describe what they were feeling as they glanced amongst each other. However, the rage reflected in their eyes said what they couldn't.

"Don't lose that image," Aiden said.

"What's that bitch up to now?" Dante rumbled.

Santiago walked over and leaned over the table. *If she takes them now, they'll never get to the orb,* he said to himself.

A low rumble rose from Bain's chest and Silas took a slight step back and clenched Dante's shoulder. "How could we have let this happen?" was all Silas could muster.

Dante looked at him, but the torment he was feeling severed his ability to speak.

"That bitch is crazy! I will not face her. I don't have the powers to go toe to toe with her, even in her lair, should I get them back," Aria asserted.

"She has her weaknesses and this time I'll do more than break her fucking back," Jadis replied.

The stories did not do her justice. Amsi feared whatever choice they made would not end well. "I'm with you. I don't have any control right now and I'm not at all confident I can defend myself, much less fight her face to face."

"Our only mission is to get the orb and get our mates here," Jadis stated.

"After seeing her in the flesh, I don't even know how you fought her to begin with," Amsi stated.

"I didn't have a choice, and I think we can get the orb before we face her again."

"Thinking and doing are two different things," Aria argued.

"Well, let's hope it doesn't come to that. She is the worst kind of snake there is. She bites before she rattles," Jadis seethed. *I'm not confident myself and I fear I may lose the battle this time. Not to mention, dealing with Arkyn is going to be a bigger problem.*

Aria looked at Jadis and raised her eyebrows.

"What?" Jadis asked.

"Remind me not to hang around you anymore. Our mates are correct. You are nothing but a shitstorm of trouble," she joked.

"I never, for one minute, imagined I would be sucked into a portal, much less an entirely different realm when I met you" Amsi winked.

"Well, here we are." Jadis chuckled meekly. "We have no choice but to leave tonight."

"How are we going to get out?" Amsi asked.

"I can feel its energy waning. Not sure if it's our mates or Arkyn," Jadis replied.

The girls looked at the mountain and watched the ostentatious, glowing river of orange wind its way down the side.

"That doesn't look good," Aria stated.

"No, it doesn't," Amsi agreed.

"Let's hope Evanora doesn't throw us in," Jadis said. She then rested her head on her knees and listened to the whispers of ghosts and the ancestral spirits echo all around her. "Do the two of you hear the whispers?"

Aria nodded. "Yes, but I can't tell if they are from the living or the dead in this place."

Just as the darkness fell over the jungle, the storms rolled and once again the girls were at the mercy of the relentless rainfall, but just as they suspected, the lone guard left and returned to the circle as soon as the altar lit up. He turned his back to the girls and squatted down on his feet.

As much as the girls loathed the rain, they were hoping it would help them escape, not to mention cover their tracks.

Jadis swung her legs up and gripped the bamboo with her hands just above her head. "What are you doing?" Aria asked.

"While you were busy catching fish, I cut the toes of my boots open. I sharpened small stones and inserted them into the rubber and bound it with cimruta, something Silas taught me."

"Well, shit, why haven't you done that for the last four days?" Amsi snapped.

"Like cut the vines while we were being watched? That would have been a bright idea."

Aria rolled her eyes, but the adrenaline coursed through her body at the mere thought of escaping. "If they see you, Jadis, we are dead."

"Shhh—just watch them and let me know if they look over."

The vines frayed and split and after another minute, they snapped, freeing her wrists. "Here, cut your vines."

Aria and Amsi began feverishly rubbing the vines against the sharp tips while Jadis untied her ankles.

She rubbed her wrists and called Mag and Limi, while Amsi and Aria untied their feet. Mag and Limi had indeed broken a few of the bars at the base of their cage and were sliding through. Jadis quieted them down telepathically, so they didn't alert the tribesmen. As soon as they slipped through, they ran over to the girls and began chewing on the bamboo. It didn't take long before their powerful jaws snapped the posts.

CHAPTER 10

The girls pulled at the broken bamboo and crawled through the opening sideways, starting with their shoulders, followed by their hips, and then their legs. Once they were free, they plunged themselves into the darkness as quietly as they could.

They made it to the tree line just beyond the village and their hands collided with wet, rough surfaces as the thundering of the rain pounded on the canopy of vegetation.

Jadis leapt over a boulder, and it caught her shin, creating a large laceration. She no longer knew if it was the rain or her own tears flowing down her cheeks. She hated to have to drag along this sniveling, frightened child she felt she had become. I won't allow myself to succumb to any weakness, she thought as she quieted the tormented thoughts and the pain. Her body's ability to heal was also taking longer than it had before, as she had only been taking the minimal amount of blood from Aria and Amsi since they had eaten very little and needed for their bodies to heal more than anything.

They couldn't see over five feet in any direction because of the density of the foliage and heavy rains. A bolt of lightning tore through the jungle and landed a few yards ahead of them, revealing the surrounding space; they were only a few steps away from falling into a ravine.

The girls tried to stop. However, they slipped on the saturated, muddy ground. Amsi let out a deafening scream, having caught herself when she grabbed onto a tree root. She hung from the top of the ravine, which appeared to drop about fifty feet to the turbulent waters below.

Aria and Jadis dropped to their knees and grabbed her hand before standing back up. Jadis would have been strong enough to pull her up if she could get a foothold, but she kept slipping on the mud and rotten vegetation, as did Aria. They sat on their asses and dug their heels into the mud to pull Amsi up. Jadis was afraid if she or Aria slipped again, they would plunge to their deaths.

"Jadis!" Amsi screamed.

Every time she dug the toes of her boots into the saturated canyon wall to climb up, she also slipped, slamming stomach first into the wall. She felt like she was losing her grip and she looked down into the abysmal darkness, the weight of her body pulling her down the slippery vine, beckoning her to fall.

"Discendant!" Jadis yelled, trying to stop Mag and Limi from barking and potentially alerting anyone or anything that may be tracking them.

"We're not letting go. Grab us with both hands," Aria yelled.

Amsi reluctantly let go of the roots one hand at a time and grabbed Jadis's and Aria's wrists.

Jadis and Aria fell onto their backs, with Amsi on top of them after pulling her to safety.

"Holy shit, that was too fucking close!" Amsi was shaking like a leaf. She rolled off the girls and covered her face.

The three of them lay in the mud as the rain pounded on their faces, contemplating how many times they had almost died, and they were still nowhere near their destination. After gathering their composure, they decided they had no choice but to follow the edge of the ravine at a safe distance, as the foliage was less dense, making it easier not to mention safer walking in the dark.

Each time the lightning forked its way through the abysmal, churning sky, claps of thunder fracturing the air followed, making them duck and yelp multiple times.

Aria's and Amsi's mortal eyesight was useless. They relied on Jadis's keen night vision to lead the way and kept a firm grip on her shoulders, carefully following her steps.

Jadis tripped on Aria's foot and almost fell. "What the hell? Stop stepping on my heels!"

"I can't help it. I can't see if you hadn't noticed!" Aria snapped.

"That's like the third goddamn time." Jadis tried to sound serious, but her chuckling gave her away. "Maybe I have a solution."

"What's that? You going to give me your night sight?" Aria asked sarcastically.

Jadis grabbed her and tossed her over her shoulder and began walking.

Aria and Amsi couldn't help but laugh aloud. "Aiden—I mean, Jadis, put me down," Aria demanded.

"Don't step on my foot again and I'll think about it."

"Jadis, put me down!"

The rains had stopped during the night and by the time dawn came, they had escaped the village and were far away; at least they hoped they were far enough the tribesmen wouldn't follow. It appeared it would take them at least a couple of days to hike up the mountain to reach their ultimate destination. It was, however, on the other side of the river that appeared to be impassible because of the constant, torrential rains.

"I don't know about you, but there is no way I can cross that shit," Aria stated.

"I can pull you both across if we can find a calmer area." *Not that I'm going to say it, but I'm also questioning my ability to get across with everyone in tow as turbulent as the water is,* Jadis thought.

"Jadis, this isn't safe. What if there are more of those snake-like things in there?" Amsi trembled.

"*Probably pull us across*? I'm not sure I like that answer. And how will you keep a hold of me, Amsi, Mag, and Limi? The wolves can swim, but the current will pull them downstream," Aria stated.

Aria's correct. There is no way I can get them all across at the same time. "What if I take you one at a time?" Jadis suggested.

"That might work. Let's walk a little farther. If it stays like this, I assume we won't have a choice," Amsi agreed.

They walked for about thirty minutes and the landscape became sickly. The dirt barely covered the high peaking bones that should've remained hidden. It was as if they had emerged from the valley into a dense wasteland of death.

"What the hell is this?" Aria kicked at the ground that was concealing the bones with the toe of her boot.

"I don't know," Jadis stated.

"This is bad." Amsi bent down and pushed some of the mud off the bones.

"Whatever lies here was consumed by something enormous based on the long scrapes on the bones and how they've been snapped in half," Jadis stated.

The girls stopped momentarily to consider their new predicament as they bent down and studied the partial skeletons.

Aria placed the piece of bone she had picked up back in its place. "Something ate them. This place looks like a feeding ground."

Jadis tossed the bone she was holding back down and stood, gaping at the vastness of the boneyard.

Amsi was already walking away. "Let's get the hell out of here before we become its next meal."

They had become used to the deafening sounds of the jungle, but here, there was nothing. It was as if all life had disappeared from the area. They knew the vast boneyard they had hiked through was the very reason, and it felt like a double-edged sword. They hadn't come across anything trying to kill them. However, the reason for that scared them just as much; whatever it may be was not far away.

Once night set in again, they found a place to rest, having pushed their bodies beyond their limit. Aria and Amsi could no longer hike any farther and knew there was no way to climb down the ravine in the darkness.

"Jadis, I need to stop. I'm parched," Amsi stated.

"Maybe I should turn you," Jadis joked.

"Maybe you should get me a drink," Amsi said.

"Okay." Jadis grabbed a handful of banana leaves and leapt from the edge of the ravine down to the river.

"Jadis!" Aria screamed.

She and Amsi waited a few heart-pounding minutes and heard nothing.

"Jadis—" Amsi called again, only hearing her own echo in return.

Jadis landed behind them with a thump on the ground. They jumped and let out a high-pitched scream.

"What the hell are you doing?" Amsi demanded.

"Getting you water, here." She handed them a folded-up banana leaf full of fresh water from the river. She put two more down for Mag and Limi.

Aria punched Jadis in the shoulder. "I'm thankful, but never leave us like that again!"

"What the hell? That's the thanks I get?" Jadis joked as she hit her back.

They curled up with Mag and Limi, allowing the heat of their bodies to keep them warm throughout the night. They hadn't even realized they had fallen asleep until the rays of the sun peeking through the canopy woke them.

"Shit! We can never fall asleep like that again," Jadis scolded.

Amsi rubbed her face and sat up. "That was too goddamn dangerous."

"We need to get across the river. I can't keep trekking through this fucking place." Aria had removed her boots, set them in the sun, and began rubbing her wet, blistered feet.

Amsi had also removed her boots and placed them in the sun. "Jadis, my feet are so raw the skin is peeling off. I don't know if I can walk, much less run today."

Jadis's chuckling pissed Aria off. "I don't know what you find to be funny about it?"

"I just keep forgetting you're not a vampire. I can help unless you want to keep being salty?"

"*Salty*—really? I believe the only reason I'm in this shit hole to begin with is because of you," Aria chided.

"I was ready yesterday," Amsi stated.

"Here, take my wrist." Jadis bit her wrist and let the blood drip from the punctures.

"You want us to drink from you again? Won't that turn us seeing how this has become a regular routine?" Aria questioned.

"Really, Aria, I wouldn't turn you if you asked," she joked back. "Plus, it doesn't work like that anyway, just don't take too much."

They reluctantly took Jadis's wrist and drank a small portion of her blood. Their feet healed after a few minutes; as did the rest of their cuts, scrapes, and bruises.

"I'm not used to being around someone so helpless," Jadis joked.

"Helpless? I believe we've been feeding you for a weeks now," Amsi replied in jest. "On a serious note, do you need to feed?" Amsi asked.

"If you don't mind, yes."

Amsi smiled and held out her wrist and Jadis took just what she needed.

After walking for what felt like a mile, they found a relatively safe place to climb down the ravine.

"It looks like this is the best we're going to get. Besides, the farther we go, the farther we're going to have to backtrack to get to the mountain on the other side." Jadis looked at Aria and Amsi to see what they were thinking.

"Worst case, like you said, you can take us across one at a time," Aria stated.

They took a deep breath and looked down; the ravine plunged into a dense fog bank and they could no longer see the river below.

They crept down the damp, slick embankment, sliding on their butts through pea-soup mist. The only sounds accompanying them were those of dripping water and shifting rocks beneath the weight of their bodies.

As they made it to the river bed below, the fog was just as dense. They could hear the water, but Aria and Amsi couldn't see more than a foot.

"I don't know about this, Jadis, I can't see for shit," Aria admitted.

"I know. You're just going to have to trust me. We'll grasp each other's forearms and no matter what happens, neither of you let go."

"Trust me—if I drown, you drown." Aria winked.

"We will not drown," Jadis said. "I can see and it can't be more than waist-high."

"Waist high can be deadly," Aria argued.

"Relax," Jadis said as she rolled her eyes.

"Well, here goes nothing." Amsi took a deep breath and grabbed a hold of the nape of Mag's neck in order to keep him from being pulled downstream.

Aria grasped Limi's fur, and Jadis, Aria and Amsi grasped each other's forearms as they waded through the swift current.

They stumbled across the waist-high river and Amsi fell face first and struggled to get to her feet. Jadis pulled her up and allowed her to regain her footing. Even though Aria and Amsi had slipped more than once, Jadis, as well as Mag's and Limi's ability to swim across, kept them from being swept downstream.

"I'm not doing that shit again," Aria mumbled.

"I told you I wouldn't let go—remember, you drown, I drown." Jadis winked.

"Never again," Amsi stated as her hands trembled.

Aria smiled before looking toward the embankment they had to climb up. "I still can't see a damn thing."

"Don't worry about it," Jadis replied. "Now let's get off the river before we run into other problems."

Aria looked at Amsi and Jadis, and they all felt the same way and began running in a panic to the edge. They kept a tight hold on Jadis's T-shirt, letting her lead the way.

They scrambled up the muddy slope as quickly as they could, as their imaginations were getting the better of them. Their feet continuously slipped out from underneath of them most of the way up. Aria and Amsi had landed on their stomachs so many times Jadis couldn't help to be amused by their constant cussing and words of frustration.

"Keep laughing," Amsi snapped.

"Or what, you'll keep falling on your face?" Jadis replied. She climbed up the steep embankment by grasping exposed tree roots and vines dangling from the cliffs above. She had to stop every few steps to help pull Aria and Amsi up the slippery incline, and it ended up taking them twice as long as they thought it would.

The fog began lifting as their approach to the top ended. Aria let out a fear-filled yelp as her feet slipped out from underneath her and she slid back down the embankment on her stomach.

"Aria!" Amsi reached for her arm, but it was muddy and slippery, and she couldn't get a hold of her without losing her own grip.

Aria's and Amsi's yelling snapped Jadis out of her train of thought; she leapt down the cliff, letting the vine she was clinging to slip through her fist. She grabbed Aria's arm and pulled her up to her.

"You two should go in front of me and I'll climb up behind. It might be safer," Jadis offered.

"Whatever works. I'm over this shit." The adrenaline was coursing through her body and all Aria could think about was feeling like they were on an unrelenting, soulless journey.

The girls traded places, and Jadis positioned herself below them and leaned all the way back, holding the vines, and plunged the toes of her boots into the soft mud.

Once they made it to the top, Mag and Limi, who had already made their way up, were looking down at them. They plopped down a few feet from the edge, and sat peering down into the density of the fog, realizing just how far they had climbed.

Aria looked at Jadis, who seemed to have something else on her mind. "What's wrong, Jadis? Other than the obvious."

"The thought of facing Evanora, do not be fooled, she's an unforgiving bitch. If we don't get to that orb, we're screwed and most likely dead."

Amsi felt another wave of anxiety in the pit of her stomach. "Not what I wanted to hear—next time lie."

"Just remember our mates have a plan," Aria said, trying to calm her own racing thoughts.

"I know and if you guys are rested, we need to go. It's a long way." Jadis let out a heavy sigh as she stood up. *If it were just me,* she thought, *I'd be too scared to go any farther. I'm grateful to have them with me. I'll take the slowness of our trek any day over being here alone.* "Hey, I'm sorry I have pulled the two of you into this, but I'm grateful you are here with me," Jadis stated.

"You don't need to apologize. This isn't your doing," Amsi replied as she smiled and squeezed her hand.

"I'm glad we're here with you. I can't imagine you facing this by yourself—again," Aria added.

They had walked the rest of the day and the shadows were once again taking form with the setting sun; the vegetation and trees becoming darkened silhouettes. After another mile or so, an incredible architectural formation appeared before them. Hiding within the ancient trees and vines at the base of the mountain lay the ruins of an ancient city, with sandstone block and pillar structures.

"Holy shit, check it out," Aria announced.

"Let's hope whoever used to live here is far gone," Amsi whispered.

They explored the hidden city, following the overgrown paths, and were fortunate to find a freshwater spring within the ruins and an abundance of fruits and nuts. Thankfully, it seemed to have been abandoned for years based on the crumbling, weathered structures and overgrown foliage. Its inhabitants had either left or rested in the boneyard they had stumbled across.

Jadis placed her palm on one of the worn stone pillars and closed her eyes. She absorbed its energy and listened to the whispers of a past long gone. Life and death remained cloistered in the crumbling rock and the pictures flickered through her mind like a runway slide show.

"What are you doing?" Amsi asked.

"Just looking into the past. This was once a place of beauty and tranquility. I wish you could both see what I see," she replied.

"Well, we can't, so tell us like you did in the graveyard in Fréyonne," Aria suggested.

"Just try. You're brujas. Place your palms on the stones and listen."

Jadis placed her hands over Aria's and Amsi's and helped them to pick up the energetic pictures.

"Wow," Amsi whispered. "I can faintly see broken images."

Aria smiled, having captured the past as well.

"Whoever lived here at one time, lived in peace and prosperity. This place provided all they would ever need, or so they thought," Jadis explained.

"What happened to them?" Amsi asked, only having a vague image.

"Selfishness and greed. They took more than the area could provide, causing a war amongst tribes." Jadis slid her hand off the stone with a heavy sigh.

"It figures," Aria answered.

They walked over to the freshwater pond and Aria picked a handful of berries from a nearby bush. She tossed them into her mouth one at a time and looked at Jadis and giggled.

"Why are you looking at me and laughing?" Jadis asked.

Aria rubbed a berry between her fingers. "When was the last time you ate a berry?"

"A long time ago."

"Well, here, try one." Aria tossed her a berry and chuckled at the speed with which Jadis caught it.

She popped the berry into her mouth and savored the taste. "Damn!" It's amazing. "Give me another one. I almost forgot what it tastes like."

Amsi tossed Jadis a few more berries in different directions, watching her snatch them out of mid-air, cracking her and Aria up.

"If you're doing that on purpose, you can stop," Jadis said.

"No, this is more entertaining." Aria tossed three more into the air in different directions and Jadis caught them as well, to their continued amusement.

Jadis reached into the cool water and splashed it in Aria's and Amsi's faces.

Aria squealed and wiped the water from her eyes. "So that's how it's going to be, huh?" She laughed before trying to splash Jadis in the face. However, Jadis efficiently dodged the spray of water.

After screwing around and cleaning up, they stayed for the night in a crumbling stone hut before taking on the mountainous cliffs. They cleared out most of the debris and lit a small fire. They lay down and listened to the hauntingly quiet jungle. The only sounds were those of the rumbling mountain and the tremors that followed.

Jadis took the first watch and lay on her back, peering through the disintegrating roof; the infinite dome looked as if it had been splattered with sapphire dust.

Jadis hadn't realized she had dozed off, only to be woken by what sounded like roars off in the distance. The three of them sat straight up and looked at each other in silence, waiting to see if what they had heard was a living creature or just rumbles from the angry mountain.

"What the hell was that?" Aria whispered.

"Hopefully it's just the mountain," Jadis stated.

"Ohhh—I don't like this at all," Amsi added.

They clung to each other as the roars and trumpeting grew in intensity; the sounds came from something flying far above the canopy. The hackles on Mag's and Limi's backs stood at attention, and they snarled at whatever it was flying around overhead.

"Whatever those things are, they are getting closer," Jadis whispered.

They sat strangled with fear and apprehension; they could feel the gentle breeze blow over them through the opening in the once thatched roof each time the creatures swooped down; bringing with them the subtle scent of sulfur. The trees overhead swayed, and the leaves rattled as if they were being blown by the winds of an encroaching storm.

Jadis placed her forehead on her knees, hoping whatever was making the horrific noises would soon move on; unfortunately, they flew overhead all night before disappearing before dawn.

Aria was lying on her back, rubbing her face. "I'm so tired."

Amsi sat up and wiped the sleep from her eyes. "My entire body aches."

"I would give anything to be in bed with Silas and Dante right now." Jadis rolled over onto her stomach and rested her face on her arms, exhausted and emotionally worn out.

"A warm, soft bed and Aiden sounds amazing. I feel like we've been in hell for months now." Aria sighed.

Jadis sat up and began rubbing her shoulders. *My whole body is sore and achy and the minimal amount of blood I've been taking from them is leaving my system almost as quickly as I take it in,* she thought.

"I'm going to grab some breakfast, if you can call it that, before we leave." Aria stood up and wiped the dirt from her butt and legs.

"I'm hungry too and berries are better than nothing," Amsi agreed.

"Would it be a problem for me to have a drink from one of you?"

Aria held her wrist out with an enduring smile. "You already know the answer—take whatever you need."

"If you need more, take mine as well. Without you, we would have never made it this far," Amsi offered.

"Without me, the two of you wouldn't even be in this godforsaken situation."

"It's a moot point, Jadis," Aria stated.

Amsi smiled and held out her wrist as well.

After another tumultuous hike, they had made it to the base of the mountain and its steep, rugged canyon walls rose before them like an impenetrable iron barrier.

"We can't climb here." Jadis studied the steep crevices and knew Aria and Amsi, as well as Mag and Limi, would never make it.

"I'm so sick of fucking rock climbing. Remind me to never go to Sagvon with you," Aria joked.

"If we ever make it to Sagvon, I promise all we'll do is hang in the sulfuric springs. After this, I think I'm done rock climbing myself." Jadis chuckled.

"I don't know if swimming with you again is in the cards either," Amsi teased.

"I might never leave the oasis after this," Jadis stated.

The girls searched for about an hour before finding a spot Jadis hoped they would all be able to climb. They began the slow ascent and once again humped their asses up what felt like a mile-long serpentine. Precarious boulders jutted their way outward, forcing them to either climb up and over or slide under on their stomachs, and Mag and Limi could barely claw their way through, lying on their sides under some passages.

"This is a screwed-up land more suited to hobbits and goblins than climbers," Jadis rumbled.

"You forgot the evil queen," Aria said, breathless.

"You okay?" Jadis asked.

"Yeah, I just need a minute," Aria replied.

They stopped to take a break before resuming their climb and the closer they got to the top, the more the gnarled undergrowth forced them to plant each boot on the loose rocks, some of which tumbled down the steep slope before being swallowed by the canopy below; the sounds echoed up from the violent impact of stone hitting stone.

The volcano let out another tremor, and the girls had to stop and hang on as the ground shook and trembled beneath them. Loose gravel and rock would vibrate off the cliffs and rained down the slope from above; all they could do was duck their heads in order to keep the debris out of their eyes.

Once they made it to the top, they rested on a large ridge sitting just below what they assumed was Evanora's lair.

"The entrance should be around the bend." Jadis looked at Aria and Amsi, and they had the same dreadful look on their faces as she did.

"I'm not sure about this anymore," Amsi admitted.

"Neither am I and the more I think about it, the more I realize every time I faced Evanora, Abigor was there to intervene."

"Didn't you break the bitch's back with no one intervening?" Aria said.

"Yeah—I guess I did."

"You did that on your on." Amsi smiled.

"It was the only altercation we got into without Abigor being right there," Jadis replied.

"Just one of many reasons she hates you," Amsi mumbled.

"Ohhh—you have no idea," Jadis replied.

"Jadis, I need you to remember that. Don't lose your confidence now. We all know if we come face to face with her, you're the only one who stands a chance," Aria acknowledged.

Jadis let out a heavy sigh, wishing more than anything they weren't in this situation to begin with. "Well, we should go. The sooner we get the orb, the sooner we see our mates."

They stood on the ramshackle trail threading its way along the steep cliffs, preparing themselves for the inevitable.

"Jadis," Aria whispered.

"What?"

"Think you could conjure me a couple of crack knives?"

Jadis laughed until a wave of debris rained down on them. A primitive warning sounded in the back of her mind; she looked up but didn't see anything.

"Do you hear that?" Amsi whispered.

"Yes. Evanora?" Aria questioned.

They, too, were looking in the same direction, expecting to see her standing above them.

"Shit, look at that thing—it's massive and the girls have no clue they are being stalked by a it," Bain warned.

"Dante, you need to get to Jadis again. They are going in the wrong direction," Silas demanded.

"I realize that!" Dante stated firmly. *"Jadis—Jadis, baby, can you hear me?"*

They stood in anticipation as they looked into the orb and watched the girls as they stood on the ledge. After a couple of heart-pounding moments, Jadis cocked her head to the side.

"Dante?" she questioned.

Aria watched as Jadis appeared to be listening again. "Dante?" Aria mouthed.

Jadis nodded as she reached out again. *"Dante?"*

"Yes, baby, it's me. I have little time. Go the other way!"

"The other way? What are we looking for?" she questioned.

"There's a small cave. Get to it and hide. There will be an entrance into Evanora's lair from there and it's closer to the orb."

"Okay, but what else are you not saying?"

"The thing above you is a dragon. You are headed right for it," Dante stated.

"Dragons? You have to be fucking kidding me!"

"Baby, you need to go and now—as in run!"

Jadis shoved Aria and Amsi and yelled for them to run.

"What the hell now?" Amsi replied along with a scream.

"A dragon!" Jadis shouted.

"A fucking *dragon*?" Aria snapped back.

The girls rounded the ledge and Aria slipped on the uneven, loose gravel and landed on her hip; Jadis grabbed her arm and wrenched her back to her feet.

As they continued running, they could hear what sounded like heavy footsteps thumping on the ground above them. The dragon was grunting and snorting, and they could smell the smoke and see long flames flickering outward beyond the ledge from above with every heavy, throaty growl.

Rocks and gravel rained down from above as the dragon continued stalking them. They ducked and dodged the debris and just as they rounded another corner, there was a small cave about five feet above the trail.

Jadis leapt into the air and landed on the ledge with Mag and Limi. Aria and Amsi had jumped all the way up out of sheer panic, knocking Jadis over. They gathered themselves together and ran into the small cave and hid as far back as they could get.

Closer and closer the dragon crept toward them and their adrenaline pumped faster and faster with each heavy thud of its feet.

Jadis clenched her fists and could feel the connection to her powers for the first time, and she felt the cimruta seep from her palms. She threw it onto the ground at the entrance, waved her hand, and lit it on fire, hoping the flames would keep the beast out.

"Jadis—your powers, do you have them back?" Aria questioned.

"It seems so and I'm afraid the only reason is that we are within Evanora's lair."

"She knows we are here," Aria rumbled.

"Of course she does and I don't even want to know what she has planned."

"If you have your powers, that means we have ours as well. We will face her together," Amsi asserted.

They waited in the back, staring at the fire burning near the entrance. Time seemed to slow as the gravity of the situation grew; they didn't know how long they sat in what felt like a suspended animation fixated on the entrance.

Suspiciously the trickles of debris, along with the grunting, snorting, and footsteps quieted.

Jadis turned to Aria and Amsi, and they looked like they had been holding their breaths as beads of moisture dripped down their foreheads. None of them were ready to face the horror that would be waiting as soon as they stepped out of the small entrance.

Aria wiped her face with her raggedy T-shirt. "What now?"

"Hell if I know, but I'm not about to step out there," Amsi replied.

"Night will be here soon, and based on last night, I think it's safe to assume they will be out in full force," Jadis reasoned.

They sat staring out of the entrance as the night crept in and Jadis couldn't help but think how beautiful the moon looked, glowing against the slate gray sky.

"A full blood moon is growing. It's a bad omen," Amsi whispered.

"The moon is always here," Jadis offered.

"Not like this—I know you feel it too." Amsi pulled her knees tighter against her chest as they watched the swirling calypso, red colors overtaking the bright, silvery moon; it was ominously mesmerizing.

It looks like the moon did the night Silas and I mated. Jadis let out a heavy sigh, wanting nothing more than to be in his arms.

"If this is the cave Dante was talking about, there has to be another entrance to the main cavern." Jadis stood up to see if there was another opening. "I won't sit here like this all night."

Aria and Amsi stood and joined her, and they began feeling their way around.

Jadis felt the subtlest wisp of air. "Here."

Aria and Amsi walked over and held up their hands, and Amsi gave them a look of acknowledgment.

Jadis placed her palms against the stone and shoved. An enormous boulder rolled out of the way, and a nauseating breeze of sulfuric acid blew past their faces, choking the air from their lungs.

"My god, that reeks," Aria stated as she held her hand over her mouth and peered into the hole. "I'm afraid to go in. What if she's waiting for us?"

"We either face the dragons or we face Evanora. Now that we have a grasp on our powers, we will kill the bitch. If we face the dragons out there without our powers, we might find ourselves sleeping with the rest of the dead in that boneyard," Jadis reasoned.

Aria and Amsi were less than enthused with either option. However, they reluctantly climbed through the hole and stood on the floor of the vast cavern. The only light came from the bubbling, molten river about a hundred feet below from where they stood.

Aria and Amsi could barely see beyond the red glow; they held Jadis's arm and she could feel Amsi trembling.

"Let go for a minute. I'll give you some light." Jadis clenched her fist and spun in a circle. She swung the cimruta, and it splattered against the walls. She then flicked her wrist and lit the substance on fire.

Beneath the flickering flames, the could see a large platform on the other side of the crevice with what appeared to be a large nest holding six giant eggs.

"Please tell me those are gigantic bird eggs!" Aria whispered.

"They are not birds," Jadis replied.

They backed away and walked to a small opening at the other end and stopped mid-stride when they heard a large puff, followed by a gigantic roar that reverberated off the rocks, vibrating the ground beneath their feet. They turned toward the noise, only to see a dragon drop from the ceiling.

The dragon crept closer and lowered her head over the nest. As she snorted and growled, the sounds rose and fell in short puffs and miniature clouds of smoke disappeared into the dimly lit cavern with each breath she exhaled.

The girls stood wide-eyed and held their breaths, and Jadis had to quiet Mag and Limi, fearing they would only anger the beast before them.

Its claws alone were large enough to lacerate even the fiercest of enemies and her eyes were endless pools of swirling crimson streaked with intelligence. She stood over her nest and wrapped her gigantic tail around the outer edge.

All Jadis thought was one toss of her tail could break through the cavern wall. *If she swings it at us, that will be the end.*

The dragon stretched her wings out and placed the pointed tips on the floor of the cavern; they were obsidian black and leathery like that of a bat and her scales were multicolored shields that slid over one another in triangular patterns.

The dragon swung her head around and stared at the opening. Just as the girls took another step toward the opening, a shadowy form appeared. Out of nowhere, Evanora stepped into the cavern and slowly clapped her hands together.

"What took you so long, Petra? I'd like you to meet my dragon and should you say one false word, her next meal will be your friends," she threatened.

The dragon stared at Evanora and seemed to wait for a command. *Evanora is controlling her*, Jadis thought.

The girls glanced at each other, not knowing what to do; they were no match for what stood between them and Evanora. The next thing they knew, Evanora waved her hand, and Mag and Limi whined incessantly as a thick raven black collar appeared around each of their necks.

Jadis and Aria grabbed the collars, but Mag and Limi swung their heads in their direction and snarled. Aria jumped back, confused as hell. As Jadis tried to rip them off, Evanora yelled, "Idvam!"

Mag and Limi wrenched themselves from Jadis's grip and took off toward Evanora. As Jadis ran after them, Evanora shouted, "Zadrŭzhte gi!"

The dragon blew a large breath of fire between Jadis, Mag, and Limi. Jadis stopped so fast she slipped on the cavern floor and fell on her ass. She held her hands up to her face to shield herself from the heat of the dragon's breath. She screamed for Mag and Limi to come to her, but they failed to respond.

Jadis jumped to her feet, and Evanora had Mag and Limi standing at her side. "You took all that I had. Do not think I have forgotten. I will now take what is most precious to you," Evanora seethed.

"I will fucking kill you!" Jadis screamed, all the while calling Mag and Limi.

Evanora let out a hate-filled laugh as she turned to the dragon and yelled, "Ubiĭ veshtitsata, zapazi!"

Jadis understood what she said, so she launched her body in between Amsi, Aria, and the dragon. "Get out!"

The girls lunged for the hole they had come through, but the dragon knocked Jadis and Amsi away with one swipe of its tail, sending them flying across the cavern.

The dragon moved with brutal strength and agility. She clamped her enormous jaws around Aria's leg and pulled her back into the cavern. Aria's attempt to escape was futile as she screamed and clawed at the ground. The dragon loomed over her body and rested a gigantic foot on the cavern's wall, partially covering their only exit.

Jadis launched herself between Aria and the dragon just as the flames escaped her mouth. She conjured up a shield spell Dante had taught her in order to save Aria from a fiery death. The flames were reflected into the dragon's face; she lifted her head and shook it back and forth. Jadis and Amsi grabbed Aria and seized the opportunity to run toward the entrance Evanora had disappeared through.

The dragon let out a deafening roar and took one swipe toward Aria and its tapered claw cut across her midsection. She screamed as she fell to the ground; with trembling hands, she tried to stop the blood flowing from the gaping wound.

"Aria!" Amsi and Jadis screamed.

The dragon stood face to face with the girls and they knew it was about to annihilate them. Jadis leapt into the air and landed on the back of its neck. It was enough of a distraction it diverted its attention to Jadis.

It tried to knock Jadis off by thrashing its head back and forth. She ducked down, evading a deadly blow from its front foot, and noticed a collar similar to the ones that appeared around Mag's and Limi's necks. She grabbed a hold and let the cimruta seep from her hands. The collar melted beneath her grip and she ripped it off.

"Sile! Sile!" Jadis demanded.

After a few minutes, the dragon appeared to be settling down. She leapt off and landed next to where Aria lay in a pool of blood, with Amsi doing her best to stop the bleeding.

"Sile! Sile!" Jadis yelled again, demanding it be still. It appeared to be working, so she focused her attention on Aria.

"I can feel myself growing colder—the dirt is black. I can see it," Aria whispered as she choked on the blood pooling in her mouth and trickling down the side of her cheek. "The Crows are circling," she mumbled.

"We will not let you die, hang on," Amsi cried.

"Aria, listen to me. You need to take my blood. You can't die, not like this!" Jadis could tell by her bubbled breath she didn't have time to heal by taking a few drops. "I'm going to *turn* you. Do what I say, agree," Jadis demanded.

Aria nodded in agreement, and Jadis didn't think twice. She bit down on Aria's wrist and took her blood. After taking what she thought would be enough, she slit her wrist and demanded Aria take her blood. "Agree, Aria, let me turn you."

Aria whispered, "I—a—agree."

Jadis let the blood flow from her vein into her mouth while Amsi held her head up enough for her to swallow.

Twice, Jadis had to hold her mouth shut so she could swallow. In between her coughing and her labored breathing, she drank.

Amsi and Jadis held her in their laps for what seemed like hours before Jadis could see the gaping wound heal. Aria took a few deep breaths and opened her eyes.

"You're going to be okay," Jadis whispered.

Aria responded with a gentle smile before falling back asleep.

Amsi looked at Jadis and let out a sob-filled breath of relief.

The dragon had remained in her nest the entire time. Not knowing what else to focus her attention on, Jadis called her Nuri after she nearly lit them on fire.

For hours, the dragon and Jadis stared at each other, and it was as if Nuri was trying to communicate with her.

Jadis closed her eyes, held out her hand, and Nuri stretched her long neck toward her and inhaled. She let out a few gentle puffs of smoky breath before tilting her head as if studying Jadis. She placed her hand on her face and spoke telepathically, using visions, not words.

Amsi stared at Jadis in shock. *It seems as if they're speaking to each other?*

"You will no longer be chained or enslaved. Help me and I will see to your freedom. You will once again roam your world as you choose," Jadis relayed.

Nuri appeared to understand and nodded before lying back down. She peered deep into Jadis's eyes and she hers.

They are beautiful; the entire world seems to be reflected in the serene, sapphire color. She's ancient, her intelligence beyond words, Jadis thought.

Nuri was adorned with pentagonal teardrop-shaped emerald scales running down her body like a jeweled coat of armor.

With a slight touch, Jadis could feel and see all that Nuri had carried since Evanora had captured and bound her, and she pitied her. Jadis listened to her loud, gentle growls. *It sounds like she's purring,* she thought before she felt the tears drip from the corners of her eyes, thinking about Evanora having taken Mag and Limi. The tears became a steady flow as she stared at Aria. "No matter what it takes, I will kill that bitch!"

"Jadis, she's going to be okay. Your blood has healed her," Amsi offered. "By the way, are you speaking with Nuri?"

Jadis dragged her hands down her face, wiping away the tears as she replied. "Yes, sort of—it's more like shredded images."

"That's crazy."

"She didn't mean to hurt Aria. Evanora was controlling her."

"Can I touch her?" Amsi asked.

"Yes." Jadis smiled.

CHAPTER 11

Evanora brought the Dire Wolves to her chamber and settled in. "Well, aren't you two beautiful?" She kneeled down and ran her hands through their thick gray fur.

As they whined and scratched at the collars, Evanora calmed them down. "Shhh—quiet," she whispered. "Soon enough you will forget all about Petra."

"Bring them food and water," she demanded.

Dolog nodded and brought the enormous creatures food and water before leaving Evanora for the night.

Evanora and Mun peered into her orb and watched as the dragon dragged Petra's friend by her foot and sent Petra and the other gril flying across the cavern.

She laughed as she refilled her cup with the fermented juice and continued watching. The dragon let out a breath of fire, which Petra shielded. "Well, I'll be dammed! The little bitch has picked up a few tricks of her own," she stated.

"She is powerful," Mun answered.

They watched the entire scene. "Oh—that had to have hurt!" Evanora said, regarding the dragon slitting Aria open.

"She'll be dead soon," Mun replied.

"What do we have here?" a voice asked.

Evanora and Mun spun in his direction. "What the hell do you want?" Evanora snarled.

"I don't care what you do with the girls, but Petra is mine," Arkyn said.

"We have a deal. If I get us out of here, you're supposed to leave Petra to me!"

"I've changed my mind and I've decided to take her with me, and then you can fuck off."

"She's not getting out of here alive!"

Arkyn stepped toward Evanora, and Mag and Limi lunged. He evaded the attack and pulled his sword. Evanora leapt between them. "Sile! Sile!" she yelled before addressing Arkyn. "They are mine!"

"You've got to be fucking kidding me." Arkyn laughed aloud. "You want Petra's mutts? I think Avenolon has put you out of your goddamn mind!"

"Leave me!"

"Ti si luda kuchka," he rumbled. "If you get in my way, you're finished," he added before leaving.

"Get out!" Evanora yelled.

Mun nodded and closed the door behind her.

Evanora lay on her bed and called to the wolves; Magi and Limi hopped up and curled together at the end of the bed. "Good—good, settle in." *I need Arkyn out of my fucking way. There has to be something I can do.*

"Jadis?" The sound of Aria's voice startled the girls.

"Aria! Tell me you're okay," Jadis said.

"How do you feel?" Amsi asked.

"I feel strange. Did you really *turn* me?"

"I did and I'm sorry. I had no other choice. I panicked," Jadis admitted.

"It's okay. I know I was dying. Your blood alone wouldn't have saved me."

Aria reached her hand down to feel for the gaping wound, only for it to have healed. As soon as she looked over and saw the sleeping dragon, she gasped and jumped to her feet. Jadis followed and snatched her out of the air.

"How the ever-living hell did you just move like that after being slit open?" Amsi questioned.

"She's Nosferatu now," Jadis answered nonchalantly.

Nuri opened her sleepy eyes and peered in the girl's direction, as if uninterested.

Aria let out a yelp and jumped back the moment the dragon looked at them.

"Aria, it's okay. She won't hurt us. She was wearing a collar Evanora used to control her. I ripped off."

"What the hell? Are you controlling that thing?"

"Sort of. We made a deal." Jadis chuckled.

"You never cease to amaze me," Aria replied. "I can't believe how strong I feel."

"There will be a lot you'll discover, but right now we need to get to that orb," Jadis stated matter-of-factly.

"Yes, we do," Aria agreed as they looked around, trying to figure out their next move.

"So, before we head out, is there anything I should know now that I have *turned*? Other than how fucking amazing I feel—did I mention that already?" Aria laughed.

"Shit, there is so much I don't know where to begin," Jadis admitted.

"How about the basics? That might be a nice place to start," Amsi replied.

"The major difference will be your strength and speed. You will move with the speed of the winds and have the power of the tides. The slightest of threats will force you to *turn*. Other than that, I'll leave the teaching to Aiden." Jadis then began chuckling.

"What's so funny?" Aria questioned.

"Thinking about the looks on our mates' faces when they find out I *turned* you."

Aria let out a belly laugh. "Oh, shit!"

"We should have a party," Jadis joked.

"What do you mean, a party?" Amsi asked.

"We'll explain later, but let's just say when my reveal took place, it didn't go smoothly," Jadis replied.

"You're crazy. You know that, right?" Aria stated before turning toward the dragon. "Can I?" Aria looked at Nuri.

"Nuri," Jadis called as she held out her hand.

Nuri lifted her enormous head and swiveled her neck in their direction and smelled Jadis's hand and then moved to Aria's. She let out a low growl and a large puff of smoke, scaring Aria. She yanked her hand back before reaching back out. "Holy hell."

Nuri sniffed at her hand, lowered her head, and Aria placed her hand on her face with a gentle caress. "I can read her thoughts—well, whatever they are."

"You will feel a lot now. Close your eyes and look with your mind," Jadis instructed.

"Well, I'll be dammed. I can see, feel everything."

"Yes, I imagine so—you'll get used to it."

"Aria, that is crazy," Amsi replied.

Aria stood, both amazed and bewildered by Jadis's powers. "I still can't believe you befriended her—now that she's not trying to kill us, she's stunning."

"Yes, she is, and she only wants what we do."

"What's that?" Aria asked.

"To live in peace," Jadis replied.

Aria cocked her head and stared at Nuri. "As soon as we kill Evanora, we'll all have that."

"Don't forget about Arkyn. He's here. I can feel him. But more importantly, how do we find the orb? It could be anywhere. It's not like the bitch is going to leave it lying around," Amsi stated.

Jadis looked at Nuri and had a thought, so she walked over to her and placed her hands on her face and read her visions.

Aria and Amsi stared at Jadis. "What are you doing?" Amsi asked.

"Shhh—I'm taking her visions. She knows where the orb is—in a roundabout way."

After a few moments, her knowledge flooded Jadis's mind. *The orb is deep within the volcanic cavern.* She could see what appeared to be the outline of a map of sorts.

"There's a small opening behind her nest," Jadis stated.

"Are we doing this? Maybe we should wait." Amsi knew it wasn't logical to sit and do nothing, but she was frightened.

"Wait for what? Dante told us what we needed to do," Jadis reasoned.

They walked around the outer edge of Nuri's nest as she followed the girls by swiveling her neck.

The cave branched out into two tunnels. One looked nearly impossible to get through, so the girls chose the larger alternative. They took their time since they had to either crawl on their hands and knees or slide sideways through the tight crevices. They could walk where the cave widened, but the two extremes made searching for the orb even more difficult.

The girls heard what sounded like a waterfall and the ground became wet, slick, and the water was ankle-deep. They climbed down the sides of the cavern only to find a dead end after traversing for almost an hour; they had no choice but to go back the way they came.

They got turned around more than once, retracing their steps, and on the third attempt, the sound of rushing water grew louder. The stone floor was thick with mud and the ankle-deep water that was there on the way down a few hours earlier was up to their knees.

"I think we're lost. How is that possible?" Aria snarked.

"Evanora," Jadis replied. She could feel the shifting energy and knew she was controlling the cave. "We have been going in circles for hours."

"Of course we have," Amsi answered.

Jadis closed her eyes and saw a pulsing, red energy off in the distance. The same map she had seen in Nuri's mind was present. However, the only problem; the way they had come had since morphed.

Jadis placed both her palms on the rock and looked at Aria and Amsi. "Can you feel that?"

"What? I can't feel anything other than being fucking lost," Aria snarled.

"I don't feel anything either," Amsi admitted.

"Aria, use your abilities, feel the rock—listen to the cave," Jadis instructed.

Aria placed her palms on the rock and stood next to Jadis. "Holy shit, I feel it."

"Amsi, do the same thing. It's like controlling the winds when you need to grasp that power," Jadis explained.

Amsi placed her palms on the stone wall and looked at Jadis and Aria in awe. "I got it!"

They realized they were stuck in an ever-evolving puzzle. The cave was metamorphosing on its own. There was now a solid stone wall blocking the way they had initially entered.

"It's a labyrinth," Amsi snapped.

Jadis looked at them and felt the walls shifting around. "Can I cry now?"

Aria snapped her head in her direction. "Jadis, not now—I can't handle it. When we get back to the oasis, you can cry all you want. I'll even give you a box of tissues."

"Well, that was unexpected. The bitch *turned* her friend," Evanora snapped.

"It should not be a problem. They are still no match for you, enchantress," Mun surmised.

Evanora sat back and ran her hand down Mag's and Limi's heads. "At least they're trapped. I wasn't expecting the sudden *turn* of events, but it's of no consequence." She chuckled and glanced at Mun who didn't get it. She casually waved her hand. "You're all so fucking boring."

Evanora enjoyed watching Petra and her friends struggle to find their way out of the labyrinth she created. "A few more twists and turns and they'll soon find themselves in the heart of the volcano."

"We need the sacrifice. Without it, the gods of the crag will destroy us all," Mun stated.

"You will have Petra's friends—toss one or both of them in for all I fucking care. Now go and get ready to appease your gods and bring me Petra!"

"There are a hundred ways for us to fail and only one way to get out." Jadis looked at Aria and Amsi before focusing on the cave; she heard what sounded like hushed whispers.

Aria looked at Jadis and cocked her head. "What? I don't get it."

"What we see isn't real. Look and listen for the slightest flicker in the rock or a gentle whisper." Jadis walked straight ahead and through what seemed to be a solid stone wall; Aria and Amsi reluctantly followed.

"Well, shit," Aria stated.

"What the hell?" Amsi whispered.

"I told you she is a master of deceit. Nothing she does is what it seems."

Amsi looked at Jadis, feeling uneasy about continuing on. "One step at a time, Jadis, one step! I've fallen off a ledge too many times and none of us can see what's on the other side."

"I promise—one step at a time, together," Jadis agreed.

The girls stopped to let Amsi rest. She leaned against the wall, feeling hopeless. "We've been doing this for hours now."

Aria wiped the sweat from her brow. "It's hot as hell in here."

Jadis also wiped her brow. "I have a bad feeling we have been descending into the depths of the crater."

Amsi pinched the bridge of her nose and closed her bloodshot eyes. "It's getting too hot to go much farther, not to mention the sulfur is making me sick."

"We'll be okay, Amsi. Take a little of my blood. It will give you some relief." Jadis bit her wrist and held it to her.

After what felt like another hour or so, they took one more carefully planned step through another discolored stone wall and found themselves looking down into a furious, boiling lake of molten lava; they had indeed hiked into the fiery heart of the active volcano.

There were multiple entrances into the cavern and many ledges jetting out above the boiling lake. The enormous, vertical walls were discolored with a pungent yellow and brown sulphur and rose up, forming a deep chimney slot.

"If you tell me we have to climb again to get out, I choose any other alternative, regardless of what it may be," Aria whispered.

Jadis couldn't help but chuckle. "You seem to forget you are Nosferatu now. You won't need my help."

"I will—no way in hell I can climb that," Amsi stated.

Aria looked up at the light peering from the top of the chimney slot. "Let's get the hell out of here."

Jadis grabbed Aria's arm and held her steady. "Wait, listen, do you hear that?"

Aria looked around and closed her eyes. "Yes, the rattling? Is that what you mean?"

"Yes, cloak yourself and now," Jadis demanded.

"What? How?" Aria questioned.

Jadis kept their arms in a tight grip, and they faded into the background. "Evanora. It's a trap—she's here."

They walked to the edge of the ledge and looked as far over as they could. And what appeared to be another altar was sitting on top of a large mantle stretchig out above the churning liquid.

"Looks like a sacrificial altar," Amsi whispered.

Shells and bones hung from braided vine and rattled each time the boil let out a large burp of gaseous air. Drawings made from blackened ash covered the walls, depicting scenes of life and death, gods and dragons.

"I have a feeling we're the sacrifice. Let's get the hell out of here," Jadis demanded.

Just as they took a step, a voice from behind penetrated their bodies like an icy wind. They spun around only to be face to face with Evanora.

"Going somewhere, Petra?"

"I'm *going* to kill you, if that's what you're asking," Jadis snarled.

"We shall see. I noticed you *turned* your friend. How charming!" Evanora laughed.

Aria *turned* at the threat and let out a deep-chested growl. "You bitch!"

Jadis grabbed her forearm and held her steady without speaking.

An exquisitely decorated aboriginal woman, with braided hair of black and red that appeared to be more human than the rest of the tribe, walked next to Evanora from behind and gazed at them. Jadis noticed the black jeweled amulet she wore around her neck. The script was odd, and she didn't recognize it or its symbols.

Even though the girls were startled by loud drumming and a burst of ritualistic cries that broke out from below, they didn't take their eyes off either Evanora or the strange woman.

"I would like the two of you to meet Manewa. She has arranged for your friends' welcoming, or should I call them the sacrifice."

Dolog's tribe of aboriginal beings who were holding spears, bows, and arrows surrounded Manewa and Evanora and waved their weapons in the air threateningly. They were looking around to see who Evanora was speaking to.

It was obvious to Jadis, Aria, and Amsi they couldn't see them, but Evanora and Manewa certainly could.

Jadis squeezed her fists together and raged into Evanora's face as she unleashed the cimruta with a harsh wave of both arms.

Evanora raised her hands in response and shielded herself and Manewa.

Aria lunged and felt a crack radiate across her cheek, which sent her tumbling backward. She caught herself and readied herself to attack again.

The girls appeared as if out of nowhere and the tribesmen let out warning calls and ran back into the multiple openings, hiding from the creatures fighting before them.

"Seems you're being abandoned," Jadis growled.

Evanora and Jadis began throwing and heaving energy back and forth. They matched and evaded each other blow for blow.

"Is there not a creature amongst you who will not cower to this bitch? This is not your destiny! There is no order—she has enslaved you all!" Aria raged.

"There is destiny and order and it's mine. That is all that matters!" Evanora bellowed in return.

Evanora raised her arms and a black molten net fell over Aria, Amsi, and Jadis, entrapping them on the hot stone ledge.

The cimruta in Jadis's palms melted the net as soon as she grasped the twisted vine. She ripped it open, rose to her feet, and watched as Evanora took two steps back. Manewa stood with her back against the stone, looking nothing less than terrified, and the tribesmen behind them had also backed into another entrance, trying to get out of the line of fire.

"Take your sacrifice!" Evanora roared.

Manewa nodded and ordered the tribal warriors to grab Aria and Amsi from behind. "Take them to the morung!" It was a bamboo structure built on stilts and sat at the edge of the ledge.

"Let Petra watch her friends' deaths—tie her!" Evanora roared.

Aria and Amsi spun around and faced the oncoming threat while Jadis continued to face off with Evanora.

Aria bared her canines and let out a guttural growl, and the tribesmen froze in place, terrified of the monster before them.

Amsi stood in place with her hands at her sides, ready to attack side by side with Aria. She stretched her arms out to her sides, flung them forward, and sent a rippling tide of energy in the tribesmen's direction, which sent them flying about the volcanic cavern; some of whom were sent over the edge, splashing into the magma.

Aria looked at her in shock once again. "Holy shit!"

"You will be the only sacrifice!" Jadis threw another energetic ball at Evanora and she held up both hands and shielded herself from the blow, which knocked her back about two feet.

Jadis took two steps forward and before she knew what happened, Evanora's body slammed into the stone wall and she tumbled to the ground.

Arkyn! Jadis thought as a fury of anxiety and fear coursed through her veins. *Fight or flight, Jadis, what you going to do?* she asked herself.

Arkyn materialized and walked in a slow circle around Jadis. He slid his hand across her stomach and around her back and stopped only when he met her face to face. "It seems our worlds have collided once again, Petra."

"I see you're still talking out of your ass," Jadis snarled.

"Well, hell, you still have an uncanny inability to keep your fucking mouth shut. I've missed it," he replied in jest. He grabbed her jaw, moved her head to the side, drug his face up the side of hers, and inhaled. "There it is," he whispered in her ear. "Watching you all this time has given me a certain itch, just a reminder in case you've forgotten." He then grabbed a fistful of her hair and planted his mouth on hers.

He bent over and released a belt of air as her knee met his crotch while the force of his blow knocked her sideways.

Arkyn grabbed her arm, pulled her toward him, and stood chest to chest. "You and I have some unfinished business. You're the fucking reason my brothers are no longer with the living. Make no mistake. I will not repeat Abigor's missteps where you're concerned."

Aria and Amsi stood motionless, watching the altercation taking place between Jadis and Arkyn.

"She's mine, you fucking traitor!" Evanora thundered.

Arkyn grabbed the front of her dress and tossed her over the ledge. "Your time is done!"

Just as the sounds of her high-pitched scream reverberated off the crater walls, there was a large rumble, and the rock above their heads crumbled and came crashing down. Arkyn and the girls ducked and lunged in different directions.

After the dust settled, they could see through the side of the volcanic chimney and Nuri was peering at them from the opening. She swept her large, clawed foot in Arkyn's direction, and he slid into another small entrance while Manewa dropped to her knees and grabbed Evanora's hand, helping to pull her back onto the ledge.

A grimace crossed Nuri's face as she drew her lips back and inhaled. Jadis grabbed Aria and Amsi and ran toward Nuri, who released a pyrogenic wave toward Evanora and Manewa, who darted into another tunnel, escaping the flames.

"Let's get the hell out of here," Jadis yelled.

She and Aria grabbed Amsi by her arms and leapt onto the vertical walls. They grabbed whatever foothold and handhold they could and climbed as quickly as they could with Amsi in tow. They reached the top and plunged themselves through the hole and landed on the solid stone floor. Nuri backed up and let out a gentle grumble before meeting the girls face to face. She then swiveled her head to her right, so the girls ran in that direction.

They came to the end of the cave and peered through a crevice, which opened up into another large room. The gap was just wide enough for them to squeeze through sideways.

"I'll go first," Jadis offered. She slipped her left arm in, followed by her left leg and then the rest of her body. She scanned the large stone room; it was lined with ramshackle shelves and a few archaic tables. Aria and Amsi slipped through the crevice and stood beside Jadis.

"Holy shit," Amsi stated as she looked around.

"What now? There are a shitload of goddamn orbs in here," Aria snapped.

Jadis let out an exasperated sigh. "I don't know where to begin. Do we pick the ugliest, the prettiest, the biggest, what the fuck?"

"Can you talk to Dante? I don't know what we're even looking for." Amsi placed her hands on her hips and shifted her weight from one foot to the other, looking as confused as Aria and Jadis.

"What should we do now?" Aria asked.

"I guess we start looking. Use your abilities and feel for anything out of the ordinary," Jadis suggested.

"Amsi, it seems you're pretty powerful. Feel for a difference in energy," Aria added.

"This will take a day to feel every one of these fucking things." Amsi sighed.

"What choice do we have?" Jadis heard someone call her name, and she held her hand up in the girls' direction.

"Silas, they found it," Dante announced.

"They're standing in her egregore, but they won't know which orb we need," Bain stated.

"Talk to Jadis again," Silas said.

Dante and Bain began another complex incantation, and the milky mixture swirled and the same mysterious symbols appeared.

"Jadis, baby, can you hear me? Jadis?" Dante called.

"Dante?" Jadis answered.

"Yes, love, the orb you need will look like cooled magma. Get it and concentrate on opening a portal. Weave its energy into the fabric of your world and we will connect it to the fabric of ours."

"'Like lava'? Do you realize there are hundreds of black orbs in here?" Jadis snapped.

"Yes, baby, you will know it when you see it—go now, darling," Dante urged.

"Okey dokey—just find a specific looking lava ball in a volcano, no big deal."

"You can do this, baby," Dante assured her.

"Dante—Dante?" Jadis called.

The vision ended before Dante could answer.

"They've done it and they're okay." Santiago smiled.

"Yes, it appears so," Silas replied.

"At least Jadis and Aria haven't killed each other yet," Lars joked.

Silas was pacing back and forth at the edge of the cenote, waiting for any sign that would indicate the portal was opening. "We need to be ready. At the first sign of movement, we need to go. Father, Eden, I need you to mind the orb for us from here."

Dante, Aiden, Bain, and Sigurd moved next to Silas and waited.

"We've got this," Eden replied.

"What did he say?" Aria asked.

"We need to look for one that looks like lava." Jadis shrugged her shoulders in response to the absurdity of the whole situation.

"Okay, *lava*, huh?" Aria looked around and went wide-eyed when she realized just how keen her eyesight had become. "Damn!"

Jadis chuckled in response. "I told you lots of things would change."

"Here goes nothing," Amsi stated.

They began their search and after a couple of hours, Jadis noticed a black, shiny orb that looked like molten glass. "That has to be it. Doesn't lava create black obsidian?"

"Yes." Aria leapt up and grabbed the orb off the shelf.

Jadis took it from her hands and rolled it around in her palm. There was nothing which made it stand out from the numerous others. It was plain and unremarkable; its surface was smooth and devoid of any intricate designs or patterns. However, despite its unassuming appearance, the energy emanating from the ball was potent and intense. *Damn, if it wasn't for its energy, I would have no reason to give it a second glance.* "Have either of you ever created a portal with your covens?"

Aria and Amsi shook their heads. "I've studied it, but I've never done it," Amsi admitted.

"I have never even contemplated the idea," Aria stated.

"Just do what I say. We don't have the time it would normally take, but I'm assuming the orb will do most of the work?"

Amsi and Aria nodded in agreement.

Jadis sat the orb down on a long, worn table. "It's essentially a rip or tear in the fabric of reality between time and space. We need to bend the fabric in order to create a door, two doors to be exact, one on either side of the portal itself. We will need to chant in unison three times, Via temporis, iam clamo ad te via spatti. Te ubio, aperire, aperi."

"I got it." Aria followed Jadis's lead and began swirling her hands over the orb in unison with hers. Amsi also joined in and did as Jadis instructed.

"Via temporis, iam clamo ad te via spatti. Te ubio, aperire. Aperi! Via concurssus, tempos spatium admi ut imperio." They chanted in unison three consecutive times and a green, gaseous substance began swirling within the orb before a multitude of odd black symbols appeared.

"I think it's working," Jadis looked at Aria and Amsi and took a deep breath.

"Shhh," Aria whispered.

"What?" Jadis asked telepathically.

"Someone's here!"

The girls turned toward an entrance at the opposite side of the room and waited a few moments.

"Am I interrupting?" Evanora said as she materialized and stood at the entrance with Mag and Limi at her side.

"Mag—Limi, veni!" Jadis demanded. Their only response was the intensity with which they snarled at her.

"I told you I would take what you hold most precious," Evanora stated. "It looks like I'll have to kill the three of you myself. What's the mortal expression? If you want something done, do it your fucking self!" she roared.

With each beat of Jadis's heart, she wanted to see Evanora's stop; she wanted to watch her eyes become glossy and vacant. "You are nothing more than a sad, lonely kuchka in a meat-covered skeleton! You are dead inside. You have no humanity and now I will show you how little humanity I have!" Jadis raged.

"Ataka!" Evanora yelled.

Mag and Limi lunged for the girls, and Aria and Jadis grabbed Amsi's arms and leapt into the air. They hovered above the ground, watching in shock as Mag and Limi jumped up and down, intent on killing them.

"Mag—Limi, Etiam!" Jadis yelled.

Mag and Limi would stop to shake their bodies and claw at the collars before resuming the attack, but Evanora continued demanding they attack; she then lunged for Jadis and met her mid-air before taking her to the ground. Jadis rolled over and swept her elbow across Evanora's cheek and scrambled to her feet.

Evanora jumped up and grabbed her by the throat. "Now you die!"

Aria and Amsi felt a large breeze blow through the room and Silas, Dante, Aiden, Bain, and Sigurd were standing below them, looking up in shock to see Aria and Amsi hovering above their heads.

"Holy shit!" Aiden mumbled.

Before they had time to assess the situation, Dante looked over and Mag and Limi headed in their direction, hell-bent on attacking.

They leapt out of the way, and Dante and Bain came down on top of them and ripped the collars off. Mag and Limi let out a yelp before feverishly shaking their entire bodies.

Evanora slammed Jadis down and ran toward the entrance. Jadis rolled to see what had caused the sudden disturbance. "Silas, Dante!" she yelled.

The room shook and trembled, and dust and dirt rained down from the ceiling. Multiple orbs fell from the shelves and shattered on the stone floor. Evanora grabbed the edge of the door and looked around, as confused as everyone else appeared to be. Nuri crashed through the wall and let out a deep-chested roar.

Silas, Dante, Bain, Aiden, and Sigurd turned to face the dragon; all of whom were in shock at the entire situation.

Jadis noticed Dante and Bain ready themselves to attack Nuri. "Nooo," she yelled as she jumped in between them and Nuri, holding one hand toward Nuri and the other toward Dante and Bain. "She won't hurt anyone!"

Aria and Amsi rushed to Jadis, and they too held up their hands toward Dante and Bain, who stood motionless, with their eyes deadlocked on the dragon.

Jadis turned her attention to Evanora, who also stood in disbelief. "How do you like your fucking dragon now, you bitch!"

Their mates, as well as Sigurd, also turned their attention to Evanora.

Nuri let out another roar and released a breath of deadly flame aimed straight for Evanora. She ducked, screamed, and held her hands in front of her face in order to shield herself from the searing heat as she disappeared into a dark mist before the flames took her life.

As soon as Evanora disappeared, Silas, Dante, Bain, Aiden, and Sigurd turned around and glanced at each other and were at a total loss for words. A dozen Mortem warriors, dropped in from the portal's entrance and took various positions around the cavern.

"Go!" Silas demanded as he pointed toward the entrance, near where Evanora disappeared.

Jadis jumped into Silas's arms, and he wrapped her in a protective embrace. "Baby, we're here now," Silas whispered in that velvety voice she loved so much.

"What took you so goddamn long?" Jadis cried.

Dante moved in and pulled her from Silas and cradled her in his arms. As he held Jadis, he let out a tremendous sigh of relief, feeling as though he had been holding his breath for a month. "You don't know how relieved we are to hold you again."

"Arkyn is here," Jadis blurted out.

Dante glanced over at Silas and could barely contain his rage.

Aria didn't speak. She leapt into Aiden's arms and clung to him, feeling safe for the first time.

Bain rushed to Amsi and swept her into his arms, and she cried hysterically. "Do you have any idea what we've been through? They almost killed us—Jadis had to give us her blood," she rambled on, having too much to say, and not enough words to express her feelings.

"I'm so sorry, my love, but you're safe now," Bain whispered.

Their mates set the girls down and began rattling off a hundred questions in unison; at the same time Aria, Amsi, and Jadis were yelling at them for taking so long and all the things that had and could have happened. No one could decipher what the other was saying at this point. They stopped talking and just looked at each other.

After a few minutes of silence, Aria and Jadis walked over to Nuri, who had rested her head on the ground as if she was watching the entire scene unfold. They rubbed her enormous face before turning their attention to the stunned crowd.

"I'd like to introduce you to Nuri," Jadis offered.

"Why, Dante, Bain, you're speechless. Who would have thought?" Jadis joked.

"What kind of fuckery have you gotten into now?" Aiden questioned, unable to take his eyes off Aria and her stunning transformation.

Aria and Jadis shrugged their shoulders and glanced at each other. "Well, I almost died. Nuri slit my stomach open, so Jadis had to *turn* me. We didn't have a choice," Aria answered bluntly.

"I didn't set out to *turn* her, Aiden, and Nuri didn't have control of herself. Shit just happened." *Hell, I don't know what else to say; it's the truth. There isn't much more to it,* Jadis thought.

Dante and Bain walked toward the girls and stopped in front of Nuri.

"I'll be dammed." Dante picked Jadis up in his arms again as he studied the beautiful creature before him.

Bain reached out and ran his hand up and down her face. "There are no words," he admitted as he pulled Amsi into his arms again.

Silas, Aiden, and Sigurd had also walked over and were staring at Nuri.

"I'm sure there's a long story, but we don't have time right now. We have an Enchantress we need to take care of once and for all," Dante stated as he turned to Silas and set Jadis down.

Jadis grabbed a hold of both their hands and pulled them close. She wrapped her arms around Silas as Dante stood behind her, his sturdy body pressing against hers.

Dante, Silas, Bain, Aiden, and Sigurd privately spoke with each other so the girls couldn't hear their conversation.

"Jadis did more than turn Aria," Dante stated.

"Aye." Sigurd agreed.

"Yes, they took too much of each other's blood. Unfortunately the moon is twice as powerful here," Bain replied.

"Are we all thinking the same thing?" Aiden asked.

"Yes," Silas answered. *"We won't tell them until we're back home."*

"They need nothing else to worry about right now," Dante replied.

"What are the four of you talking about?" Jadis questioned. "I can tell you're speaking, so fess up," she demanded.

"Nothing you need to worry about, baby. We are going after Evanora," Silas answered, avoiding the actual answer.

Aria, Amsi, and Jadis looked at each other with the same expression; utter relief.

We no longer have to face Evanora alone, nor will we have to fight her. We will watch as our mates unleash their wrath, Jadis thought.

The girls looked adoringly at their mates, who had only one thing on their minds; *Evanora's death.*

Evanora appeared in her chamber and began throwing and destroying everything within reach. She screamed at the top of her lungs and flipped a table into the wall.

"That kuchka! I will fucking destroy her!" she yelled as she clenched her fists and brought them down on her mattress, flames roaring in her eyes.

She left after gathering her thoughts, knowing she didn't yield the powers needed to defeat the Silas and his clan. *I'll hide for the time being,* she thought, having already made preparations for a worst-case scenario; this was undoubtedly a worst-case scenario.

"Where's Arkyn? We're leaving!," she yelled.

"He is waiting," was all Mun said.

CHAPTER 12

Keket was sitting on the stool in an old bar on the outskirts of Thebes, sewing her seeds of regret as she did every night. She spun her empty glass on the bar when the bartender approached.

"Another refill?"

She reached into her pocket and pulled out a couple of crumpled dollar bills, and looked at the bartender, all the while rubbing them together in order to make them appear as if they were tens. She had done this many a night hoping he wouldn't notice until they were already in the till before turning back into ones.

"Nice trick," a smooth voice said from behind.

Kekat's body stiffened, and she turned her head in his direction. "What trick?"

He took a seat next to her and nodded toward the bartender. "The bills."

"I have no idea what you talking about," she mumbled.

He placed a hundred-dollar bill on the bar and nodded to the bartender.

"What can I get you, sir?" he asked.

"I'll take whatever the young lady is drinking and bring her another."

"I don't know what your game is, but I'm not interested," Keket mumbled.

"No games, just a casual drink between new acquaintances."

"I'm not interested in making your *acquaintance*, so what do you want?"

"A drink and maybe some company is all." He had been watching her, studying her for a week, and knew everything he wanted to know about her and her sister's.

"You'll find better company elsewhere," she replied.

"Maybe, but I'd rather enjoy yours."

"Suit yourself." She lifted the glass to her mouth and took a large swig before motioning to the bartender to refill it.

"You drink as if you're drowning a broken heart."

Her eyes snapped in his direction and she stared at him, stunned by his audacity. "You know nothing about me."

"I know you're drinking alone, and I know you look like you either lost your best friend or had your heart broken."

"You're pretty bold."

"Maybe, but I know heartache when I see it. I too, am suffering from the same affliction."

"Oh, please—look at you. I highly doubt some girl broke your heart. I assume it's the other way around."

"What do my looks have to do with being deceived by a woman?"

"You don't look like you do and not have a hundred *women* lined up to heal your so called *affliction*."

"If only it were the case."

"Why me? There are plenty of other women here tonight."

"You looked lonely sitting over here and you sound as if you could use a friend."

"I have no such needs, and I'm waiting for my sister's."

"Until they arrive, how about a conversation—that can't hurt?"

"I don't have much to say, but you're welcome to sit there."

"Alright then, some progress is better than none," he chuckled.

She rolled her eyes and took another drink. "Look, I appreciate the offer but I'm not in the mood."

"How about you sit and I talk?"

"Suit yourself."

He looked down at his glass, twirled it around and tried to appear as solemn as she was."

She side-eyed him and wondered who put him in such a damper. "Okay, what gives?"

"I met someone and thought it might be a go until the husband I didn't know existed showed up." He casually waved his glass at nothing in particular and took another sip.

"That sounds pretty fucking familiar."

"You too, huh? Girlfriend or wife?"

"She is a mate."

"Did you know he was *mated*?"

"Unfortunately, yes," she admitted.

"I can assure you that won't be a problem where I'm concerned."

"I'm sure." She chuckled in jest and took another drink.

"She can laugh after all—well, sort of," he teased, as he tipped his glass toward her.

She returned the gesture and a soft smile crept out from under her scowl.

Easy as catching a fish out of water, he said to himself. "Tell me your name, sweetheart."

"Kekat, and you are?"

"Thaveus."

The door of Kekat's apartment slammed open, and Thaveus was carrying her in his arms as their tongues ravaged the other. Thaveus kicked the door closed and shoved her back against the wall, knocking a picture partially askew. He ripped her shirt and bra off over her head and cupped her breast in his hand. He grabbed her hair, pulled her head to the side, slid his tongue down her neck, and lingered over the heightened beat of her rabid pulse.

Not yet, he told himself. He pulled her away from the wall and walked over to the small kitchen island and knocked the random items onto the floor. He then laid her down, crawled over the top of her, and pushed her onto her back. She kicked off her tennis shoes, and he pulled her jeans off her body, along with her panties.

"Wait," she whispered.

"Wait? Wait for what?" He slowed down and moved with a bit more caution. He slid his hand up her thigh and slowly moved it upward between her legs. He then brushed her nub with his fingers and stared into her eyes, looking for her reaction.

The gentle caress caused her body to respond with an appetite for his sex that pooled within her core. "Oh shit," she moaned.

Exactly what I want to hear. His mouth fell to hers and he could feel her tormented, desperate state of mind.

"Damn, I want you," she moaned.

"Then you shall have me." He spread her legs apart with his knees and thrust his hips forward, giving her what she was so desperate for.

She let out a belt of air and placed her hand on his hip, but he grabbed her wrist and pinned it beside her head as he continued rotating his hips.

She felt the rising swell of her orgasm. "Oh, fuck!" she exclaimed, as her release took over her body.

"Just one more thing," he mumbled. He turned her head to the side, sank his canines deep into her vein, and aggressively thrust his hips.

"W-what are you doing? Stopp!" She cried out only to have her voice lodged within his bite. She was unable to fight back and remained pinned beneath his powerful body as he continued fucking her.

He held her steady and tasted the fear marching through her veins. He released his grip momentarily, lifted his head, and seductively licked his lips. "I love it when they put up a fight."

"Stop! You never told me you were one of them!" she yelled.

He chuckled, dropped his head, and continued to satiate his hunger before taking a moment to bathe in her angst. He then ran his hand over her head and wiped her memory.

Her body relaxed as she slid her hand down his ass and pulled him closer. "You feel—umm," she mumbled, sounding confused.

She let out a belt of air when he rocked his hips and shoved himself deeper. "Izdŭrpaĭte kostta!" He let out a deep, feral snarl as his own release pulsed inside her body.

After a few moments, he slid himself out, rolled off the island, and grabbed his pants. She sat up, feeling perplexed and dazed. It was as if she had been pulled in and out of her sub-conscious mind. "Where are you going?"

"Home. I thought we had an understanding?"

"We do," she agreed groggily.

She slid off the island, picked up her T-shirt, and watched as he sat on the arm of the couch and laced up his boots. He then tossed his shirt over his shoulder and headed for the door. He looked back before shutting it behind him. "Until we meet again."

She plopped down on the couch and covered her face with her arm, trying to stop the tears welling up for reasons she could not discern.

Kekat woke to the sounds of thunder in a drunken stupor. She rolled onto her back, pulled the blanket over her naked body, trying to remember all that had happened. The only light in the room was from the streaks of lightning snaking their way through the tattered curtains. She rolled off the old leather couch and used the coffee table to stand up. She stumbled around the couch and the pain from the wooden chair leg she tripped over radiated through her foot.

"Goddammit!" she shouted, before she fell to the floor. She bent her leg and wrapped her hand around her throbbing toe. After a few minutes, she stood up and limped to the kitchen sink. She turned on the water and filled a glass she grabbed off the counter. She then bent over, turned on the faucet, and splashed the cold water on her face. She limped to her bedroom, fell into her bed, and fumbled around the nightstand, feeling for her cell phone; 4:00 am it read.

By the time she woke up again, it was 5:00 pm. She got into the shower and stood under the hot water for about thirty minutes. She reached for a towel and wrapped it around her body before placing another around her hair. She stood in front of the vanity and wiped the fog from the cracked mirror with her hand. After putting herself together, she noticed a considerable amount of bruising around the left side of her neck. *What the hell?* She slid her fingers over the bruise and looked for any signs of an injury.

Kekat was sitting at the kitchen table eating a bowl of soup when there was a knock at her door. *Who the fuck can that be?* She sat quietly before hearing the knock again, as well as a muffled male voice.

"Kekat, it's Thaveus."

Her heart leapt into her throat. *Shit! He came back?* She hurried to the door and undid the locks she hadn't remembered fastening. He was standing there dressed in worn jeans hanging loosely on his hips and a tight grey T-shirt. *Damn,* she said to herself. "What are you doing here?" she stammered.

"I figured you would need something to eat after last night. Your kitchen looked a little bleak." He handed her a bag, and the aroma wafted into her stomach.

"Thank you, and come in."

"You look surprised to see me."

"Well—I mean—yes, I didn't expect you to come back."

"Here, sit." She hurried over to the table and moved some items out of the way. "Sorry, I know it's a mess, but I've been really busy lately."

"Think nothing of it."

"Would you like a drink?"

"Sure."

She opened the half empty bottle of bourbon that was sitting on her counter and filled a glass. "It's not top shelf, but it's all I have."

"It's fine. What's with the limp?"

"I stubbed my toe is all." She took a seat and pulled the food from the bag. "Would you like a plate? I feel bad eating in front of you."

"I fed myself already, so enjoy."

"*Fed*?" she chuckled, "Your accent, where is it from?"

"Bergelême."

"Then you must be familiar with the war that took place?" She asked.

"Yes, I've heard the gossip, not that it matters to us mortals."

"You refer to yourself as a *mortal*?"

He tilted his glass at her. "Isn't that what their kind call us?"

"Yes, I've just never heard a person call themselves that," she chuckled.

"You are not mortal then?"

She paused momentarily, nervous to reveal the truth.

"Tell me, I have no judgement."

"Well, I am partially mortal. I'm actually a bruja," she replied nervously.

"What are you doing with me? Doesn't your kind gravitate toward Nosferatu?"

"Yes, but I've been there and done that," she huffed.

"Hence the reason for your solemn attitude last night?"

"If you don't mind, I really don't want to talk about it."

"I'll let it go, for now."

She took another bite of her toasted beef sandwich and casually covered her mouth. "So, what brought you here?"

"You, what else? I thought you might like to go out for another drink, unless of course you have plans already?"

"No, I don't have any plans, and I'd love to."

"Why don't you invite your sister's? I'd like to meet them."

Just as Kekat was about to take another bite she paused momentarily and stared at Thaveus. "Why?"

"Why not? You talked about them fondly the night we met."

"I don't remember that."

Thaveus chuckled. "You did have quite a bit to drink."

"That's true. I'll call them and see what they say. I'd like for them to meet you as well."

Jadis turned to Dante. "Baby."

"What is it, mon amour?"

"Can you and Bain protect Nuri? I can't let her be chained by Evanora again."

Dante chuckled and kissed the top of her head. "My love, there is nothing I would deny you."

Jadis looked up adoringly at her wizard. "Thank you." She stood on her tiptoes, grabbed the back of his head, and pulled him in for a much-needed kiss.

"Bain, let's cast a dimensional lock on her. Evanora won't be able to break it, nor will anyone else."

"Sounds good. Let the bitch try. Nuri will kill her before she ever figures it out."

They all backed up as Dante and Bain approached Nuri. They moved their hands in unison with each other in a gyroscope type of motion and waved them in her direction. A light enveloped her before disappearing at the tip of her pointed tail. She shook her entire body before diving from the ledge and flying away.

"We need to find Evanora," Silas said before addressing Jadis. "Darling, I want the three of you to stand back and let us handle her."

"You don't have to tell us twice," Jadis replied.

Silas smiled, bent down, and took her mouth with his.

"Milord," Sigurd said as he returned.

"I assume she's gone?" Silas replied.

"Yes, for now."

Everyone turned back to the entrance when they heard the faint sounds of bugling off in the distance. Nuri had returned and her large wings blew the air in a whirlwind all around them as she hovered outside. She tossed her head in the air and made strange noises and without warning, a large pack of dragons were hovering behind her.

"What's she doing?" Aiden asked.

Jadis stood on the ledge, stared at Nuri, and pulled her thoughts.

"What is it, baby?" Silas asked.

"For a lack of words, she wants Dante and Bain to protect them all," she stated.

Dante and Bain glanced at each other and walked to the edge next to Jadis.

"You know what I want," Jadis said.

Dante and Bain leapt out of the cave and hovered within Nuri's pack. They cast the same spell on each of the dragons.

They searched the interior of the volcanic mountain in its entirety, for days looking for Evanora and Arkyn, even though they knew they would not have stuck around.

"They've covered their tracks, milord," Sigurd said.

"They could be anywhere. How long should we look for them?" Dante asked.

"I think we need to get our mates out of here and back home. They won't escape this place if we take the orb and destroy everything," Bain reasoned.

"The last time we let them get away, look what happened," Jadis snapped. "I'm more afraid of leaving Evanora and Arkyn alive than I am staying here."

"Baby, whether we stay or go, this isn't over. I think it's best to get the three of you out of here." Silas looked at Jadis and wanted nothing more than to get her home.

The girls knew they had no say. It was clear their mates were not going to waver.

By the time they cleared the egregore, night had fallen once again. Aria, Amsi, and Jadis looked at each other, dreading one more night in Avenolon.

Silas smiled and ran his hand down Jadis's cheek. "You will be in our bed tonight, mon chéri. Now let's get the hell out of here."

"I want to say goodbye to Nuri," Jadis said as she looked at Dante for reassurance.

"Nuri will be fine, love. They're well protected. Evanora nor anyone else will ever control them again," Dante confirmed.

Jadis called to Nuri and waited for her to appear while Dante and Bain opened the portal back to their world.

Nuri landed before Jadis, carrying something in her mouth. She set two eggs down at Jadis's feet and nudged her body.

"Oh, hell no!" Aiden exclaimed.

Jadis rolled her eyes and looked back at Nuri. "Dante, why are they here—in Avenolon?" Jadis asked.

"According to Santiago, they were captured and sent into here when the Great War began in order to save them."

Nuri let out a few large puffs of breath and nudged the eggs closer before taking flight.

Jadis turned to Silas and Dante, who stood statuesque.

"Jadis, you cannot take those things home," Dante stated.

"I can and I will."

"Baby, what are you going to do with two dragons?" Silas asked, sounding somewhat amused.

"We're going to take them back to the oasis. They can live freely there," Aria interjected.

"You are not bringing dragons home," Aiden stated.

"Bain, please." Amsi smiled.

"Jabari will lose his shit if you bring those things back." Bain chuckled.

Aria placed her hands on her hips and cocked her head. "I can handle Father. Regardless, we are not leaving them."

The girls stood in place with the eggs, refusing to waver.

Dante let out an exasperated sigh. "Jadis, you are going to have to control those things. You realize that, don't you?"

"We've spent days with Nuri. I think I know what to do," she argued.

"I won't stand here all night arguing. It's clear they've made up their minds," Aiden rumbled.

"What are you going to feed them?" Bain asked.

Jadis looked at Dante and ran her hands up his chest and smiled. "Baby, you can do something, can't you?"

Aiden, Bain, and Sigurd laughed, knowing Dante would not deny her a thing.

"I know what you're doing, love." He cupped his hand over hers and looked at Silas.

"I'm not one to speak. I can't say no to our little pain in the ass, either. Let's go, we'll deal with this later. Worst case, we can bring them back," Silas mumbled.

Jadis grabbed Dante by the back of the head and pulled him in for a kiss before doing the same to Silas. "Thank you!"

"Let's get the hell out of here," Aiden said as he wrapped Aria in his arms.

"Thank you, baby." She smiled.

"Thank me when this becomes a disaster." He chucked before bending down and taking her mouth with his.

Santiago heard the subtle sounds of moving water, and the cenote churned and bubbled. "Be prepared for anything," he warned.

"Here we go," Eden replied.

Eden and Santiago kept the portal open on their end while Jabari, and dozens of Silas's Mortem warriors, as well as Kilark, guarded the pool in case Evanora tried to escape.

The water crashed against the ceiling and Silas, Aiden, and Bain appeared with Jadis, Aria, and Amsi; Sigurd and his warriors were right behind them, having brought Mag and Limi.

Jabari slowly clapped his hands together the moment he saw Aria. He grabbed her and picked her up in his arms.

"Daughter, you have returned!"

Aria wrapped her arms around his neck. "Yes, but there are a few things I need to tell you."

"Tell me later. I just want to hold you."

Eden pulled Jadis from Silas and held her. "You're back. We were so worried about the three of you."

"We're okay, Eden, and thank you for everything," Jadis replied with tears of relief.

Adelrik ran to his daughter. "Amsi!" he stated as he swept her into his arms.

"Father!" As soon as she saw him, she couldn't hold back the tears.

Adelrik nodded at Bain, grateful he had brought his daughter back.

Jabari pulled Aria's head back and stared into her eyes. "Why do you look so different?" He set her down and looked at Silas.

"Not sure you're ready to hear what's transpired." Dante chuckled.

"What are you and Sigurd holding?" Eden asked.

The girls glanced amongst themselves, waiting to see who was going to tell them they brought back two dragons.

Santiago walked over and took the large egg from Dante and rolled it around in his hands. "Don't tell me these are what I think they are?" he rumbled.

Eden took the other egg from Sigurd and looked at Jadis. "Baby girl—" He paused. "What the ever-loving hell have you done now?"

"They were a gift." Jadis smiled.

"A gift?" Adelrik looked at Amsi, and she shrugged her shoulders, smiling.

"A gift? I see two gifts. "I'm curious. Who the hell gifted you, of all Nosferatu, two dragon eggs?" Eden demanded.

"Their mother." Jadis laughed, not able to hide her amusement at their expressions any longer.

"*Their mother?*" Santiago repeated.

"Yes," Silas replied.

Santiago, Eden, Jabari, and Kilark looked at Silas. "The four of you allowed this?" Santiago questioned.

"When does anyone ever tell Jadis no when she gets something in that stubborn head of hers?" Silas pulled Jadis into his arms and looked down at his beautiful mate.

Jadis began chuckling when Eden rubbed his temples after handing the egg to Jabari. "You realize this is going to be a disaster?"

"Where are you going to keep those things?" Jabari looked at Aria, afraid of her answer.

"Here, the oasis is the perfect place. We can raise them here and keep them hidden from the rest of the world. No one will ever find out, Father."

"Really? No one is going hear the rumors about two dragons flying around?" Eden replied.

"Do you realize how much they will eat?" Santiago interjected.

"Yes, Dante said he would feed them," Jadis stated.

Dante snapped his head in her direction. "I offered to feed your dragons? I don't believe that's what I said."

"You did sort of tell her you would." Aiden laughed.

If looks could kill, Aiden would have been buried based on the look Dante shot his way. "I didn't hear you tell Aria no, more than once."

"They'll be fine. Aria, Amsi, and I will take care of them." As soon as the words left her mouth, every head in the pyramid snapped in Jadis's direction.

"Jadis, need I remind you how many times you have pulled us into an uncontrolled situation?" Eden snapped. "And the three of you are going to raise two, count them—two dragons?" Eden began laughing before interlocking his hands behind his head, exasperated.

"I believe the four of you are going to need a lesson on how to tell those three no at some point," Santiago stated firmly, scolding Silas, Dante, Aiden, and Bain. "I think it's best if you take them back."

"Hell no," Aria and Jadis said in unison. However, the look on Santiago's face was all it took to silence them as they backed into their mates.

"*Hell no?*" Santiago repeated as he took two steps toward his defiant daughters.

"My apologies, we didn't mean to be rude, father." Jadis said as she looked up at Silas, her eyes pleading for him to force Santiago to let her keep them.

"Father, they are keeping them—for now anyway," Silas stated.

"This is not your decision, son. It's up to Jabari."

"Father, please, you don't understand what all happened. We have to keep them," Aria pleaded.

He's going to tell Aria no, Jadis thought.

"Maybe I need a lesson on saying no myself. If you want to keep them here in the oasis, there will be very strict rules."

Aria jumped into his arms. "Thank you!"

"Rules?" Eden laughed. "Has Aria, much less Jadis, ever followed even the simplest of requests? And we don't yet know how defiant Amsi is going to be."

Amsi's mouth dropped open, not expecting the accusation.

"She will follow the rules," Bain replied, along with a wink in Amsi's direction.

"Eden, it will be fine. You can help Dante feed them," Jadis joked.

"Say what?" Eden stated. "I can assure you I won't." He chuckled.

"On a side note, I think Aiden and Aria have *a little announcement,*" Silas said.

"Oh shit! Dare I even ask?" Eden replied.

"Come, we shall finish this conversation in the temple." Jabari motioned for everyone to follow him home.

CHAPTER 13

They entered the main temple, and Maddie, Skye, and Ivory squealed with delight and ran to the girls. And they hugged and cried.

Sindri and Badru ran for Jadis, and she kneeled down and grabbed a hold of them. "My little ones, it's so good to see you," she whispered to her cubs as she held them.

As soon as Luciana approached, Jadis stood up. "Come!" She held out her arms and Jadis rushed to her. Her warm, tight embrace said more than any words could. After a few minutes, Luciana reached for Aria and Amsi.

"Before you all jump for joy, you should know they brought back two dragons," Eden stated bluntly.

Maddie, Skye, Ivory, and Luciana looked at each other, trying to figure out if they had heard Eden correctly.

"*Dragons*?" Skye questioned.

"Yes," Dante replied as he and Sigurd held out the enormous eggs.

"Hole shit, like actual dragons?" Ivory asked.

"Yes." Jadis chuckled.

"I need a drink." Luciana waved her hand, and one of her ladies handed her a drink.

"They're your daughters." Santiago smiled.

"My daughters? I believe you indulge them as much as their mates," she replied.

"I think I'll join you in a drink, my love."

"Hell, I think I need a drink." Jadis laughed.

"Shit, you and me both! Jadis was pretty useless in Avenolon. She couldn't conjure a simple bottle by herself," Aria joked.

"Me? You and Amsi couldn't light so much as a small fire."

"Shit was wet," Amsi replied.

"And I was rendered powerless," Jadis stated.

"Come, let us celebrate!" Jabari waved the staff over and they handed everyone a drink before moving into the main parlor. They took a seat, ready to hear all that had transpired.

Dante and Bain set the large eggs on the floor and Jadis, Aria, and Amsi wrapped a couple of cashmere blankets around their base.

Ivory, Skye, and Maddie kneeled down and studied and felt the eggs, not believing they were real. Maddie looked at Eden and cracked up.

"What's funny, darling?" Eden asked.

"I wish I'd been there to see the look on your face."

"Jadis, I assume you will be here permanently, to raise those things?" Jabari asked after calming his laughter.

Jadis looked at Silas and Dante for an answer, as she hadn't thought about it.

"Yes, if you will have us, we will remain here for the duration," Silas answered.

"As will Amsi and I if it's not inconvenient," Bain suggested.

"Of course! You are family. There is no question. I have quite a nice-sized temple off the main garden. You are all welcome to it," Jabari offered.

"Your generosity is much appreciated," Santiago replied.

"Since that has been settled, want to explain how you acquired the dragons?" Eden asked.

"I think you may want to know what else the girls have not said," Aiden offered with a coy smile.

Aria landed a quick slap to his stomach; her movements and the speed at which she smacked Aiden didn't go unnoticed by anyone in the room.

"Oh, fuck," Eden snapped.

"Aria, what have you *not said*?" Jabari questioned.

Aria looked at Jadis, urging her to tell them.

"You tell them," Jadis replied as she raised her eyebrows.

"Me? You're the one who *turned* me."

Eden spat out his drink and Jabari about dropped his glass. Skye's, Ivory's, and Maddie's mouths dropped open.

"Jadis, you *turned* Aria?" Eden questioned.

"Yes, but it's not what you're thinking. It's a long story, but I had to in order to save her life."

"May your gods help us," Eden mumbled as he stared at Aria. "So, you and Jadis—Nosferatu, huh?"

"I'm assuming Silas and or Dante taught you how to *turn* someone properly—yes?" Santiago questioned.

"Well, no, but it wasn't hard, and it was under a full Blood Moon," Jadis replied.

"A full Blood Moon in Avenolon—" Eden began when he heard Silas in his head.

"Don't ask too much. They don't know," Silas stated.

Eden looked at Silas, Dante, and Aiden and spoke privately. *"Please tell me she did this properly."*

"Not exactly, and do not reveal your suspicions," Silas replied.

"I assume the three of you prepared to deal with this situation?" Eden replied, heeding Silas's warning.

"So, I'm just another *situation*, huh?" Jadis looked at Eden and cocked her head.

"Jadis, not this again, you've been back for an hour." His statement caused everyone to break out into another bout of laughter.

"Jadis, Aria, and two dragons, well, this is going to be bloody fantastic! I think I'm moving in as well. I don't want to miss a moment of this," Lars replied, unable to quell his amusement.

Aiden looked at Eden and then back at Aria. "Brother, it will be fine. You worry too much."

"Worry too much? Where the hell have you been?" Eden snapped back.

"Eden, how about you and Maddie move to the oasis as well?" Bain said.

"I'm hoping you didn't *turn* Amsi as well?" Eden stared at her, studying her appearance before letting out a sigh of relief.

"No, Jadis didn't *turn* me." Amsi chuckled.

Adelrik smiled at Amsi and let out a vast sigh of relief.

"We should unite our clans. All are welcome," Jabari announced. "I can provide you all with your own living quarters if you choose to stay."

"For now, no one will leave the oasis. Not until we locate and put an end to Arkyn and Evanora. Eden, I suggest you and Maddie pack your bags," Santiago stated firmly.

Leave it to Santiago to bring us all back to reality, Jadis thought as she rolled her eyes. She heard Santiago chuckle and assumed he saw her.

"Yes, I saw you. You have a thing for rolling those eyes, darling," Santiago replied.

Jadis was curled up in Silas's and Dante's laps with her posse curled up, sleeping at their feet. *I couldn't be happier than I am right now,* she thought.

"Mon amour, you don't know how happy we are right now." Dante pulled her head back and stole a heated kiss.

"I love you, wizard."

"And I you."

She looked over at Silas and smiled as she cupped his cheek in her hand. "Do you know how much I missed you?"

"As much as I did you?" he whispered as the warmth of his tongue met hers.

Silas pulled away and looked at Dante. "I don't know about you, but I'm ready to call it a night."

"I'm with you," Dante replied.

They stood and reached for Jadis's hands and pulled her to her feet.

"It's been fun, but I'm sure Jadis needs her sleep," Silas suggested with a seductive smile.

"I agree, bed sounds amazing." Aiden stood and pulled Aria into his arms and headed upstairs.

"Wait, the eggs," Jadis stated.

Dante and Silas rolled their eyes at her in jest and picked them up; she couldn't help but laugh at their mockery as they headed up to bed. They put the eggs on the large fireplace hearth in their room and Dante conjured two nests to keep them safe until they hatched before they headed straight for the shower.

Aiden picked Aria up in his arms and took her mouth with his. "I have other ideas and sleeping is not one of them." He carried her into the shower, removed their clothes, and tossed them onto the floor.

Aria reveled in the spray's warmth, as she hadn't had an actual shower in over a month. "I can't believe I'm home."

"I was so worried about you, my love."

"Take me, Aiden," she replied in a desperate whisper.

Aiden stroked her wet hair and cupped her face in his hands. She looked up at him and he watched as her canines slipped from her gums for the first time, and his body responded. "Damn," was all he said as he rubbed the tip of her canines with his finger. "You are stunning." He watched, mesmerized, as her green eyes swirled and came alive with a newfound hunger and lust.

He grabbed her thighs and picked her up, and she wrapped her legs around his body. He lowered her onto his hard shaft and let out a raspy moan as he slid himself into her heated, wet core.

"Do you have any idea how happy I am to be back in your arms?" She smiled and ran her hands over his perfect shoulders, admiring his tattoos and muscle-laden body. *Perfection*, she thought.

"You are what's *perfect* and you are mine. Say it."

"I am yours," she growled.

Aiden listened intently. "Your voice." He chuckled. "I think we should head to bed now. I want to hear you moaning with that deep drawl."

"Santiago, we have a lot to deal with, my friend." Jabari crossed one leg over the other and adjusted himself in his seat, pondering the entire situation.

"It seems so," Santiago replied as he rubbed Luciana's back. "Our daughters are going to be a lot to deal with and have I mentioned the dragons yet?"

"Yes, dear, more than once." Luciana chuckled. "I never thought I would see one. It's said that after the Great War they had disappeared from Avenolon."

"Neither did I, and yes, no one knew they were still there. Leave it to Jadis to bring them home with her," Jabari replied.

"Aye, you should have seen their mother. She was majestic, beautiful, and dangerous," Sigurd offered.

"I'm sure she was. I might have to take a trip," Santiago added. "On a serious note, Eden, we need to deal with the dragons. Your brother can handle Aria."

"Really? Aria and Jadis together before she *turned* were a lot to handle. Can you imagine the trouble the two of them and two dragons are going to cause?" Eden chuckled.

"I would say it won't be that bad, but I think I'm with you on this one, my love," Maddie agreed.

"Jabari, the oasis is the size of a large state. Do you think it's adequate for two dragons?"

Santiago became serious again, knowing the damage they could cause should they not be handled properly and, god forbid, they somehow get out of the oasis.

"Yes, it's more than enough for them. My genuine concern is the rules the girls are going to have to follow when it comes to raising and caring for them. The oasis will have to be sealed from here on out," Jabari replied.

"Amsi, I assume you had something to do with bringing them back?" Santiago asked.

"Well, yes," she agreed, looking at Bain for reassurance.

"Bain, I assume you, Silas, Dante, and Aiden will be in charge of all of this?" Eden questioned.

"The dragons will be the responsibility of our clans. Eden, you can help feed them," Santiago joked.

"Don't pull me into her fuckery." Eden laughed.

"Darling, you've been in the middle of her *fuckery* since you thought it best Aiden look out for her, IF we're being honest," Maddie stated.

"You find it funny, do you?"

"I will never again question Jadis's ability to amuse or shock us all," Maddie replied.

"Adelrik, it seems we are also going to have a celebration to plan," Luciana offered, skipping the current subject.

"It seems so." Adelrik smiled and looked at his daughter with a full heart.

Amsi looked up at Bain and rested her head on his shoulder and gave him a heartfelt smile.

"You look exhausted, darling." Bain smiled.

"I am." She wanted nothing more than to be naked and in his arms.

Bain stood and pulled Amsi to her feet. "We're going to head to bed."

Adelrik stood and gave her another tight embrace. "Until tomorrow, my love." He kissed the top of her head, handed her over to Bain, and grasped his forearm. "I will be forever grateful for all you have done to bring my daughter back to me."

"Think nothing of it. I will do whatever it takes to ensure her safety, whatever it takes." He nodded.

Adelrik nodded back and kissed Amsi on either cheek.

After they had finished their *reunification*, they were lying wrapped in each other's arms. "Baby." Aria lifted her head from Aiden's chest and looked at him. "I need to see Jadis. Think Silas and Dante would mind?"

"Not at all. Is everything okay?" Aiden called Silas telepathically to give him a heads-up.

"Yes, I just want to talk with her."

Aiden smiled and rolled out of bed. Aria followed and put on a T-shirt and a pair of shorts. She was thinking about all that had happened and all they had been through, and figured Jadis would be the one who would understand the most. *Hell, she's been possessed, nearly killed by a creature from the underworld, not to mention kidnapped by Abigor,* she thought. *After everything we have been through in Avenolon, I know she will understand.*

Bain carried Amsi to the shower in order to let her wash off the chaos of Avenolon. He picked her up in his arms and she wrapped her legs around his body and cried.

"It's okay, baby, I've got you now," Bain said.

"I was so scared."

Bain pulled her head back and peered deep into her eyes. "Tell me everything and I can help calm the memories for you."

"I don't want to forget. I just need you."

He pressed his lips to hers and parted her mouth before speaking. "And I need you more than you know." He carried her out of the shower, laid her down on the bed, and crawled on top of her. He caressed her thighs and settled his body between her legs.

She arched her back, wrapped her arms around his powerful body, and could feel the flush grow between her legs. She closed her eyes and inhaled the evocative scent of his body. "I desperately missed you," she whispered.

"And I you." He lowered his mouth to hers and moved his hand between her legs.

The warmth of his touch, the power of his broad, muscular chest pressed against hers, sent a wave of desire through her body. She slid her hand down his back, over his ass, and pulled him closer, needing to feel all of him within her.

He slid himself into the slick heat of her core. "No one but me will ever know your body," he whispered.

"No, they won't," she moaned.

He ran his hand over her slim waist, up the arch of her ribs and began to knead her breast in his hand.

She pulled his head to hers and he shoved his tongue into her mouth as he gave a hard thrust. She let out a belt of air as the pain surged between her legs. "Oh, shit—" she groaned.

"Do you need me to be careful?" he murmured.

"No, and it won't take me long if you keep doing that."

"Well then, let me finish you."

The harder he rocked his body and the farther he drove himself in caused the orgasm wound tight within her to uncoil.

Bain felt her wet, swollen core throb around his shaft and it nearly undid him. With another hard shove, followed by another, he could feel the orgasm take over her body.

He pulled out and flipped her over and entered again. "My turn," he rumbled.

After another long romp between the sheets, he fell on top of her and laid his head next to hers. "I can never get enough of you," he whispered.

She lay there, reveling in the ecstasy she never knew she needed. "I never imagined it could feel this amazing and you mean everything to me."

He rolled over and pulled her body against his. "And you have captured my heart in every way."

"Will you ever take another?"

He turned his head to face her so she would see the truth in his eyes. "Never, but if *another* looks at you, or touches you ever again, I will take *another* life."

CHAPTER 14

Thaveus leaned against the wall staring out the window of Kekat's apartment. He could feel the tattered curtain and the cool wisps of air brush against his naked body with each violent gale that rattled the neglected pane. A lone street lamp cast a dim yellow glow on the alley as the torrential rains swept across the cobblestone street. He took a sip of the amber hued brandy and watched the lightening snake its way across the turbulent, rotating sky. He looked over at Kekat, who was peacefully sleeping and stared at the scars marring her back. *She's been laid bare and broken. It won't take much coercing.*

The sudden flash of light and crack of thunder tore through the fragile veil of silence, startling Kekat. She reached out and felt for Thaveus, who was no longer next to her. She rolled over and noticed his silhouette leaning against the wall. "I didn't expect for you to still be here."

"The storms rolled in. I didn't feel like venturing out."

Kekat, sat up, adjusted the pillow beneath her head, and pulled the covers up. "Why don't you come back to bed."

"I'm not the cuddling type." He walked out of her room, strolled down the hallway, and into the kitchen. He refilled his glass and poured another for Kekat.

Kekat rubbed her face and swung her legs over the edge of the bed. She reached for the black cotton robe and wrapped it tightly around her body, shielding herself from the chill of the drafty room. *Damn,* she thought. *You can't 'cuddle' with me, but you have no problem fucking me.*

She wandered into the dimly lit kitchen, and leaned against the counter. Thaveus handed her a glass and walked into the living room, and took a seat on the couch. Kekat followed and sat at the other end. She pulled her knees to her chest and tossed the end of the robe over her feet.

After a few deafening moments of silence, Kekat spoke up. "What do you want from me Thaveus?"

"What makes you think I want something?"

"Just a feeling. I don't know why you're still with me?"

"I thought we were enjoying ourselves?"

"We are, that's not what I meant. It's the way I catch you looking at me at times, is all."

"How do I look at you that makes you feel uneasy?"

"I don't know—you seem closed off?"

"You should understand more than most. At least I thought you would, having been betrayed yourself. If I make you uneasy, I'll show myself out."

"No. Please don't go. I'm sorry, I didn't mean for it to come across that way."

"You want me to stay then?"

"Yes."

"If I'm being honest, there may be a hint of truth behind your concern," he admitted.

"Like what?"

Thaveus scooted over, pulled her legs across his lap, and stroked her hair." *She's so desperate for a pittance of attention she'd drop to her knees at me feet if I demand it,* he thought. "Tell me about the scars on your back."

She nervously took another drink, feeling too embarrassed to reveal the truth. "It's nothing."

"They look like more than nothing. Tell me, you can't scare me off that easily." He winked.

She thought momentarily, contemplating whether or not to reveal the truth.

"Darling, whatever it is you can trust me."

Kekat barely looked at him as she tried to quell the nerves assailing her body. "I—my sisters, a friend and I—well, we were banished from the oasis."

He pulled her head toward his and parted her mouth. "Tell me all of it," he whispered after pulling away.

"I, we were at the stables and a bruja named Jadis and her mates weren't happy about it."

"There's more to it than that, Kekat. How are we to trust each other if you can't be honest with me?"

"It's embarrassing Thaveus," she muttered.

"If I know the truth, maybe we can help each other out."

She tilted her head and stared at him. "How?"

He gently ran his hand down her cheek. "Tell me the story."

She looked down at her glass and cupped it with both hands. "We thought we could catch Silas or Dante alone," she admitted softly, having failed to make eye contact as she spoke the words.

Thaveus stopped himself from laughing aloud. He lifted the glass to his mouth and took a large drink as he peered at her over the rim. *She thought she could bed a Montiago?* "And the scars?"

She wiped away the tears streaming down her face. "It was Silas's commander, Sigurd. After he took us to the cells, he gave us a lashing."

Sigurd? She's lucky all she got was a lashing. "Well shit," he sighed, trying his best to sound disturbed rather than amused.

"Now that you know the truth, what did you mean by *we can help each other out?*"

"How does a bit of well-executed revenge sound? It seems we both have a hatchet to grind."

"Why do you have a problem with them? You've never mentioned anything before."

"We have a long history, but the details are not important."

"I don't know Thaveus. I'm not sure it's a good idea. You're simply a mortal how will you handle them?"

"Let me worry about the details. Would you sister's be agreeable for a sizeable amount of money and my protection?"

"Would you really protect us?"

"Of course. You and I are together, are we not?" He smiled.

She felt her heart skip a beat with his sudden admission. *We're together?* "Are you saying we're together—together?"

He leaned over and took her mouth to his. He then pulled back slightly. "Yes, *together, together*. Are you in or not?"

"What do you have in mind?"

Silas, Dante, and Jadis were sitting in bed, playing around and drinking after a much-needed reunion. Silas and Dante got up, put their sweatpants on, and Silas tossed Jadis his T-shirt. "Put this on."

Dante held out her underwear. "You might want these as well.'

"What's going on?"

"Aiden said Aria wants to see you," Silas replied.

"Is everything okay?"

"I assume so. Aiden said nothing else."

"It seems we are going to have to deal with the consequences of Jadis turning Aria sooner than later," Silas stated to Dante privately.

"Now is as good a time as any," Dante replied.

There was a quiet knock. "Jadis, can we come in?"

"Yes," Jadis replied as she walked to the door. As soon as Aria saw Jadis, she wrapped her arms around her.

"Are you all right?" Jadis asked, along with a tight embrace.

"Yeah, is it okay if we hang in here for a bit?"

Jadis held her and rubbed her back momentarily before she let go.

"Of course, come sit with me." She jumped into the bed and motioned for Aria to join her. They sat in the middle and crossed their legs while Jadis waited for her to speak.

Silas, Dante, and Aiden took a seat at the table across the room, allowing the girls their privacy.

Jadis patiently waited in order to let Aria get her thoughts together. "Silas, will you get us a drink, please? I think Aria could use it."

"How did you ever get your shit together after all that you have been through?" she asked bluntly and heavy-hearted. "Thank you," she said as Silas handed them a drink.

"I don't know? I can't control what's happened, but Silas has never wavered and now Dante, too, is there no matter what. They have been my anchor in the shit storm my life has been."

Aria smiled warmly, but Jadis could feel her confusion.

"Aiden's got you. You need to rely on him. They have been through shit like this for hundreds of years. He is as loyal as they come and there is nothing he wouldn't do for you."

"He is pretty amazing," Aria replied.

"You will be fine. It just takes time. You have been there for me too many times to count. I'll be here with you all the way. Whatever you need, whenever you need it, you've got it. I believe someone said that to me once." Jadis winked.

"Would you have a problem? More like would Silas and Dante have a problem if Aiden and I stayed in here with you tonight?" she whispered.

Jadis looked at Silas and Dante, who nodded in her direction. "Of course, however, the bed's too small for the five of us," Jadis joked as she patted the plush duvet. "Wizard, I think we need a bigger bed and I assume you can do something?"

"I think I can muster a little something up," he replied with a wink. "The two of you might want to get up first."

The girls moved off the bed before it rumbled, shook, and disappeared; it suddenly appeared twice its size. Aria and Jadis yelped in unison, to everyone's amusement. *I can never get over the powers Dante yields,* Jadis thought.

The two of them climbed into the massive bed and wrapped a couple of large cashmere blankets over their laps while the posse curled up next to them.

Jadis looked at Dante and Silas and patted the duvet. "Come, mates," she demanded coyly. She knew Aria could use Aiden by her side; knowing, of course, he would never crawl into her bed, mated to Aria or not.

Silas nodded at Aiden and the three of them climbed into bed, along with a couple of bottles of Molatto's Whiskey.

"Be careful demanding we come," Dante joked.

"Dante!" Jadis stated, after having choked on her drink.

Aria let out an embarrassed chuckle and diverted her eyes from Dante.

Silas and Dante leaned against the massive headboard with their legs casually stretched out while Aiden sat behind Aria leaning against the large footboard.

"Thanks for letting us stay here," Aria spoke, avoiding the sexual undertones Dante was shooting Jadis's way.

"Anytime. We can have a sleepover whenever you want," Jadis offered.

"Sleepovers can be fun in more than one way," Silas blurted out, winking in Aria's direction.

His statement shocked Aria and Jadis, and both their faces flushed a warm crimson while Silas, Dante, and Aiden laughed.

"Jesus, how do you put up with them?" Aria joked. "Soo—I assume the three of you—together?"

"Yes," Jadis replied. "As Eden told me once, and I quote, 'sex to us is nothing more than that. We have all taken part with one or more partners. I believe all of us have shared a woman, in the same bed at some point'."

"I can't believe he said that to you. Eden, of all the Nosferatu." She chuckled, having never seen or heard him joking around. "I think I for one will refrain from an orgy."

"We'll see," Aiden teased.

"I didn't expect this to turn sexual. I just wanted to hang with you, and I'm sure as hell happy I did." Aria laughed. "There's something about being with you that puts me at ease."

"I feel the same way. It's probably because I turned you?" They looked at their mates for clarity.

"The two of you are as bonded as Dante and me. When you *turned* Aria and drank from each other, a little too much, I might add, you bound yourselves together as if you had mated. It's not much different from you and Aiden being mated," Silas explained.

"That's what happens when you play around and are just a pup in the woods. Next time, ask someone who knows what they're doing." Dante chuckled.

After a few moments of laughter and drinking, the thought hit Jadis. She tilted her head and stared at Aria.

"Why are you looking at me like that?"

Jadis ignored her and let her canines slip from her gums as she *turned*.

"Jadis, stop!" Aria slid back into Aiden's lap. "Aiden, make her stop that right now." Aria let her own canines slip from her gums and she also *turned* feeling threatened.

Silas, Dante, and Aiden stared at Jadis and Aria, not sure what was happening.

"Well, well, well. Apparently, I'm your sire and I expect you to bend the knee," Jadis snarled.

Silas, Dante, and Aiden bellowed in laughter.

Jadis rose up on her knees before Aria. "I suggest you bend the knee."

Aria met her chest to chest, as if challenging her. "And if I don't?" She defiantly cocked her head at Jadis.

"Then I'll have to force you." Jadis grabbed a pillow and cracked her across the head.

"Are you serious?" Aria laughed, before clocking Jadis upside the head with a pillow of her own.

The girls were in hysterics as they fell into a full-fledged pillow fight while their mates rolled in laugher.

Jadis winked at Aria, and they spun around, pillow in hand. Aria hit Aiden right upside his head and Jadis hit Dante in the face, reeled the pillow back and crossed Silas's body. "What exactly are the two of you laughing at?" Jadis joked.

Before Jadis knew it, Aiden cracked her across the body. "You certainly have a thing for pillows." His statement forced them both to laugh at the inside joke.

Jadis swung her pillow at Aiden's face, only for him to grab it and rip it from her hands. He tossed it to Mag and Limi, who used it for a game of tug-of-war.

The three of them lunged for Aria and Jadis, who screamed, leap from the bed, and took off across the room.

Silas, Dante, and Aiden grabbed Aria and Jadis and tossed them onto the bed on their backs and pummeled them with pillows.

"Okay—stopp!" Jadis laughed. "Clearly we were not winning this fight!"

"Aiden, I give up!" Aria yelled through her laughter.

They tossed the pillows down and looked at each other deviously, deciding they had more on their minds than a pillow fight. It was obvious to the girls what they were up to by the way they all crawled onto the bed and hovered over them.

"Aiden, no." Aria chuckled nervously.

Silas took Jadis's mouth with his and placed his heavy body on top of hers before Dante moved in.

Aiden had repositioned Aria farther down on the bed and forced her mouth open.

Aria placed her hands on either side of Aiden's face. "Aiden, we have company if you hadn't noticed," she whispered.

"It makes no difference. Don't worry about it. I'm taking you now whether you like it or not." He pulled her t-shirt over her head, tossed it aside, and cupped her breast in his hand. He then moved his body down hers and gently sucked her nipple into his mouth.

She barely looked at Jadis, who was already naked beneath both Silas and Dante.

Jadis caught Aria's eye and winked, letting her know it was fine.

"Well, shit, if we can't beat them, we may as well join them." Aria grabbed the back of Aiden's head and pulled him in for another heated kiss, her body melting beneath his.

Aria moaned beneath him as she reached down and wrapped her hand around his hard shaft and rubbed up and down, using the drops of liquid dripping from his tip.

He groaned with each firm stroke of her touch and pushed her legs apart. He pulled one of them higher over his waist as he settled farther between her legs.

She let out a heavy, moan-filled breath. "Aiden, I need you inside me now."

The entire situation had her mind and body spiraling. The nervousness of being in the same bed as Jadis, Silas, and Dante was nerve-racking. However, she found herself turned on more than she cared to admit.

Aiden dragged his canines along her neck and hovered over her throbbing pulse as her blood coursed through her veins.

"I think I need a drink. This time I'll have my fill." Aiden gently turned her head and playfully nipped her ear.

"Mmm—I'm hungry too," she whispered.

He sank his canines deep into her vein and gave one hard shove and was deep inside her wet, heated core as he pulled her blood into his mouth.

She sucked in her breath and held it before the pain subsided and the pleasure took over. He continued slowly rocking back and forth as he took as much of her blood as he needed to satiate his thirst.

He let go of her neck and licked the few droplets with the tip of his tongue before watching the punctures heal themselves.

She could feel the warmth of his breath in her ear. "You always taste like the desert smells after a gentle rain," he groaned.

"My turn," she whispered.

He turned his head for her, offering his vein. The sharp tips puncturing his flesh seared throughout his body. He continued to rock back and forth as she drank from him, holding his neck steady. He couldn't believe the sensations rocking his body feeling her feed from him.

"I think I am going to come in that mouth of yours," he whispered before he pulled his neck from her, forcing her to release her grip.

He slid his tongue across the tips of her canines, pulled out, and straddled her. He bent on top of her and planted one palm on the footboard and wrapped her hair in a tight grip. She slid her tongue along his shaft before sliding it into her mouth.

Dante brushed his lips against Jadis's before slipping her his tongue while Silas moved between her legs.

Dante sat up and straddled her; he placed the palm of his hand on the headboard while she took him into her mouth. He stroked her face and grabbed her hair as she sucked and teased his pulsing shaft with her tongue and hand.

"My god—that—you feel amazing," Dante rumbled.

The sensations quickly rose from between her legs as Silas sucked her sex and drove his fingers deep into her core; teasing the perfect spot with his finger.

The feeling from Silas's and Dante's sexual rapture was intoxicating. She let Dante's shaft slip from her mouth as she let out a deep, moan-filled gasp and planted her head into the pillow and arched her back.

Dante moved over to the side as Silas made his way back up and lay on his back, then pulled Jadis on top of him. The warmth of his mouth found hers.

"You know what I want more of." He put his hand on her shoulders and pushed her lower. She moved down and took his sex into her mouth and gently stroked his shaft with a tight grip.

"Shit!" Silas held the back of her head with his hands and released a guttural groan when the tips of her whites scraped the sides of his shaft.

Dante lifted her hips and shoved himself into her heated, throbbing core.

Aiden flipped Aria over and lifted her onto her knees and pushed her face down into the bed.

"Fuck," he mumbled from beneath his breath. He hadn't been in bed with others in years and the fact Silas and Dante were taking Jadis next to him brought out an age-old desire, one he hadn't felt in ages.

He rubbed his hand up and down Aria's back before he reached for his shaft and teased her sex with the wet tip. The sounds of her growls only ramped up his desire as he thrust his hips forward.

She let out a belt of air. "Damn, Aiden," she gasped.

He rocked himself back and forth and forcefully shoved himself in and out with one powerful thrust after the other.

"Goddamn, you are so tight, so wet," he growled. He reached around and began teasing her sex with his fingers.

Her moans intensified, and he felt her swollen nub throb beneath his fingers and her tight core clench his shaft.

"Don't stop," she moaned as her orgasm cracked to the surface.

The more she orgasmed, the wetter she became; Aiden could barely hold himself from getting off. As soon as she finished, he flipped her onto her back and shoved himself back in, ready to come himself.

"Come for me again, baby," Aiden whispered.

"Keep that up and I will," she groaned.

"Ahh, mon chéri," Silas moaned as Jadis continued to suck harder and cupped his shaft in a tighter grip as her hand followed the motions of her mouth.

"Fuck me," Dante stated as he climaxed.

Jadis let out a guttural groan as the feeling rippled to the surface again.

"That's it, baby, come with us," Dante moaned.

Silas grabbed her head, forcing her to take him deeper. His vein pulsed, and he could feel her body convulse as she swallowed. He let out a deep-throated growl that vibrated the bed beneath them.

Dante shoved one more time, bringing about his own orgasm. He felt the slickness of her release around his shaft and he let his seed fill her core.

"I got off so hard the last orgasm actually hurt," Jadis whispered. Dante and Silas were rougher than normal and she reveled in the pain-filled pleasure.

They fell into a heap on the bed, their breathing heavy and labored, and Jadis could hear Aria's and Aiden's heavy breaths as they too came down together.

Aiden rested his body on top of Aria and continued gently rocking back and forth, letting their racing hearts calm. He pulled out and rolled over, taking her with. She laid her head on his shoulder and felt relaxed for the first time in what felt like months.

Silas, Dante, and Aiden finally propped themselves up against the headboard and footboard on a bunch of pillows, letting Jadis and Aria decide when it was time to face each other. Dante reached his hand out and handed Silas a glass. He conjured another and handed it to Aiden before getting himself a drink.

"So—this really happened." Jadis chuckled to Aria privately.

"It sure the hell did." She chuckled back. *"Who's going to face who first?"*

"At the same time." They casually rolled off their mates, propped themselves up on a few pillows, and faced each other. They could feel the warmth of their cheeks, realizing they were all buck naked without so much as a sheet covering one of them.

Silas, Dante, and Aiden chuckled at the embarrassed looks on their mates' faces.

"Your shyness is adorable," Dante teased as he handed Jadis a highball glass.

Aiden handed one to Aria and winked.

Silas and Dante didn't cover up the fact that they were eying Aria's naked body and Aiden was making it all too obvious he was reveling in looking at Jadis'. There was an unrelenting lust behind his eyes Jadis picked up on immediately.

The girls grabbed the large cashmere blankets to cover their bodies from the burning stares of their mates. They were utterly embarrassed, which only increased their mates' amusement.

"I have a few ideas coming to mind," Aiden stated as he winked at Jadis.

"As do we." Silas and Dante looked at Aria with the same devious smirk.

"Oh, hell no," Aria and Jadis stammered at the same time.

Jadis backhanded Silas and Dante, only for them to grab her wrists in a vice-like grip.

Aria landed a hard smack on Aiden's chest and he grabbed her wrist and pinned it at her side. "Still feisty? Maybe another round?"

"If you think we are going to partner swap, you all have another think coming." Jadis chuckled.

"Aiden, do not for one minute think about it," Aria said. Silas and Dante always intimidated her, and she couldn't fathom giving her body to them. *Hell, I don't know how Jadis can be with Silas to begin with. He's so fucking intimidating. All he has to do to send my soul into hiding is to cock his head at me,* Aria thought to herself.

They began teasing the girls and enjoyed every minute of their embarrassment. The girls, however, were nervous and unamused, knowing if Silas and Dante were willing to let Aiden have sex with Jadis and them with Aria, only the gods knew the reason behind it.

Aria and Jadis refused, which only ramped up their taunting. They both felt the jealous pangs just thinking about their mates being with another.

"At least we're basically mated, which would keep us from killing each other," Jadis stated to Aria silently.

"Yes. Aiden, however, will be at the mercy of Silas and Dante, who would put him in the grave," Aria replied.

"I believe we have a couple of jealous lovers on our hands," Aiden quipped.

"Ahh—don't be jealous, mon chéri," Silas teased.

"There is a solution," Dante offered.

"Stop," Jadis demanded, trying her best to sound serious.

"I don't want to know," Aria replied nervously.

"Maybe we should tell them?" Silas looked at Dante and Aiden with a coy smile.

"There is that," Dante stated as he raised his eyebrows at Jadis.

"You're freaking me out, Aiden. Make them stop," Aria pleaded.

Jadis tried to get up, but Dante and Silas pinned her between them. "Going somewhere?" Silas rumbled.

"Let's do it," Dante stated.

That put Aria over the edge. She tried to jump out of the bed, only for Aiden to snatch her around the waist and pull her back down. "Hell, why not," Aiden agreed.

"Do what?" Jadis demanded.

"If we all take each other as a mate, then we can *partner swap*," Dante added.

"What are you talking about?" Aria asked.

Aria and Jadis remained pinned in place, not knowing what to think, what to do, or what to say. Silas's, Dante's, and Aiden's inability to stop laughing at them only caused Aria and Jadis to join in on their amusement.

After a few minutes, they all settled down. "On a serious note, we should think about it," Silas admitted.

"You can't be serious, Silas," Jadis protested. "I'm not okay with that by any means."

"I'm with Jadis on this one," Aria agreed.

"Listen, baby, the Blood Moon in Avenolon is twice as strong as it is here. You and Aria are bonded and she will be in our bed more than you realize. The only problem is that she and Aiden are mated as well. The two of you will feel the pull to be with each other almost as much as you do with us," Dante explained.

Silas, of course, took it to a more serious level. "If you choose to not let us mate, it puts the five of us in a precarious situation. One false move on Aiden's part—let's just say it wouldn't end well."

"We'll leave the decision to the two of you," Aiden added. "Just know the underlying consequences should you choose the alternative."

"We have no problem abiding by your wishes. We will also do everything in our power to not let it come to that. However, things can go awry and we will not make false promises. We've been around far too long," Dante said.

Jadis and Aria looked at each other. They hadn't realized they had essentially mated.

"Why can't you just conjure something up, Dante? I've seen what you're capable of," Jadis suggested, looking for any other alternative.

"Darling, as much as I would love to, the bond of a mate goes beyond even what I can control. It's a deep-seated, powerful bond sealed in blood. It goes beyond the realm of any archaic powers I possess. I could cloak us, but, if the veil should drop at the wrong time for even a moment, it could be disastrous. Mating is the one thing we cannot control."

"I really messed up, didn't I?" Jadis sighed.

"No, baby, not at all. You saved Aria's life and we will always be proud of you," Silas stated.

"And I am beyond grateful," Aiden added.

"There was no way for you to know, and had you not been in Avenolon, it would have been a normal *turning*," Dante said.

"Well, fuck," Aria belted out, looking less than enthused.

Jadis glanced out the window at the swirling, red colors of the Full Blood Moon, thinking back to when she and Silas had mated, and then with Dante in the cave, and then with Aria in Avenolon. "Well, shit, I don't know if I can do this," Jadis was so confused. "How am I to deal with three of you? You two suffocate me enough as it is."

"Maybe three of us will get you under control." Dante rolled his eyes at her in jest.

"Maybe a little backup wouldn't hurt." Silas chuckled.

"You are both ridiculous." Jadis laughed.

"You two talk it over, but now is as good a time as any. Hell, we're all naked already," Aiden teased.

Jadis thought back to all that had taken place over the years. *Dante and Silas no longer hold any animosity toward Aiden, but this?*

"Does that mean I have to—with the two of you?" Aria asked.

"Yes, and Jadis will be taken by Aiden," Silas answered truthfully, but looked less than thrilled.

Jadis knew Silas and Dante were holding their authentic emotions back, and it scared her. The entire situation sent her mind spiraling into a million and one jealous thoughts. *If Aria and I weren't bonded, I'd want to kill her based on the mere thought.*

Aria wasn't in love with Silas and Dante, and she couldn't see herself letting them take her at the same time. A jealous thought crossed her mind. *I know Aiden's in love with Jadis. Allowing them to have sex with each other would be out of the question under any other circumstance.*

"Feel that, baby? That's how Dante and I feel when Aiden looks at you. Hence the reason the situation is so dangerous. If the two of you feel you cannot do this, you and Aria will need to abide by very strict rules." *Shit, Jadis never follows the simplest of requests. This will be a disaster should they decide not to do this,* Silas thought.

"Jadis following rules? That's tantamount to kissing a dragon." Aiden laughed.

"Seriously, Aiden—I believe I've already kissed the dragon," Jadis retorted.

"You sure as hell did," Dante replied before he stole another kiss.

"Let's let them speak privately," Silas suggested.

The three of them got out of bed buck naked, not having a care in the world; modesty was not in their nature.

The girls stared at the naked trio, admiring their gorgeous sculpted bodies. Once their mates put their sweats back on, they turned their attention back to each other.

Dante turned back to Jadis before heading out the door. "Take your time and let us know when you've decided."

"Make your decision, mon chéri, and *choose wisely*." Silas winked.

CHAPTER 15

Jabari was sitting with Lars in the main parlor when Silas, Dante, and Aiden headed down the stairs.

"What's going on?" Jabari asked.

"Nothing, we decided to join you for a drink," Dante replied.

"Bullshit. I can smell them all over the three of you. What the hell have you been doing all night, or dare I ask?" Lars asked.

Jabari tossed Aiden a bottle. "I assume there's something else going on?"

"The three of you look like the girls before they pull some kind of fuckery." Lars chuckled.

"Let's hear this," Jabari motioned for them to continue. "What have they done now?"

"Should we tell them?" Aiden asked as he crossed one leg over his knee and sat back.

"They will find out tomorrow at some point. We may as well." Dante swung one leg over the arm of the chair and sat back.

"Is this some portal, possession, or evil villain fuckery?" Lars laughed.

"Nothing like that." Silas chuckled.

"We're waiting," Jabari said, urging them to fess up.

"Silas, they're waiting for you," Dante said.

Silas adjusted himself in the chair, crossed one leg over the other, and took a drink. "The girls have a decision to make. As you know, Jadis and Aria have bonded. I'm assuming you can guess the rest."

After a few moments of contemplation, Jabari realized what they were and weren't saying. "Oh—hell," Jabari stated as he laughed aloud.

"What's going on?" Lars asked.

Jabari looked over at his clueless friend. "You'll figure it out, eventually."

"Aiden, are you going to mate Jadis after all you have been through with that girl?" Jabari questioned, remembering back to how many times she had enraged him.

Aiden tipped his glass to him. "I'm ready. I can handle her."

"Really? When has any one of us *handled* Jadis?" Dante replied jokingly.

"Three against two. Sounds like an easy fight," Silas said.

"Easy my ass! The three of you are gluttons for punishment," Lars stated.

"You understand the consequences of your decision where the entire clan is concerned—yes?" Jabari asked.

They knew he was giving them a subtle warning. "You're essentially partaking in pack sex, and the rest of our clan will eventually feel the pull."

Aiden looked at Silas and Dante. "I hadn't thought about it that way," Aiden admitted.

"He speaks the truth," Dante agreed.

"They'll figure it out should they feel the pull," Silas stated unemotionally.

"Jadis, I can't believe this is happening right now. I don't know how to be with Silas and Dante, not to mention Aiden is suffocating."

"If you think Aiden is suffocating, you don't know what you're in store for. Silas and Dante are on a whole other level."

"You and I have one of two choices. Either we do as they suggest, or we risk Aiden's life. We both know he is no match against the two of them together." Aria sighed.

"No, he wouldn't stand a chance and I don't trust for one minute Dante, much less Silas, wouldn't lose it at some point. Silas's words of warning were enough. Hell, did you feel his and Dante's energy at the mere thought of letting Aiden take me?"

"I did! I think I was holding my breath."

"You and me both."

"What did Silas mean by *choose wisely*?"

"Remember when Skye, Ivory, and I snuck into the portal and spoke with Hecate, our mother?"

"I remember."

"She told me I would be pulled between worlds and would have to make a choice. She said, *choose wisely*."

"I still don't understand."

"During my little possession, I was between the realms of light and dark. I could either succumb to the Bakale and give my life to them, or I could choose to remain with Silas. I chose Silas. Hence, the meaning, *choose wisely*."

"You never told us that."

"I know. I never thought about it, there was never any question I would choose my vampire."

"I get that, but what do we do now? If I'm being honest, they terrify me."

"Aria, I don't know myself. For whatever reason, I'm as nervous as you are, but regardless, we have to make a decision together. One we will never regret."

Aria and Jadis were wrapped in their blankets, leaning into one another, trying to make the life-changing decision. They sat contemplating all that the mating between the five of them would mean and everything it would entail. They stared at the eggs and looked at Mag and Limi curled up with them on the bed, which brought about dismal memories of Avenolon. They pulled Sindri and Badru into their arms for a bit of comfort.

"At least this is familiar. Can you imagine what would have happened to us if we hadn't had Mag and Limi?" Aria said.

"No, and I don't want to think back to all that transpired," Jadis replied.

Aria sat quietly, thinking about the fact she was about to mate the two most menacing, jealous, and controlling vampires she had ever met.

"You do realize we will live the rest of our days like a couple of birds in a gilded cage?" Jadis chuckled.

"How did our lives come to this? I don't feel anything toward Dante and Silas other than they are Aiden's cousins and your mates."

"I know, I get it—can I be honest with you?"

"Really? After all we have been through, do you have to ask?"

Jadis was contemplating her words when Aria nudged her with her shoulder. "Just say it. Don't get shy with me now."

"Okay, but don't be mad—the mere thought of you being with Silas and Dante sexually is a problem. In fact, I think I might hurt you." Jadis couldn't look at her and the guilt she felt sat in the pit of her stomach like a brick.

"You too? I'm so relieved you said that! I feel the same way about Aiden."

Jadis looked at Aria, feeling relieved. "Really?"

"Hell yes," Aria said as she looked around the room.

"What are you looking for?"

"Just making sure there aren't any crack knives lying around," she joked. "I don't know, Jadis, maybe it's time for me to let the old ways die and take more than one mate? You did. And like you said, *as Nosferatu we run in packs.*"

"I remember."

"It's now or never. We should call them back or I'll never have the nerve again." Aria finished her glass and refilled it.

Jadis motioned for the bottle and Aria handed it over and she took a large drink, not bothering to fill her glass.

"Call Aiden back."

"What? No, you call Silas and Dante."

"Shit!" Jadis took another drink, as did Aria.

"Are we both in agreement?" Jadis asked.

"We are, and I'm as ready as I'll ever be." Aria took another large swallow and Jadis could see her hands trembling.

"Silas—Dante," Jadis whispered telepathically.

"It seems our mates have decided," Silas announced.

"Are they really going to take each other as mates?" Lars asked as soon as they were gone.

"I'll be dammed." Jabari laughed.

"How are they going to control Jadis and Aria together? Those two are fucking crazy," Lars stated through his laughter.

"That they are," Jabari agreed. "Silas, Dante, and Aiden are about to get themselves into a storm of reckoning."

"Being that Jadis is a Dhamphyr, she could probably bend the tides if she demanded. Now, with Aria at her side, those three are screwed. I can't wait to see the shit they are going to pull over on them." Lars couldn't wait for the fallout to begin. "I know I'm never leaving."

"Let the games begin!" Jabari shouted. "I wouldn't miss this for anything," Jabari added as he tilted his glass toward Lars.

Silas, Dante, and Aiden appeared at the edge of the bed, and Aria and Jadis looked at each other, not sure they made the right decision. They didn't know how to feel, and the heavy silence felt thicker than the tension in the air surrounding them.

"I assume by the expressions on your faces and the way you're cuddled up, you've decided the safer alternative?" Silas asked.

Neither of them could get the words out; their silence let their mates know what they had decided.

The three of them crawled across the expansive bed and Jadis felt Aria's body go stiff as soon as Silas and Dante looked at her.

"Wait, I don't know if we should do this," Jadis heard the shakiness of her own voice, exposing her trepidation.

"Shhh—both of you need to be still. Your minds are running wild right now." Dante couldn't help but chuckle at the befuddled mess the girls were.

Aiden looked at Aria and tried to hide his own amusement; he had never seen Aria look so timid.

Silas looked deep into Jadis's and Aria's eyes and stroked their cheeks with the back of his hand. "What heart has ever loved without madness? We're uniquely different in our shadowed forms. Some days you will be our flowers, other days you will be our thorns. We shall whisper wicked words and hum enchanting tunes. We shall walk through forbidden places and play under the moon. We shall become lovers in the night and warriors during the day."

Silas bent down and took Jadis's mouth before looking at Dante and Aiden.

Aria looked at Jadis and spoke telepathically. *"Silas is a fucking poet?"*

"Amongst other things, one of which you don't want to see," Jadis warned.

Silas reached for Jadis's and Aria's ankles and pulled them toward himself, Dante, and Aiden.

"The two of you need to relax and let us do what we know," Silas said before claiming Jadis's mouth again.

I've longed for this since the night I first laid eyes on her, Aiden thought.

"The three of us will bond first to make sure this goes smoothly," Silas assured the girls as he and Dante held out their wrists to Aiden before taking his.

The girls watched as they took each other's wrists to their mouths and drank. It was as if their eyes became a reflection of one another and a predatory look came over them. Their features sharpened and their gaze intensified as if they were drawing strength from one another.

"Shit," Aria mumbled as she scooted back.

They then turned toward the girls and they found themselves being consumed by their mates. They were side by side while Silas, Dante, and Aiden moved on top of them.

Silas nodded at Aiden. "Take Jadis."

Aiden looked down at Aria. "It's time, baby. Let them take you. I'll be right here—well, sort of," he added with a wink.

Aria's heart leapt out of her chest, knowing it was time to let Silas and Dante have their way with her.

"Don't worry, we'll be gentle." Dante winked.

Jadis tried to quell her feelings, but the jealousy consumed her and she let out a guttural, dangerous snarl and bared her canines.

"Jadis—stop!" Aria demanded.

"Shhh—" Silas whispered. "Calm, baby, soon enough you won't feel like this. We'll make the mating quick."

"We need to do this now," Dante stated privately.

"Yes, I give Jadis two minutes before she lunges for Aria," Silas replied.

Aiden cupped Jadis's face in his hand and turned her head, pulling her attention to him and away from Aria.

Her eyes met Aiden's and the nervous anticipation of mating him subtly overtook the overwhelming jealously she was feeling.

He pulled her from Silas and Dante and rested his heavy body on hers, pinning her beneath him, and his mouth fell to hers.

Dante moved in next to Aria and pinned her body between himself and Silas.

"It's okay, Aria. All you have to do is say yes. Dante and I will do the rest," Silas said.

"Yes," she whispered.

"Give me your vein," Silas requested.

She reluctantly turned her head and closed her eyes. Silas sank his canines deep into her flesh, and her sweet, warm blood pooled into his mouth. After taking enough to create the bond, he released his grip. "Take my vein."

The power flowing within Silas's blood was like nothing she had ever felt. *I feel as though I'm being offered a forbidden sip of cruor from the devil's chalice.*

"Take your other mate," Silas whispered. He pulled his neck away and moved to the side and let Dante take over.

Aiden scooted Jadis away from Silas, Dante, and Aria. It was time he took what should have been his all along. After everything that had happened, this was the last thing he had ever expected, and the anticipation was killing him. *"You don't know how long I have wanted this,"* he said telepathically.

Jadis looked into his eyes and felt calm for the first time since making this decision. *I've never understood why he didn't make a move on me the entire time we slept in the same bed.*

Aiden read her thoughts and answered. *"Bain cloaked me. I wanted to take your body more than you can ever imagine,"* he admitted. *"Can you see the chains I've carried for you? The ones that have bound me to you all these days and nights? I can finally put them down. I should have never walked out that door and I will never let you go again."*

"I know and you're right, you should have never walked out. I lay in that empty bed in tears all night. When you said goodbye and tossed my bag on the bed, I felt it in my soul."

"I know, baby, and I will make it up to you for the rest of my life. The night you left, I felt so tormented without you by my side. I searched endlessly for you. You have to know that."

"Aiden, you need to know I would never give up one second of my time with Silas and Dante. I love them with all that I am."

"That's obvious. You and I mating will not change that and I will do nothing to disrespect your mating."

The soft warmth of his tongue lit her body on fire. *By the gods, I want him.* She felt the nervous desperation pool between her legs.

Aiden pulled his mouth from hers and peered into her eyes. "I've sure missed my bunkmate."

Jadis chuckled. "As have I."

"Say it, baby, agree to become my mate. I don't want to wait one more fucking minute."

"I agree, Aiden." She turned her head, exposing her vein. The force of his bite and the depth in which his canines sank into her flesh forced her to let out a pain-filled gasp.

He savored every drop and could barely contain himself when the sweet hint of Jasmine caressed his tongue. After he took enough to complete the bond, he reluctantly let go, struggling to contain his arousal.

Jadis finally understood why Silas suggested this. *My own jealously toward Aria scared me. I can't imagine how Silas and Dante felt.*

"Take my vein, baby." Aiden turned his head, and he felt the stabbing pain from her eight canines.

He tastes just like he smells, musky, earthy, and powerful.

After she finished, he rested on top of her and took her mouth to his again. "You are now mine. Say it," he demanded.

Her mind became a pool of dizzying emotions as his blood pumped through her veins with each heavy beat of her heart. "I am yours, Aiden."

He reveled in the taste of her and the warmth of her tongue. *I now own her. She is mine and nothing, no one, will ever separate us again.* He loved her more than he would ever have dared to admit before tonight.

CHAPTER 16

After they mated, Aiden, Silas, and Dante sat up and repositioned Aria and Jadis onto the pillows between them. As they waited for the girls' bodies to complete the bond, they conversed amongst themselves while Jadis and Aria slept peacefully.

"This is an unexpected turn of events, no pun intended," Dante joked.

"I hadn't realized how much Jadis would spin my life upside down," Silas replied.

"Shit, I never, for one minute, expected to be in bed with the two of you. Who would have ever thought this would happen?" Aiden replied.

"Aiden, you realize you've just mated an aphrodisiac laced with venom?" Silas chuckled.

Aiden tilted his glass toward Silas and Dante. "I know exactly who I mated. I've gone a few rounds with her, in case you've forgotten."

"That you have." Dante laughed. "What's your brother going to think?"

"Can you imagine that conversation?" Aiden chuckled.

Jadis opened her eyes and looked around. She rubbed her face, trying to wipe the sleep from her mind. Aiden's blood was more powerful than she had anticipated.

"Hi, baby, how are you feeling?" Silas asked.

"A bit foggy. Otherwise I feel great."

Dante nodded at Aiden. "Your mate is awake."

Aiden's smile lit up the room as he held his hand out.

Jadis slid over Dante, and he and Aiden lifted her over Aria so they didn't disturb her.

Aiden pulled her into his body and she straddled his lap and wrapped her arms around his neck and their tongues met in a gentle lover's tangle.

He pulled her head back and stared into her eyes. "You're mine."

She smiled and rested her face in the crook of his neck. "And you're mine," she whispered before she dozed off in his arms.

Jadis felt Aria gently rustle next to her, and she woke, only to realize she had fallen asleep on top of Aiden. She turned her head toward Aria.

"Aria, how do you feel?" Dante asked.

"Tired and a little out of sorts."

"That's normal. It's from the power of our blood combined," Silas said.

"So what happens now?" Aria asked, looking at Aiden.

"If you're asking, I have a few ideas." Aiden winked.

Aria looked over at Silas and Dante, who also had a *I want to fuck look*. Her face immediately turned a warm pink.

Jadis chuckled in response. "So, where's the bruja with the crack knives? I don't know this shy vampire."

Aria also chuckled as she rolled onto her back and rested her arm behind her head. "I don't have them on me right now if you hadn't noticed. I think what I am is thirsty."

"I have something for that," Silas replied jokingly.

She wasn't quite ready to go that far with them; she had only mated them in order to protect Aiden. She sat up and looked down at Aiden and smiled.

Aiden patted Jadis's naked butt, and she knew he wanted to accommodate Aria. She crawled off him and Dante reached over and pulled her back in between himself and Silas, as always.

Aiden reached over and pulled Aria into his body.

Jadis noticed the entire bed was round now. "What the hell? When did that happen?"

"Well, shit, that's new. Dante, I assume it was you?" Aria asked.

"Yes, now that we'll have five of us in bed together, we thought this would accommodate us better."

"How long have Aria and I been asleep?"

"You slept through the night and all day," Silas answered.

"So how does this work?" Aria asked, not sure what to do at this point.

"You do whatever you want, as Dante and I told Jadis on our first night together. The two of you will always choose who to be with and when. Aiden will also be the one to make the final decision when it comes to you. Dante and I split that decision when it comes to Jadis."

Jadis rolled her eyes as far back as they would go. "You have no idea what you have gotten yourself into, Aria." She chuckled.

"How about we show them?" Dante replied.

"I'm all in." Aiden looked at Jadis and spoke telepathically. *"Do you realize how badly I want to take your ass right now?"*

"And I you, milord." She could feel the burning desire she had for Aiden, her mate.

"I have a little something on my mind," Aiden answered aloud.

"I believe we all want the same thing. Shall we play under the moon with our new mates?" Silas flicked his wrist and a dark waltz began playing in the background as he, Dante, and Aiden repositioned the girls' bodies.

Jadis's pulse raced with the anticipation of having sex with Aiden for the first time.

Aiden laid Aria on her back and cupped her breast in his hand. He gently massaged it and slipped her his tongue.

Dante picked Jadis's body up and moved her to the middle of the bed and shoved his tongue into her mouth before releasing her to Silas.

Aiden looked at Dante, who nodded in agreement and switched places with him.

Silas pulled back and let Aiden move in, who took her mouth with his and the soft warmth of their tongues rolled together.

Aiden let up, and Silas slid his face next to hers and nipped her ear. "I'm going to leave you to your new mate, but I'll be back."

Jadis smiled nervously and nodded in agreement.

"I finally have you and best of all, I have you naked," Aiden stated after Silas moved to Aria.

"A little bit naughty is a whole lot nice. Show me what you got," she whispered.

"Baby." Aiden chuckled. "I have every intention of showing you."

He settled in between her legs and began teasing her nub with the tip of his hard shaft and he could feel her pulse quicken, as well as the desire she had for him.

"By the gods, I want you," she mumbled.

He teased her sex with his fingers before sliding them deep into her wet core. He moved them in and out as he rubbed her nub with his thumb; all the while his tongue rolled with hers. He moved down her body and suckled the hard pink bud like he had wanted so many times before. He then moved up and licked the throbbing pulse in her neck. "I am going to take my time with you. Not only do I want you begging, I think I need another taste."

He turned her head to the side, and the harsh pricks were as erotic as they were painful, and she felt the liquid pool between her legs.

He released her throat and offered his vein. The stab he felt from her double set of canines nearly undid him. "Fuck me," he snarled as she continued to feed.

Dante and Silas lay next to Aria, each taking turns claiming the soft warmth of her tongue. After a few moments, another need rose, so Dante, rolled beneath her and pulled her body on top of his.

Silas moved behind her and lifted her hips and teased her wet opening with his tip. He could feel her trembling and listened to her nervous thoughts, which only heightened his arousal. Slowly, he slid his fingers into her warm, wet core.

Aria cupped her fist tighter around Dante's enormous shaft and rubbed her hand up and down, following the movements of her mouth.

She never imagined how much she would want them both, sexually, and never thought for a moment mating them would make her desire them so deeply.

"The mating is powerful," Silas replied to her thoughts in only a rumble.

Aria tried to breathe calmly, but her body had other ideas.

Silas moved back and Dante pulled Aria's head off his shaft, knowing Silas wanted to trade places.

Silas lay on his back and pulled Aria on top of his body and pushed her down. Aria stopped to tease both his nipples with her tongue before moving lower. She wrapped his shaft in her hand and massaged it with a firm grip, using the wetness of her mouth. He let out a deep-throated groan and grabbed the back of her head, moving it up and down as she took as much of him as she could.

"Damn," he moaned.

Dante reveled in her anxious anticipation. He placed his hand on her back and slid it up to her shoulder, ready to dominate her from behind. He thrust his hips forward, which forced Aria to pull Silas's shaft from her mouth as she gasped.

Aiden could feel her arousal surface and pulled his fingers from her core.

"Aiden, don't stop," she begged.

"Not yet, baby." He kissed his way down her body and flicked his tongue over her pink buds before trailing it down her stomach until he was in between her legs.

Aiden glanced up and could see the desperation on her face and in her eyes as she peered down at him. He pushed her knees apart and sucked her sex into his mouth and swirled his tongue around the throbbing nub.

Her moans intensified when she felt his hot breath and the wet heat of his mouth as his tongue tantalized her sex.

"Aiden—I need you inside me."

"I'm going to hurt you," he groaned.

As soon as he felt her finish, he moved up and settled between her legs and with one hard shove, he thrust himself into her body with a year's worth of pent-up tension.

She let out a guttural moan. *Shit, that hurts,* she thought, as she arched her back and moaned. She placed her hands on his hips, trying to stop him from penetrating so deeply, so quickly.

Aiden was not about to let Jadis hold him back; he gently grabbed her wrists and pinned her arms above her head with one hand. "I told you I was going to hurt you," he moaned.

He bent down, and their mouths met with another desperate, heady need. He forcefully rocked back and forth, needing to feel her pain, her pleasure, and, most of all, the desire she had for him.

"Aiden—shit," she whispered.

"Take it, baby," he groaned.

"I'm about to—," she mumbled.

"Then let me finish you off."

"Oh, damn, by the gods," she groaned.

"Holy fuck, Jadis—" As soon as he came inside her, he let out a deep-throated growl that matched her moans. He continued thrusting his hips back and forth as his shaft pulsed with its release. "Damn—I want to crawl inside you," he rumbled.

After their orgasms tore through their bodies, he fell on top of her, trying to catch his breath. "Holy hell, that ripped through my dick so hard it almost hurt." He chuckled.

"Hurt you? Shit, I thought you were going to break me." She laughed.

He could feel her heart frantically beating against his chest, as well as her heavy breathing. He finally had all he had ever desired, and it was everything he had imagined it would be.

"You intoxicate me," he whispered.

"Just a wisp of your scent turns me on," she replied.

"Do you know how much I wanted to do this to you the night you snuck out?"

"Yes, it was pretty obvious." She chuckled.

Silas looked down at Aria as her low moans vibrated his shaft, forcing his own orgasm to the surface. "Shit."

Dante felt her body pulse and clench his shaft, so he let his own orgasm flow into her core. After a few minutes, he pulled out and Aria moved up and fell on top of Silas. He placed one arm behind his head and cupped her butt cheek in his hand.

Dante plopped down on his back next to Silas and rested his arm over his stomach and looked over at Jadis, wrapped in Aiden's arms.

Aria rolled off of Silas and glanced at Jadis.

Jadis felt more than one set of eyes on her and she lifted her head and laid it back down on Aiden's chest, facing Silas, Dante, and Aria. *Damn, I'm afraid to look at them.*

Silas and Dante winked at her, letting her know everything was okay. She smiled from ear to ear and let out a sigh of relief.

Aria, Dante, and Silas sat up and scooted against the expansive headboard and adjusted the pillows behind them.

"I assume you need a real drink?" Silas asked as he handed Aria a glass.

Aiden rolled over and consumed Jadis's body beneath his. "Not sure I'm ready to let you go. Maybe we should go for round two?"

She grabbed the back of his head and pulled him in for another long-awaited kiss.

Before letting her up, he peered deep into her eyes. "I love you," he whispered.

"And I you."

"Do you have any idea how happy I am right now?"

"If it matches mine, then yes, I do." Jadis smiled.

She again looked at Silas and Dante, and Dante held his hand out. "Come here, mon amour."

Silas grabbed a blanket and tossed it over the three of them, having felt the coolness of Jadis's skin.

Aiden sat up and reached for Aria, who crawled across the bed and into his arms. He grabbed another blanket and tossed it over them and she snuggled into his warm body and pulled the blanket up.

"Why's it so cold?" Jadis asked, feeling the chill in the air.

"Apparently, you've been too busy to notice the storm that's moved in," Silas answered.

Jadis looked out the windows and watched the flashes of lightning, and listened to the rolling thunder and the relentless rain pinging off the expansive windows; not to mention the wind gusts howling outside.

"Well, shit, no wonder it's cold. Can't you do something, baby?" Jadis asked.

"I think so." Silas flicked his wrist, and the flames rose within the stone fireplace across the room. "Better, baby?"

"Yes." She smiled.

Silas placed his fist under her chin and lifted it up and stole a heartfelt kiss and Dante stole another for himself as soon as Silas pulled away.

"I don't know about you all, but I'm ready again." Silas chuckled, looking down at Jadis.

"Well, hell, let's go." Dante winked.

"I'm all in," Aiden agreed.

Jadis and Aria looked at each other and rolled their eyes.

"Shit, I can't take any more right now." Aria chuckled.

"I just need an hour." Jadis squinted her eyes at Aiden, along with a quick wink and a coy smile.

"Do you have any idea what you all just did to us?" Aria joked.

"Based on the sounds the two of you were making, yes." Silas chuckled.

Jadis's and Aria's cheeks became rosy, realizing they had been listening to the two of them moaning and groaning. Their mutual thought brought about a heap of laugher from their mates.

"Well, shit, I never would have thought the two of you would become a couple of shy little pups from one little tryst," Aiden joked.

"We must have fucked the fuckery out of them," Dante added with a hearty laugh.

"If this is all it takes to control the two of you, you're never leaving this bed," Silas joked.

Silas and Dante placed a gentle kiss on Jadis's lips before she felt them slip out of bed, waking her immediately. "Where are you two going?"

Silas bent down and kissed her forehead. "We need to meet with father," he whispered. "Go back to sleep, baby."

Aria woke to the sounds of Jadis's voice and saw Aiden standing at the edge of the bed. "Aiden, what are you doing?"

Aria and Jadis looked at each other, confused. They both felt the elusive energy swirling around their mates.

Jadis grabbed onto Silas's and Dante's wrists. "Don't buy it. What are the three of you not saying?"

Dante ran his hand over her forehead and rubbed her shoulder.

"Stop, Dante, you're not pulling your sorcery crap on me. What are the three of you doing?"

Aiden looked at Silas and Dante as he buttoned up his jeans. "You may as well tell her. She's not stupid."

Jadis turned and gave him a warm smile, and he winked with a half-cocked smile.

Silas and Dante shot him a look of warning, which he paid no attention to.

"Tell me you're not planning on going after Arkyn and Evanora," she demanded.

"Oh, hell no!" Aria snapped. She and Jadis were both sitting up on their knees, demanding an answer.

"If you go, we go," Jadis demanded.

"Not this time, my love," Silas stated sternly.

"The two of you will stay put," Dante added.

"The hell we will," Aria protested.

"As Dante and Silas said, neither of you is going back to Avenolon. We've already decided." Aiden pulled his shirt on, waiting for the backlash.

"We'll see about that," Jadis snapped.

"Listen, right now we're simply meeting with father. You two need to go back to bed or hang out, but whatever you do, you will do it here." Dante looked at Jadis and cocked his head.

The girls jumped out of bed and tossed on a T-shirt and a pair of underwear, not wanting to continue arguing buck naked.

Silas, Dante, and Aiden ignored the girls as they finished dressing, having grown tired of the argument.

"Do we still have the chamber below?" Aiden asked.

"Yes, and we'll use it if needed." Silas looked at Dante, who nodded in agreement.

"We'll just add a bigger bed." Dante chuckled as he continued to tie the laces on his leather boots.

"Do the three of you ever listen to anything but the sound of your own voices?" Jadis growled.

"Yes, the sound of your incessant disobedience," Silas grumbled.

"Jadis, let them go. I'm sure between the two of us and your Dhamphyric abilities, we can easily follow them," Aria reasoned.

"I agree." Jadis turned back to her mates, who were currently ignoring them. "Go if you will, but don't think for one minute we won't follow."

"You can't argue with a leopard while your throat is in its mouth," Aiden stated.

Jadis squinted her eyes at Aiden. "I don't even know what that means."

Silas side-eyed both Dante and Aiden. *"Shall we?"*

"Yes," Dante and Aiden answered telepathically.

The next thing Aria and Jadis knew, Silas and Aiden snatched them up, threw them over their shoulders, and headed out of the bedroom.

"Silas, put me down right now!" Jadis demanded.

"No can do, mon chéri."

"Aiden, let go of me," Aria hissed.

"Sorry, darling, not happening. If you think the two of you are going to defy us, you have another think coming," Aiden stated sternly.

Jabari, Lars, and Eden were sitting in the main parlor when they heard the commotion at the top of the stairs. They burst into a heap of laughter when they saw Silas and Aiden carrying Jadis and Aria over their shoulders.

"Apparently they aren't listening very well," Eden announced, enjoying the altercation now that he wasn't involved.

"I assume they found out we're leaving," Jabari stated.

It was clear Silas, Dante, and Aiden were taking Jadis and Aria to the sealed chamber.

Lars sat back and pulled his leg over his knee. "That didn't take long. I'm so glad I stayed."

Aria and Jadis continued to protest, which, of course, was of no use. Dante walked in front of them and flicked his wrist, and the door to the chamber opened and slammed shut behind them.

They tossed the girls onto their backs on the bed and the three of them stood at the edge, staring at them.

"You two will learn one way or another you don't make the decisions around here," Silas stated.

"Sit tight, baby, we'll let you out when we feel like it," Dante said before the three of them turned and walked out.

Aiden glanced back. "Have fun," he added as he shut the door behind him.

Aria jumped to her feet. "Jadis, open the door. I've seen what you can do."

"It's not that simple. Jabari's wizard, Mercari, helped Dante and Bain seal this room." Jadis plopped onto her back and rubbed her face.

Jadis watched Aria pull at the door, trying to break the incantation surrounding it. "Good luck. Welcome to my world. At least I have company this time."

Aria snapped her head in Jadis's direction. "Aren't you even going to at least try to get us out of here?"

"No." Jadis cracked up at the look on her face.

"What's so funny? I'm not letting them control me like this."

"Really?" Jadis replied.

Aria couldn't help but begin laughing with Jadis. "I'm questioning our decision."

Jadis couldn't have laughed harder if she tried. She was holding her stomach with one hand and wiping the tears with the other.

"Jadis, be serious, get us out of here."

"I—seriously—I can't."

"You're actually serious?" Aria asked.

"Yes."

Aria walked over and plopped on the bed and as soon as she looked at Jadis, she let out another belly laugh. Jadis was being ridiculous and her amusement was contagious.

"How long will they keep us here?" Aria asked.

"Until they decide they've put us in our place."

CHAPTER 17

Eden, Jabari, and Lars looked up as the trio appeared from around the corner.

"It looks like the three of you only lasted seventy-two hours." Eden laughed.

"Your family never ceases to amuse," Jabari replied.

"Silas is late yet again," Lars quipped.

"Are we meeting with father or not?" Silas questioned, ignoring the jabs coming their way.

"I don't know. You tell us," Lars replied.

Silas, Dante, and Aiden ignored the entertained group and headed down the hallway.

They walked into the main hall where Santiago, Sigurd, Kilark, Agaeus, and Syth were waiting.

"Well, hell, based on the bellows of laughter following the three of you, not to mention you're late, I assume you're having a few issues with your mates?" Agaeus questioned.

Silas, Dante, and Aiden took a seat, trying to ignore the incessant joking bullshit.

"We've handled them," Silas stated, sounding unamused.

"Aiden, you having fun yet?" Eden joked.

"Where's Bain?" Dante asked, ignoring the group.

"He'll be here. Apparently, he's having a hard time pulling himself from Amsi," Santiago replied.

They took their seats and Eden conjured a couple hundred dollars and tossed it onto the middle of the table. "Anyone up for a little wager? How many hours before Jadis and Aria convince their mates to take them with us?"

"I got four hundred and five hours." Jabari tossed his cash in. Everyone else tossed their money on the table and shouted out different hours.

Silas, Dante, and Aiden couldn't help but to chuckle at the absurdity of everyone's amusement at their expense.

"Laugh it up. They're not going," Dante stated.

"Tell us that in a couple of days. I think we've heard that a time or two," Eden replied.

"A time or two? Should we go all the way back to the night Jadis snuck out on you and Aiden when you told her she wasn't leaving?" Lars added.

"If you all are done, can we get back to business?" Aiden rumbled.

"We're just getting started, as are Jadis and Aria." Lars chuckled.

"What's so funny?" Bain asked as he took a seat.

"Jadis and Aria," Eden stated.

Bain held up his hand. "Say no more."

"All right, enough of the joking around," Santiago stated, trying to get his clan to focus on the matter at hand.

Aria and Jadis were joking around when they heard a gentle knock on the cell door. "What are you two doing locked in here?" Amsi asked quietly.

"Amsi," Jadis stated as she got up and waked over.

"Our mates locked us up. They're planning on going after Arkyn and Evanora," Aria explained.

Amsi chuckled, looking at Jadis and Aria on the other side of the bars. "Can't the two of you get out?"

"No," they answered in unison.

"Maybe if we work together we can open the door?" Amsi suggested.

"I doubt it, but what the hell," Jadis replied.

They grabbed each other's hands and began an incantation. A cool wind blew in behind Amsi and as she turned around, Bain and Dante were standing there, which caused Amsi to yelp.

"The three of you assume you can break our spell?" Dante questioned.

"My dear, what exactly are you doing down here?" Bain stepped forward and cocked his head.

"I was—well—" Amsi didn't have time to answer before the door opened.

"I think it's safer to keep them together, at least until we figure out what they are capable of when joining forces." Bain looked at Dante, who simply nodded in agreement.

"Wait—Bain, you're not actually going to lock me up?"

"I am, my love. I lost you once. It won't happen again." He stepped forward, causing her to step backward into the cell. He cupped her face in his hands and gently kissed her lips. "This happens when you choose to run with those two."

"Dante, you're being ridiculous. We aren't going anywhere. If all you're doing is talking about it, what's the problem?" Jadis argued.

"Mon amour, we're making sure you understand no means no."

"Dante, come on, this is stupid."

"Just a little warning, love." Dante winked.

"Welcome to the world of chains, cages, and anklets, Amsi," Jadis stated before she and Aria fell into another heap of laughter.

Amsi ignored their laughter and noticed they were only wearing T-shits and their underwear. "Care to explain your lack of clothing?"

"We didn't have time to dress before being sequestered," Aria answered.

"I see Amsi's prepared to follow those two anywhere," Lars stated. "You're not even mated yet, and she's already locked up."

"I'll leave her for thirty minutes just to prove a point," Bain answered.

"And the girls?" Jabari chuckled.

"We haven't decided yet. We know giving Jadis her freedom is tantamount to unleashing a hurricane," Silas replied.

"Good luck saying no. I can hear the arguments already," Eden joked.

"Amsi will obey me," Bain stated.

"I wouldn't be so sure. Amsi is as impetuous as they come. I don't think it will take much coaxing for my daughter to follow the girls." Kilark chuckled.

"We need to get back to business. The sooner we finish here, the sooner you all can get back to taunting your brothers," Santiago stated firmly.

After what felt like a couple of hours, the door unlocked, and the girls jumped to their feet, expecting their mates to be standing there.

Aria looked at Amsi and Jadis. "I wonder if it's a trap," Jadis joked.

"Does this mean we can leave?" Amsi asked.

"I assume so," Jadis said as she walked to the door.

As soon as they made it through the doorway, the three of them ran down the long hallway. "Run!" Jadis yelled jokingly.

They came to the main hall and peered around the corner to see if anyone was around seeing how she and Aria were in nothing more than a T-shit and their underwear.

Aria pushed Amsi toward the entrance into the main temple. "Amsi, look around. Is anyone near the stairs?"

"Push me again and I'll scream—you will have an audience." Amsi laughed as she peered around the corner. "It's clear."

They ran around the corner, up the stairs, into their bedroom, and shut the door behind them.

"I assume them locking us up was nothing more than them screwing around?" Aria stated.

"Yes," Jadis replied.

"Care to explain?" Amsi asked. "Like all of it, including why the two of you are in your underwear?"

"You know I had to *turn* Aria, but we didn't realize we would end up bonding—" Jadis began.

"Are we all in with the plan?" Jabari asked.

"Before we head back to Avenolon, there is a meeting with the Circle of Lords. I've decided Aiden and Dante will accompany myself and Jabari. You should represent the family now that the two of you are titled," Santiago said.

"I couldn't agree more," Silas replied.

Jabari nodded in response. "We leave tonight and will be back in three days' time. We'll finish our business with Arkyn and Evanora upon our return."

"Before we depart, there is just one other matter we need to attend to," Santiago added.

Silas leaned back in his chair and had a daunting feeling it had something to do with Jadis. "Speak, Father," Silas stated bluntly.

"It's about Jadis—" Before Santiago could finish his sentence, there was a resounding "No," from Silas, Dante, and Aiden.

"You need to hear the Circle out. They would not endanger her nor use her Dhamphyric abilities for their own gain should she attend the meeting with Dante and Aiden. They are well aware she faced face Abigor, Vidar, and Arkyn. She may have knowledge which will be helpful in locating the rest of Arkyn's clan. She saw the maps, after all, not to mention she was with them at all times."

"No," Silas stated.

"I'm with Silas. What makes you think the questioning wouldn't bring up unwanted memories? Jadis doesn't want to relive any of that. Do not forget what Abigor did to her," Dante added angrily.

"I understand and I have not forgotten," Santiago replied sternly.

"There is not one vampiress that will be in attendance. Her allure alone will pull our kind to her. Walking into such a large clan of Nosferatu would make her more than uncomfortable and it's not happening," Aiden agreed.

"They are our brethren and they would not disrespect her, although I understand your concern. The pull she had on many of the warriors the night of the ceremony didn't go unnoticed by any of us," Santiago admitted.

"She will not be going. There is nothing Dante and I don't already know. We have retained her memories. Every last infuriating one," Silas rumbled.

"They need to know about the dragons as well. They are going to need the protection of the Circle. This will also undoubtedly bring up questions regarding Jadis's ability to control them," Jabari added.

Silas knew Jabari was speaking the truth regarding the dragons and Jadis's powers. However, he would not change his mind. "Again, there aren't questions Dante and Aiden can't answer. I agree they will need to be informed about the dragons, but Jadis will not be in attendance."

"It's clear the three of you aren't going to waver. She is your mate, and the decision is yours," Santiago agreed.

"How is it that bitch is untouchable?" Evanora bellowed.

"You fucked up. My brother was right—you are fucking worthless!" Arkyn roared.

"I fucked up? You had Petra in the palm of your hand and couldn't keep a hold of her!" The blow from the back of his hand nearly knocked her over.

"Mind your fucking tongue. I will not tolerate your shit any more than my brother did!"

"I should have never fucking trusted you! You said you would help me."

Arkyn grabbed her by her throat, seething with anger. "Your memories are misguided. I never agreed to this. The only reason I'm here is because Abigor sent me after you when the attack happened and you somehow sucked me into the fucking portal with you. All you have done is reveal our whereabouts!"

"Strakhlivet," she yelled.

"*Strakhlivet*? I will not be called a coward by you. It was never my plan to bring Petra here," he roared into her face.

"I know damn well you want nothing more than to bed that kuchaka and I didn't hear you arguing otherwise."

"Do you not realize who's coming for us? Are you ignorant enough to think they will not come back seeking revenge?" *Silas and Dante will be back sooner rather than later and I know full well I, too, will end up paying for your catastrophic fuck-up.*

Evanora shoved him toward the entrance of the small cave. "Get out!"

Arkyn picked her up, body slammed her onto her back on the ramshackle bed, and leaned over her. "Your mind is so besieged with thoughts of revenge against Petra, you have made catastrophic mistakes. You no longer control the dragons. Petra does. And you no longer control Avenolon. The Mortem Warriors do."

Arkyn turned his hip, avoiding the blow to his crotch when Evanora tried to kick him. "So, you want to play Enchantress?"

With both hands, he grasped the low-cut neckline of her dress and tore it open. She rolled over and scrambled across the small bed on her hands and knees. Arkyn grabbed her ankle, pulled her toward him, and then flipped her over. With a quick swipe of her hand, Arkyn's head snapped to the side. "This is nothing more than an excuse to release the ache in your cock for Petra!"

"The only *ache* I feel is in my ass whenever you're in my presence," he snarled as he pulled a dagger from his waistband and placed it against her throat before dragging the sharp blade down her chest.

She lay frozen beneath his dark, surreptitious, soulless glare before she glanced down and watched as the colorful linen fell open, exposing her olive-colored flesh. He yanked away the remaining material, ripped off his shirt, and hastily untied the laces on his leather trousers straining against his cock. He shoved them off before dropping his naked body onto hers. She planted her palms on his chest to hold him back, but his mouth fell to hers.

As much as she fought and protested, a strange, familiar sensation began stirring and uncoiling like a sleeping serpent, and she could feel the warm dampness pool between her legs as she squirmed against his muscular body. The unexpected reaction thwarted her desire to continue fighting, and another, more powerful need consumed her as their tongues rolled together.

Arkyn slid his face down her body and despite the fight for dominance taking place between them, he noticed her nipples were absurdly erect. "My brother always said the only way to get you to shut your fucking mouth was to spread your legs," he rumbled.

"I will never be your whore," she mumbled.

She arched her back when she felt the heat of his breath and the warmth of his tongue dominating her nipple and his fingers penetrating her core with one harsh shove after the other. And she hated herself for wanting him, wanting Abigor.

"And yet here you are," he snarled.

Her eyes rolled into the back of her head and visions of Abigor's face replaced that of Arkyn's beneath her lids. *Your lust for Petra is what destroyed us and this will be the last time I'll pay for your sins,* she said to herself, as if speaking to Abigor.

Arkyn felt the warm, humid breeze blow through the tattered piece of material covering the cave's entrance and, for a brief moment, he smelled a subtle fragrance being carried with it. *Jasmine, if only it were you,* he thought, while muffled moans and drips of desire calmed his bitterness. He spread Evanora's legs with his knees and shoved his cock into the slickness of her core with a brutal assault.

She wrapped one arm around his body and grabbed his ass with her free hand and pulled him closer, all the while her hips matched the rhythm of his. For all the hatred she felt for Arkyn, she found herself willingly spread out beneath him like a concubine *desperate for a pittance of attention.*

With each harsh thrust, he felt another wave of wetness pool around his cock. He let out an animalistic growl as his orgasm snuck up on him. "Maïnata mi," he groaned.

Evanora cried out and mumbled unintelligible words when a riptide of ecstasy consumed her.

He fell on top of her moist body with labored breaths; after a few minutes he pulled out and rolled off of her; they quietly lay on the bed side by side, hating each other and longing for another.

Once they had finished with their meeting, they found their mates sitting in the gardens playing with Badru and Sindri.

"I see you stayed put," Silas stated.

Jadis sauntered over and poked him in the chest. "Funny—was it really necessary to lock us up in the first place?"

Silas grabbed her finger and pulled her in for a tight embrace. "Yes, just making a point."

"Point proven." Jadis chuckled.

"Mon amour," Dante smiled as he held out his hand and pulled her in. "Aiden and I need to leave tonight. There is some business we need to attend to with the Circle of Lords."

Jadis looked up at him. "Why, has something happened?"

"It's just a meeting and yes, we will discuss Arkyn and Evanora, but to put your curiosity to rest, we are not going after her—just yet." He winked.

"We've only been back for a week. Can't someone else go?"

"No, Father and Jabari thought it necessary Aiden and I attend to represent the family."

"You sure about that?"

"Yes, darling."

Jadis sighed ."I haven't seen you in what feels like months."

"I know, baby. I'd rather stay in bed with you, but business calls as does our fealty to the lords."

"I get that. I'm just going to miss you, is all."

He cupped her face in his hands and kissed her forehead. "And I you."

Aria sighed. Having been listening, she wrapped her arms around Aiden and looked up. "You're leaving for three days?"

"You'll be fine, baby, Silas will be here to look after you. You are his mate after all." He winked.

"You know he intimidates me. What if Jadis pisses him off?" she whispered.

"If the two of you can refrain from pulling any fuckery for a few days, you should be fine," Aiden replied.

Silas, Dante, and Aiden couldn't help but be amused when they saw the look on Aria's face and how Jadis sneered at Aiden and cocked her defiant head.

Aiden smacked Aria on the ass jokingly and jogged toward Jadis. "Stand fast, baby, Silas will keep an eye on you."

Aria laughed and tried to grab Aiden's arm, but he quickly dodged her grasp, grabbed Jadis, and moved her in front of him like a shield.

Silas and Dante jumped in a silly stance toward Aria and she flinched and took a few steps back, forcing everyone to laugh.

Aiden looked at Aria and winked, then tossed Jadis over his shoulder and walked away.

"Come, walk with us," Silas offered gently. He and Dante held out their elbows, and she took hold of their forearms and glanced up. Silas and Dante seemed to tower over her as they walked arm in arm.

"Do you like to ride?" Dante asked.

"Yes, is that what we're doing?"

"Yes," Silas replied. "We also want to put your mind at ease and speak to you regarding all that's transpired. The three of us know we took each other as a mate, for Jadis's and Aiden's sake as well as your own, and we have no expectations." Silas looked at Aria, reading her expression and thoughts.

"I am so glad you said that. You know I only mated the two of you to protect Aiden."

"Awe, you know you want this," Dante stated as he stretched out her arm and made a few seductive dance steps, joking around.

"Those moves serve you well in the past?" She laughed.

"Gets them every time, darling." He winked.

"Now that you've seen Dante's dance skills, we also want you to know that as your mates we will protect you with our life, but we will always stand at Jadis's side, just as you're expected to stand at Aidens."

"What you have done for your mate is admirable and you should not fear us nor cower before us. We will never take you without your permission and or your own desire. The choice will always be yours to make," Dante added.

"We are also no longer a threat to Aiden, so you can relax." Silas winked.

"Thank you. I really appreciate the two of you telling me this. I never expected for this to happen and I have no idea how it's supposed to work." Aria let out a sigh of relief, feeling relaxed around them for the first time.

They walked into the stables, and Silas and Dante grabbed their reins and bits and put them on Lucidus and Helios.

"They are magnificent." Aria rubbed Saga's face, admiring her beauty and size.

"Yes, they are." Dante smiled.

"Why are you too looking at each other like that?"

"We have a little mating gift for you," Dante replied.

Aria heard hooves behind her and turned around just as two beautiful black and white Friesian Stallions were being led into the stable.

"Are you serious?"

"Yes, Aiden told us what color to get for you and he wanted one for himself," Silas answered.

"I don't know what to say." *This means more to me than they realize.*

"You should give her a name," Silas offered while Dante put the bit in her mouth.

"Chione." She looked at them for approval.

"Mythical daughter," Dante said. "It's perfect."

"Chione it is." Silas smiled.

"I don't know how to thank you."

"No need, you deserve nothing less," Dante replied.

"Do you think Aiden would like the name Mangera?" She smiled warmly as she admired the beauty of Aiden's stallion.

"Yes," Silas agreed.

Dante picked Aria up and placed her on Chione. "Are you okay to ride bareback?" he teased, with a wink and a coy smile.

"Yes, just don't run." She chuckled a bit embarrassed by the sexual undertone.

Silas and Dante gracefully mounted Lucidus and Helios and walked out of the stables, keeping Aria between them.

Silas looked at Aria. "We would genuinely like to get to know you better. We know Jabari thinks of you as his daughter. Tell us how the two of you came together."

Aiden pulled Jadis from his shoulders and she wrapped her legs around his waist and he parted her mouth with his. He laid her down on her back on the plush, velvet cushions covering the original stone bench in the bathhouse and fell on top of her.

She suddenly felt a pang of jealously knowing Silas and Dante were alone with Aria. She never expected their bonds to be as strong as hers and Aria's.

"Je t'aime. They are only talking to her. They had asked me to give them some time with her in order to put her mind at ease. They also have a mating gift for her."

Jadis let out a sigh of relief. "Good, she needs that—what did they get her?"

"We picked out two black and white Friesian Stallions."

"She is going to love them. I wish I were there to see her face."

"As do I, but Dante and Silas wanted to make the gesture themselves to let her know they see her as a mate."

"Awe—that's perfect."

"I agree."

"I feel guilty. Aria asked me how I felt about you while we were in Avenolon."

"What did you tell her?"

"I told her the truth. At least I tried to. I told her I loved you, but that a lot had changed since you and I first met."

"Don't feel bad, darling, it's my fault she asked."

"Why?"

"I'm sure she felt my desire for you during the ceremony. No matter how hard I tried to hide it, you have never left my heart. Eden felt it, so I assume she felt something."

"So what happens now?"

"I love Aria and I will stand beside her and put my life on the line if necessary. The love I have for you is different. I suppose it has to do with all you and I have been through. You also need to know that when we're all together, I will stand at Aria's side first."

"And I will stand with Silas and Dante." She smiled nervously.

"As it should be. You don't need to be nervous, but you and I will need to walk a careful path. However, never think you aren't on my mind."

The warmth of his tongue and the desperation in his kiss turned her on immediately. "Take me," she mumbled into his mouth.

He pulled her shirt and bra over her head and cupped her breast in his hand, then bent down and suckled the pink bud. "I need to be inside you," he growled.

She removed his shirt, and the warmth of his hard chest on hers felt amazing. She ran her hands up his back, feeling the strength and density of his muscles with each movement of his perfect body.

He pulled the rest of her clothes off, admiring her slim, toned figure as he removed his own jeans. "Damn, you're perfect," he whispered, his eyes swirling with desire. He ran his hand down her waist and found her sex with his fingers as he kneeled over her and stroked her desire.

"I want you as badly now as I did then," she whispered.

He ran his cheek up the side of her face and whispered into her ear, "Bain may have put a stop to it physically, but the desire never left my mind."

She slid her hand across the back of his neck and pulled him to her while her other hand gently glided up from his butt and over his back. "I want you now." She nipped his neck, letting him know she also wanted to feed.

He turned his head and offered his vein. "Ahhh—Je t'aime," he moaned.

She released his neck and turned her head, and the sting from the sharp pricks seared through her body like a drug, and she could feel the desire swell between her legs. The rumble rising out of his chest caused her entire body to vibrate and her moans to intensify.

He could feel her heartbeat drumming against his chest as he pushed her legs apart with his before sliding his erection in. He reveled in the intensity of the moans in his ear and the way her body enveloped his shaft. "Goddamn, I can't get enough of you," he whispered.

She wrapped her arms tightly around his neck and dug her fingernails into his shoulders as their bodies moved together in unison.

Her body melted beneath his, and it wasn't long before a wave of pleasure washed over her. "God, you feel amazing," she moaned.

He could feel the swell within her core as it throbbed around his shaft, bringing about his own orgasm.

"Shit, I'm going to come," she said in a sensual whisper.

He rocked his hips and didn't slow his movements as he drove himself deeper. She clamped her legs around his hips and her orgasm rolled through her body.

"Ah fuck," he snarled.

They lay wrapped in each other's arms, not wanting to let go. After all that had happened over the last few years, they were finally together in every way.

Jadis hadn't realized she had dozed off until she heard Aiden's warm voice. "As much as I would like to stay like this forever, let's go sit in the garden for a bit before I have to leave."

"I wish you and Dante didn't have to go," she mumbled.

"I know, baby." He bent down and swept his lips across hers. "Come, darling, get up."

"If you insist," she rumbled.

"I have some good news," Aiden said.

"What is it?"

"We've decided to allow you all to accompany us to Avenolon."

"Really?"

"Really." Aiden smiled.

Aiden was sitting against a palm tree and Jadis was lying next to him with her head in his lap when they heard voices approaching. She rolled over, and Silas, Dante, and Aria were headed their way.

She sat up, and Dante and Silas held out their hands and pulled her to her feet. "How about a drink before we head out?" Dante suggested. Jadis wrapped her arms around his waist and let out a heavy sigh.

"Don't look so solemn. We'll be back before you know it, mon amour," he replied.

"Maybe, but I don't have to like it. We have a history of shit ending up being weeks or months," she stated.

"That we do." Dante chuckled.

CHAPTER 18

"Why don't we go out for a while, mon chéri? We haven't been in town for quite some time. We should have everyone join us," Silas suggested.

"Really? I'd love to. It's been so long, I forgot what it feels like."

Silas slapped her ass and laughed. "You should put some clothes on first."

"Ow—Dammit, Silas!" She grabbed his wrists and tried to pin his arms above his head. However, he flipped her body over, pinning her beneath him. "Silas, I can't breathe." She laughed.

"I like you naked beneath me. Maybe going out was not the best option after all," he teased.

"We can finish this later. Take me dancing."

"Whatever your heart desires." He jumped from the bed and pulled her with him.

They sat with Eden, Maddie, and Aria waiting for everyone to join them before heading into town.

"Jadis, may I make a suggestion?" Eden asked.

"This ought to be good."

"Can you refrain from killing anyone tonight?" he joked.

"Eden!" Maddie chuckled.

"As long as some random bitch doesn't touch my mate, it'll be fine. You all draw a lot of unwanted attention," she teased.

Silas raised an eyebrow. "We draw unwanted attention? Have you forgotten your own history?"

"Did I hear someone accuse us of *drawing unwanted attention*?" Bain asked.

Jadis turned around in Silas's lap to see Bain and Amsi joining them. "It's about time. We thought we were going to wait all night on the two of you."

Aria stood and grabbed Maddie's hand. "Can we go now?"

"Aria, stop." Maddie laughed. She about tripped and fell when Aria pulled her from Eden's lap, screwing around.

"Where are my sisters?" Jadis asked before calling them telepathically. *"Let's go, dammit!"*

"For shit's sake, have patience," Skye replied as they appeared from the gardens.

They arrived at an old stone tavern in the downtown area known as Sumtra. It was a classy upscale tavern known for its high-end beverages, unique drinks, and odd décor; it resided in a three-hundred-year-old villa. They were escorted to a private area on the large rooftop allowing them a panoramic view of the Sacré River. The colorful lights flickered amongst the palms gently swaying with the warm evening breeze, and the chatter and laughter from the bustling streets below echoed off the stone walls.

"How do you feel about mating Bain in a few weeks?" Maddie asked Amsi.

She looked at Bain and smiled. "I'm thrilled."

He squeezed her hand. "As am I, but I think there will be rules where Jadis and Aria are concerned." He chuckled.

"A lot of them." Eden laughed.

"You already put me in a cell and I had done nothing more than to go check on them." Amsi laughed.

"If I'm not mistaken, the three of you decided to see if you could break the ties that bind, so to speak," Silas replied.

"Maybe we should keep them apart and let them have supervised visitation with each other," Bain joked.

"Zip it, nanny," Jadis replied in jest.

Bain laughed aloud. "I believe my nannying days are over."

Silas placed a firm hand on his shoulder. "From painful experience, I believe you are just getting started."

Jadis poked Silas in his chest. "*Painful*, huh?"

"A big old pain in the ass is what you are," he teased as he grabbed her hand and pulled her into his body.

She slid her hand around his back and grabbed his ass. "What an ass it is." She winked.

"I like the way you think," he replied as he handed her a drink.

"Thank you, baby." She tried to take the cup from his hand and he pulled it back, joking around.

"A kiss for a drink," he said.

Maybe." She smiled coyly.

"*Maybe* I should demand a bit more," he whispered into her mouth.

"Later I'll give you all you want."

"I have every intention of taking you up on your offer."

They took a seat amongst their family and the drinks, laughter, and casual conversation were what they needed.

Bain, Agaeus, and Syth pulled the girls to the dance floor to give Eden and Silas some time alone.

Silas and Eden leaned back and watched the girls enjoying themselves.

"They seem to be intoxicated." Eden chuckled. It was apparent by their boisterous laughter and how the girls slurred their words.

"I'm a bit surprised it's affecting Jadis and Aria being that they are Nosferatu." Silas stated.

He and Eden looked at each other inquisitively before they picked up the girls' glasses and smelled them.

"Anything?" Silas asked.

"No, just alcohol." Eden looked as puzzled as Silas, who couldn't help but chuckle at the look on Eden's face.

"You know, with Jadis, anything is possible," Eden said.

Silas tilted his glass to Eden. "That it is."

The girls' lighthearted laughter and playful banter had Bain fully entertained. He grabbed Amsi's and Jadis's hands and spun them around his body before grabbing Maddie and Aria and doing the same.

"Well, aren't you just sturdy and ready? Who knew you could take so many partners at once." Amsi laughed.

"Are you suggesting we make this a family night?" Bain joked.

Aria laughed. "Jadis pulled that shit already."

"Me? You came to our bed," she teased back.

Amsi cracked up. "Whatever freaky you got going on in your bed keep it. Bain and I will not be partaking in your sexual festivities."

Skye wrapped her arms around Amsi. "Our family is your family."

"If we do, it should be with Eden and Maddie. I don't need you under the influence of those two more than you already are." Bain smiled coyly, nodding at Jadis and Aria.

"Bain, you are crazy and you will not be sharing our bed," Maddie stated firmly.

"We'll see about that," Bain teased as he grabbed Maddie's and Amsi's hands and twirled them around.

"I see things have progressed smoothly between you all," Eden said.

"Surprisingly so—Jadis has certainly proven herself to be my equal. She is a formidable opponent not only in my heart but on the battlefield as well."

"She has the heart of a lover and the tongue of a warrior." Eden tipped his glass to Silas. "I never thought I would see the day you let Aiden anywhere near Jadis, much less allow him to share your bed. Dante taking her as a mate was a shock, but Aiden?"

"Dante and Aiden hold her to the highest regard. They treat her like a queen and for the first time since finding her, I can go into battle with some sense of peace rather than dread. Should anything happen to me, she will be well taken care of, not to mention protected at all costs."

"If I'm being honest, there are times I also would like to see Maddie take another mate. We live in a dangerous world. Any one of us could be struck down."

"Have the two of you spoken about it?"

"Yes. However, talking and doing are two different things."

"Isn't that the truth? After coming so close to death in Bergelême, the only comfort I had in that dark moment when I felt the world fade was knowing Dante was taking her as his mate. Watching the tears fall from her eyes, her desperation, and her reaction to thinking I was dying almost broke me."

"I have to give you credit. You have never wavered when it comes to her. You are to be commended—in case I haven't said it."

"Don't swoon on me now, cousin."

Eden laughed and looked at the girls. "On that note, I believe we should join our mates on the dance floor," he suggested.

Santiago, Jabari, Dante, and Aiden had arrived in Athonia, where the Circle of the Lords was gathering at the palatial estate owned by Zanthos, known as Meodian. It sat along the celestial, blue coastline with a view of the Ronovia ocean before it and the lush mountainous landscape behind it.

Zanthos was the lord of his clan and a few years older than Santiago and Jabari. His father, Moneur, fought alongside Santiago's and Jabari's fathers during the Original War; Zanthos, Jabari, and Santiago were just fledglings at the time.

Moneur eventually settled his clan in Athonia after the war ended and he was appointed Reining Lord of the Circle. Moneur met his death in a battle at sea six hundred years ago with Zanthos at his side. They were defending Athonia from a rogue clan of warriors sent by Abigor's father. There was no one that wanted to put an end to Abigor and his son's reign more than Zanthos.

"Milords, welcome!" Zanthos grasped Dante's and Aiden's forearms with a warm greeting.

"Santiago, it's good to see you." He and Santiago grasped forearms and gave each other a solid pat on the back.

"And you as well," Santiago replied.

"I thought we had put Bergelême to the grave."

"It seems the old wars are springing to life once again." Santiago nodded.

"Just like the old days, and your family has quite the reputation amongst all clans."

"Yes, they do," Santiago agreed. "We can no longer ignore the inevitable. The enemies of our history have returned."

"In full force. We have lived behind the smokescreen of peace for far too long. It's time we all to join forces with you," he replied as he reached for Jabari's forearm.

"Jabari, my old friend, it's good to see you."

"And you as well. We've obtained a few spoils of war I believe you will be pleased with," Jabari stated as he looked at Dante and Aiden.

"And that would be?" Zanthos questioned.

Jabari patted his shoulder. "I will reveal all tomorrow."

Zanthos nodded. "Come, then, let us move into the main hall and begin with a drink.

Jadis looked over and Silas and Eden were making their way toward them. Silas sidestepped in her direction with one hand on his stomach and the other bent with his hand held up; he took one long step before sliding across the floor to her.

She laughed at his silly demeanor and playful steps. He slid into her body, picked her up, and spun in circles. "You're in a good mood, assassin."

"Always when I am with you—there are some days, however." He winked.

"You're ridiculous," she replied before feeling dizzy. "Silas—"

"Yes, love?"

"You should stop spinning me around."

"Someone tipping the cup a bit too much?" He chuckled.

"No—no, I don't think so. Maybe I'm lustrusterously drunk?" Jadis replied.

"*Lustrusterously*? I didn't know that was a word. Do you mean lustfully?"

"Whatever you want to call it."

"I believe our girls are tanked," Syth stated.

"I'm not drunk. I'm slightly slurred." Skye laughed.

"*Slurred*?" Ivory questioned as she stumbled over Agaeus's foot.

Bain looked at Eden and laughed. "Oh, boy."

Amsi slid her hand up Bain's stomach and walked the tips of her fingers up his chest. "I believe I want you naked."

"That sounds enticing." He grabbed the bottom of her shirt and acted as if he was going to pull it off.

She let out a squeal and grabbed his hands. "Not right here!" She bent a bit too far back and about fell over; Bain caught her and laughed all the more.

"Maddie leaned into Amsi—your ass is blocking the dance floor."

Amsi couldn't help but to laugh at Maddie cussing. "*My ass?*"

"That's a clear sign Maddie's drunk. I believe it's time to get them home." Eden chuckled.

"Eden, when have you ever wanted to leave early?" Jadis questioned.

Silas cupped her face in his hands. "Since you're all stumbling and fumbling."

"What are you saying, vampire?"

"Maybe I want to take you to bed." He winked.

"Ooo to bed?" Aria stepped closer to Silas, joking around.

Jadis looked at Aria, wrapped her arms around Silas, and snarled before laughing at the look on Aria's face.

"Jadis, stop it! You know I hate when you do that shit," she scolded.

"I see a mate fight coming," Maddie yelled.

Zanthos stood and greeted the Circle. "Milords."

"Aru—Aru—Aru," they chanted.

Zanthos took his seat at the head of the table. "There is much to discuss, and our first order of business is regarding Mercia and Aisley. It's time to deal with them,. You are all aware they helped Evanora trap Jadis, Aria, and Amsi. If there are any amongst who disagree, they will remain imprisoned for life.

"It will come as no surprise our clan chooses the blade," Santiago stated.

"I speak on behalf of my clan and we are also in agreement," Jabari replied without hesitation.

"Are there any amongst us who choose imprisonment?" Zanthos asked.

"Our mates are sacred, and I believe I speak for the rest of us. They shall meet the blade," Radul stated.

"The Circle has spoken. Mercia and Aisley have chosen their fate," Zanthos said.

Everyone was in agreement. "Aru—Aru—Aru!"

Zanthos nodded. "Very well then on to the next matter at hand. We have received word that Abigor's warriors who escaped Bergelême are regrouping."

"The Circle needs to send a unified message. We stand together as one clan and their raids will not continue nor will their threats," Santiago added.

"Where were they located?" Dante asked.

"They have a fleet of warships and have been gathering in the Black Sea east of the Balkoni Islands. We suspect Arkyn is with them," Zanthos stated.

"You've been misinformed. We know for a fact he is in Avenolon with Evanora," Santiago replied.

"You know this how?" Zanthos asked.

"He spoke to Jadis," Silas replied.

"That makes it easy for us to take the head of the snake," Radul replied.

"After which, the rest will fall," Moneur added.

"Speaking of Jadis, we would like to speak with the Dhamphyr. We would appreciate her assistance in locating the rest of his clan and we could use her in Avenolon to lure Arkyn and Evanora out of hiding."

"*Lure Arkyn and Evanora out?*" Dante questioned.

"I understand your hesitation—" Zanthos began before Aiden cut him off.

"What makes you think we would allow our mate to take a part in any of this?" Aiden asked.

Dante nodded to Aiden in agreement. "I'm curious as to your plans," Dante replied.

"Again, it's the reason we would like to at least meet with Jadis, given your permission, of course. She may know more than she realizes," Zanthos reasoned.

"We know everything that took place in Avenolon," Dante stated firmly.

"Dante—Aiden, on my honor, she will not be used for our benefit. I would like for her to at least come here to meet with us. If that is not an option, we would be prepared to travel to Seba and meet with her there," Zanthos offered.

Santiago, Jabari, Dante, and Aiden glanced at each other, knowing they needed to reveal to the Circle they had two dragon eggs in their possession.

Dante motioned for his glass to be filled. "We will send the best tracker from each clan, but we will not waver where our mate is concerned."

Zanthos casually waved his hand. "It seems we are at an impasse and I will not press the issue. I understand your desire to protect her."

Faris spoke up first. "You cannot keep the Dhamphyr hidden if she can be of service to the Circle."

A few of the other lords agreed with Faris and argued the decision as well.

"The sooner we put an end to Arkyn and Evanora, the better off all will be. If the Dhamphyr can be of any help, you should not stand in the way," another argued.

"It's not in your best interest to challenge me," Dante warned.

"Our word is all that matters. If you challenge Dante, you challenge our clan," Aiden added.

Radul held up his hand, silencing the argument. "Dante—Aiden, I have known you and your brothers for hundreds of years. We have fought many battles side by side. I can't imagine what Jadis must have endured at the hands of Abigor. I was there when Silas nearly lost his life. What she faced is unspeakable, and no one here will continue to question your decision. I stand with you."

"I understand she is your mate—" another began.

"Enough." Zanthos held up two fingers, stopping him mid-sentence. "I support Dante and Aiden's decision, as will the Circle."

Jabari nodded. "Let us not fall into a heated discussion. They will not waver, nor will I."

"We are all aware of our plans to return to Avenolon. However, there is just one minor matter we need to discuss in lieu of that." Santiago took a drink, contemplating what they were about to reveal. *I know without a doubt, once word gets out, they will want to see the dragons for themselves,* he thought.

Jabari looked at Santiago and shook his head before speaking. "This will be a moment you will not soon forget—ah, the spoils of war!"

Santiago tilted his head to Dante and Aiden and spoke privately. *"I understand your hesitation. Not only will this bring attention to Seba, it will put Jadis forefront in everyone's minds—more than she already is."*

"I am well aware," Dante replied telepathically. He then spoke aloud. "Dragons—they are alive and well and living in Avenolon. There is no other way to say it."

Everyone glanced at each other; what they were hearing was untethered to truth and reality.

"It can't be—dragons?" Radul asked. "I thought they had disappeared."

"We all thought that," Jabari stated.

"There are quite a few, in fact," Aiden added.

"Go on, I assume there is more to the story?" Zanthos questioned.

"Evanora was controlling them, one of which attacked Aria. Had Jadis not *turned* her, she would've succumbed to her wounds. Jadis also released the dragon from her bindings and could communicate with her and control her. At least that's the gist of it."

The lords sat frozen with various expressions of shock and bewilderment on their faces. No one so much as uttered a word trying to comprehend what they were being told.

"The Dhamphyr can control and speak to dragons?" Faris questioned.

"Her name is Jadis, and yes," Aided replied.

"It's not possible—on all accounts," Argur stated.

"It is possible, it is a reality, and yes, Jadis's powers are what we assumed they would be. This information will not leave this room and as a ranking member of this Circle, I'm not asking," Santiago ordered.

Zanthos held up his hand, stopping the brewing questions and defiance. "We have sworn our fealty to one another. Whatever is discussed will remain between us."

"How is it possible?" another questioned.

"After Jadis *turned* her powers increased tenfold. She's always been able to control wild creatures, so it's no surprise she can indeed control the dragons as well," Dante reasoned.

"You said she—the dragon is a female, which means she can reproduce?" another asked.

"Yes, we were there. We saw her as well as dozen others," Aiden replied.

"They will need our protection, as will Avenolon," Jabari added.

Zanthos nodded in agreement once again. "We will secure Avenolon. If word gets out, we are all aware of the consequences. Well, then Arkyn is certainly aware of their existence and he won't hesitate to exploit them."

"We will need to send a group of ranking members from each clan to Avenolon, which will now be under the control of the Circle," Zanthos ordered.

"Silas's Mortem Warriors are still there," Dante stated.

"Before we leave for Avenolon, we will choose the warriors who will accompany us and remain in Avenolon for the duration. Are we all in agreement?" Santiago asked.

"Aru—Aru—Aru," they chanted.

"There is just one more thing you need to be aware of," Dante admitted.

"What more could there possibly be?" another asked.

Aiden took a drink and chuckled to himself. "We have two dragon eggs in our possession. They were given to Jadis by the one she calls Nuri."

Once again, the silence was deafening. Not only were the mythical creatures alive, they had also been brought back to the new world.

"I assume they will be secure in Seba?" Zanthos asked.

"Yes, we have made all the arrangements," Jabari answered.

"We would like to see them," Radul replied.

"We will reveal them to the Circle. However, we don't know when they will hatch," Dante replied.

Santiago looked at Zanthos. "It has been a long couple of days and there is still much to discuss, but let us adjourn for the evening."

"We shall gather in the main parlor for drinks and enjoy the rest of the evening causally," Zanthos stated.

"Aru—Aru—Aru."

They were catching up on all the events that had taken place within the various clans, from taking new mates, births, deaths, and the ensuing battles before them and behind them. There were also a hundred friendly questions about the dragons and Jadis's connection to them.

"It seems Jadis has outdone herself." Radul chuckled.

"She has, and she never ceases to amaze us," Dante agreed.

Radul handed his glass to the barkeep and shook his head. "And how are you going to raise two dragons?"

"It'll be interesting." Aiden laughed.

"We would like to invite you and Zanthos to the oasis after they hatch," Dante offered.

Radul placed his fist on his chest. "I would be honored. And I would love to make Jadis's acquaintance again."

"It would please her to see you as well," Dante replied.

"None of us ever thought Silas would be mated, much less settled." Radul chuckled.

"She infuriates him," Aiden joked.

"Infuriates Silas? Is that right?" Dante asked jokingly. "You have certainly had your fair share of fights."

"As have you," Aiden replied.

"From what I've witnessed, she can stand toe to toe with anyone," Radul stated.

"That she can," Dante replied.

Radul took a drink and leaned against the bar. "Hearing about the dragons was certainly unexpected."

"Seeing the girls standing with Nuri will be something we will never forget," Aiden stated.

Radul noticed a feeder sneaking around a temple column. He looked at Dante and Aiden and nodded toward the girl. "We have company."

Dante rushed over and grabbed her arm and pulled her front and center. "What are you doing sneaking around like a rat?"

She yelped and held up her hand. "Milord," she stated, along with a small curtsy.

Dante looked at Aiden and Radul and spoke telepathically. *"She is up to something. We need to alert the rest. She wasn't here earlier."*

"Dante, m—may—have a-a moment of your time?"

"Not interested," Dante replied coldly. He turned his back to her ever so slightly, having felt a threat. He looked at Aiden and Radul and spoke telepathically. *"Ready yourselves. Something is off with her,"*

Aiden and Radul nodded and Radul announced telepathically to the rest of the Circle. *"Heads up, we have an issue."*

The entire crowd was staring at her from where they stood without having moved or drawn attention to themselves.

"Milord, I am not he-here offering my blood," she stuttered. "I—I—am here—" Her body trembled, not having expected to get caught. She could not complete her sentence and froze.

Dante, Aiden, and Radul looked at each other in shock at her audacity. They *turned* and set their drinks down.

"You are a brazen fool," Dante snarled.

Santiago, Jabari, Zanthos, and Aiden now had her surrounded.

"How did you get in here?" Zanthos demanded.

I can't do this, think—think—how the hell am I going to get out of this? she thought.

"Speak now," Dante demanded.

"I-I am here to give you a message," she stuttered.

Santiago took one slow step toward her. "*A message*? From whom?"

She backed away, too terrified to carry out her orders. Dante grabbed her arm and met her face to face. "Speak or I'll force it the fuck out of you."

She looked to her left, then to her right, and realized she had nowhere to run. *It wasn't supposed to happen this way! What the fuck did I agree to?* she thought.

"What *wasn't supposed to happen this way? And what did you agree to?*" Dante demanded.

She nervously eyed the crowd, knowing there was no way out. *Just tell them you agreed to be a feeder and get out,* she told herself.

Santiago cocked his head and took one step forward. "Her name is Kekat. She wants us to believe she is a feeder."

Zanthos slipped his dagger from the sheath hanging on his thigh and spun it in his hand. "The message and now," he stated menacingly, calm.

She stood terrified and trembling when she felt a strange presence in her head, urging her forward. "This is in retribution for Arkyn!" she shouted, as if unable to control herself. She reached under her flannel shirt and threw a small metallic device into the crowd and ran.

Dante grabbed the back of her shirt while Aiden lunged forward. He caught the device and tossed it toward Dante. "Dante!" he called out.

Dante shoved it into her stomach. He then wrapped her body in an energetic bubble in order to contain the blast. The entire crowd disappeared in various directions and cloaked themselves. Once the smoke and ash cleared, there was nothing left but pieces of Kekat's body and only the floor where she once stood showed any signs of damage.

Jabari looked up and noticed a chambermaid jump to her feet from where she had been crouching down in the upper hallway. Just as she darted down the hallway and around the corner, Jabari swept her off her feet and leapt over the railing. He landed in the center of the parlor, and shoved her into the middle of the crowd.

Zanthos stepped forward and low rumble rose from his chest. "Chose your words wisely, Siria."

"M-Milord, I—I d-did not know of Kekat's intensions," she cried as her body shook and the tears streamed down her face.

"Miguel take her," Zanthos demanded.

Miguel nodded and dragged her away, terrified, crying, and pleading for her life.

"Please! I beg of you—this was Kekat. I didn't know! I thought she wanted to be a feeder, is all," she wailed.

Dante rushed forward, grabbed a fistful of her hair, and snarled in her face. "You have made a grave mistake."

"How the hell did she get past the guards?" Aiden asked.

"We shall soon find out and the chambermaid will pay for her part in this," Zanthos answered.

"Silas and Eden need to be notified," Santiago stated.

"I'll inform them," Dante replied.

"Silas—"

"Dante?" Silas motioned for Eden to listen in as continued dancing with the girls.

"There's been an explosion."

"What the hell happened? Is anyone hurt?"

"No, everyone's fine. I'll explain it all, but you need to be aware it was Panya and Kali's sister, Kekat."

"Shit! You're sure you are all okay?"

"Yes. Kekat, however, is all over the place." Dante chuckled. *"Is Jadis hearing this?"*

"No, she and the girls are a little sideways," Silas replied.

"We'll be home tomorrow, but you need to secure her sisters. They either had something to do with this or they knew about it. Kekat said it was a message from Arkyn. This was treason against the Circle."

Silas glanced at Eden and Bain, who had been listening in as well. *"We'll handle them."*

"We'll be back tomorrow night," Dante said.

"We'll be waiting—be well, brother."

Silas called to Sigurd telepathically. *"Sigurd."*

"Milord?"

"There's been an explosion. Someone with ties to Arkyn sent Kekat to relay a message to the Circle. I want Kali and Panya in the cell tonight."

"Aye, Milord."

"We need to keep this to ourselves for the time being," Silas requested of Eden and Bain.

"I didn't see this coming. It never occurred to me the girls would take such drastic measures after being banished," Eden said.

"It seems Arkyn's warriors found a hole in the wall," Silas replied.

"Yes, they did," Bain agreed.

Zanthos stood before the Circle, pulled the amulet from beneath his tunic, and let it hang from his neck. "If there is anyone to be held accountable, I will take full responsibility for Kekat's acts of treason. My fealty resides with the Circle."

Santiago placed his hand on Zanthos's shoulder. "As an elder member of the Circle, I speak on behalf of us all. We will not be divided. The amulet of Nosferatu will remain around your neck. We will deal with the infiltrators as we always have."

Zanthos grasped Santiago's forearm. "Milord." He nodded.

"Aru—Aru—Aru!" the lords chanted as an acknowledgment they stood in unity with Zanthos.

Zanthos motioned for a few of his warriors to follow. "I'll take the information from her myself," he snarled.

Radul rubbed his boot across the burnt spot on the floor. "This was unexpected."

"That it was," Dante replied.

"I suppose we will have to deal with Panya and Kali tomorrow?" Jabari asked.

"I assume Silas will see to them before the sun rises," Aiden replied.

"I have no doubt." Radul laughed.

"Siria's death was swift and just," Zanthos announced as he returned.

"How did Kekat convince the girl to help her?" Santiago walked over and grasped his forearm.

"She snuck her in through the tunnels beneath the east wing. Apparently, Kekat and Siria have been sharing a bed for quite some time," Zanthos explained.

"It's always the lover," Jabari shouted.

Radul tipped his glass to Jabari in agreement. "Mortals' hearts and minds are so easily manipulated."

Zanthos stood before the crowd and raised his cup. "Warriors!" he shouted. "The enemy has come to our door in a barbarous act of treason against the Circle. We shall carry with us the blood of our ancestors when we take our leave. The darkness has yet to pass and we shall face our enemies with iron and steel!"

"Aru—Aru—Aru!"

CHAPTER 19

Kali and Panya snuck down the dimly lit alley outside of Kekat's apartment, carrying only their backpacks. They glanced up at her window but continued walking until they found a service door that was partially obscured by a dumpster. They slipped past the dumpster and stood with their backs against the metal door.

Panya pulled her black hoodie tighter around her face and clenched her fists tightly inside the pockets, doing her best to brush aside her trepidation. "I don't see any signs of movement. Should we go in?"

Kali looked at Panya and then back at the window. "I suppose so. Thaveus told us to meet him here tonight."

"It's too quiet. I don't like this at all," Panya said.

Kali looked up and down the dark and empty alley one more time. "Let's go in. If he's not there, we'll leave."

"And then what?" Panya asked, sounding worried.

"I don't know, but we can't stand here all fucking night," Kali said.

"Okay, let's go," Panya replied.

They snuck back down the alley and entered the building through the back door Kekat said she would leave unlocked. They jogged up the stairs to the third floor and rushed down the hallway to Kekat's apartment.

Panya was breathing heavily as she shoved the key into the door; they hurried into the apartment and quietly shut the door behind them.

"Thaveus?" Kali whispered harshly.

Panya pushed the hood off her head and unzipped her hoodie. "He's not here."

"Maybe something went wrong?" Kali replied, as she looked at the two empty glasses sitting on the coffee table.

They rummaged through her apartment, looking for any sign Thaveus had been there recently. As they walked into her bedroom and looked around, they noticed a couple of her dresser drawers were partially pulled out, her closet door was open, and it appeared as if she had packed in a hurry based on her clothes and the random items strewn about.

Kali glanced into the bathroom and then looked at Panya. "How long should we wait?"

"I don't know?" Panya replied as she shrugged her shoulders.

"I say we wait a half an hour. If he doesn't show, I'm out," Kali said.

They walked back into the living room, and Kali set her backpack on the table and took a seat.

Panya pulled a bottle from the cabinet and filled two glasses, and handed one to Kali. "I'll never forgive myself for agreeing to this if something has happened to Kekat."

Kali took a drink and then gasped when she looked across the room and noticed a barely discernable silhouette in the corner.

"What the hell?" Panya exclaimed.

The girls jumped to their feet when Sigurd materialized and stepped forward, along with four other warriors they had never seen before. "If you're waiting for your sister, she won't be returning," Sigurd said.

"What have you done to her?" Kali threw her glass at Sigurd and it shattered against the wall when he knocked it out of his way. He rushed forward, grabbed a handful of her hair, and wrenched her head back. "Fear not lass, you will be reunited your sister sooner than later."

What the fuck was she thinking? Panya thought as she stood motionless. She was afraid to speak, afraid to move, and most of all, she was afraid of what Sigurd might do to Kali in this moment.

Sigurd shoved Kali toward his men. "Take them."

Silas, Bain, and Eden arrived back in the oasis and headed for the temple, hoping to get the girls into bed, but as they walked past the bathhouse, Aria got an idea. "Jadis."

"Aria?" Jadis replied.

"Let's go for a swim." Aria lunged for Jadis and jumped into the pool, taking her with her.

"I'm in," Amsi laughed as she pulled her shirt off over her head and tossed it at Bain's face. Skye, Ivory, and Maddie followed suit and also jumped in.

"Looks like tonight is going to end up being a family event after all." Bain chuckled as he caught her shirt.

They stood watching their mates screwing around in the pool and removing their clothes. Shirts, pants, bras, and shoes were all being tossed their way, and they caught and dodged the onslaught of wet clothing.

"We should join them," Bain suggested as he pulled his shirt off and sealed off the bathhouse.

"Well, this is enticing," Agaeus said as he and Syth removed their clothes and jumped in.

"Where's my assassin?" Jadis yelled.

Silas swam up behind her and wrapped his arms around her chest. "Right here with a knife to your throat," he joked as he slid his finger across it.

She let out a yelp and splashed him in the face.

"Who's up for a game of chicken?" Aria asked.

"We're one mate short. Sigurd, where is he?" Jadis questioned.

"Around here somewhere," Silas replied. "Sigurd, come join us at the bathhouse for a game of chicken," Silas called.

Sigurd appeared, looking confused. "Milord? You want me to fetch you a chicken—and put it in the pool?"

"Not a real chicken! We are short a partner." Maddie laughed.

"I'll show you." Silas sent him a mental image of the game.

"This will be interesting," Sigurd replied, amused with the stupidity of it all. "I'm assuming you're all wearing at least your undergarments—aye?" he asked as he tossed his clothes aside.

"Yes, but tops are optional, as you can see," Eden replied.

Aria swam over to Sigurd, and he ducked under the water before appearing with her on his shoulders. "I always win, lass."

"As do I."

"Wait, there have to be rules. Jadis and Aria, you're not allowed to use you vampiriery strengths," Maddie joked.

"*Vampiriery*?" Sigurd repeated as he cocked his head. "You mean vampiric?"

"They're suffering from the effects of Avenolon," Silas explained.

"Ahh, makes sense."

They backed up into a circle with their mates on their shoulders. "Let the games begin!" Bain yelled.

They rushed into the center of the pool and the girls latched fists and fought to knock each other off their mates' shoulders. While the girls were tousling with each other, their mates were wrestling below the water, trying to pull each other off their feet.

Jadis and Aria knocked Amsi and Maddie down, and as soon as they fell, Bain and Eden lunged and tackled Silas and Sigurd, sending Jadis and Aria tumbling into the water.

After a few hours and multiple games of chicken, they retired for the night.

"It's been interesting. Not exactly the battles I'm used to, but the next time you all want a rematch, count me in," Sigurd said.

"Since Silas and Jadis are one up, a rematch is in order," Eden stated.

"We'll take you up on that," Sigurd agreed as he and Silas jumped out of the pool and pulled Jadis and Aria with them.

"Next time, lass, we shall win." Sigurd winked.

"We sure will," Aria agreed.

Jadis was resting on Silas's shoulder when she woke up, and Aria was passed out on the other side of the bed.

"Morning, mon chéri," Silas whispered.

"I feel like I'm still drunk."

"It will take a few more days, my love." Silas placed one arm behind his head as he played with her hair with the other.

Jadis lay with her arm across his chest and her bent leg across his crotch. "What should we do today, baby?" she asked.

"Whatever you'd like, darling."

"How about we take the stallions out?"

"Perfect."

"Is everything okay? I feel like there is something you're not telling me."

Silas thought momentarily before speaking, knowing how she would react when he told her about the assassination attempt.

"Silas?" She sat up on one elbow and looked down at him. He smiled and moved her hair from her face and placed it behind her ear.

"Everyone is fine, love. However, there was an explosion last night during the meeting at Zanthos's estate."

"Are you kidding me? And you're just now telling me this?"

"It's okay, darling. Dante contained the blast. No one was hurt, and last night not one of you was in any shape to hear about it."

"What the hell happened?"

"Panya and Kali's sister, Kekat, happened," he stated matter-of-factly.

Jadis flopped across Silas's body and slapped Aria's ass to wake her. "Get up!"

"What the hell, Jadis? That shit hurt!"

"Someone needs to die today."

"What are you talking about?"

"Kekat tried to kill Dante and Aiden and everyone else."

Aria sat straight up in bed. "Are you fucking kidding?"

"Wait—Silas, did you take care of them last night?" Jadis asked.

"After I finally got the two of you to bed, Dante, Aiden, and I decided to let you have a say."

"Then we go now," Jadis stated.

They jumped out of bed with Silas, dressed, and headed for the cells.

Kali and Panya jumped up and shrieked when the cell door slammed open and Silas, Jadis, and Aria appeared.

"Wha-what are you doing here, mi-milord?" Kali asked nervously enough. However, her tone was nothing short of hate-filled.

"Say nothing!" Jadis let out a guttural growl and slowly walked in their direction, with Aria at her side.

They walked in a slow circle around Kali and Panya in opposite directions. "You think you could succeed in killing our mates?" Aria questioned.

"Wait—w-we did not. We have been locked in here," Panya stuttered.

"How could we?" Kali reiterated.

"We know about Kekat's attempted assassination. Unfortunately for the two of you, her failed attempt will now result in your deaths as well," Silas stated.

"Wait, we're allowed a trial by the Circle," Kali pleaded.

Panya cried. "We didn't know, milord, pl-please!"

Silas stood blocking the exit while Jadis and Aria continued to circle them. Jadis slid her hand across Kali's stomach, making her body lurch before she ran her hand over her shoulder. She moved her hair to the other side of her neck. "There will be no redemption for someone whose soul has been marred by insanity and this IS your trial!"

"I feel your panic building—I dare you to move," Aria whispered into Panya's ear.

"We are innocent! I d-did not—"

Aria cut her off and wrapped her arm around her chest from behind.

"You may bleed red, but you will die black." Aria looked at Silas, who gave her a slight nod of approval.

She pulled a dagger from the back of her waistband and plunged it into her flank multiple times. Panya let out a deafening, pain-filled scream while Kali watched in horror.

Aria held her up as her knees buckled beneath her. "We are your absolution and what awaits your soul is far more terrifying than my blade," Aria snarled as she let her fall to the floor.

Jadis shoved Kali onto the floor next to Panya, who lay dying in a crimson pool of her own regret. "This is what happens when twisted secrets manifest and sinners are punished." Jadis held out her hand to Silas, and he tossed her his sword.

"I beg of you. Please—you don't have to do this!"

Jadis stood over Kali, watching her squirm. "When the warmth leaves your body and the cold sets in, there will be no light, no wings, no pretty things. You will bathe in the darkness of your mortal sins. Atone and I may find it in my heart to show you mercy." Jadis snarled and bared her canines. As she looked into her eyes, she could see the terror within her dilated pupils and smell the adrenaline coursing through her body.

Kali sobbed, terrified and stuttering. "I-I want to—"

Before she could finish responding, Jadis cut her off. "Too late!" She spun the sword above her head with one hand before she dropped to her knee and plunged it through her heart.

Her eyes went wide and she let out a blood-curdling scream. Jadis watched as they glossed over and listened to the rhythm of her heartbeat as it slowed; one sluggish thump after the other.

She stood up, walked over to Silas, and wrapped her arms around his waist. He took his sword from her hand and slipped it back into the sheath on his back.

"I think I'm going to promote the two of you to executioner in arms," he joked.

Aria smiled, bent over, and used Kali's pant leg to wipe the blood off of her blade.

"I couldn't have done better myself," Sigurd stated.

Jadis looked behind Silas, and Sigurd was in the doorway. "How long have you been standing there?"

"Long enough, milady, to know one would be foolish to cross the two of you."

"Shall we?" Silas smiled and held out his hand to Aria.

Sigurd winked at Jadis. "You're gaining quite the reputation amongst our legion of Mortem. Maybe one day you may join us, lass. Unless of course *it's too late*?"

They joined the rest of their family, who were already sitting in the garden enjoying the warmth of the mid-morning sun, while Maddie, Skye, Ivory, and Amsi ate breakfast.

Eden stood and greeted them and nodded in approval toward Aria. "Well done, Aria. I heard how efficient you and Jadis were."

Aria smiled and took a seat next to Skye.

He walked over and placed his hands on Jadis's shoulders. "You are like a snake shedding her skin, only what emerges is anyone's guess." He winked. "I believe we would all choose to stand beside you in battle rather than before you."

"Thank you, Eden." Jadis smiled.

Eden kissed her cheek. "You are becoming quite the warrior."

"Sooo—no more headaches?" she teased.

"I wouldn't go that far, baby girl." He chuckled.

"I think it's time to put this all to rest and take the stallions out," Silas offered.

"Shall we?" Bain stood and held his hand out to Amsi.

"What are we going to ride?" she asked as she took Bain's hand in hers.

"Dante and Aiden won't be back until later. We can ride Helios and Mangera."

"I don't know if I can control either of them. They are huge," Amsi stated.

"It'll be fine, darling."

"It will be when she's on her ass," Jadis joked.

"I believe you were flat on your back," Silas offered.

"Oh snap." Jadis chuckled.

"Are we going to double up?" Maddie asked. "There are only five stallions."

Eden held out his hand. "We'll figure it out."

Bain and Eden moved behind Amsi and Maddie and covered their eyes with their hands and guided them into the stables.

Amsi wrapped her hands around Bain's forearms. "What are you up to now, my love?"

"You'll see, darling."

"Is it what I think it is?" Maddie asked, her excitement clear based on the tone of her voice.

They uncovered their eyes and there stood two Nisean horses and two Andalusian horses; one stud and one mare of each breed.

"Bain! They are stunning. Did you purchase these for us?"

"I did, *cariño."*

"Cariño?" Amsi questioned.

"It means darling." Bain winked. Watching everyone else riding brought back some very fond memories. I thought we should have a couple for ourselves."

"I have never seen horses like these. What breed are they?"

"They are Andalusian. They come from the Iberian Peninsula. Their ancestors have lived and been bred there for thousands of years."

"I don't know what to say." Amsi turned and wrapped her arms around Bain. "I love them."

"And I love you."

"Have you named them?"

"I thought I'd let you have the honor." He smiled.

Amsi contemplated thier names for a few minutes. "How about Mandisa for mine and Faraji for yours?"

"Perfect."

The moment Maddie saw their horses, she squealed in delight. "Eden, they're beautiful!"

"I'm with Bain. We couldn't exactly watch everyone else ride, now could we?" Eden walked her over to the horses and admired their beauty and size.

"I don't recognize their breed either," Maddie stated.

"They are Niseans, once considered a sacred breed in the Achaemenian Persians. They were the horses of royalty and are almost extinct. I bought a male and female, different genetics of course. I thought we could breed them."

"Eden, I don't know how to thank you. You never cease to amaze me."

"The look on your face is thanks enough. How about a name?"

After a brief moment of consideration Maddie smiled. "Bellus for mine and Balder for yours."

"Perfect, my love."

They admired the fresh additions, and Eden's and Maddie's Niseans were stunning; their lush, cream-colored manes and tails stood out against their muscular, chestnut-colored bodies, while Bain's and Amsi's Andalusians were a beautiful hazelnut color with coal-black, wavy manes and tails that looked as if they had been braided at one time. Each of their horses was wearing a black leather halter encrusted with diamond-shaped emerald studs.

They saddled up the horses, headed out of the stable and into the oasis. Eden and Bain stayed next to Maddie and Amsi in case they needed to grab the reins.

"A green rider on a spirited horse always ends in disaster." Maddie chuckled.

"Just hold the reins lightly and use them to guide her. Rely on your thighs to hold on, not the reins, and if you lean forward, she's going to think you want to go faster," Eden explained.

"Maddie, would you be mad if I gave her a little smack on the ass?" Jadis joked.

"Don't you even think about it," Maddie stated firmly.

"You know, Amsi, if we decide to race, your horse will follow," Aria teased.

"If you do that, I will kill you later," Amsi replied.

Silas winked at Aria. "I think we'll take it slow. There's been enough killing for today."

"Maddie, have you never ridden before?" Ivory asked.

"Not in sixty-plus years and even then I was nervous, and those horses were nothing compared to these beauties."

"Amsi, I assume you don't ride either?" Skye asked.

"I have, but I'm not a professional by any means. The last time I rode was on a small Arabian with my father years ago and he was very gentle and well trained."

"Well, this will be interesting," Skye replied.

After riding for about an hour, they walked the horses to a natural spring and let them have a drink. The spring was the size of a small lake and was surrounded by lush foliage and tall grass, while a small sandy beach separated the grass from the crystal-clear water. The horses were pawing at the water, wading in the shallows and making soft snorting sounds.

Amsi and Maddie were having a harder time controlling their horses than the rest of the family, who were seasoned riders.

"Maddie, I think you're about to go for a swim." Ivory laughed.

"Eden, help me." Maddie laughed.

"You're fine, baby. Pull the reins toward the shoreline and use your thighs to help guide her."

"I'm trying!" She laughed.

Bellus walked farther into the spring, ignoring Maddie's futile attempts to stop her. She stood in the water up to her stomach while Maddie tried lifting her legs up high enough to not have them dangling in the water. Saga had been standing near Bellus, while Jadis let her paw at the water.

"Maddie, what are you doing?" Eden questioned.

"Trying to not get drenched," Maddie stated.

"You won't control her with your knees tucked against your chest like a jester." Bain laughed.

Bellus knelt down and then rolled over. "Eden!" Maddie yelled before being submerged.

Eden jumped off his horse, leapt into the spring, and pulled Maddie out from under Bellus. He had a grip on Maddie's bicep with one hand and Bellus's reins in the other. Maddie slipped and fell into the water trying to get out; she was laughing so hard she was having trouble getting back on her feet.

"You look like a drowned rat," Skye exclaimed.

Ivory placed her hand over her stomach. "That was the funniest shit I have ever seen."

Jadis couldn't stop laughing, and Maddie turned around and splashed her in the face. "You think it's funny, do you?"

Jadis tried to lean far enough over to splash her back, but Saga swung her head to the side and bucked, and Jadis ended up sitting sideways with half her body dangling in the water.

Silas laughed, hopped off his stallion, and waded into the water to grab Saga's reins and offer Jadis a hand. "I hope one day you'll learn to keep your ass on the horse."

"Can you imagine the girls trying to ride into battle?" Bain stated.

"No. It would be a disaster," Agaeus answered.

"They can't keep their asses in the saddle on a standing horse, much less riding with one hand while wielding a sword in the other," Syth joked.

"Mon chéri, if you're ever going to be a true warrior, you need to stop falling off your horse," Silas teased.

"Maybe you should be a better teacher," she joked back.

"Jadis has an uncanny knack for tripping over her own feet," Skye replied.

"Me? I believe Maddie just went for a swim," Jadis stated.

"Don't bring me into this. I didn't fall off, she rolled over."

They made it back to the stable and a half a dozen stablemen led their horses away to wash and groom them while the clan headed to the temple to clean themselves up.

After they showered, Aria decided to take a nap while Silas went with Bain, Eden, Syth, and Agaeus to discuss Athonia.

"I'll be back later. Are you going to nap with Aria?" Silas asked.

"No, I want to groom Saga myself." She smiled.

"Of course you do," Silas replied before pulling her in for a kiss and stealing a little tongue. "Would milady allow me to walk with her?"

"Hmm, let me think about it." She walked away, joking around.

Silas grabbed her and threw her over his shoulder, and she let out a yelp.

"Are you going to carry me all the way to the stables?" She chuckled.

"H*mm, let me think about it.*"

Mag and Limi were jumping up and down, trying to reach Jadis, while Badru and Sindri were pouncing down the stairs before them.

Dante stood in the doorway of the barn, watching Jadis brush Saga's mane; she turned in his direction and cocked her head as if curious before turning back to Saga. He snuck over and wrapped his arms around her waist and pulled her in tight.

She jumped and let out a yelp.

"Hi, baby." He picked her up, and she wrapped her arms and legs around his body. "Did you just get in?"

"Yes, and I've missed you, mon amour."

"And I you, wizard."

"Standing there watching you tend to your stallion brings back old memories. You look like a proper Naserian Lady." He chuckled.

"Shall I show you how a lady greets her lord?"

"In every way, milady."

Aria was sleeping when Aiden walked into the bedroom; he undressed before crawling into the bed next to her.

Aria felt Aiden slide into the bed and she rolled over. "When did you get here?"

"We just got in."

"I missed you, baby," she whispered.

"And I you, my love."

"I can't believe Kekat blew herself up. She could've hurt or worse killed you all."

"It was nothing. Dante is quick with the hand," he replied.

"Thank the gods."

"We watched you and Jadis execute Panya and Kali. It was quite the show."

"You watched—like everyone watched?"

"No, just our clan and Zanthos, who said your tongues are sharper than your blades."

"Next time you leave, Jadis and I are coming with you.

"After your little execution, you will probably have a personal invite. It was quite impressive."

"Tell me about your meeting, other than the bomb," she joked.

"Later. I have something else on my mind."

"I'll take it."

Aiden rolled over and pinned her body beneath his before turning her head to the side. He slid his tongue across her throat and lingered there before sinking his canines into her soft flesh. He licked the trickle of blood from her neck before offering his vein to her.

As she pulled his blood into her mouth, he spread her thighs apart with his knees and she let out a moan and released his neck.

"Damn, I want you," she groaned.

Dante carried Jadis to the back of the stable and grabbed a blanket off the iron rails as he walked; he tossed it on a pile of hay before laying her down. The soft warmth of her tongue met his and his body responded.

He ran his hand up her waist and under her bra, cupping her soft breast in his hand while his thumb slid over her hardened nipple.

She pulled away, grabbed his shirt, pulled it over his head, and glanced over his muscular body. She ran her hand over his shoulders and thick biceps, admiring all that was hers.

"I hate when you have to leave me," she whispered.

He pulled her shirt over her head and reached around, unlatching her bra before tossing it aside. "If I had a choice, I would never leave."

As she unbuttoned his jeans, he sat up, straddled her, and unbuttoned her shorts. After pulling them off, he glanced up and down her body, admiring her toned thighs. He then ran his hand up and down her legs and squeezed the soft flesh.

"You are stunning."

She cupped his face in her hands and pulled it to hers.

He settled himself in between her legs and she let out a gentle moan and cupped his shaft in a tight grip.

"Goddamn, I want you," he mumbled.

"And I you." She grasped the back of his head and pulled him in for another heated kiss.

As he laid his heavy body on hers, he could feel the rapid beat of her heart thumping against his chest. He kissed and licked his way down her body, then placed his face between her legs and slid his fingers into her impatient core.

The gentle movements of his fingers matching the rhythm of his tongue forced her to release a guttural moan as she raised her hips, desperate for more.

"I needed this."

"Come for me, baby," he mumbled.

"Dante—"

"Let it go," he demanded softly. He sucked her sex harder and felt the moisture pool around his fingers.

"Damn," she growled.

He crawled back up her body, pulled her thigh over his hip, and shoved himself inside. "Ahh stercore." He grabbed her hair, pulled her head to the side, and sank his canines into the warmth of her jasmine-scented flesh.

The more he pulled her blood and the more she moaned, the faster his own need rose to the surface. He rocked back and forth, sliding in and out of her body, reveling in the heat and tightness surrounding his vein.

She glided one hand over his ass and the other around his muscular back. *He's perfect in every way, and I can't get enough of him.*

He responded to her gentle groans and drove himself farther, trying to get as deep inside her as he could.

"Oh, damn—" She put a hand on his hip to hold him back.

He pulled her hand away and pinned it above her head. "Take it all in, baby, pain is pleasure," he moaned.

"I'm going to." The sensations of her orgasm rocked her body.

"Together, baby," he growled.

He felt her tremble around his shaft, and he dropped his head next to hers and let out an animalistic growl as he pulsed inside her.

He fell on top of her, his chest rising and falling with hers. "Exactly what I needed," he whispered.

They lay wrapped in each other's arms and all she could think about was losing him.

"You will never lose me, baby."

"She could have killed you, Aiden, and anyone else that was near the blast."

"She didn't stand a chance." He chuckled.

"If I had lost you or Aiden, I would have died inside."

"Trust me, baby, we will never leave you. I'm more careful now that you are mine than I ever have been." He sat up on one elbow and looked into her swirling, sated eyes. "By the way, have I told you how amazing you and Aria were?"

"What do you mean?"

"We watched the execution by trial." He chuckled.

"You did?"

"Of course, we all did. Silas projected it to us."

She felt the warm flush of her cheeks at the mere thought of who all witnessed her and Aria killing Panya and Kali. "Like everyone?"

"Not everyone, just our clan and Zanthos."

"Good to know."

"Although we should have let the Circle watch, they too would have been proud. Zanthos said your tongues were sharper than your blades."

Jadis hadn't realized they had dozed off until the laughter of a couple of stable hands walking outside startled her. "What time is it?"

"It's about dinner time for the girls, anyway. I assume you'd like to go see Aiden."

"Yes." She smiled.

"I know he's excited to see you too," Dante said as he smacked her ass.

"What the hell?"

"Where there's a bare ass, there's a bare hand." He winked.

They made their way into the main parlor, where everyone was already sitting around with a drink. Aiden stood up and headed in Jadis's direction.

Dante let go of her hand and she leapt into Aiden's arms.

"There's my girl," he whispered.

"I missed you, baby."

"I missed you too, Je t'aime." He gave her a tight embrace, happy to have her in his arms again. He kissed her shoulder and the crook of her neck before taking her mouth to his.

While Jadis was greeting Aiden, Aria walked to Dante. "Dante." She smiled.

"Come." He smiled and pulled her in for a tight embrace.

"It's good to be home with our mates."

Aria looked up at Dante and smiled. "We're all together again."

"As it should be." He cupped her face in his hands, bent down, and kissed her forehead.

They took a seat with the rest of their family while the waitstaff brought dinner and drinks.

"The newest additions to the stables are stunning," Dante stated.

"Yes, they sure are," Aiden agreed.

Silas chuckled to himself before looking at Eden, who joined in on his amusement.

"I assume there is a story?" Aiden asked.

"There sure is," Agaeus answered.

"It seems Maddie and Jadis can't stay on their horses," Eden replied.

"Baby, again?" Dante asked.

Jadis rolled her eyes in response.

"Sort of. Maddie and Jadis took a little swim today," Syth said.

"I'll project it," Silas offered.

"I would have loved to have seen that in real time." Dante laughed.

"That is some funny shit," Aiden added.

Dante kissed the back of Jadis's hand and winked. "What else have we missed other than the girls swimming and the hangovers?"

"A chicken fight," Agaeus answered.

"A what?" Aiden asked, not sure what they meant.

"In the pool, once we got the girls back here, they weren't ready to go to bed," Silas explained.

"Not only that, but Sigurd joined us. He was Aria's partner," Jadis added.

"Sigurd? No shit?" Dante chuckled.

Aiden motioned with his hand. "Again, you need to show us."

Aiden looked at Jadis. "So, you and Silas are one up?"

"They didn't play fair. She and Aria took us all out," Ivory stated.

"They weren't supposed to use their natural strength, but try telling Jadis and Aria not to do something," Skye added.

"We're in better shape, Nosferatu or not," Jadis teased.

"Bullshit." Ivory laughed.

"Jadis, I believe you tossed Skye about five feet across the pool. That's immortal strength," Maddie replied in jest.

"As for you, Aria, you jumped off Sigurd and tackled me." Amsi laughed.

"And you screamed like a little girl," Aria joked.

Dante looked at Aiden. "It seems we are going to have to even the score."

Aiden nodded in agreement. "A rematch it is. We just need a partner for Sigurd."

"I have an idea," Jadis replied as she winked at Aiden.

"Oh shit, I think it would be better if we found him a partner," Bain suggested.

"Really? It looks like you and Amsi are hitting it off," she replied.

Bain winked at Amsi. "I can't deny that."

"Dare I ask who you have in mind so we can prepare ourselves?" Eden asked.

"Do you remember Giovanna?"

Eden cocked his head. "Yes, and I hope you're talking about a partner, not a mate. I'm not sure Sigurd has ever had relations that lasted more than a night or two."

"I don't think setting Sigurd up is in the cards, my love," Silas stated.

"It's a game of chicken," she replied as she furrowed her eyebrows in a joking manner.

Dante raised one eyebrow. "Baby, you always have ulterior motives. I highly doubt your idea is simply setting them up as partners for a game of chicken."

"I've already invited her. She'll be here in two days," Jadis admitted.

"Does that mean you won't be arguing about going with us to Avenolon?" Silas asked.

"Maybe? I'm tired of being locked up anyway," Jadis replied.

"Dante, I assume you've done something to her?" Eden asked.

Dante shook his head. "No, and this is too easy. I think there are games afoot."

Jadis and Aiden glanced at each and Aiden winked at her.

CHAPTER 20

Mag and Limi let out a low growl and Jadis, Aria, Silas, Dante, and Aiden sat straight up, their eyes darting amongst each other before lunging for the stone hearth. The girls were so excited they practically fell over each other trying to be the first to see the dragons.

Aiden and Silas grabbed Aria and Jadis and tossed them across the bed.

"What the hell?" Aria squealed.

Dante threw a pillow at Jadis's face while Aria lunged from the bed. Her foot got caught in a blanket and she tumbled to the floor in a bout of laughter. Once the girls joined their mates at the hearth, there stood two tiny dragons with small, raspy roars and gentle puffs of smoke. They stretched out their leathery, emerald wings, shook their bodies, and hopped out of the half-broken shells.

"They are beautiful—they look just like Nuri," Jadis beamed.

"Look at them." Aria reached her hand out and let them smell it. They snapped at each other and darted their heads back and forth, puffing, hissing, and screeching.

Aiden placed his hands on Jadis's shoulders and stroked them. "Dire wolves, leopards, stallions, dragons—what's next?"

"They are stunning, but this is going to be one hell of a ride." Dante chuckled.

Silas gave Dante a few hard pats on his shoulder. "Your job is just beginning. I think they're hungry."

Dante looked at Silas with an over-exaggerated eye roll before conjuring up small bits of meat. "I believe this is a family affair," he stated as he tossed everyone a piece of meat.

They each took turns feeding them, and it wasn't long before they seemed to be sated and sleepy. Their eyelids fluttered before covering their brilliant, garnet and emerald infused irises.

Jadis looked at Dante and smiled. "Baby, they need a bigger nest."

He wrapped one arm around her chest and she held on to his forearm while he waved his other hand. A large round nest appeared in the center of the hearth. "That should do."

Silas and Aiden carefully picked them up and placed them in the nest. The dragons moved in slow circles before settling down with their bodies intertwined and their pointed tails wrapped around each other.

They kneeled in front of the hearth and stared at what was once nothing more than myth and legend sleeping amongst them.

"We should call the family. They have been waiting for this," Silas suggested.

"We should throw some clothes on first," Aria replied.

Silas's words woke Bain up. *"They did?"*

"What is it, baby?" Amsi asked groggily.

"The dragons. They've hatched."

Amsi sat straight up and grabbed Bain's arm. "Really?"

They jumped from the bed and headed to see the new arrivals.

Once they entered the hallway, the others were all heading in the same direction.

"The dragons. I can't believe it," Maddie exclaimed.

They all began walking faster, joking around, trying to beat each other to the bedroom. The girls were laughing and grabbing each other, trying to slow the other down.

Amsi tripped Skye and ran ahead of her, trying to beat Maddie. "Dammit, Amsi." Skye laughed as she fell into the wall.

Bain and Eden stiff-armed Syth and Agaeus, shoving them into the railing, and jumped ahead of them before grabbing Amsi and Maddie.

"Bain, stop." Amsi chuckled as he picked her up from behind.

Eden wrapped his arms around Maddie and shoved his knees into the back of hers, forcing her to take huge steps forward.

Within minutes, there was a large commotion outside the bedroom door that sounded like a herd of animals headed their way. Their whimsical laughter and jubilant voices resonated from the other end of the hallway.

Aria looked at the door. "What the hell are they doing?"

"Apparently they're shoving each other around from the sounds of it." Aiden chuckled.

"Go figure. It must be a family trait," Jadis joked.

The door opened, and the girls rushed toward the hearth while their mates casually followed behind.

"I can't believe it," Maddie whispered.

"Unbelievable," Skye said.

Silas, Dante, Aiden, and the girls backed up and let the rest of their family move in for a closer look. They kneeled down and stared at the sleeping dragons.

"I'm not sure we are ready for this," Bain stated.

"Can I touch them?" Amsi asked.

"Of course," Silas answered.

Amsi reached out and ran her fingers down their bodies. Their skin rippled with her touch, acting as if they were being tickled. "I can't believe they are real."

The dragons stirred and lifted their sleepy heads. They tilted them in the family's direction and seemed to study them as much as they were studying the dragons.

"Damn," was all Agaeus could muster. He, too, was having a hard time believing they were real.

"I hear they've hatched," a smooth voice stated from the doorway.

They turned around to see Sigurd walking in.

"Aren't they gorgeous?" Jadis replied.

Sigurd stood in disbelief. "They are remarkable, milady."

He stood stoic as always, and it was hard to read his emotions. "What do you think, for real?" Aria asked.

"I'm not sure what to think, milady."

"Can you imagine what they are going to look like fully grown? It's scary if you ask me," Ivory admitted.

"Scary, why?" Aria asked.

"They are dragons if you hadn't noticed." Ivory chuckled.

"Nuri was very sweet," Jadis replied.

"Didn't she try to kill the three of you?" Skye asked.

"That was not her doing," Jadis replied.

"How are you going to control them?" Ivory asked no one in particular.

Jadis shrugged her shoulders. "We'll have plenty of time to learn while they grow."

"Great plan," Aiden teased.

She rolled her eyes and chuckled. "I know what I am doing."

"I beg to differ," Aria replied.

"What have we here?" Santiago asked from the doorway.

Aria smiled at Jabari. "Father, they're here."

"By the sounds of your thundering footsteps and laughter, we could only assume they have hatched," Luciana replied as she kneeled down and stared at them. "Oh, my lord, they are something else."

Santiago looked at Jadis. "If you're not prepared for this, it could be a disaster."

"It'll be fine," Silas replied.

"I sure hope so."

Luciana held her hand out to Santiago. "Come, darling."

Santiago took her hand and kneeled down beside her. "In all my years, I never thought I would see a living dragon again, much less in my home."

Luciana turned to Jadis. "Have you named them yet, dear?"

"No, not yet."

"Well, what should they be called?" Luciana questioned.

They looked amongst each other before everyone started tossing out names.

"Beyorn for the male?" Sigurd offered.

"Why, Sigurd, who would have thought?" Jadis joked.

He winked at her with a half-cocked smile and kneeled down next to Santiago.

"I like it," Silas answered.

"Beyorn it is," Dante replied. "And the female?"

After a few moments of silence, Luciana spoke, "How about Andisa?"

"Yes." Aria smiled.

"Beyorn and Andisa it is," Aiden said.

Santiago stood and looked at Jabari. "I assume the oasis is ready? We will also need to lock down the immediate area. These two little ones are going to cause quite the stir."

"It's taken care of. We have limited the access to the temple and the surrounding oasis."

"They can roam freely for about a half a mile. Bain and I will seal off the area so they can't wander any farther without running into an energetic barrier," Bain interjected.

"There will be one entrance and exit at the end of the main walk that will open to anyone coming and going. We will have it under guard at all times and sealed at sundown," Dante added.

"Good, good. And the barrier, is it up now?" Santiago asked.

"No, we'll put it up first thing in the morning," Bain replied.

"I would feel better if you sealed it tonight."

"Bain and I will get on it," Dante agreed.

"And the guards?"

Sigurd nodded at Santiago. "Only the best, milord. They will be ready at a moment's notice."

"Let's get it done then." Santiago nodded.

"Bain, we can get it done in an hour. Jabari, if you would like any additional security added, let us know."

Jabari placed his hand on Dante's shoulder. "I'll go with you. I would like to see the area for myself."

"I'll accompany you as well," Sigurd offered.

Santiago placed his hand on Luciana's lower back. "I believe it's time for us to retire for the rest of the night. Luciana and I will leave you to your dragons."

Luciana turned back around before shutting the door. "Maybe you all can keep your excitement to a dull roar." She smiled.

The girls sat on the bed while Silas, Aiden, and Eden moved some of the furniture around facing the hearth. Silas opened a large cabinet containing a wet bar in their bedroom and pulled out ten glasses; he dropped a round ice cube in each glass from the small freezer and filled them halfway with Macallan Whiskey.

"I wonder if they'll sleep through the night," Jadis questioned no one in particular.

"They're nocturnal, so I assume they will be awake all night," Silas replied as he handed her a highball glass.

"Where are you going to house them? You can't keep them in your bedroom as they grow," Eden questioned.

"I was thinking we could add a door to the back wall with a long hallway that would lead to a large enclosure," Jadis answered.

"So, you want access to the dragon's lair from your bedroom?" Skye chuckled.

"Why not?"

"Jadis, you are crazy," Ivory stated.

"Baby, we are going to have to discuss that," Silas replied.

"It's not a bad idea," Aria agreed.

Aiden cocked his head. "I'm not sure your father would appreciate us knocking a hole in the temple wall and adding an enormous enclosure on the other side."

Dante, Bain, and Sigurd returned about an hour later. "We've sealed the entire area," Dante stated.

"No one gets in, no one gets out without our knowledge. The guards are at the entrance as we speak," Sigurd added.

They headed for the wet bar and filled their glasses before taking a seat.

"Did Jadis tell you about her idea for their housing?" Amsi asked, looking between Bain and Dante.

"By the way in which you ask, I can't imagine," Bain replied as he took a seat.

"She wants you all to create a hallway between the bedroom and the dragon's lair," Amsi said.

Dante raised his eyebrows and looked at Aiden and Silas, not sure how to respond.

"Milady, do you have any idea how big that enclosure is going to be?" Sigurd wasn't really asking.

"Yes, and there is plenty of land behind the temple. Our bedroom faces the open space. It's the perfect place."

"It will take up a couple of acres," Dante offered.

"And? There's nothing back there but land," Jadis replied.

"She is right, we can keep them close at all times," Aria agreed.

Sigurd looked at Jadis and shook his head. "Milady, the ideas running wild in that head of yours."

Beyorn and Andisa stirred in their nest and opened one eye at a time. They stood up, stretched their bodies, and shook like wet dogs as they spread their wings and began flapping as if trying to fly while standing upright on their hind legs.

"Well, shit," Silas stated, sounding amused.

Syth leaned forward and placed his elbows on his knees, enthralled with the dragons.

They hopped out of the nest, reared their heads back, and let out raspy noises.

"I think they are trying to roar." Jadis chuckled.

Maddie was smiling from ear to ear. "They sound more like puppies than dragons."

They used the pointed tips of their wings to hold their balance as they took a deep breath, stretched out their necks, and tried to release a stream of fire. However, there was nothing more than small puffs of smoke.

Ivory took a sip and thought momentarily. "They're already trying to burn us alive."

"Just wait until they're fully grown. They'll burn everything to the ground," Skye joked.

They began hopping around the room, exploring their new environment; the girls got up and sat on the floor, letting Beyorn and Andisa get used to their presence.

"There's a storm stirring within them," Aiden stated.

"Yes, there is," Bain agreed.

Jadis held out her hands, and they stepped toward her. With each cautious step, their wings followed as if they were a set of walking sticks.

"They're incredible," Amsi whispered.

"They sure are," Maddie replied.

Beyorn and Andisa stopped just short of Jadis; they stretched their necks out and darted their heads back and forth, smelling the air before feeling comfortable enough to jump into her lap.

"There you go, little ones." She stroked their backs, letting them get used to her touch.

"Can I?" Maddie asked.

"Of course, you don't need to ask. They belong to us all." Jadis smiled.

Skye reached out and ran her hand along Andisa's back. "They feel like lizards."

"Their mother was as solid as stone and her scales felt like iron shields," Jadis replied.

Maddie scooted back and rested her forearm on Eden's leg. "How fast do they grow?"

Eden reached out and ran his hand along Beyorn's back. "I don't think any of us truly knows."

Andisa jumped onto Jadis's shoulder and looked at Dante and Silas, who were sitting behind her in their armchairs. They tossed them bits of meat Dante conjured. They snatched them from the air and tossed the pieces above their heads before swallowing the small chunks whole. Andisa's claws dug into her shoulder, making her wince and chuckle every time she caught the meat. Jadis pulled Andisa off, and she let out a loud screech in protest.

"What's the matter, little one?" She folded her wings to her body and held her tightly in her arms to calm her down; she let out little growls that sounded like she was purring.

Beyorn and Andisa looked at the posse and lifted their noses into the air.

"Better make sure they get along before they become the next meal," Syth teased.

"Syth!" Jadis gasped. "They will not eat them."

"Better keep them full," Maddie joked.

Silas bent over and picked up Beyorn, and Aiden stood and held his hand out to Jadis to help her up, since she still had Andisa in her arms.

They placed them in their nests and waited a few moments to make sure they settled down.

"This has been a night full of surprises," Sigurd stated.

"That is has," Silas agreed.

Sigurd headed for the door. "Until tomorrow then."

"Sigurd," Jadis called.

He stopped in the doorway and looked back. "Milady?"

"Thank you for picking the guards. I'm worried about all the attention they're going to get."

Sigurd smiled. "Think nothing of it, milady. They will be well protected. You have my word."

"Good night."

Sigurd nodded. "Sleep well, milady."

Eden stated and pulled Maddie to her feet. "I think it's time we all get some sleep. Tomorrow's going to be a long day."

They were sitting around in the main parlor when Jadis looked at her girls and then at Silas. "Silas, will you ask Sigurd to join us?" Jadis asked.

"Here we go," he replied before reaching out. *"Sigurd?"*

"Milord?"

"Come join us for a drink."

"Aye."

Shani walked in and interrupted their conversation. "Milady, you have a visitor."

The girls jumped up from their chairs and followed Shani to the door to greet Giovanna.

"I'm so glad you made it," Jadis stated, along with a hug.

"So am I. I've missed you all."

Skye and Ivory greeted her in the same manner. "It's so good to see you again," Skye said.

"It's great to be here." Giovanna smiled.

Jadis grabbed Giovanna in another tight embrace. "I can't believe you're here again."

"Neither can I. It was hell getting father to agree." She chuckled before seeing the dragons following the girls. "Wow, look at them."

"Aren't they beautiful?" Maddie replied.

"Yes. Can I touch them?"

"Sure." Jadis kneeled beside her and called them over. They hesitantly approached the girls before letting Giovanna reach out to them.

She held her hand and let them smell it and after a few moments, Andisa and Beyorn hopped away. Giovanna stood up and watched them in awe. "Never in my wildest imagination did I think I would see much less touch one."

Aria moved in and gave her a hug as well. "Sigurd is here."

"Does he know?" Giovanna asked.

"No." Maddie winked.

"Shit," Giovanna stated under her breath.

"It's fine and once you get past his stoic demeanor, he's surprisingly fun." Maddie chuckled.

"He was very polite when we were dancing, although he seems quite austere."

"I don't know how to describe him." Jadis chuckled.

Aria reached for her hand. "Come, we just sat down for pre-dinner drinks."

"Are you hungry?" Amsi asked.

"Yes, and thirsty."

"Perfect," Amsi replied.

The girls walked back to the main parlor while an attendant took Giovanna's bags to the room Aria had arranged for her.

Jadis could feel Giovanna's trepidation. "Don't be nervous."

Giovanna looked at her and smiled. "I'm fine."

Their mates stood to greet Giovanna as she strolled over to the table with the girls.

Sigurd pulled an empty chair out for her and nodded. "Giovanna, it's nice to see you again."

"And you as well." She took a seat and looked up at him. "Thank you."

"Aye," he replied.

"Darling, this could be a disaster," Silas stated privately.

Jadis looked at him and smiled. *"They spent some time together during the ball. They're not strangers."*

"You're not talking about a dance," Dante chimed in.

"The two of you worry too much."

"Jadis, you certainly have some grand schemes," Aiden interjected.

"She's perfect for him," Aria added.

"Does this mean you've decided to stay here rather than go to Avenolon with us?" Silas asked telepathically.

"No," Jadis replied.

Silas, Dante, and Aiden side-eyed each other, having the same unrelenting feeling. *"Is Giovanna aware she will be here alone for a few days?"* Silas asked.

"Let us worry about Giovanna," Jadis replied.

"If you're up to what I think you are, it's out of the question," Silas said.

"What have you been up to?" Giovanna asked, interrupting their telepathic conversation.

"Just riding our stallions and hanging out," Jadis replied.

"There was a game of chicken the other night," Aria said.

"Really? You all played chicken? Sigurd, you too?" Giovanna couldn't fathom the girls' mates playing such a mortal game, especially Sigurd.

"Aye, Aria and I lived to fight another day," he joked.

"You can be Sigurd's partner this time." Jadis winked.

Sigurd cocked his head at Jadis and raised his eyebrows, realizing why Giovanna was there.

"Something you would like to fill me in on, milady?"

Jadis shrugged her shoulders and looked at Giovanna, who was squinting her eyes at her, trying to hide her embarrassment.

"Well, there it is," Aiden stated aloud.

Sigurd tilted his glass toward Jadis and winked at Giovanna. "Giovanna looks like she could handle her own. We might just take you up on the offer."

One of the waitstaff approached the table and looked at Silas. "Milord, dinner is about to be served. Will you be dining here or in the main hall?"

"This is fine," Silas answered.

"Milord," he replied, with a subtle nod.

Sigurd looked at Giovanna. "I assume you're hungry after your travels?"

"Yes, it felt like an endless flight."

"And your father, Agustos, how is he?" Silas asked.

"Fine. He asked me to thank you all for allowing me to stay here."

The staff brought in dinner for the girls, and a plate of cut fruit, which was the one thing Aria and Jadis dined on, to the amusement of their mates.

"I still can't get over the two of you enjoying eating mortal food." Dante chuckled.

After dinner, they moved to the antique love seats and settees in front of the expansive fireplace. The warmth of the fire and soft glow of the flames created the perfect atmosphere for the girls to get Sigurd and Giovanna together.

CHAPTER 21

It had been a week since Giovanna had arrived and she ended up sleeping in Sigurd's bedroom on the second night.

Giovanna felt Sigurd rustle next to her, waking her up. She rolled over and wrapped her body around his.

"Good morning, lass."

"Good morning," she answered groggily.

"You're not an early riser?"

"No." She smiled.

"You know what they say about waking early?"

"The early bird gets the worm?"

Sigurd thought momentarily. "Nye, but it makes sense."

"What were you going to say?"

"Wake early if you want another man's life or land."

Giovanna laughed aloud. "I don't want another man's life or land."

"Then how about breakfast?"

"Sure."

"There's another reason to rise before breakfast." He rolled on top of her, took her mouth with his, and spread her legs apart with his knees.

Jadis rolled over and laid her head on Silas's shoulder, then reached for Dante, who was behind her. "What's on your mind, baby?" Silas asked.

"We leave for Avenolon tomorrow."

"Are you worried about it?"

"No, I was just thinking—"

Dante cut her off mid-sentence. "You *just thinking* is never a good thing."

"Ha-ha-ha-ha," Jadis stated, mocking Dante. "I think we should bring Giovanna with us."

Silas raised his eyebrows. "What the hell are you thinking?"

"Do any of us ever know what goes on in that head of hers?" Aiden chuckled.

Dante rolled onto his back and placed his arm behind his head. "I told you!"

"Baby, that's a terrible idea. Agustos would lose his shit," Silas offered.

Jadis plopped her body across Dante and Aiden so she could slap Aria's ass, but Aiden smacked her ass cheek as soon as she plopped on top of him. "I'm with Silas on this one."

"Shit, Aiden!" She chuckled as she landed a hard smack on Aria's ass.

"Dammit, Jadis, stop doing that! A simple 'hey, get up' would be great!"

"Back me up here."

Aria rolled over and laid her head on Aiden's chest. "Back you up on what?"

"Taking Giovanna to Avenolon with us."

"I agree. Now can I go back to sleep?"

"You two don't get to *agree* to this and think it's going to happen," Dante replied.

"Sure, we can," Jadis answered.

"*Sure, you can't,*" Silas replied.

"What's so wrong with it?"

"There's a lot wrong with it," Aiden interjected.

"It's not like she is in danger with all of you around, not to mention Sigurd."

Silas moved his arm behind his head and repositioned Jadis's body between his and Dante's. "First off, you're lucky they hit it off. Secondly, I don't think Sigurd would appreciate the distraction—shall I continue?"

"Nope, because Aria and I already decided."

"We have *decided* nothing, mon amour," Dante rumbled.

"We will see about that. This is a family affair, lest you forget," Jadis joked.

"*A family affair*? I'll show you *a family affair*," Dante teased. He and Silas rolled over and tossed Jadis on her back, and Aiden repositioned Aria beneath his body.

Giovanna and Sigurd were already sitting in the garden with a pitcher full of mimosas. "What are you doing out here so early?" Jadis asked as she approached the table.

"Sigurd thinks it's a good idea to wake with the sunrise." She chuckled.

"Aye, and my lass here would sleep until the roosters called it a day."

Silas filled their glasses as they took a seat with them. "Jadis and Aria would sleep all day if we let them."

Jadis squinted her eyes in jest. "Let us? You're always telling us to go back to sleep."

"You're not wrong. It's the only time our minds are at ease," Aiden replied.

Aria and Jadis refrained from arguing any further, not wanting to disrupt the opportunity to ask about Giovanna.

"Why so quiet?" Eden asked as he sat back.

Maddie looked at Jadis, and Aria and tilted her head ever so slightly toward Eden.

Eden caught Maddie, motioning to the girls. "Okay, what are you all not saying?"

"Go ahead, tell him." Dante chuckled.

Eden waved his flute toward everyone. "I don't want to know. I'm just going to say no and save you all the trouble."

"You don't even know what it is, my love." Maddie smiled.

"Whatever it is, I'm still saying no."

Sigurd looked at Giovanna and she gave him a quick side-eye before staring at her plate, pretending to pick at the food. "Lass?"

Giovanna smiled and glanced at Jadis with pleading eyes, telling her to ask.

"We want Giovanna to go to Avenolon with us," Jadis stated boldly.

"Say that again, milady?" Sigurd asked.

"We're taking Giovanna with us," Aria replied.

"Says who?" Bain asked.

Amsi shrugged her shoulders and squeezed Bain's thigh. "*Says* us."

Bain looked at Amsi, a bit shocked; he didn't think she was bold enough yet to question his authority. "You have been around the girls for what, a couple of months and now you side with them?"

"I'm not siding with them, baby, I'm simply agreeing."

"I told you it wouldn't take long." Aiden laughed.

"Agustos would never agree," Dante added.

"My father doesn't have a say in what I do or where I go," Giovanna replied politely.

"I understand your desire to stay with the girls, but I don't think it's a good idea, not under the current circumstances," Silas reiterated.

"You don't, huh?" Jadis questioned as she sat back and took another drink.

"Jadis," Dante stated sternly.

"What?"

Aria looked at Dante. "There's no reason she can't go with us."

"There are a hundred reasons, and then some," Aiden added.

"Aye, lass, I would love for you to accompany me, but they are correct, it's not safe."

"I understand." Although Giovanna smiled, her disappointment was clear.

Sigurd found himself caught off guard by an unfamiliar feeling creeping over him. The rational side of him was telling him to deny her, while a flicker of emotion he didn't understand was telling him to take her with.

Silas chuckled to himself when he saw the look of confusion that crossed Sigurd's face.

"Milord?" Sigurd asked.

"I suppose the decision should be yours," Silas replied, offering no help at all. However, he was curious what Sigurd would decide.

As soon as Silas left the decision to Sigurd, the girls sighed and looked at each other. They weren't about to argue with Sigurd.

"What's the matter? Not one of you has anything to say? Well, isn't that the shit?" Bain laughed.

"I think hell has just frozen over," Aiden joked.

Giovanna spun the stem of her flute in her fingers, trying to come up with the nerve to argue the issue for herself, but didn't want to disrespect Sigurd, or anyone else for that matter.

Jadis sneered at Silas and squinted her eyes, realizing him leaving the decision to Sigurd was nothing more than a calculated move on his part.

Once again, the girls looked at each other, knowing someone better speak up and fast.

Giovanna sat back and felt bad Sigurd had been put on the spot. She ran her hand across his thigh and gave it a squeeze. "I'm sorry. I didn't mean for this to upset you," she said.

"You didn't upset me, lass." He placed his fist under her chin so she would look at him. "It's dangerous, is all."

"You're one of the most notorious warriors out there. You could protect me."

"Ahh shit," Silas stated telepathically to everyone but the girls and Sigurd.

The rest of them had to hide their amusement. They all knew Sigurd was about to lose his first battle.

"She just laid the damsel card on the table," Bain replied.

"Aye, I would, lass, but that's not the point."

"He's still in the game," Dante added.

"Five hundred he crumbles," Eden replied.

"I'm all in on Giovanna," Aiden stated.

"Since the girls are all going, what could it hurt? Unless, of course, you don't want me to go with you—in that case, I would understand," she said.

"Nice emotional counter," Silas stated.

"It's not that I don't want you to join me. It's a dangerous land and we are heading there to face our enemies."

"I should have asked you in private. I apologize. I didn't mean to impose."

"Uh-oh, here comes the final blow." Bain chuckled privately.

"Don't think you're imposing. That's not what I am saying."

"I just thought we—I mean—the last week has been amazing. I'm not ready to say goodbye to you, but I certainly understand." She looked down at her lap and wiped a piece of lint off, not wanting to face him; it embarrassed her they had an audience.

"And there's the death punch," Silas replied.

Sigurd pushed his chair back and reached for her hand. "Come, walk with me." As soon as they were out of sight, everyone broke out into a bout of laughter.

"I guess that means she will accompany us." Silas looked at Jadis and furrowed his eyebrows.

"The more of us that go, the safer Amsi, Aria, and I would feel," Jadis argued.

"Nice try, my love. We all know you're not afraid of anything." Dante chuckled.

"Jadis, you get into enough shit to need a squad of warriors at your side and now you're bringing your friend to Avenolon, as if we are going on a vacation," Aiden said.

Jadis motioned with her hand toward all the girls. "Hold up, we—not just me. We all decided to bring her with us."

Maddie nodded at Jadis. "It's true. We all want her to come with."

"All the more reason she shouldn't," Eden replied.

"Maddie and I are going. What's one more going to matter?" Amsi asked.

"That's different. You have been there and deserve to be there when we put an end to them," Bain replied sternly.

"What difference does that make?" Jadis chuckled.

"Sigurd may like her, but that's no reason to put her forefront in the upcoming battle with Arkyn and Evanora," Silas replied.

Jadis cocked her head at Silas. "I thought we were to hang back and let you all deal with them? Neither of them stands a chance against one of you, much less all of you."

"You're trying our patience, mon amour," Dante rumbled.

"And you mine. I know what she is capable of and the more of us there are while you are going after Arkyn and Evanora, the better off we are."

"Jadis is right. You know Giovanna is a powerful bruja. It's not like she can't hold her own," Aria argued.

"Trying to reason with you all is like pulling blood from a stone," Eden huffed.

"I could say the same about you, my love." Maddie winked.

Giovanna truly felt bad. She had no idea Silas would leave the decision to Sigurd like that. "I am sorry. I didn't mean for you to be put on the spot."

"Apologies aren't necessary, lass. I find myself torn and I don't know how to respond."

"What do you mean?"

"I'm not sure myself," he replied.

"If you don't want me to go, I am fine with it—I promise."

"It's not that. I've been thinking about asking you to stay here and wait for my return."

"Really?" she asked with a radiant smile and a sigh of relief.

"Aye, now I struggle with another decision."

"I won't try to influence you. I want you to decide what you want, no matter what you decide. If you don't want me to go, I would still be happy to wait for you."

He stopped walking and turned to face her. "You have been a surprise I wasn't ready for."

"As have you." She smiled and looked up at him.

He pulled her into his body for a heated kiss, and she wrapped her arms around him. The mere thought of him leaving her tied her into knots.

He looked down and stared into her beautiful, umber brown eyes and there was a simple truth behind them; she was falling in love with him.

"I would like for you to join me in Avenolon. However, you will do as I say."

"Wait! You really want me to go?"

"Aye, lass, I'd rather not leave you behind. It doesn't sit right."

She jumped into his arms and parted his mouth with hers before pulling back ever so slightly. "As for Silas and the rest of them, are they going to be mad? I certainly don't want to upset or anger them."

Sigurd chuckled. "They will be fine, don't give it another thought. I'm sure they're expecting the outcome." Sigurd pulled her face to his and stole another heated kiss.

After a few minutes, he pulled away. "We should head back and let them know my decision."

"You're sure about this?"

"Aye, I am."

They walked back arm in arm, chatting, and came across a group of brujas who were partying around on the bank of the Sacré River in their bikinis and sarongs. They looked at Sigurd and smiled before they began giggling and whispering to each other.

"Hey, Sigurd!" one of them yelled.

"Join us for a drink?" another called out.

Giovanna casually looked at Sigurd to see how he would respond and he nodded to them but remained emotionless, his expression never changing.

"Friends of yours?"

"Nye, they are witches from the surrounding areas, members of other covens."

"So, you don't know them?"

"Nye, lass, why do you ask?"

"I don't know? They seem to be pretty interested in you."

"Aye, pay no attention."

Giovanna chuckled to herself; his brief answers were more sincere than any long-winded explanation and she found it absolutely charming.

They dropped from the portal and landed on the stone floor in the same volcanic cavern where the girls had their first run-in with Nuri. The Mortem warriors who had remained behind greeted Silas and his clan while the girls walked toward the ledge; the only thing on their minds was Nuri.

The familiar stench of sulfur and sting in their eyes they had become all too familiar with brought back dismal memories like a tidal wave of emotional torment. It felt as if they had stepped back in time. Aria, Amsi, and Jadis looked at each other with the same expression and mutual acknowledgment of all they had suffered; it was as if part of them had remained in that cavern.

Jadis walked to the edge of the ledge and called Nuri telepathically while the girls stood behind her with bated breath.

"Are they here?" Maddie whispered.

Jadis smiled. "Yes, I can feel her. She's coming."

It wasn't long before they heard the faint, trumpet-like calls of the dragons before they could see them. They stared off into the horizon that was bathed in a wash of indigo and could see their dark silhouettes appear off in the distance.

Giovanna stood. "Holy shit, how many are there?"

"Ten—that we know of," Aria replied.

As their silhouettes took shape, their colors became more apparent. Chartreuse, crimson, and bronze bodies flew past the entrance before Nuri appeared. Their roars and grunts reminded the girls of a pack of lazy lions awaking at dusk.

Nuri let out a ground-shaking roar as she hovered before the girls; her enormous feet met the stone and her claws stretched from her toes like non-retractable, curved thorns. With each slow beat of her emerald wings, the air blew their hair back as if they were standing in blowing winds.

Once Nuri appeared, everyone in the cavern stood behind the girls in a half circle, gaping at the lethal and stunning creature before them. Nuri stretched her long neck out and ran her face up the side of Jadis's, Aria's, and Amsi's bodies, almost knocking them over.

Maddie stood in utter disbelief. "My god, they are incredible!"

Nuri let out short puffs and deep-throated growls when Jadis ran her hand over the side of her face and spoke to her telepathically.

"Hi, beautiful girl, I have something for you." Beyorn and Andisa leapt toward Nuri as if they already knew who she was. Nuri let out another gigantic roar and stepped forward. Beyorn and Andisa screeched nonstop and rubbed their bodies against the bottom of Nuri's face.

Within minutes, there were at least a dozen other dragons behind Nuri, dipping, diving, and hovering just beyond the entrance.

"Milord, I hate to interrupt, but we have something we would like to show you," Seain stated.

Silas turned around and motioned for everyone but the girls to follow him. He walked to Jadis and pulled her in for a tight embrace.

"You don't need to worry. We're going to stay here."

Silas cupped her face in his hands. "I'm leaving a few of our warriors behind, but under no circumstances are any of you to wander."

"I have already been here and I have no intention of trekking through Avenolon ever again."

Sigurd walked to Giovanna. "I need you to stay put, lass."

"I will. I promise."

They stood over the wood table, staring at a map of Avenolon and Seain pointed to a plateau beyond the volcanic mountains. "We believe Evanora and Arkyn are there. There is a small cave that has been occupied recently."

"How far is it?" Dante asked.

"A day's trek. Other than our physical strength, any other powers we're accustomed to using are limited outside this cavern," he stated.

"Evanora is also powerless out there. She'll be an easy target. Arkyn, however, will be a problem," Bain acknowledged.

"The nights are dangerous and the landscape and creatures are unforgiving. I still can't fathom the girls spent a month here alone in the wilds," Seain stated.

Dante let out a sigh. "Neither can we."

"She's not going anywhere and it will be dark soon. I say we leave at first light," Eden suggested.

Silas thought momentarily as he stared at the map. "We need to keep our mates as far away from Evanora's egregore as possible. We know they are going to try to escape and that's the only way out at this point."

"Aye, milord," Seain agreed.

Arkyn and Evanora had circled back toward the volcanic chimney. "You are such a stupid kuchka and if you would listen to me, we can make it out of here!" Arkyn hollered.

"And how—exactly how are we to do that, you imbecile? Their entire clan has arrived! We would have already been caught if we hadn't left the cave when we did!"

"I believe we can recreate the portal."

Evanora paced back and forth, knowing she shouldn't trust Arkyn. "How? They destroyed everything."

"Not everything. That's all you need to know."

"You want me to believe you intend on taking me with you? You must think I am a fucking idiot. You are the blood of your brother."

"I will take us both, and yes, in order to get the hell out of this fucking place, we need to trust each other."

"How do I trust you won't betray me?"

"The same way I have to trust you won't fucking betray me," Arkyn snarled.

"We need to get from here to the egregore and past Silas and his men. How do you fucking plan on that?"

"If we can make it to the base of the volcano, the sulfuric air should hide our scent long enough for us to remain hidden."

"And what about the guards?"

"Goddamn it, you try my patience! We can get in through the tunnels."

"So, we hide right next to the sleeping dragons and hope they don't sense us?"

"Yes, Evanora, we hide in the mouth of the volcano. I assume they will wait until the sun rises before tracking us. That's what I would do in this godforsaken place."

Evanora knew he spoke the truth but didn't trust him any more than a rat trusts a sleeping snake.

Silas and his clan crept through the small opening. It was a mid-sized cave and only the remnants of someone having been living there remained. A few pots near the fire, a wood stool, and a dirty, tattered mattress sitting on a bamboo base.

Dante looked behind the makeshift bed and noticed the chains on the floor. He kneeled down and picked them up. "Jadis, this is where Arkyn planned on keeping her."

Silas kicked a small pot into the stone wall as he assessed the surroundings.

"They couldn't have gotten far," Eden stated.

"If you were in Evanora and Arkyn's position, what would you do?" Dante asked.

Aiden walked to the mattress and stared at the worn blanket. "I would fucking run."

"The only way out of here is the egregore. Granted they would need another orb," Bain replied.

They each looked at the other with the same inquisitive expressions before the realization hit Aiden. "They've circled back."

"Even a moment in time would be long enough for them to slip through a portal should they open one," Sigurd agreed.

"Shit, the girls," Silas announced.

They took off without hesitation and headed for the cavern. Even running at full speed, it would still take them a few hours to make it back.

As they ran for the caverns, Dante looked at Silas. "Now I understand what Jadis meant when she said using her powers was tantamount to pulling them through a tar pit."

The landscape might have been dense and seemingly impenetrable, but to them it was nothing more than an obstacle to movement; for Evanora it would be a dangerous disadvantage; for Arkyn, it would be a welcome means of concealment.

Evanora and Arkyn slipped through a hidden tunnel leading from the bottom of the volcano's main chamber to just beyond the boiling pool of molten lava. It was the same passageway she had trapped Jadis, Amsi, and Aria in.

"Which way is it? It's a goddamn maze down here," Arkyn rumbled.

"If you would see fit to let me lead the way, we might fucking make it in time."

He grabbed her arm and spun her around to face him. "If you try to betray me, I will kill you myself."

She tried to wrench her arm from his grip. "Get your hands off me!"

He shoved her forward but kept a grip on her arm. "Fucking move!"

Aria noticed Jadis tilt her head and stare toward the entrance. "Jadis, what is it?"

"I don't know. Do you feel anything?"

"Like what?" Aria asked.

Amsi glanced at the girls before addressing Jadis. "Should we be concerned?"

Jadis looked at Nuri, who was curled up in her nest with Beyorn and Andisa sleeping next to her. "They look peaceful enough. Maybe I'm being paranoid."

"You didn't answer my question. If you're feeling something, say it," Aria demanded.

"Milady?" Seain asked.

Jadis looked at Seain and then back at the entrance. "Something's off."

Seain motioned with his hand, and he and his warriors pulled their swords and crept toward the entrance.

"The egregore," Jadis whispered, following along.

"Milady, I need you to stay back," Seain ordered.

"No, if that bitch is here, I am going to finish her once and for all," Jadis *turned;* the only thing on her mind was killing Evanora.

"Milady, stay here. Arkyn will be with her."

"Jadis, listen to him," Giovanna pleaded.

"If you go, I go," Aria had *turned* as well and stood next to Jadis.

Seain grabbed Jadis's arm. "I will stop you."

"Jadis, listen to him!" Amsi demanded.

"We gave our word we would not wander," Maddie scolded.

"The longer we stand here arguing, the more likely it is they will pull some bullshit," Jadis replied.

She ripped her arm from Seain's grip and headed for the egregore with Aria. However, the next thing they knew, they were in the arms of his warriors, who were restraining them.

"Hold them!" Seain ordered before he and a few others slipped through the entrance.

"Get off me," Jadis snarled.

"I have my orders, milady," Deion stated.

Jadis spun around in his arms and broke free, but he tackled her.

"Get off me!"

Aria was also trying to get away, to no avail. "Let me go!"

"Stop it! The two of you cannot face them again," Amsi yelled.

"Please, Jadis, calm down—let the warriors handle this," Maddie begged.

"Maddie, the bitch has tried to kill me too many times to count." Jadis seethed.

"I understand, I really do, but you need to let them handle this!" Maddie demanded.

"The hell I do," Jadis snarled.

Giovanna kneeled down, doing her best to quell Jadis's and Aria's fury. "Listen to us. Your mates will handle it."

Arkyn soon recognized the area. As he glanced around, he noticed a soft magenta hue glowing at the end of another passageway. "We need to get to the lava pit."

"Why? What haven't you revealed to me?"

Arkyn didn't answer as he pulled her arm and headed for the cavern. The air became thick with the pungent smell of sulfur and waves of sweltering heat radiated off the hot stone walls. They rounded another bend and a large chamber opened before them. Evanora spun her body sideways in an act of defiance the moment Arkyn released his grip.

Arkyn glanced up and down the crater and watched as the hot magma drizzled down the blackened rock each time the pit let out a gaseous burp. He pulled a stone from the wall and removed a mid-sized piece of brown material that had been bound with a fibrous chord.

It became chillingly clear to Evanora; *all this time, no matter how many times he denied it, he indeed hid the sole remaining orb, the last* remaining *connection to the portal.* "I'm curious. How many times have you tried, or should I say failed, to open the portal without me?"

After finding their way to then cavern situated below the egregore, Arkyn opened the sack and placed the pulsing orb on the floor. "Now," he demanded.

Evanora began her incantation. "Aperire abricate temporis. Peto deos superos coniungere temporis et spatii. Non seu januam prohibebere!"

The incantation served as the catalyst to combine the energies between the realms. The air waned and there was a shift in the energy surrounding them, and the moment the opening appeared, Arkyn, back handed Evanora, grabbed the orb, and jumped in.

"Arkyn, you kopele!" Evanora shouted as she jumped to her feet and ran toward him.

Arkyn's foot landed squarely in her chest, propelling her backward. Her head hit the stone wall and she tumbled to the ground.

"I'm sure your death will be a painful one," Arkyn said with a decrepit laugh.

Evanora could barely make out the blurry image of Arkyn disappearing as the portal's entrance closed behind him, as well as the sounds of the orb shattering on the ground next to her body. She tried to gather her senses while a wave of nauseating panic overcame her. Having been left to defend herself, she rolled over, stumbled to her feet, and ran back into the passageway.

The commotion woke Nuri and she lifted her head languidly and looked toward Jadis. She swung her massive head in her and Aria's direction and let out a guttural growl of warning along with a few puffs of short flame.

Deion and Elian slowly rose to their feet, backed away from Jadis and Aria, and held their hands out in front of them.

Aria and Jadis jumped to their feet and Jadis held her hands out to calm Nuri down. "It's okay, cessabi, cessabit," she stated softly.

"Jadis," Maddie whispered. She was standing against the wall with Amsi and Giovanna, terrified Nuri was going to kill Deion, and Elian.

Nuri swung her head from side to side and let out another rumble of warning.

"What the hell is going on?" Silas demanded, having entered the cavern amid what appeared to be an altercation between Jadis, Aria, Nuri, and his men.

"Milord, there's no time to explain. The egregore. We need to get there and now," Deion stated calmly, not wanting to upset Nuri any more than she already was.

They didn't hesitate, nor did they wait for an explanation. Dante mumbled under his breath when they saw the empty room and felt the waning energy.

Seain was kneeling above pieces of shattered glass when they entered. "Milords, they have escaped. We made it here as soon as possible, but it was too late."

Bain walked over and crunched some of the obsidian shards beneath his boot. "Shit!"

Jadis closed her eyes and walked to where the portal door had been and held her hands out.

"The only exit will be in the pyramid, but at least Jabari is lying in wait," Eden added.

Aiden walked over to Jadis and ran his hands down her arms. "What are you sensing, darling?"

"Evanora, she didn't make it."

"No, she didn't," Bain agreed. "I can still smell her."

"There's a passageway behind that bend," Jadis offered as she pointed toward the entrance.

They lifted their heads and took in the scent; there was still a faint trail of energy following Evanora.

Sigurd glanced at everyone standing around. "She can't be far. We can track her faster than she can run through the jungle."

Jadis walked to Silas and placed her hands on his chest. "I want to go with you."

"I'm assuming the mess we interrupted has something to do with this?" He looked at Seain for an answer.

"Aye, we had to stop them from coming here. The dragon, she reacted on behalf of Jadis and Aria, milord," Deon answered.

If looks said anything, how they stared at Aria and Jadis, words were unnecessary. Their faces were stone-cold and absent of any emotion other than the furrowed brows and dilated pupils.

Aria and Jadis took a few steps back and side-eyed each other.

Jadis pointed toward the small opening. "Evanora went that way."

"Shh—" was all that escaped Silas's mouth.

"We will deal with the two of you later," Dante growled.

"Evanora is out there. We need to go after her," Bain interrupted.

Silas looked down at Jadis and Aria. "You want your revenge?"

"Yes," they replied.

CHAPTER 22

Evanora ran barefoot through the entanglement of the jungle brush and tripped and fell more than once. She was dirty, bleeding, and terrified. She ran as far as she could before her journey abruptly came to a halt, having run to the edge of the river. "Noo—shiban kopele!" she bellowed in her native tongue. She fell to her knees and slammed her palms onto the hard dirt and dug her nails into the ground and wailed.

"That bitch, that fucking bitch!" She thought about how much she hated Abigor for fucking up so badly she was here in the first place and how much she hated Jadis for having survived, and how much she hated Arkyn for betraying her. "What a fucking fool I was," she roared as she grabbed a handful of her hair on either side of her face and fell forward onto her elbows with guttural wails of despair.

The snapping of brush behind her let her know it was the end; there would be no escape this time. Having lost the will to go on, she rose to her feet to face the inevitable.

Silas and his clan appeared from the density of trees and brush and stepped forward.

"We finally meet again," Silas snarled, baring his canines.

"This time there will be no bargains," Dante growled.

"I've brought along an acquaintance of yours," Silas offered.

Her eyes went wide when Jadis and Aria appeared from between their mates' bodies.

"Remember me?" Jadis snarled.

"You may take my life, bitch, but Arkyn has escaped. He will come for you." *Fuck Arkyn,* Evanora thought.

"You think we don't know that?" Silas asked as they pulled their swords from the sheaths on their backs and circled Evanora. They didn't want her to take the easy way out and leap to her death; her life was theirs to take.

"Arkyn won't be with the living much longer," Aiden stated.

"Silas and Aiden tossed Jadis and Aria their swords. Your death is theirs," Silas stated.

"If you spare me, I can take you to Arkyn's entire clan. I know where they are."

"Take us to Arkyn? Why the fuck would we need you?" Dante asked, not really asking.

"I know of his whereabouts."

"As do we," Eden answered.

Nuri let out a deadly roar and flew overhead along with three other dragons.

"Another acquaintance of yours," Jadis growled.

Jadis spun the sword in her hand as she and Aria approached her. "Someone once told me I would die at her feet. Looks like she will now die at mine. This is for my mates, my friends, and my own fucking life!" Jadis and Aria plunged their swords into her abdomen.

Evanora didn't feel the initial blow as her panic had set in. She felt nothing more than a burning sensation; it was as if the steel had short-circuited her brain, but it wasn't long before the searing pain hit her. She fell forward and grasped Jadis's shirt in one hand and her shoulder in the other. Jadis and Aria slid their blades from her body and watched as she slumped to the ground at their feet. Jadis cupped Evanora's hand in hers and wrenched it free from her shirt.

Evanora covered the gaping wounds with her trembling hands and began taking shallow, labored breaths as she looked up at Jadis.

For the first time, the fear in her eyes is real, Jadis thought. She felt the adrenaline surging through her veins and smelled the salty beads of moisture covering her skin.

"Someone else is here for their revenge." Jadis looked up at Nuri and nodded; she swooped down and looked as if she was grinning, revealing rows of colossus, ivory skeans.

Jadis and Aria looked at each other and couldn't help but to chuckle at the way in which Evanora screamed. Nuri began tossing her body between the other dragons before dismembering and consuming the bitch they used to refer to as the Enchantress.

"There's another body for their boneyard," Jadis said.

"Aye, lass. I have seen many an execution wrought in iron, but that was an exceptional way to give up the ghost."

Aria handed her sword to Aiden. "I bet she never saw that coming."

The fresh water in the cenote bubbled and churned before a tidal wave of water appeared; it spread out along the stone ceiling as if the pyramid was upside down.

Jabari jumped into the spinning waters and came down with his blade; although he couldn't see his enemy, he knew without a doubt the wafting form in the center was Arkyn.

Arkyn felt the cold blade cross his thigh as he headed for the entrance, barely evading the ensuing warriors. He created a wall of sand and dust so thick one couldn't see anything if it was right in front of their faces.

"Span out and strike," Jabari ordered.

"Aye!" multiple warriors shouted in unison as they gave chase.

They could feel Arkyn's presence ahead of them, but they couldn't see him. They draped their scarfs over their mouths and noses, which they had kept looped around their necks. Jabari and his warriors felt the air wane and a heard the sounds of others approaching from the distance.

Arkyn's clan members had been waiting for his arrival and had cloaked themselves beneath the desert sands using a prismatic illusion.

The clanging of metal meeting metal, deep voices shouting out orders, and the moans of the fallen pierced the air.

"Retreat!" Jabari and his warriors heard, and it wasn't long after the torrential blowing sands calmed. They looked around to assess the situation as the sands rained down around them and the thick, dust-laden air cleared. Multiple warriors lay bloodied and dismembered, including two of Jabari's own warriors.

Jabari couldn't detect so much as a trace scent of Evanora. "Evanora was not with him."

"Aye, that can only mean she is either dead, or she didn't know of his plans?" Ammon replied.

Jabari headed back to the pyramid entrance. "She knew and I'm assuming Arkyn left her behind on purpose."

"We shall find out when the others send word." Ammon nodded as they all headed back to the cenote.

Bain and Amsi had mated under the Full Blood Moon in Avenolon, and Sigurd had asked Giovanna to move into the temple with him permanently. Of course, she agreed.

Aria, Amsi, and Jadis wandered through the ruins they had discovered; everyone was curious as to the places they had hidden, fought, and slept.

For the first time, exploring Avenolon was not a life or death situation. The girls had their mates and were free to walk back through the memories without fear or trepidation; in a way, it was their redemption.

Jadis closed her eyes and leaned back into Dante's and Silas's bodies. She took in the fragrant smells, listened to the sounds of the now familiar creatures, the dripping water, and the rustling of the canopy.

"You okay, baby?" Dante asked softly.

"Yes, it's crazy how both familiar and unfamiliar it all seems to be. It's changed with all the fresh growth."

Silas cupped her chin and kissed her on the forehead. "You're safe this time, mon chéri."

Sigurd glanced into the small, crumbling structure. "That is where you all slept, milady?" Sigurd asked as he stood behind Giovanna with his arms wrapped around her.

"Yes, and it's the first place we heard the dragons flying overhead," Jadis answered.

Amsi thought back to how scared they had been all night and now they had two dragons. "I never would have imagined things would have turned out this way. I thought we were going to be their next meal."

"You and me both," Aria agreed.

Aiden pulled Aria in closer, remembering back to how desperate they had been to get to them.

"I have to give it to you all. To survive here was nothing short of incredible," Eden said.

"Jadis, I'm sorry for yelling at you. After seeing all of this, I understand your need to go after Evanora," Maddie apologized.

"It's nothing," Jadis replied. "You were right after all, but the need to confront her was stronger than my ability to control the pull I was feeling and I'm sorry if I directed my anger toward you. I meant no disrespect."

"Think nothing of it. I never fully understood until now." Maddie ran her hand down Jadis's arm. "I can certainly understand why you reacted that way after seeing everything you, Aria, and Amsi have shown us over the last couple weeks."

"I believe we all do," Giovanna added.

"Is there anywhere else you all want to go back to?" Aiden asked.

Jadis, Aria, and Amsi looked at each other and their surroundings for a few minutes.

Jadis thought about how far they had hiked to get to where they were now. "No, most of it is too far away. I don't know about the two of you, but I'm good."

"As am I," Amsi agreed.

"Unless we figure out how to regain our powers here, this is as far as I'm willing to go," Aria said.

"I say we leave this all behind and head home," Silas suggested.

"We can come back from time to time—yes?" Jadis questioned.

"Of course, as long as we accompany you." Dante winked.

Maddie wrapped her arms around Eden. "I'm ready to go. This whole place creeps me out."

Bain smiled at the girls and nodded. "Whenever you're ready, Dante and I will get us home."

"Shall we?" Silas smiled.

It had been a month since Arkyn had escaped Avenolon and he was sitting in his galleon along with the most prominent members of his clan; at least those who managed to survive the Bergelême war.

Arkyn motioned toward his cup out. One of his concubines rushed over and filled it. "The plan has been set in motion. We will cross the gray mists and sail right into the heart of Vlakura."

"Are you sure this is going to work?" Thaveus asked.

"As long as the kuchaka can follow directions, there shouldn't be a problem." Thaveus nodded.

Yordan waved his cup back and forth in Arkyn's direction. "And what is the plan? Should she raise suspicion?"

"Then we deal with the aftermath," Arkyn replied casually.

"The way in which Abigor and Evanora did?" Vasil rumbled.

"Fucking say again?" Arkyn snarled.

Vasil waved his hand, not wanting to push him. "Your brother and Evanora underestimated their entire situations—did they not?"

Atamas looked amongst the warriors before speaking. "That was a serious aftermath and we may all suffer the same fate should she fail."

"Don't fucking tell me you're turning white. That's as serious as it gets around here," Arkyn said.

"I fucking fear no one, but I think we need a second passageway. Should your plan fail, Silas and his clan will come for us in open waters.

Vlakura is our destination and we need to cross the veil one way or another."

Stoyan looked at Arkyn and then back at Atamas. "Your cowardice is showing."

Atamas lunged for Stoyan and placed his dagger to his throat. "Call me a fucking coward and I will enjoy watching my blade cross your throat!"

Stoyan spun his arm and caught Atamas's arm in the crook of his elbow before landing a blow to his face. The sounds of chairs being upheaved and cups of ale falling to the deck stole everyone's attention from the matter at hand. Stoyan and Atamas wrestled each other to the floor, trading blow for blow.

"I'nəf!" Arkyn shouted. "Nyama shibani poveche!"

The others separated Stoyan and Atamas and tossed them to either side of the galleon.

Arkyn threw a chair blocking his way as he rushed toward the separated warriors. "The plan stands. If either of you step out of line again, it will be my blade that crosses your throats!"

Continue reading with
The Legends of Mortem Book 4 | Coming soon.